Twist and Turn

Tim Tigner

Copyright © 2018 Tim Tigner
All rights reserved.
ISBN: 9781728822075

For more information on this novel or Tim Tigner's other
thrillers, please visit timtigner.com

This novel is dedicated to the sweet little mouse
also known as Kristina Victoria Tigner.
So is my heart.

AUTHOR'S NOTE

If skepticism strikes while you're reading this novel,
please follow the links supplied at the end.
But beware, spoilers exist there.

ACKNOWLEDGMENTS

Writing novels full of twists and turns is relatively easy. Doing so logically and coherently while maintaining a rapid pace is much tougher. Surprising readers without confusing them is the real art.

I draw on generous fans for guidance in achieving those goals, and for assistance in fighting my natural inclination toward typos. These are my friends, and I'm grateful to them all.

Editors: Suzanne Barnhill, Andrea Kerr, Judy Marksteiner and Peter Mathon.

Technical Consultant: Eric Weissend, M.D.

Beta Readers: Errol Adler, Dennis Attig, Martin Baggs, Dave Berkowitz, Doug Branscombe, Kay Brooks, Anna Bruns, Diane Bryant, Pat Carella, Ian Cockerill, Robert Enzenauer, Hugo Ernst, Rae Fellenberg, Geof Ferrell, Emily Hagman, Jim Hutchins, Cliff Jordan, Margaret Lovett, Debbie Malina, Ed McArdle, Joe McKinley, Dick Norsworthy, Michael Picco, Lee Proost, Robert Rubinstayn, Todd Simpson, Martha Smith, Ronald Spunt, Gwen Tigner, Robert Tigner and Sandy Wallace.

PART 1: TWIST

Chapter 1: *In the Dark*

Location Unknown

WAS I DEAD? Had I died? If this was the afterlife, then I'd been deemed lacking. Less than sufficient, or sub-saintly at least.

I had killed. The Lord knew that Kyle Achilles had violated the Sixth Commandment on more than one occasion—therefore I shouldn't be surprised by His judgment.

But I was.

I guess I'd expected an exception. A pass. A nod. My kills had been righteous, after all. For the greater good. I'd dedicated much of my life to fighting the honorable fight. The battle where the good had to do bad to win.

And Katya. Poor Katya. She was now alone again. I'd failed her ... somehow.

These thoughts all raced around my mind, bouncing off the walls and sending reverberations through my soul, in two sticky blinks of my crusty eyes. I continued blinking as my other senses shucked off slumber and attempted to tune in to the waking world.

A new world.

A world like none I'd known before.

My eyes gave me nothing. Literally nothing. They funneled no information through my optic nerves and into my brain. They didn't hurt. They didn't feel different. They just reported black, like a television without power.

Was that it? Had someone or something used a drug to

pull the plug? To chemically sever a connection? As logical as that seemed, my mind didn't buy in. It took a different turn because my ears were also off-kilter.

Strain as I might, I heard nothing beyond my own biology —and the breathing of others. Not a sound. No passing cars or chirping crickets. No humming appliances or rustling leaves. Beyond the breathing, my auditory world was also dead. But the breathing was enough, enough to know that my system was online, while somehow, some way, the rest of the world was turned off.

My nose reported next, and it flooded my flummoxed brain with joy. The otherwise stale air held a familiar fresh, floral scent that never failed to warm my heart and lift my mood. Katya's shampoo.

As I shifted my position to reach for her head, my kinesthetic awareness kicked in. I was resting in a three-quarter prone position, with my legs bent and interlocked and my head braced by both arms. It was close to a standard sleeping posture, but a bit too awkward and precise to be casual. The alignment even had a name.

Recovery position was used by medical professionals and knowledgeable laymen to prevent unconscious people from choking due to a closed or obstructed airway. The ensuing conclusion was inescapable. Like a piece of furniture, I had been arranged.

I reached slowly toward the scent, at once eager and hesitant, longing yet fearful of what I might find. I felt nothing. Nothing but thin air, rising adrenaline and a dropping stomach.

Propping myself up on an elbow, I became aware that I was lying on a floor rather than a mattress. A hardwood floor. I added that fact to the astounding array of puzzle pieces I'd been sorting in the seconds since first opening my eyes.

I extended my hand further toward the sweet scent and found my reward a few inches later. Silky soft strands with a slight curl.

I slid closer.

Her body was warm, her chest rising, her heart beating.

She, too, had been situated in the recovery position.

I'm not sure why we strive to be quiet in silent situations. Probably residual programming, written in the lizard brain to keep us safe at night. In any case, I found myself compelled to whisper directly into her ear. "Katya. Katya, wake up."

There is, perhaps, no more contented feeling than lying beside the woman you love and burying your nose in her hair. Despite the extreme and alarming circumstances, now that I knew my love was safe by my side, that simple act put me at peace.

I had no idea where we were.

I had no idea how we'd gotten there.

But by her side was where I wanted to be. The rest was reduced to the status of *details*. For the moment at least.

As I whispered, I became aware of something tucked into my cheek. Something small, circular and metallic. I carefully expelled it into my hand and instantly identified the familiar object. I'd studied it often in the preceding weeks, with a smile on my face and a swelling in my chest.

It was Katya's engagement ring. Or at least, it was going to be. I hadn't actually given it to her. Hadn't quite proposed. At least, I didn't think I had.

The last thing I remembered from before waking up in the black was reaching for that ring. That overpriced piece of metal and stone that would symbolize our union—if she agreed to make me the luckiest man alive.

I'd put my hand into my pocket while preparing to drop to one knee—and found it missing. Panic had shocked me like a Taser strike, a horrible, all-consuming visceral pain and then … nothing. My memory ended there like a cut comic strip.

Somehow in the span since that unfortunate event, we had ended up in the deathly darkness that now enveloped us, and rather than onto her finger, the ring had found its way into my mouth.

2
Savings Account

One Week Earlier
San Francisco, California

DR. BRUCE DEVLIN had never fought for his freedom in court. He'd never waited for a jury to announce his fate. Never had his future precariously poised on a single word. A judgment. A decision. But as he waited for his attorney to call, Bruce knew exactly how people in that position felt.

Fortunately, his attorney wasn't of the criminal type. Bruce's future wasn't in the hands of the Justice Department. Angus MacAskill, Esquire, specialized in manipulating a different branch of the federal government. The Food and Drug Administration, to be precise.

Today, the FDA was scheduled to announce its decision on Bruce's innovative acoustic anesthetic. If AcotocA, pronounced *A-koo-t-ka*, was *Approved*, he and his executive team would become wildly rich. If, however, permission to market AcotocA was *Denied*, the four would have nothing but bills and a bad reputation. Making matters worse for Bruce, this was his third time at bat as a startup CEO. If he missed, he would be out—and he'd never get another swing.

Developing new medical devices was very risky business. High-stakes roulette. They typically cost millions of dollars to design and tens of millions more to test. Only after all that money was on the table, riding on a single spin, did the FDA decide whether you could sell your invention. Or not.

After collecting hefty fees and taking their sweet time, a bunch of agency bureaucrats—underpaid academics who couldn't make it in the corporate world—would render their decision from on high. Thumbs up or thumbs-down. Billions or bust.

It was maddening.

Like the other three founders seated around the small conference table in their Potrero Hill office, Bruce stared alternately at the phone and the silver bucket bearing four bottles of iced champagne—and speculated. Not on defeat, but on success. On the unbelievable transformation that would take place once their bank account balances boasted an additional comma.

"Will you finally tell us exactly what you think they'll offer?" Seb asked. The *they* to which AcotocA engineer Joel "Seb" Sebastian referred was Galantic Pharmaceuticals, the gorilla in the highly lucrative general anesthesia market.

Bruce noted that his other engineer, Milton Webb, also appeared eager to bathe in the sweet words. So he obliged them with his best bit of speculation. "Galantic earned 1.2 billion off their injectable anesthetic last year. I figure they'll lose half of that to us the first year AcotocA is on the market, and half again every year thereafter as the death spiral continues. But they won't let it come to that. They've run the same calculations we have. They have no choice but to buy us out. For Galantic, it's buy or die."

Bruce knew that wasn't an answer, but at the moment, he wanted to focus on that imagery. On the sweet sensation of vanquishing his enemy. And that's what Galantic was. Not just a competitor, but an enemy, on account of their CEO.

Picking up on his mood, Webb asked, "You know Galantic's CEO inside and out, right?"

Bruce had indeed seen the dark depths of Kai Basher's mind. He'd worked at Kai's right hand for years. Basher was smart, slick and a total prick. It would feel euphoric to grab his former boss where he hurt most—and squeeze. "I do. Kai will follow the numbers, and they are unambiguous. As much as it hurts his wallet and pride, he'll do whatever it takes to save his company."

"But how much?" Seb pressed. "Will we get two billion?"

As co-founders, Seb and Webb, each owned six percent of AcotocA. Bruce understood their eagerness to complete that equation. As the CEO with a ten percent stake, he had run the numbers many times. Add in the eight percent owned by his wife, Danica, the Chief Medical Officer, and the Devlin family was looking at a very pretty picture regardless of the valuation method used. "My best guess is three. Three billion dollars."

As the ensuing calculations sucked all the air from the room, the phone rang.

Bruce grabbed the neck of a champagne bottle with his left hand and hit the speaker button with his right. Trying to control his enthusiasm, he said, "Talk to us, Angus."

"Bruce, how nice to hear your voice. It's Kai calling."

Kai's voice hit Bruce like a sucker punch to the gut. Not so much the words as his tone. The best word for it was *mocking*. Bruce endeavored to hide his discomfort, to camouflage the feeling that the bottom had just been ripped from his stomach and acid was flowing over his bowels and down his legs. "It's good to hear from you, even if your call is a tad earlier than anticipated."

"Forgive my temerity. I just wanted to be the one to share the news. AcotocA's approval for sale—has been denied."

"No!" Danica gasped, bringing a hand to her mouth as Seb and Webb buried their faces.

"Afraid so," Kai continued. "Looks like my company just saved three billion bucks. Have a nice day."

3
Reversal

Napa, California

DANICA DEVLIN reached over and grabbed her husband's wrist as he began to exit their white Range Rover. "Don't do it, Bruce."

He tugged, but not violently. He didn't put his weight into it. Angry as he was, Bruce wouldn't cross that line. Not with her.

She'd seen her husband clean a few clocks during the dozen years they'd been together, always late at night and over silly stuff. Pissing contests came with the high-testosterone territory. They went part and parcel with the drive to win that had thrice put him at the helm of Silicon Valley startups. But he'd never, ever, raised a finger in her direction. "What do I have to lose?" he asked.

It hurt her heart to see him suffer this way. Not as much as losing eighteen percent of three billion dollars, but it rivaled the news that they could never have children. It was the pain of a dream being ripped away. "Your pride. Your reputation. Your self-respect."

Bruce didn't close the door, but he released the handle and turned his fiery gaze her way. "Kai didn't call just for the satisfaction of being the one to deliver my death blow. He didn't call just to hear the anguish in my voice. He called because he couldn't help himself. He had to let me know that he'd orchestrated the rejection. He found a way to rig the game, either through bribes or through extortion. I can't just sit back and do nothing."

"You can't be certain of that, Bruce. AcotocA's safety

data *is* marginal."

Bruce snorted. "You're talking about a man who legally changed his name from Charles to Kai, in order to be Kai Basher. And that's exactly what he did to me—to us. He put the kibosh on our hopes and dreams. It's not like he needed more money, either. He's already got a jet and two yachts and more vacation property than I can count. And now we've got nothing."

"We've got each other."

"I've got three strikes, Danica. And no runs. I'm out of the startup business—and in debt."

"We'll figure something out."

"Yes, we will. And as the first step in doing that, I'm going to go into that fancy restaurant and rattle Kai Basher's golden cage." Bruce stepped out of the Range Rover and slammed the door.

They were parked beside Cinquante Bouches, the famous Michelin three-star restaurant perched high in the hills overlooking Napa Valley. Catering to the Bay Area's elite, *Fifty Mouths* sold out reservations for its fixed-menu dinners two months in advance. If you wanted to score one or more of the fifty available seats, you had to be online within minutes of the booking period opening—and pay in advance.

Of course, few of the elite diners jumped through the virtual hoops themselves. Bruce knew for a fact that Kai had his executive assistant secure him four seats every Friday night. Failure to do so was a firing offense.

Danica and Bruce had occupied two of Kai's four seats some eight years back. At the time, Kai was freshly separated from his third and final wife, and Bruce was his favored lieutenant. As Danica recalled, Kai had spent the evening regaling his date with tales of his business triumphs. Danica wondered who he had in there tonight. Was the woman, at that very moment, listening to how Kai had outmaneuvered his old protégé to the tune of three billion dollars?

Danica hustled across the finely crushed gravel to catch her husband before he opened the door. When she reached his side, she held out her left hand, not to block him, but to take his.

He looked over and gave her a smile. "Thank you."

"I'm thinking we should just slip in and see what we can overhear," she suggested.

"That sounds—very sensible."

"But before we go in, do me one favor." She led him a few steps from the door to where the travertine walkway turned toward the valley. Stopping there, she said, "Just look at that."

The twilight view was magnificent. The lights of Napa Valley shone far below even as the stars were becoming visible higher up in the midnight blue sky. Surrounded by a lush forest, they were both connected to the human world and yet a million miles from it. Aside from the fifty diners behind them, and the supporting restaurant staff, there probably wasn't another soul for miles around. The crickets were contentedly singing their songs, and the air was serving up a fresh pine scent. "It's beautiful, but what's your point?"

"Just wanted to take a second to broaden your perspective beyond today's problems. Nobody out there has ever heard of Kai Basher. Don't let him rule your life."

Bruce squeezed her hand. "Point taken, and I thank you for the second of serenity. But the fact of the matter is, we don't live in the stars. We live in civilization. Life on Earth requires economic resources—and Kai just stole ours. I refuse to let him walk away unscathed. I wouldn't be a man if I did."

Danica wasn't about to argue with that. At their core, men were hunters—and she'd latched onto one of the best. Even though her husband's next move might not be a wise one, deep in her heart Danica felt proud that her hunter refused to roll over and take it. "I understand. And I love you."

The restaurant resembled a French chateau, with an elegant white façade and a steeply sloping slate roof. Originally designed for entertaining by a wealthy winery owner, Cinquante Bouches was now Northern California's most exclusive restaurant. Under the inspired management of the owner's daughter, Michelin granted its first star on the fifth anniversary of its opening, the elusive second star six years after that, and the exceptionally rare third star during the restaurant's fifteenth year. Rumor had it that Cinquante Bouches now made ten times more money than the family's wineries ever had.

Bruce and Danica walked through the oak doors and into the sounds of a dozen quiet conversations and the clinking of silverware against china. Visually, they were shielded from the dining room by the reception area and bar, both of which were now empty given that everyone ate at the same time, and the nine-course service had commenced.

"Apparently they don't anticipate anyone arriving without a reservation," Danica whispered, attempting to insert a speed bump.

"It's too remote to stumble upon," Bruce replied, leaning in. "And everyone who knows it's here will have been advised of the rules. The exclusivity is half the allure."

"I thought it was all about the food and ambiance."

"Don't be silly," Bruce said with a wink.

The gesture momentarily raised Danica's hopes that her husband might abandon his career suicide quest, but he continued toward one of the archways. She hastened to his side and peered into the fine dining room.

The tables were all round and sized for the party. Each was covered with white linen and genuine candle arrangements. The guests were a mixture of couples and professionals. All were nicely dressed for Napa, which meant expensive but not necessarily traditional. This was, after all, the land where billionaires showed off their status with hoodies and jeans. There were no hoodies on display tonight, but Danica saw a fair share of denim.

She soon spotted the shaved head of Kai Basher. He wasn't with a woman. The other three at his table looked more like bankers. All wore smug expressions as they sipped the wine the sommelier had paired with their foie gras appetizers.

She prayed Bruce wouldn't march across the floor and slug him in the face. Well, for the most part anyway. Her darker side would be happy to see their nemesis lose a few teeth.

Danica returned her attention to her husband and saw a familiar look on his face. A contemplative look. His gaze was shifting from table to table as if assessing missile strikes. What was he thinking? Surely he wasn't going to go postal and work out his frustrations on the whole spoiled lot. Had he brought a gun? Was his Glock tucked in the small of his back?

As she reached to check, enlightenment entered his eyes, followed swiftly by a slow nod of resolve and finally the hint of a smile. He had an idea.

Bruce intercepted her hand. Without a word he turned toward the door and led her back beneath the stars.

She said nothing.

He kept walking all the way to their car.

Turning once he'd reached the driver's side door, he dealt her a second surprise. "Would you mind taking an Uber home?"

Danica was at once relieved and perplexed. "You're leaving me?"

"I'd never leave you, dear. But tonight, I need to go to Nevada."

4
Fast Action

San Francisco, California

DANICA EXPERIENCED an uncomfortable sense of déjà vu as she studied her colleagues' faces across the conference table. They were in her husband's office. Ground zero. The location where the news bomb had dropped forty-eight hours earlier. The rejection that had obliterated her hopes and dreams and laid waste to the hard work and sacrifices of the preceding six years.

Seb and Webb, AcotocA's founding engineers, looked the way she felt. Usually quick-witted and chic—at least for geeks—the matched set appeared untidy and downtrodden. Their sandy blond hair was flat, their hazel eyes highlighted by dark, puffy bags, and their faces unshaven. The sight reminded her of a paparazzi picture in which a photographer had captured a vacationing celebrity off-guard.

Although Kai Basher had caused their disaster, Danica was determined to own her reaction. Whereas the men had erupted like Vesuvius, smashing champagne bottles rather than raining ash, Danica had taken the news in stride. She was attempting to focus on the positive. While unpleasant, it wasn't cancer.

But try as she might, the slow simmer of rage ignited by Kai's call now had her anger at full boil. She needed to vent that energy. But how? Where?

Bruce's sudden course reversal at Cinquante Bouches had surprised her, but his subsequent secrecy had not. He'd always been one to contemplate in solitude, emerging only after he'd either fully fleshed out his big idea or rejected it.

He'd called an hour earlier to say that he had a plan—a plan that would both serve justice and restore the fortune Kai had stolen. He'd given no detail, just a request to gather in his office for a momentous discussion.

"We should have seen it coming," Seb said. "We were naive to think Galantic would play by the rules. The rich and powerful have never done that."

Webb nodded along. "Why pay us three billion dollars when you can bribe an official for a small fraction of that? I feel like a fool for not anticipating it."

"And there's no way we can fight back," Seb continued, bunching his fists. "Not when their breakeven point is three billion in legal fees, lobbyist contracts and outright bribes."

"Meanwhile, we haven't just lost our big payout, we've lost our salary," Webb said. "This is going to crush me. I've been anticipating a major cash infusion—and I've acted accordingly."

"Me too," Seb said. "I'm totally screwed. For the first five years I was conservative. Disciplined. But once the clinical data came in so strong, I jumped the gun a bit. You can't take it with you, you know? Old and rich is good, but young and rich is better."

Danica wanted to chastise her colleagues for their shortsightedness. *Don't count your chickens before they're hatched* was an oft-repeated idiom for good reason. But she understood the temptation. The Bay Area was full of people living large after scoring huge. When you were as smart and hardworking as Seb and Webb, it was natural to feel that you deserved to live like your successful neighbors.

She and Bruce didn't have credit card debt, but they did have a five-figure monthly mortgage payment. Savings would keep them solvent for a year or so, but it could easily take them longer than that to find acceptable employment. By drawing paychecks from the same company, they had violated conventional wisdom as well, putting all their eggs in one basket.

"So what does Bruce have in mind?" Seb asked, changing the subject.

Both engineers focused their bloodshot eyes on her.

Danica didn't have the answer. "You know my husband almost as well as I do, and I've told you all I know. One minute Bruce was studying Kai Basher and the other smug patrons around his four-hundred-dollar-per-plate table, the next he was headed for Nevada."

"What's in Nevada?" Seb asked.

"Beyond Vegas? Not much," Webb replied.

Danica didn't find that encouraging. It was practically cliché, the desperado heading to Vegas to roll the dice and either win big or end it all with a rooftop dive. She quickly dismissed the depressing thought. Surely her husband—her brilliant, insightful, courageous husband—was more resilient than that.

"Are you angry?" Bruce asked, walking into the room and catching them all by surprise.

"Yes," Danica replied in concert with her colleagues, buoyed by her husband's exuberant tone.

"Are you prepared to take action? To reclaim your rightful rung on the socioeconomic ladder?" Bruce continued, gesturing enthusiastically.

"Yes," they all replied.

"Bold action?" Bruce clarified.

"Yes!"

"Decisive action?"

"Yes!"

"Are you prepared to stoop to the level required to win? To get dirty? To take risks? To use every tool at your disposal to outwit the people and the system that effectively just stole the last six years of your life?"

Again, Danica found herself saying, "Yes!" and meaning it, despite the implied element of danger. And criminality.

"Good. Because I've figured out how to make us whole."

All three exhaled in relief before Bruce continued. "But we have to act fast. The moment we need to strike is a mere five days from now. This Friday night."

5
Big Mouths

Five Days Later
Napa, California

I FELT a funny flutter in my stomach, the kind you get when cresting a hill at speed. But I hadn't crested a hill. Katya and I were still ascending at a modest 45 mph.

It was nerves.

My body was expressing apprehension about what lay ahead, something it rarely did even under circumstances most would consider far more extreme—like working undercover for the CIA or climbing a cliff without a rope. Funny how those things work.

At the moment, I was facing no imminent physical danger. No significant chance of emotional damage either.

Not really.

I didn't think.

But there was, of course, some chance. And given the magnitude of the situation, even a small possibility of failure apparently presented as a significant threat. At least as far as my bowels were concerned.

"I know it's not a picnic, because there's no way you'd put on a collared shirt and sport coat for one of those," Katya said. "But given the state of my stomach, and the fact that we're leaving civilization ever further behind, I'm beginning to wish that was what you had planned."

She was kidding, of course. Unlike me, Katya had a camel's capacity to function without food. On the other hand, and again unlike me, she was not good at delaying gratification when it came to surprises. I'd told Katya that I was taking her someplace special for her birthday and then added to the intrigue by doing something I rarely did. I dressed up.

At least above the waist.

Below, I'd retained my favorite jeans and, of course, approach shoes. One never knew when obstacles would appear and beg to be climbed.

Katya, by contrast, looked like a million bucks with her long, honey-blonde hair coiffed to add curly bounce and her proud Slavic face lightly painted.

"Five minutes," I said, and rolled down the front windows. "Enjoy the fresh air."

We both inhaled deeply. Palo Alto was nice enough as far as climate was concerned. We felt privileged to live there. But it was a city, and this, this was God at His best.

"Bozhe moi. Pravda!" Katya said, momentarily reverting to her native Russian out of excitement as my headlights illuminated the polished brass letters on the stone wall just ahead. "You brought me to Cinquante Bouches for my birthday! How did you get reservations?"

"I planned ahead." I'd set three reminders and an alarm to ensure that I was at my laptop, credit card in hand, when reservations became available two months earlier. I had more than just a memorable birthday planned.

"I'm excited. I've heard stories and always wanted to go, but can we afford it?"

Katya made a respectable salary as a mathematics professor at Stanford, whereas my income was more hit or miss, with good consulting income occasionally supplementing the meager sponsorship money I made climbing cliffs. We'd have been relatively well off most places, but the Bay Area is a very expensive place to live. Still, I could afford the occasional nice dinner and, once in my life, a gold ring with a glittering rock. "It's already paid for. Famous French restaurateurs demand payment in advance."

She leaned over and gave me a big hug and kiss as I brought the Jeep Cherokee to a crunching halt on the gravel. "Thank you!"

"Wait till we try the food. You never know," I said with a wink.

As we approached the front door, an attractive couple was exiting a white Audi 7 with a glowing Uber sign in the windshield. The stylish pair appeared to be Middle Eastern, but were conversing in English with British accents. They sounded as excited as we were. She wore an off-the-shoulder dress—or was it a gown? I wasn't sure of the distinction. It resembled Katya's except that it was café au lait in color, whereas Katya's was emerald green. He, on the other hand, had outdone me twofold with both a vest and necktie. We'd see who was happier with his wardrobe choice if a bear wandered in from the woods.

The Uber rider reached the door first and held it open as both ladies walked through. I did the *after you* gesture, and we approached reception.

"Bonsoir," a proper French hostess said in greeting. "Do you have a reservation?"

Would anyone drive all the way up here if he didn't?

"Abdilla, table for two," the gentleman said.

Rather than consult a computer or list, the hostess simply said, "Right this way."

She returned a few seconds later and repeated the ritual with us. "Achilles, table for two," I said.

We followed her into a large, elegant dining room outfitted with a dozen round, white linen-covered tables of various sizes. To my disappointment, most appeared to be occupied by businessmen, rather than couples. In fact, other than the two we'd walked in with, I spotted only one other two-top. It was occupied by a blatantly gay couple, with matching colorful suits and glasses and "I'm with him" neck tattoos. Not the atmosphere I had been hoping for, but one hard to avoid given that Katya's birthday coincided with the annual J.P. Morgan Healthcare Conference. The invitation-only event took over the Bay Area as the rich industry's movers and shakers with their financiers and fat expense accounts descended in droves.

Alas, four of the obnoxious sort were seated just behind me, apparently already drunk. Their leader, a big blond fellow with a perfect part and over-bleached teeth, seemed to be confusing Cinquante Bouches with the dining room of the fraternity he'd undoubtedly run. Given the half-full crystal bottle of amber liquid on the table between Chip or Skip or Biff or Trey and his friends, I wasn't expecting their behavior to improve with food. Fortunately for them, I had plenty to occupy my mind.

"It's beautiful," Katya said, spinning around to take in the entire scene. "The attention to detail. I love how the number of candles coincides with the number of guests. And the way they lit each work of art. They even have Hillary Hahn playing Bach sonatas in the background. Thank you, Kyle."

Katya rarely called me by my first name. Nobody who knew me did. I took it as a sign that she was pleased, a sign confirmed a second later when she gave me a kiss before taking her seat.

So far, so good—obnoxious bankers aside.

As Bernard, the waiter, laid the napkin in my lap, I reached into my pocket for the ring.

I didn't find it.

While Bernard poured the champagne and placed puffy ping-pong ball-sized appetizers before us, my fingers continued to fumble without success. I was trying to operate under the radar of my hopefully soon to be fiancée, both in my actions and in my expression. This was supposed to be the moment. That memorable, magical experience every child anticipates at some point in his or her life.

In preparation, I had confirmed that champagne would indeed accompany the meal, and the hostess had clarified that it was served with the welcoming hors d'oeuvres. I had it all planned out. And then—what? Had the ring somehow snagged on the cuff of the cursed shirt? Was there a hole in my new jacket? Would my homeowner's insurance cover the ring's loss? Was this really happening?

"Bug bite?" Katya asked, mistaking my fumbling for scratching.

Not wanting to lie, I raised my champagne, "Happy birthday, Katya. I hope the memory of tonight will make you smile for years to come."

We clinked and sipped and savored our hors d'oeuvres. For the few seconds it took me to chew the small but sumptuous treat, I almost forgot my distressing situation. But the swallow came all too soon, and I was face-to-face with my costly blunder again.

Looking around, I saw that all the waiters had disappeared. No doubt the next course would soon be forthcoming. I ran my hands down my sides and over both pockets as if stretching. This was my final attempt to find the ring before excusing myself to the bathroom for a strip search.

I felt it!

The bulge wasn't at the bottom of my pocket, but rather further up. My fingers found it inside a tiny pocket within the pocket. As the knots in my shoulders released, I speculated that the inner pocket was intended for business cards.

Pinching the ring between the fingers of my left hand, I again raised a champagne flute with my right. Once Katya raised hers, I brought the ring into view.

Her eyes went wide.

I was about to slide out of my seat and onto my knee when an atmospheric disturbance pinged my radar.

I redirected my attention toward the source of the disturbance and watched two masked people clad in black walk into the room, H&K MP7s raised. "Everyone stay in your seats!"

6
Acoustic Camouflage

Napa, California

GASPS ERUPTED as the assailants positioned themselves at opposite sides of the room. One was obviously a woman. Neither moved like a skilled combatant, but then it didn't take a lot of skill to kill with submachine guns in a crowded room.

"Everyone put your hands behind your heads, and plant your faces in your plates," the man commanded in a menacing monotone.

As the diners glanced about, struggling to comprehend the inconceivable, he shouted, "Now! Do it now! If I don't see your nose touching your plate, I'm going to put it there. And no talking!"

I put on a calm and confident expression, met Katya's eye, and nodded for her to comply. As she did so, I made two subtle moves. I slipped the ring into my mouth and flipped my soup spoon, creating a convex mirror.

"Good. Now stay that way—still and silent," the attacker added, his voice more moderate. "If everyone plays along, nobody gets hurt."

It was a good tactical play. Start with shock and awe, instilling all kinds of fear, then offer a sense of security tied to complete cooperation. I made a note that the team was strategically savvy, even if operationally inexperienced.

The spoon helped, but it was no crystal ball. It only gave me views of objects high off the ground and on my flanks. Kinda like the side view mirrors on a car when angled upward. I could augment my field of vision with subtle head movements, but I wanted to minimize those. My goal at this early stage was to blend into the crowd.

I did, however, reach a foot across to stroke one of Katya's calves. I couldn't be particularly tender with my shoe on, but I did my best to deliver a soothing touch.

"Now, anyone in possession of a weapon, raise your left hand! You will be searched shortly, and if a weapon is found, it will be used on you, then and there, without hesitation or question."

I didn't detect any movement. Not surprising since my fellow patrons were likely big city bankers and pharmaceutical company executives. Most had probably flown to the Bay Area for the conference.

"Last chance. You have been warned."

Still no movement.

I had a 9mm with me, but it was holstered under the steering wheel of my Jeep.

After a few seconds of silence, the woman moved in my direction but stopped at the table with the gay couple. "You two, on your feet."

She marched the men in the direction of the front door, where the intervening partition would have hidden them from sight even if I were free to watch. As their footsteps faded, another unexpected event occurred. Music started playing. And not just any music—jazz music. Louis Armstrong's "What a Wonderful World."

I couldn't think of a more pleasant or uplifting song, and that was a bit freaky. Was the music intended to make us docile prior to slaughter? Or was it acoustic camouflage?

As my mind parsed the possibilities, I realized that its intent might be mental distraction. In which case it was working.

The woman returned quickly, very quickly. Again she walked to a seemingly random table. This time a group of four.

"What did we do?" a mature, gravelly voice asked.

The reply came in two parts. First, I heard cold steel cracking against bone. Then, after the resulting groan, a repeat of the earlier warning. "No talking! Not ... a ...

sound."

Hitting someone with your weapon was a stupid move. It took the muzzle off target. Perhaps only for a second, but a second was often enough. Another tactical blunder I'd bear in mind.

As the woman led two more people out, I came to an unsettling conclusion. Even with only a couple of data points, the pattern was clear. Within the next few minutes, Katya and I would be led from the room.

Napa, California

KATYA CLOSED her eyes and took a deep breath. This was not her first extreme emotional rollercoaster. Despite living an academic lifestyle, she'd suffered through quite a few stomach scrunchers.

The wild rides had begun when Kyle's brother entered her life. Katya had met Colin Achilles while completing her Ph.D. at Moscow State University. At the time, Colin had also been living and working in Russia.

Colin had eventually asked her to marry him, and she had wholeheartedly agreed to be his wife until death did them part. But on the very night of his proposal, Colin and his father had both died of carbon monoxide poisoning in an incident that Katya and Kyle had barely escaped.

It hadn't been an accident.

When the culprits had subsequently come for Katya, Kyle had raced to her rescue. Not an easy feat, given that he'd been jailed for murder at the time. Together, the two survivors had unraveled the contorted conspiracy that had ensnared his family and her fiancé.

They had ultimately rendered justice, but only after surviving attacks on two continents. During the process, their relationship had blossomed. A taboo attraction had grown. One of those irresistible, undeniable forces that they both had felt honor bound to resist.

After many months of heart-wrenching struggle, she and Achilles had mutually come to the conclusion that their union would actually make Colin happy.

But still, they had put off the final step. Until tonight.

Now, on the very night when Kyle Achilles was prepared to propose, they were again thrust into a life-threatening situation. How was that possible? As a mathematics professor, she found herself stuck on the odds.

And yet it was happening.

Was she cursed? Was there a demon determined to make her miserable? She didn't believe in such things but still the coincidences were hard to swallow without question.

Kyle kept rubbing her calf under the table while the restaurant emptied out, two by two. He was always thinking about her comfort. He did it in little ways that she rarely acknowledged but always appreciated. She wanted to express her gratitude—but not now. The penalty for clandestine communication had proven swift and harsh.

With each round, Katya struggled to hear what was happening to those who left the room. The only words she ever detected above the jazz song playing loudly on repeat were "face the wall." Presumably that was prior to a patdown. After each command, Katya strained to hear a suppressed gunshot or the thud of a dropping body, but neither ever followed.

Before she knew it, their turn arrived. "On your feet," the man commanded.

As Katya rose, she saw that they were the only two diners remaining in the room. That probably wasn't a coincidence. By saving Achilles for last, they had kept him in a passive stance until the second gun was freed to focus on his center mass.

With the woman's submachine gun pressed into the small of her back, Katya marched toward the entrance with Achilles at her side. She could feel him raring to react, plotting to turn the tables and pulverize the people who threatened his sweetheart. He wasn't one to tolerate being pushed around.

But she knew he wouldn't act.

Not now.

Not while she was under a gun.

As they entered the reception area, Katya was surprised

to see two more men waiting. She could practically feel Achilles' spirits drop at the sight. Two armed assailants was already a stretch, four was out of the question. Even for him.

The new guys were clad in black and wearing ski masks. They weren't pointing guns, however. Each held something that looked like a large pair of headphones.

"Face the wall," the man behind Achilles said.

8
Mixed Messages

Napa, California

BRUCE FELT like he was having an out-of-body experience as he guided the final pair of diners toward the door. He'd never done anything like this before. He wasn't violent or scheming and he certainly wasn't a criminal—by nature. Although he couldn't deny that whacking Kai in the head had felt fantastic.

Like the best of his species, Bruce had adapted to an unwelcome change in his environment. Now he and his people wouldn't just survive, they'd thrive.

Other than Seb and Webb, the first forty-eight diners that Danica had escorted out of the room had all been desk jockeys. Corporate captains or big shot bankers. Men who, like Bruce himself, made their money from the comfort of a chair.

This last guy was the odd man out. He was like a panther in a room of pussycats. Not a caveman or a thug—one look into his intelligent eyes told you that—but a man who could rule the jungle.

Fortunately, Tarzan was there with Jane. As long as she was under the gun, he would be neutralized. Tarzan couldn't know that his captors would never actually kill anyone—or that the cartridges cramming the twenty-round magazines in their MP7s were blanks.

"Face the wall," Bruce said, his H&K pressed to the small of the big man's spine. He kept it there while Seb or Webb —he couldn't distinguish the two with ski masks on— slipped AcotocA sedation systems over Tarzan's ears and he collapsed into unconsciousness. A second later, so did Jane.

"That's all of them," Bruce said, removing the itchy mask.

"We did it!" Seb said. "Mother of God, we did it!"

With the risky part of the operation behind them, the four exchanged high fives.

"I promised you that AcotocA would make us all rich," Bruce said.

AcotocA, a palindrome created from *acoustic*, was a revolutionary product. Instead of using chemicals to block nerve signals, their technology effectively plunged the human nervous system into deep sleep by forcing brain waves into the relatively low-frequency, high-amplitude delta waves experienced during dreaming. When powerful enough, the acoustic transmission didn't just induce immediate deep sleep, it also jammed other nerve transmissions, effectively preventing pain from registering.

With an AcotocA device on someone's ears, you could put them to sleep with the flip of a switch. And you could keep them asleep as long as the system was in place and transmitting. They'd kept rhesus monkeys anesthetized for an entire month, nourishing and hydrating them intravenously.

The FDA's stated reason for rejecting AcotocA's approval for sale was not based on efficacy. That was immediately apparent. They cited safety concerns.

According to the FDA review panel, AcotocA Inc. had not sufficiently demonstrated that there would be no long-term impact on cognitive health. They had set an impossibly high hurdle. *Cognitive health* was too multidimensional a parameter, and *long-term* was too vague a condition, to ever be overcome—if someone was bribed to rule against them. As their panel obviously had been.

No matter what Bruce said or did, the corrupt official could always say, "Not enough." One bribed bureaucrat could keep AcotocA's revolutionary product off the marketplace simply by noting that there were tried-and-true alternatives whose long-term impacts were well established. Period. Full stop. End of story. Death of dream.

Tricks like that were one way the rich and powerful

remained rich and powerful.

Well, not today.

Today, Bruce had the power. And soon, he would have the riches too.

As the four of them carried Tarzan and Jane out to the U-Haul trucks parked just outside the door, Seb said, "You were right about the demographics of the diners. I've been checking the business cards in their wallets as we load them. Most are either from Wall Street or the C-suites of Big Pharma."

When Seb hacked the reservation system at Cinquante Bouches, he obtained the names and phone numbers of every reservation holder. Bruce could have investigated them, confirmed their caliber, but time was tight with all the other prep work required. He verified that Kai Basher had his regular reservation, then moved on, trusting that the healthcare conference had put the right clientele in the other forty-nine seats. "Timing is everything," he replied.

"And thus the rush to be ready this Friday," Webb added. "Good call. Although there is one potential complication."

"What's that?" Bruce asked, his heart skipping a beat.

"One of the men at Kai's table—the tall one with a tan and thick white hair—"

"Yes?"

"He's Whip Rickman."

"Name sounds familiar."

"He's the governor of Florida."

"Crap."

"Yeah."

"Well, nothing we can do about that now. Who knows, maybe that will work in our favor," Bruce said, anticipating exactly the opposite.

They laid the last two diners on the floor of a U-Haul beside the others, sardine-style. With AcotocA systems on their ears, their cargo was completely oblivious.

"Danica, please get the restaurant staff all traditionally sedated. We want the marks on their arms and the ketamine in their veins for camouflage."

Before sedating the diners, Bruce and Danica had used

AcotocA to disable Cinquante Bouches's employees—the chefs, servers and other staff. Thus, like the diners, they would have no recollection of the event.

Memory loss was a side effect induced when AcotocA abruptly shifted brain waves from beta to delta, from waking to deep sleep, skipping the intermediary alpha and theta wave states. By disrupting the chemical process that converted experiences into long-term memories, AcotocA effectively erased the last five or so minutes of memory. The staff would have absolutely no recollection of the kidnapping process. Their last memories would be of business as usual at the restaurant—creating quite the mystery.

"On it," his wife replied.

"Seb, get to work on the restaurant's logs and computers. Make certain there are no records of any kind indicating who was here tonight."

Once Bruce had conceived of his plan—while standing there studying the rich crowd of carnivores in the remote restaurant—he had his computer guru hack into Cinquante Bouches's online reservation system and erase all records for this particular evening. He'd also picked one of the three couples that had reservations and phoned them to reschedule, thereby making room for Seb and Webb to join the party.

"On it," the engineer replied.

By this point in the evening, with the physical confrontations behind them and the rest of the operation arranged to run on rails, Bruce should have been ecstatic. His beleaguered brain should now be sipping the sweet nectar of success, enjoying that first cool trickle of the lemonade he'd made from the big lemon life had dealt him.

Adding to the emotional feast was the satisfaction of serving up revenge. Revenge against not just the individual who had stolen his dream, but also a significant sample of the smarmy elites who destroyed others' lives on a daily basis—all for their personal gain.

But Bruce found himself feeling neither ecstatic nor satisfied.

Standing there with all forty-eight hostages safely sedated at his feet, he couldn't shake the sinking feeling that something was about to go terribly, horribly wrong.

9
White Knight

Napa, California

DANICA EXHALED long and slow after completing the final anesthetic injection. She'd used veterinary-strength ketamine in combination with lorazepam to minimize injection volume while maximizing incapacitation. The restaurant staff would now be dead to the world for at least two hours and groggy beyond arousal for an additional sixty minutes.

Bruce walked in as she was closing up her bag, a bag she'd pull back out again in a few hours for a similar exercise with the restaurant's diners. He paused with hands on hips while surveying the scene. She had everyone laid out in a recovery position with mouth down to drain the drool that ketamine created, chin up to keep the airway open, and arms and legs interlocked in a stabilizing position. "Are you sure they're completely unconscious?"

"Dead to the world."

"But their eyes?" Bruce said, his face scrunched with skepticism. "They're cracked open and moving."

"The lights are on, but nobody's home," Danica replied, enjoying a moment of levity. "Eyelids at half-mast is a characteristic effect of the drug I used, as is the nystagmus —the rapid eye movement."

"It's going to be one weird experience for them, waking up," Bruce said. "With all their colleagues in a similar state and with no memory of how they ended up on the kitchen floor and with nothing else out of order."

"Except the missing reservation information," she

corrected.

"Yes, but that vanished days ago."

"It also occurred to me that they'll be able to tell from the remaining food that the dinner service was interrupted."

"And yet there will be no sign of the diners or any record of who they were. It will be baffling, for sure."

"They could run DNA tests and take fingerprints using the dirty dishes, you know," she said as yet another concern struck. Danica worried that they'd missed something critical when throwing the plan together so fast. It had been a conscious tradeoff, exchanging prep time for a restaurant guaranteed to be replete with medical industry executives and investment bankers, thanks to the big conference.

"DNA testing takes way too long to be a threat. Fingerprints are much faster in theory, but in practice the police won't spend the time or money until they have a good reason. By the time they have one, it will be too late to matter."

"Even with Governor Rickman among the missing?"

"Granted, that's an unfortunate and unforeseen complication. But I don't see it tipping the scales against us. Even the feds can't follow a trail that isn't there."

Danica hoped her husband was right. It wasn't an exaggeration to say that they had everything riding on his master plan. Of course, as AcotocA employees, the four of them were used to having everything riding on his plans. This twist, the diagnostician in her argued, was simply an acceleration. They were condensing the work and the wait from one of his plans down to hours and days rather than months and years. After three long, legitimate shots on goal, she was ready to risk a shortcut.

"If you're done here, I need your help with the cars," Bruce said. "That's going slower than I'd hoped since hardly any of the diners carpooled."

"Okay, but you didn't brief me on that part of the mission."

"Come with me and I'll show you."

He walked her out of the kitchen and into the guest parking lot, which still contained eight cars according to her quick count. She saw eight white drawstring kitchen trash bags lined up on the ground, each anchored with a set of car keys. Beside them were two Mini-Segways, compact versions of the two-wheeled, self-balancing personal transporters popular among mall cops and tour operators.

Danica knew that Seb and Webb had emptied each patron's pockets into an individual bag. Apparently, the bags that had car keys were now here.

"Grab a key and the bag beneath it," Bruce said, demonstrating. "Use the key to find the car." He pressed the unlock feature on the fob and a 7 series BMW blinked in reply.

She did the same with a Mercedes CLK.

"Now hop on a Segway, ride it to your car and pop the trunk. Empty the contents of the trunk, glove box, arm rest, and other interior items including the registration information into the bag. We're hoping to find laptops and tablets, but take everything and we'll sort it out later. Just be sure to keep the items discrete. Don't mix one person's stuff with another's."

Danica knew what was coming so this all made sense to her. "Got it."

"Leave the packed bag on the ground, put the Segway into the trunk, and follow me a mile to the clearing in the woods where we're hiding the cars."

Danica understood. "Then I ride back here on the Segway and repeat."

"Exactly. But first put the used key into the appropriate bag and drop it off in our rental van."

As Bruce spoke, Seb and Webb came into sight, returning from their latest drop-off. Unfortunately, their Segways weren't the only vehicles cresting the hill. Danica also spotted a car. A white sedan. Could it be a cop? Was their plan about to fall apart? Had they climbed a mountain only to trip on a molehill?

She looked over at her husband. Bruce had also spotted the intruding vehicle. Judging by his expression, he wasn't happy.

10
Overkill

Napa, California

AT FIRST, Bruce thought the car was a patrolling cop. Granted, they were well off the beaten path, but perhaps the restaurant used its clout to get extra protection around closing time.

That frightful notion vanished a second later when the glow in the windshield became discernible. It was an Uber, an *Uber Black* most likely, given that the vehicle was a new Audi. Much better than a cop, but still an unwelcome intrusion. A dilemma to deal with.

The A7 pulled around the circular drive and came to a stop before the restaurant's front door. In a second the driver would alert his fare to his arrival. He would, of course, receive no reply. His customer was unconscious. The associated cell phone powered off with its battery removed.

Bruce hit the push-to-talk switch on the bone induction mic in his ear. "Seb, Webb, we need to knock this guy out immediately."

"Roger that," they replied in unison.

Knocking someone out with AcotocA was as simple as slipping an active system over their ears. The effect was as immediate as firing a gun because it completely disrupted brain function. The trick was accessing the ears without interference from the fists.

With the diners, they had solved the problem by having them face the wall. While Seb moved their hands from the back of their heads to the small of their backs, Webb slipped AcotocA over their ears.

With the Uber driver, it wouldn't be so easy. For starters, they'd have to get him out of the car.

"We could just let him go," Danica said. "He'll likely drive off if his fare doesn't show. With Uber, he still gets paid."

Bruce looked over at his wife, pleased that she'd voiced her concern directly rather than over the mic so all could hear. "We can't risk it now that he's seen two guys on Segways. It's unusual enough that he might report it—especially if he's the suspicious type or has a friend or relative in law enforcement. And he's not likely to drive off without investigating. Uber drivers rely on high customer ratings. A single one-star review can crush their average."

Before Danica could respond, the driver ended the debate by exiting his vehicle.

Seb and Webb meanwhile had abandoned their Segways at the edge of the drive and were also walking toward the restaurant door.

Reminding himself that the driver had no reason to be suspicious, that he probably waited for his fares to show as often as not, Bruce attempted to remain calm. He watched the engineers time their approach to coincide with the driver's. Seb was out in front, walking a few paces faster. A man in a hurry. As he passed the driver, he looked over, smiled, nodded and tripped. He went down with a thud on the flagstone path, directly in front of the driver.

The man couldn't ignore him. To do so, he would literally have to step over Seb's fallen body.

Seb propped himself up on an elbow and began shaking his head.

The man stooped over and extended a hand.

Webb slipped an AcotocA headset from his backpack and attempted to clap it over the man's ears, but the driver sensed the aggression and swatted the system away. "What the hell is going on here?! What is that thing?"

Seb rolled onto his feet, pinning the man between them.

"Help!" the man shouted toward the door.

"It's for your own good," Webb said.

"Bullshit," the man said, dropping into a combat stance. Right leg back, right arm cocked, weight evenly distributed between two flat feet.

Seb pulled an MP7 from his backpack and leveled it at the driver. "The choice is yours. His—" he nodded toward the headset in Webb's hand, "or mine." He moved the selector on his submachine gun from safety to single shot. "Choose now."

The man glanced back and forth, unable to believe what was happening.

"Now!" Seb repeated, raising the barrel to heart level.

The man raised his hands.

Webb acted quickly, scooting in and slipping the headset over the man's ears, then catching him as he dropped.

Bruce and Danica emerged from the shadows to join them.

"What do we do now?" Danica asked. "Do we leave him with the restaurant staff or take him with the diners?"

Seb returned the MP7 to his backpack. "No sense mixing an Uber driver in with the diners, not with what we have planned."

Bruce turned to Danica. "What's your best guess on how much memory this guy will lose?"

"Looking at his unconscious body, the only thing I have to go on is age. Three to five minutes is my best guess, but it could be as little as one."

"So he might remember what Seb and Webb look like?" Bruce pressed.

"That's a distinct possibility."

Bruce turned to Webb, the hardware engineer. "Can you crank up the power on his system? Here and now?"

"Best to do it on a system that's not on his head. Given the tools at my disposal, I'll have to physically crack the case open and bypass a regulator."

"Get to it," Bruce commanded before turning back to Danica. "If we double the amperage, what will that buy us?"

"At least two minutes—but the shock might kill him."

Bruce knew death was a distinct possibility with AcotocA, as with most surgical systems, if it was misused. That was the stated reason for the FDA's denial of their application. "We don't have a choice. He's seen two of our faces."

The diners had also seen the engineers, but Seb and Webb were disguised and presented as fellow patrons. Furthermore, given the way AcotocA prevented active memory from being stored, none of the captives would remember anything that happened after they were summoned to leave the room. Not the two additional masked men. Not turning to face the wall. And certainly not the application of the AcotocA system.

"I'm going to put his car in the employee lot," Seb said. "Help add to the confusion."

"How much longer?" Bruce asked Webb.

Webb didn't answer. He was fully focused on the circuitboard laid bare beneath his fingertips. After a few seconds, he said, "Done."

He handed the headset to Bruce, who held it open around the driver's head. As Webb slid the functioning pair off, Bruce slapped the modified pair on. Given the stakes, he was surprised when nothing happened.

"Help me move him into the kitchen with the staff," he said to Webb.

"Hold on a sec!" Danica interrupted. She crouched down to check the driver's carotid pulse and breathing. When she looked up, her ashen face told Bruce everything he needed to know. The words merely confirmed. "He's dead."

11
Descent

Northern California

SEB WAS GLAD to have a job that kept him busy while he and his AcotocA colleagues drove to their destination. Sitting in the back of one of the two U-Hauls, where he could ensure that none of the diners dislodged their headphones and woke up prematurely, Seb pitied Bruce and Danica. Since they were driving the trucks, they had no distractions to keep their minds off the fact that they'd just committed murder.

Back in Bruce's office, when he'd proposed his outlandish idea, the first thing they'd agreed to was *Nobody gets hurt.* Of course the plan required them to threaten violence, but that was an entirely different affair—legally, morally and spiritually. They hadn't even bought bullets for their guns. Just blanks. Enough to make noise if need be.

With a shake of his head, Seb forced his mind back to his job, which included more than observation. He was also tasked with obfuscation.

Beside him at the back of the trailer were the twenty-four bags matching the twenty-four diners who lay sedated at his feet. His half of the forty-eight. One by one, he was matching phones with bodies using driver's licenses, then unlocking the phones with biometrics. Fingerprints or face scans. These tech titans all had the latest gadgets.

Seb was going through texts and emails, first identifying anyone who looked like a secretary or significant other, and then sending them a variant of a simple message, tailored to the tone of their chat history. "Something BIG has come up. Very exciting. But it's going to keep me off the grid for a few days. Wish me luck."

Of course, that particular ploy was unlikely to work with the governor of Florida. Someone with a schedule-keeper on staff. But what else could they do? Governor Rickman's presence added a new dimension to their security concerns, and made the need to execute a clean escape all the more critical.

Webb was performing the same texting task in the back of the second truck—undoubtedly equally happy to have the distraction. They were working quickly in order to limit cell tower usage to those between Napa and Sacramento, which was a highway hub for Northern California. Leaving no electronic indication of which way they turned when leaving the capital would make it much more difficult to track them. The tactic was far from foolproof, but it would buy time.

Time was what they needed.

Once Seb finished with the cell phones, exhaustion overtook him and he nodded off. He jolted back to consciousness sometime later when the gradient beneath the truck's tires changed from up to down. Nervous about his dereliction of duty, he glanced around to confirm that all his prisoners still had their earphones in place.

They did.

No harm, no foul.

He checked his watch and saw that they had indeed been driving for three hours. That fit with the change in gradient. They were nearing their destination.

He found it interesting that all four team members had stayed silent during the drive rather than chat away nervous energy. Seb was certain Webb wanted to talk about what happened. His buddy would want to explore their new status like a tongue probing the socket of a freshly pulled tooth. But the bone mics that connected them would bring everyone into the conversation, and no one would want to endure that emotional burden at the moment. So everyone remained silent, each in the solitude of his or her own hell.

The truck slowed, then the surface beneath the tires

switched from asphalt to crushed stone. Soon they swung around, stopped and reversed. A minute later, Seb heard Bruce's voice through the cargo door. "Everything okay in there?"

Seb wouldn't characterize things that way, but he knew what Bruce meant. "Yes."

The door rolled up and Seb found himself looking at an exquisite cabin. Even though it was lit only by the moon, the stars and the few lights Bruce had left burning, the hideout still reeked of money. It was a log cabin, if you could call it that.

From there in the driveway, Seb estimated the size to be six thousand square feet. The logs that formed the main walls must have been entire treetrunks, each long and straight and somehow preserved in a light pine color. The floorpan was no Lincoln-style box either. It featured a wraparound porch, big balconies and bumped-out suites, all protected from the mountain weather by interlocking sections of steep brick-red roof.

"No problems?" Bruce asked, grabbing the two stretchers he'd hidden beside the porch.

"None."

"How about the messages?"

"One hundred percent success."

Bruce raised his eyebrows. "I'd expected a few misses, but I guess these guys keep up with the latest toys. Let's get moving."

They grabbed the person closest to the door, lifted him onto a stretcher and carried him into the house. "I left it unlocked with the heat on and the elevator open."

Seb wasn't sure what Bruce meant by the last bit, but he saw soon enough. Bruce led him into the library located just off the atrium. It was classic in style, with floor-to-high-ceiling bookshelves lining two of the walls, complete with rolling ladders. One huge section of shelving had been pivoted aside like a gigantic door to reveal a large elevator, a small elevator and a nook.

"The nook was a gun room," Bruce clarified. "But I moved all the weapons to the garage along with the electronics from below as a safety precaution."

"Safety precaution?"

"Our prisoners will be passing through here on their way in and their way out. Figured it was best not to tempt fate." Bruce hit the DOWN button with his elbow and the doors opened, revealing a freight elevator roughly six feet square. Pressed against the back wall and spanning every inch of the width was a card table. The big makeshift shelf held nothing but a small Wi-Fi repeater, which was wired to the elevator control box. "The table lets us take two more people per trip," Bruce said, in answer to an unasked question. "Six instead of four."

Seb snagged for a second on the fact that fifty wasn't evenly divisible by six, but then remembered that he and Webb were two of the diners. He was thrilled that his boss had bothered to analyze elevator operations. If Bruce had devoted attention to the little details, then the big ones were surely covered. "And the Wi-Fi repeater?"

"You'll figure it out. Let's grab five more guests."

Leading answers like "You'll figure it out" were very Bruce. The man's brain was so big as to be a burden. Seb had come to that conclusion one evening while reflecting on another odd comment. Bruce was so smart as to make interactions with normal folk analogous to what the rest of us went through when working with dogs. It had to be frustrating and isolating.

Oddly enough, Bruce had only earned one degree. A Bachelor of Science in physics from Cornell. But he could talk medicine on par with his Johns Hopkins M.D. wife. Material science, electrical engineering and systems design on equal footing with the Stanford engineers in his employ. Seb had also seen Bruce go toe-to-toe with billionaire bankers discussing derivative operations at cocktail parties, and hold his own debating Shakespeare with a prominent theater critic.

His only meaningful weakness was politics.

Bruce had such a strong understanding of fundamental truths that he found it uncomfortable to lie. He just wasn't wired for deception. It was his Achilles' heel. At least, that was Seb's conclusion.

Fortunately, there was nothing deceptive about this operation. It was straightforward diabolical genius.

Danica and Webb had their truck backed into place by the time Bruce and Seb returned for the third body. After a bit of cold, confirmatory discussion, the four of them made two quick trips and then wedged themselves into the freight elevator with their cargo.

"Here we go," Bruce said, hitting the down button.

12
Changing Sides

Western Nevada

THE ELEVATOR hummed away, drawing them ever deeper beneath the Nevada bedrock while Seb steeled himself for what was to come. To say that he'd be standing on unfamiliar ground would be an understatement on multiple levels. Looking down, he cringed at his own unfortunate pun. The floor at his feet was literally strewn with bodies. Adding to the irony was the fact that he and Webb would soon be among them, albeit voluntarily, for they too had been diners.

The costumes they were wearing—the stylish suits, short hair, matching glasses and temporary tattoos—would both shield them from any future efforts to identify them and help keep them in character. But Seb found that they made him more uncomfortable. Particularly the glasses, as he wasn't used to wearing them.

As the surreal scene sunk in, Seb mused that he wouldn't need to work at appearing despondent when he woke up. The unfortunate incident with the Uber driver had taken care of that.

To cover and conceal the unusual murder, Danica used a very fine-gauge needle to inject ketamine directly into the driver's femoral vein. She also stuck a regular syringe in his arm and left it there. Then he and Webb drove car and driver into Napa where they staged the suicide scene at a picturesque overlook.

Although the four conspirators vowed to never speak of their vile accident again, Seb knew the shock would take days to wear off, and the images would forever haunt his dreams.

Bruce interrupted Seb's reflections by pressing a pair of surgical gloves into his hands. "The bunker is sixty-four feet down. It's constructed inside a natural cavern."

Seb accepted the gloves and voiced the question he'd been itching to explore ever since Bruce had unveiled his plan. "Why would anyone lay out the kind of money a project like this requires? It had to cost more than the mansion above, but can't be anywhere near as pleasant."

Danica and Webb perked up as well. Apparently, they too had the same question.

The elevator doors interrupted the reply by opening to reveal a large, luxurious living space served by a full kitchen and filled with quality furnishings. "The main room is backed by two floors of smaller rooms half its height," Bruce said as they lugged the first set of bodies inside. "There are four bedrooms, two bathrooms, a den and a workout room. At the left end of the bunker, there's a storage area, which runs long and deep. The right end is divided into a utility room, containing the power and filtration systems, and a greenhouse."

Bruce released the ankles of the diner he was carrying when they reached the far end of the room. "To answer your earlier question about why this is here, the owner is a prepper."

"What's a prepper?" Webb asked as they continued unloading. "The term rings a bell, but isn't in my active vocabulary."

"In general, a prepper is a person who believes a catastrophic disaster is imminent and prepares for it by creating a refuge which he stockpiles with supplies. In this case, the prepper is convinced that the United States will face a nuclear or biological war. He built this bunker to allow his family to survive in style.

"And since survival includes dealing with refugees in the apocalyptic aftermath, he hid it."

"This is where you got our submachine guns," Webb said.

"That's right. In preparation for tonight, I had to haul all the electronics and weaponry up and out. Did have to buy the blanks though. Our benefactor didn't stockpile those."

"Are you ever going to tell us who that benefactor is?" Danica asked. "And how you knew the access and alarm codes?"

Seb knew Bruce loved his secrets, so he hadn't pressed, although of course he too was curious.

"You'll know soon enough," Bruce said, and left it at that.

They completed another seven round trips with the freight elevator until all forty-eight diners were laid out on the living room floor. Aside from the suits and headsets, they looked like fraternity boys after a wild party.

Despite the danger, Seb found himself dragging. It had been a very long day. Even with the stretchers, hauling so many hostages had been physically exhausting. Now that their preparatory work was complete, he actually found himself looking forward to the next stage.

While Danica went to work injecting the diners with the same sedative cocktail she'd used on the restaurant staff, Bruce reminded Seb and Webb of their mission. He went through everything in detail for the fourth or fifth time, then added a new twist. "To avoid confusion, you'll still go by familiar names. Instead of Joel Sebastian, you'll be Sebastian Silver. And instead of Milton Webb, you'll be Webster Gold."

"Sebastian and Webster," Seb said. "Easy enough."

"Silver and Gold," Webb said. "Got it."

"Good," Bruce said.

Danica looked their way. "I've still got a dozen bodies to position. If you're done, please grab all the pill bottles and cigarette packs you can find among the confiscated belongings. We should leave them on the kitchen table to help prevent unproductive anxiety."

The guys did as the good doctor asked, using the trip upstairs to stash the AcotocA headsets in the hidden closet.

After that last group task was complete, Bruce pulled a roll of red duct tape from his backpack and walked to stand directly beneath the only electronic device in the room—a fancy doorbell some seven feet off the ground. Seb recognized it as the same model of wireless intercom with one-way video that the Devlins had in their home.

Bruce proceeded to pace out to a position seven feet from the wall. There, he used the tape to demarcate a two-foot by two-foot box on the floor.

The scene sparked an insight. "I get it now," Seb said. "The Wi-Fi repeater on the elevator. You can turn it on and off from up top by using the corresponding circuit breaker. Very clever."

Bruce nodded affirmation.

Seb and Webb assumed prone positions among the other diners.

"Sleep well," Bruce said, as Danica pinched Seb's left triceps and plunged her needle in. "A few more days of work and then you get to spend the rest of your life living the dream."

I SLIPPED THE ENGAGEMENT RING deep into the front pocket of my jeans, then gave Katya a shake before whispering for a third time, "Katya, wake up."

She didn't wake, but this time she stirred. A second later I got the second big shock of the day. The world burst into life.

Lights illuminated. Appliances sputtered. Air started to flow. All as if tripped by a motion detector.

With the urgency of a paratrooper who'd just hit the ground, I surveyed our surroundings. The room we occupied was windowless—despite being roughly thirty by sixty feet in size, with a twenty-foot ceiling. I'd have compared it to an elementary school gymnasium were it not for the high-end furnishings. Adding the still, stale and silent air to my initial observations, I concluded that we were underground.

By we, I wasn't just referencing Katya. There were dozens of unconscious bodies scattered around the floor. Familiar faces and clothes. I was looking at the other diners from Cinquante Bouches. Forty-eight of them, I supposed.

A few other guys started stirring. The younger, more athletic ones. And by guys I meant men. There were only two women in the room.

I gave Katya's arm a good squeeze.

She winced and withdrew, but didn't open her eyes. The odd reaction led me to inspect her arm. Sure enough, I found a needle mark.

I checked my own arm and found a matching red dot. Just one, thank goodness. An anesthetic, no doubt. That thought toppled another like a big fat domino. Anesthetics caused short-term memory loss.

I leaned over Katya so my face was just a foot from hers and stroked her cheek.

She smiled faintly, and then opened her eyes. Her nose crinkled and she blinked a few times. "What's going on?" she asked with groggy voice.

"I'm not sure yet, but we're together, so I'm not too worried," I replied, keeping my voice calm and low.

Her eyes widened. "The restaurant, the ring, the gunmen. I remember that—but then draw a blank."

Gunmen! The mention of them restored a few more frames of my memory. I recalled black masks and panicked people being led from the room—but nothing more.

Knowing that Katya was a processor rather than a panicker, I gave it to her straight. "We were drugged. Near as I can tell, we're in a sub-basement beneath the restaurant."

"You mean we've been kidnapped," she said, glancing around.

I hadn't thought of it quite like that, but given the gunmen element, I supposed she was right. "It appears that way. I have yet to talk to anyone else or otherwise investigate."

Katya sat up and studied our surroundings. After a few seconds, she slipped off her high heels and said, "Let's look around, quietly."

Katya had it right. Her contained and courageous reaction would surely prove to be the exception. Pandemonium was about to break out. Best to gain a basic understanding of our environment before that happened.

I stood and offered her my hand. There were two other hushed conversations taking place as we rose, but most of our fellow diners were still anesthetized. I suspected that the stressful, sedentary lifestyles led by these big time bankers and blue-chip executives had slowed their metabolism.

My first observation was that the room had lots of exits.

Both the short walls had large double doors in the middle. One long wall had ten regular doors, five at ground level, five accessed by an elevated walkway that ran the length of the room. It was the kind of construction I'd seen in only one other setting: a prison.

Suppressing the emotions that accompanied that observation, I turned my attention to the most interesting doors. Two elevators in the wall behind us. One large, one small. The poured-concrete shaft that housed both was bumped out, partially dividing the big room, with the kitchen and dining room on one side, and a lounge area on the other.

The larger elevator appeared typical at first glance. A stainless steel set of double sliders. A second glance revealed deadbolts at the top and bottom, obviously designed to prevent the doors from opening. They weren't engaged, but still struck me as odd since I'd never seen that feature on an elevator before.

More concerning than the presence of locks was what wasn't there, specifically the control panel. The place where it had been was now just a rectangular hole in the wall.

The smaller elevator had a single, hinged door that was obviously very heavy duty. Almost safe-like. It too had deadbolts. I didn't see a call panel next to it either. Not exactly. What I did see was a large ratcheted crank.

"What is that?" Katya asked, her gaze in line with mine.

"I think it's a failsafe. A manual lift." I walked over and put pressure on the crank handle. It wiggled a bit but wouldn't turn. "Locked."

Katya canted her head. A mathematics professor by profession, she had exceptional analytical skills. "Is it there in case of a power outage?"

"Or a mechanical failure."

"Why not simply install a ladder?"

"Ladders don't have cargo capability."

Katya had an answer ready for that. "You use the ladder to get out, then call an electrician. Problem solved."

I turned toward my sweetie and took both her hands in mine. "I referred to this place earlier as a sub-basement, but

I didn't mention its purpose, its function."

Her eyes grew wider. "And what's that?"

"I believe it's a bunker. A refuge designed for doomsday survival. The accompanying assumption is that no electricians will be available."

"Oh," Katya said, processing the unexpected twist like a wood chipper encountering a knotty log. "Are there any other insights to our predicament you'd care to share?"

"The control box has been removed from the electric elevator, so we can safely assume neither lift will operate."

"What else?"

"You see the red box?"

"The tape on the middle of the floor?"

"I think it's a podium."

"You mean, like a speaking platform?"

"Exactly."

"But it's not raised."

"It's not for addressing people in the room," I said with a gesture toward a piece of electronic equipment installed above the elevators. "It's for addressing whoever's on the other side of that camera."

"Oh," Katya replied, her mind continuing to chip away as her gaze came to rest on the electronic eye.

"What the hell happened?!" a voice boomed behind us.

14
Prepping

Location Unknown

KATYA TURNED to see the same blowhard banker who'd bothered her at dinner. He was sitting up and rubbing the back of his skull. The sight made her wonder if he'd been dropped on his head—either accidentally or on purpose.

"Where are we?" he continued in a voice much too loud, addressing the guys to his left and right while shaking them awake.

Katya noted that people were grouped on the floor roughly as they'd been in the restaurant. At least to the extent she could remember. The other diners had been far from her primary focus at the time. She suspected that their sleeping locations were likely the result of the loading and unloading function that got them from there to here, rather than a conscious design.

"Ignore him," Achilles said. "Let's go explore."

"With pleasure."

In the back of her mind, Katya was aware that she should be panicking, but she wasn't. Like the banker, she should be screaming and pounding, interrogating everyone around, but she didn't feel the need. It wasn't that she was an exceptionally calm or brave person, although a few extreme experiences had tempered her reactions. She owed her current composure to the fact that she was facing the unknown beside Kyle Achilles. Now and forever.

Had he swallowed the ring? This probably wasn't the best time to ask.

They were nearer the lounge than the kitchen, so they

walked toward the double doors in that direction. "You think they'll be unlocked?" Katya asked.

"They don't appear to even have a lock," Achilles replied.

He opened the handled door, revealing a storeroom. It illuminated in response to their motion.

"It's the size of a small grocery store, and packed like they are in Midtown Manhattan," Katya said, calculating the room to be about three times as wide as it was deep.

"About fifteen by forty-five feet, I'd estimate," Achilles said. "It runs further to our right than the main room by about fifteen feet, which I'm sure we'll find is the depth of the rooms along the back wall."

Katya saw the pattern too. With this second piece of the big geometric puzzle, she could now estimate that the bunker's footprint was at least a forty-five-by-ninety-foot rectangle, with the main room sandwiched by long rooms on each end, and a series of smaller rooms capping the top in the middle. Whether or not other rooms extended it further remained to be seen.

The supplies stored before them on heavy gauge wire shelves were all generic. Brandless. Brown, white or olive green boxes with plain black lettering. Multivitamins. UHT Milk. Powdered milk. Powdered eggs. Canned Tuna. Canned Chicken. Peanut Butter. Olive Oil. Chili. Sugar. Flour. Salt. Pepper.

They began walking the closest aisle.

The room was arranged with deep floor-to-ceiling shelves around the perimeter and had a similar island of shelving in the middle, creating a circuit which they now lapped. Dried Apricots. Dried Plums. Raisins. Red Beans. Black Beans. Dried Cheese. Mixed Nuts. Trail Mix. Oatmeal. Wheat Crackers. Granola Bars. Power Bars. Chocolate. Katya stopped at Chocolate. She'd seen enough. She wouldn't starve.

They exited where they'd come in and found that the main room was now awash in murmured conversation. Katya noted that all but a few of their fellow prisoners were awake or waking. Most groups were talking in hushed tones, a few others were also starting to explore. Fortunately, nobody sounded hysterical. Katya considered that a small blessing, a silver lining on the cloud of captivity.

Achilles continued to ignore the crowd. He led her up the stairway to their left. The first door off the elevated walkway opened into a bedroom, fifteen feet square. It had twin beds in two corners and a king between them in the third. All were bunk beds, creating a room that would sleep eight comfortably and many more in a pinch. There were clothes dressers as well, but they were relatively small. Dorm room or military size. "I guess the fashion needs are minimal when you're in survival mode," Katya said.

"The weather needs too," I replied. "I bet the temperature stays the same here year round."

The next door exposed an identical bedroom. Then a den full of books and desks but no computers. The fourth was a dormitory-style bathroom with multiple sinks and toilets.

"I was hoping to find one of these," Achilles said.

"Yeah, me too," Katya replied.

"Where are we?" the obnoxious banker yelled when they exited the bathroom. He was addressing them, Katya noted.

Achilles walked to the edge of the railing and she stayed at his side. The shout had turned everyone's attention in their direction.

"Looks like a bunker," Achilles said, gesturing with both arms.

"How did we get here?" the banker asked.

"I think the elevator is a safe assumption."

Achilles took her hand and headed down the staircase opposite the one they'd ascended. A flurry of quiet conversations broke out. Again, Achilles ignored them.

The second set of double doors was right there at the bottom of the stairs so they stepped inside. Although large, the room appeared to be half the size of the pantry. It had double doors on the end to their left, presumably providing access to the second half.

They were surrounded by troughs rather than shelves. Troughs of dirt at floor level, and empty plastic troughs suspended above. All were empty.

The ceiling was lined with light fixtures that varied from

those in the rest of the bunker. In the corner, she spotted what appeared to be an uninhabited chicken coop. "A farm," Katya said. "I don't know if that's a good sign or bad. While the setup is impressive, the implied timeline is discouraging."

"I don't think it's a sign at all," Achilles replied. "This facility isn't brand new, but it hasn't seen much use either. That tells me it wasn't designed for us—or people like us."

Before asking who Achilles thought it was designed for, Katya decided to ponder the problem herself.

They spent a minute walking around, touching and testing, taking it all in. "What do you think is through there?" Katya asked, gesturing toward the double doors at the far end.

"The utility room," Achilles said. "It's the only critical element we haven't yet found. And potentially, the most interesting one."

"Shall we?"

They were two steps from their destination when shouting turned them in their tracks. They ran back to the main room and saw the source of distress. The obnoxious banker had the man they'd entered the restaurant with pressed against the elevator door, swaths of shirt bunched in both fists. "If you don't get your people to let us out, I'm going to pound you to a pulp."

15
Good Question

Location Unknown

EXACTLY TWO YEARS AGO, I was in a conventional jail —awaiting trial for murders I hadn't committed. I made the most of those miserable circumstances by focusing on the unique opportunities that incarceration presented.

I became a calisthenics junkie, developing the balance and strength that ultimately took my rock climbing to a level I might not have otherwise achieved. I also trained for the U.S. Memory Championship, honing my mind in a manner that seemed likely to bring lifelong benefits.

But this was a very different kind of confinement. On the upside, the company appeared more erudite, the facilities more luxurious, and the food more palatable. All welcome improvements. On the downside, I didn't know for certain why we were here or how long we should expect to stay. And the pressure was greater. More aggravating and intense. Because I worried about Katya.

Being buried alive was also a bit unsettling.

I found myself reassessing my initial impression of the company as Katya and I burst back into the main room. The scene had changed a lot. Or rather the people. Apparently, locking humans in cages tends to bump them down the evolutionary ladder.

I'm far from a pacifist. Although intellectually I bow to diplomats and diplomacy, I'm built and wired to grab the bull by the horns. A man of action, you might say. But I'm also disciplined. Logic driven. And I have a deep affinity for fairness. So when I see injustice occurring, I tend to wade in. "What's going on?"

A circle of spectators had formed around the pair, with the banker's buddies on the inside left and the assaulted man's attractive wife on the inside right. I pushed through the crowd and placed one hand firmly on a shoulder of each man. "What happened?"

"I'm getting us out of here. I suggest you leave me to it," the aggressor replied without meeting my eye.

No way this guy would have spoken to me like that if we were alone. Mano a mano, he'd undoubtedly have melted. But surrounded by his colleagues, Biff's banker brain was blinded by simple math. Four to one.

As a military man, I knew that caliber and cyclic rate counted much more in situations like these. Four .22 revolvers were no match for a .50 machine gun.

Oblivious to the fact that he was outgunned, Biff attempted to shrug off my hand.

I dug my thumb into his brachial plexus, applying just enough pressure to give him a taste. You'd have thought I'd plunged a dagger between his ribs based on reaction I received.

He released the smaller guy and backed up to stand amidst his pack. "Are you in on it with him?" he spouted, attempting to save face.

"What's your name?" I asked.

He stared at me for a long, slow second, then straightened his back and shoulders. "I'm Harold Herbert Huxley III. Who the hell are you?"

The third. I'd been right. While not a Chip or Skip or Biff, he was a Trey.

I turned to the guy whose shirt collars Trey had seized. "And you?"

"I go by Oz," he said with a singsong British accent.

"Like the Wizard?

"I work in high tech."

"I go by Achilles. I work in low tech. What happened?"

"I believe the technical term is racial profiling."

I turned back to Harold Herbert Huxley III. "What happened?"

"This," Trey said, gesturing around.

"So to summarize, you think this is a terrorist act and are fighting back by attacking the brown guy?"

"I play the odds for a living, a very substantial living, and this was an easy call. I mean, look around. You don't need a Ph.D. in criminal psychology to pick the terrorist spy from this crowd," Trey said, looking from one colleague to another for support as he spoke.

I knew Oz and his wife weren't spies because I'd already identified those. But Trey had inadvertently opened a welcome opportunity to covertly cripple them. "If this guy was a spy, he'd have a microphone hidden in his ear. Did you spot a mic?"

Trey didn't reply.

"Did you bother to look?"

Again nothing.

As I turned to the target of Trey's ire, I subtly scanned the room. The movement I observed confirmed my hypothesis. "Where are you from, Oz?"

"I'm Maltese, not Middle Eastern. That's an EU country, if you didn't know. I studied chemistry at Oxford. My wife, Sabrina, is also an Oxford grad."

I looked back at Trey. He still wore a stubborn expression, but the fire had left his eyes. I was staring into them when the world went black. Completely black.

There was utter silence immediately following the power cut, then murmuring broke out.

The saying "It takes one to know one" is only half true. *Like* merely has an advantage in detecting *like*, not a monopoly. The advantage doesn't stop with biology. It also applies to profession. Once you've worked as a spy, once you've lived a false identity while concealing your real one, you know the tricks of the trade. The little things that make a big difference. The tiny alterations and subtle disguises. You automatically spot them on others the way fashion designers do brands.

Spend enough time living the clandestine life and you also become adept at predicting the behavior of other covert operatives. "Send a spy to catch a spy" as another old saying goes.

Because of my past profession, I knew what would happen next. I knew it the way a poker pro knows you're about to raise. The way a car salesman knows you're going to counter. The way a cop knows you're planning to run.

I closed my eyes, aimed my ears, and heard exactly what I'd expected. The mechanical mix of shifting gears and sliding bolts, followed by a sucking whoosh. Two seconds later the auditory pattern reversed and the footfalls retreated, fading back into the crowd.

I began counting down in my head. Five, four, three, two —

The lights blazed back to life as suddenly as they'd been extinguished, creating a collective sigh. As people blinked, a voice boomed forth. "What happened?"

I turned and saw the man who'd asked "What did we do?" during dinner. He now sported quite the welt above his brow. He was way over by the manual elevator, but spoke with a tone loud and authoritative enough to turn everyone's head.

He struck me as a cross between a banker and a drill sergeant. Mature, lean and fit, he had a shaved scalp and piercing blue eyes and wore clothes that likely cost more than my car. Last I'd seen, he'd been sawing logs on the floor. Apparently, he'd just come to.

His next question really riveted everyone's attention. "What are you guys doing in my bunker?"

16
Timeline

Location Unknown

I WATCHED TREY and his colleagues melt into the crowd as the man claiming to be the bunker's owner made his way to the center of the circle. It was the man who had questioned our captors in the restaurant. I could tell by his voice and the lump on his head.

He met my eye and asked, "What's going on?"

"What's the last thing you remember?"

He stopped walking well inside my personal space, as if claiming ownership to the concrete beneath my feet, but he took my question at face value. He tilted his head for a few seconds of thought, then said, "The appetizer at Cinquante Bouches. I was there with Governor Rickman and two other friends. You were there with a beautiful woman."

I didn't recall which state Governor Rickman was from but figured his presence might explain things. Didn't want to get ahead of myself though. "You don't remember the masked gunmen?"

His eyes widened. "No."

I raised my voice. "Does anyone else not remember the gunmen?"

A dozen hands rose. One belonged to a tall tan man with a patrician face topped by thick white hair. I could place him now. Rickman was from Florida.

Turning back to the owner I said, "Give it a minute. We're all missing memories, but you're missing a bit more than most." As I spoke, an idea occurred to me. Again I raised my voice. "Does anyone remember what happened after you were led from the dining room?"

No hands this time.

The owner's expression showed him to be a quick study. He backed off half a step.

"What's your name?" I asked.

"Kai—Kai Basher."

"And this is your place?"

"Hard to mistake it wouldn't you say." Even Kai's light tone sounded like shoveled gravel.

"Point taken. Where, exactly, are we?"

It was Kai's turn to address the attentive crowd. "You're standing sixty feet beneath the foundation of my hunting lodge, which is in the Carson Spur of the Sierra Nevada mountains, southwest of Reno, Nevada."

The unexpected answer sucked the air from the room.

Trey quickly jumped into the void.

"We can discuss geography later. Just show us the way out."

Kai appraised Trey and then turned back to the crowd. "There's only one way out of here and that's up. Sixty feet up—measuring from the floor we're standing on to the floor our captors occupy. The electric elevator is obviously out of commission, and if you'll try the crank on the manual lift, as I just did, you'll find that it's been blocked. We're not getting out until whoever put us here decides he wants us out."

"It can't be a coincidence that you're here," Trey pressed, puffing back up. "You know more than you're letting on."

Kai appraised his assailant with the nonchalance of a dog about to flick a flea. "While I agree that it can't be a coincidence, I have no idea who put us here or why."

"I don't believe you."

Trey was considerably bigger and decades younger, but my money was on Basher if violence broke out. And though I couldn't deny the appeal of watching Trey get clocked, I had more pressing priorities. "Kai, what can you tell us about your bunker?"

Kai half-turned in my direction. He had the hefty gaze of a man used to command, but it was more analytical than adversarial. "This bunker is constructed inside a natural cavern, which was eroded by the underground river that now supplies it with water."

"What about the elevator and ventilation shafts?"

"Like the primary facility, they leverage a natural formation—a crevasse."

"Can the rest of the crevasse be accessed?" I asked.

"It no longer exists. I had it plugged with concrete as part of the hardening process. Didn't want any contamination or radiation leaking in."

Wonderful. "Speaking of things leaking in, what's with the bolts on the elevator doors?"

Kai turned to fully face me. "Obviously, they're the last line of defense for keeping people out. Both are designed to withstand small arms fire, and they're hermetically sealed so we can't be smoked out."

I had to hand it to Kai, he was a thorough and thoughtful prepper. "Do you have the key?"

"There is no key. Keys can get lost. The deadbolts just slide."

"I'm talking about the kind of key firefighters use to open elevator doors. I'm talking about getting us out, not keeping marauders from getting in."

Kai's face contorted. "You just push the button—if it's not missing. There is no key."

I dropped it. "What's the utility situation?"

The confident look returned. "In a word, redundant. The river running beneath our feet keeps a 24,000-gallon tank topped off and powers a generator. The generator feeds a 1000 kWh battery array, which also has feeds from twin wind turbines and a solar farm up top."

"And ventilation?"

"There are eight sixteen-inch ventilation shafts. A redundant set in each corner of the main room." Kai pointed up. "Each fan can be individually configured to blow in or out, although typically they're balanced in pairs."

"How are the fans controlled?"

"Normally by thermostats. But you'll note that those have been removed with the other electronics and anything that might be considered a weapon or tool."

That they'd removed weapons was no surprise. The fact that they'd tampered with the climate control system did concern me, although I was unsure if their removal was part of a specific plan or they'd just been swept up in a blanket order. "Do you notice anything that's been added?"

"The intercom camera over the elevator is new, as is the safe bolted to the floor in the lounge. Other than that, just the stuff on the table—the calculators, stationery supplies, pill bottles and cigarettes."

Our captors had installed a safe. That was an interesting twist, one I'd surely puzzle over in the coming hours.

"What's the situation with food?" I asked.

"The pantry is stocked to feed 32 adults for a full year. Utilizing the garden will extend that indefinitely."

Trey jumped back in. "That's enough to feed the fifty of us for nearly eight months. How long are they planning to keep us here?"

The room fell silent as every captive contemplated the chilling prospect of being locked in an underground cave—forever.

17
Speculation

Two Days Later
Western Nevada

AS SHE WALKED into the gym with Sabrina at her side, Katya found herself giving credit to Kai. The man knew how to build a bunker. Located directly beneath the den, the gym contained a stationary bike, a treadmill, a universal weight machine, and space for floor exercises.

They headed for the mats.

Katya was spending the bulk of her time with Achilles, and much of the rest with Sabrina—the bunker's other female resident. Oz's wife was smart, fit and pleasant, if not a bit mysterious.

Achilles was the gym's only other occupant. He was pounding away on the treadmill at a pace that would wind her in seconds.

After forty-eight hours in the bunker, most of the captives were beginning to adapt to life "down under." The forty-eight hours was just an estimation based on their collective biological clocks. Their captors had confiscated all watches and removed not only the wall clock but everything with a time display. In fact, kitchen appliances aside, there wasn't a piece of electronic equipment to be found, other than the video intercom, which Kai told them wasn't his. The reason for that action and everything else remained a mystery. They had not heard one word from above ground.

"What's the crowd's latest thinking?" Achilles asked, pressing a button that took the treadmill down a notch.

"People are beginning to speculate that we'll never hear

anything. That we'll be buried underground until we die of old age or someone stumbles upon us," Katya replied.

"Don't count on anyone finding us," Kai said, walking into the room and plopping down on the bench press. "The elevators are expertly concealed. They're tough to find even when you know they're there. Trespassers could live in the cabin for years oblivious to the bunker below."

"What about the utilities?" Achilles asked.

"The solar panels and wind turbines also service the house, so they don't provide a clue, and the ventilation shafts are well hidden."

"People are proposing all kinds of crazy ideas," Sabrina added. "Sebastian or Webster—I always forget which is which—suggested that we could be here for organ harvesting."

"That's terrible," Katya said. "Why would someone speculate like that out loud?"

"It gets worse," Sabrina replied. "The other one floated the idea that we were inventory to be used in snuff films. Said he'd recently read a bestseller where that was the big reveal."

With that conversation killer hanging in the air, Katya turned to the mat. She began a pre-yoga stretching routine, and Sabrina joined in.

Everyone had changed out of their formal wear and into the dark blue surgical scrubs Kai had stockpiled. Katya found the plain cotton clothes comfortable for both casual wear and exercise. With everyone wearing matching medical garb, the bunker now resembled the breakroom at an elite hospital. The outfit also seemed to put people in a professional mindset. She wondered if that was an intended effect. Kai was clearly a very clever guy.

Despite their now uniform appearance, cliques had formed. That was inevitable, she supposed. There was a *banker* clique, led by Trey, an *executive* clique, co-led by Kai and the governor, and an *other* clique. She and Achilles were *others*, along with Oz, Sabrina and the group of four software startup guys who shared their bedroom.

The clatter of iron plates announced the end of Kai's

second set of chest presses. He looked over at Achilles. "I'd like to know your theory on why we're here."

Katya was also curious to hear Kyle's latest thinking. She was certain that his mind had been churning as fast as his legs.

Achilles answered the question with one of his own, as was often his way. "Who knew you'd be dining at Cinquante Bouches?"

Kai smiled. "Nice idea, but it doesn't lead anywhere. I have a standing reservation. This time of year, I'm there almost every Friday night. The restaurant staff obviously know that, as do most of the people I've dined with over the years. My habit has even been mentioned in an article or two."

"Articles about you or the restaurant?"

"Both."

"How about the bunker?" Achilles asked. "Your earlier comments imply that you've kept its existence secret."

Kai chewed on that one for two shakes. "Not really. Making something difficult to discover is different from keeping it secret. I'm worried about the wild herd. The looting mob. The people I've shown my secret bunker to aren't the types who'll pick up pitchforks and firebrands after the bombs drop."

Kai obviously had no firsthand experience with war. Nothing changes people like the prospect of an untimely death. "What about house keys and the alarm code? Who has access to those?"

"There are no metal keys, just a keypad. I didn't want to risk being locked out when the missiles launch."

"Do other people know the codes? Former guests, for instance? How often do you change them?"

"I've never changed the codes. And yes, my former guests know them. Or knew them. Who remembers that kind of thing?"

"So you didn't use a mnemonic device? A passphrase or the like?"

Kai's face dropped. "Look, even if we could construct a Venn diagram and draw up a list of suspects from the overlap, what good would it do us? We'd still be completely at their mercy."

"You're probably right," Achilles replied. "But one thing is certain: complacency won't get us anywhere. Speaking of which, what does it look like upstairs?"

"Like a cabin in the mountains. A very nice, very isolated cabin."

"What about the bunker entrance?"

"It's hidden behind a big built-in bookcase. You'd never know the elevators are there. You'd never stumble on them either. People don't randomly try to pull built-in bookcases from the wall."

That wasn't encouraging. "So how did our captors find it?"

"Back on that topic, are we? Obviously, they already knew it was there." Kai folded his arms across his chest. "Now, you still haven't answered my initial question."

He was right, I hadn't. "Surely, you already know why we're here."

"Why do you say that?"

Achilles grinned. "You're a smart guy with two eyes."

"I don't follow." Judging by Kai's expression, Katya concluded that he really didn't. She didn't follow either for that matter.

"Look around. Who do you see?" Achilles asked.

"Prisoners."

"Perhaps you've been blinded by familiarity, Kai. When I look around, what I see is rich people."

Kai clenched his broad jaw. "You think we've been kidnapped? As in for ransom? A mass kidnapping?"

"That's the way I'd do it, if I were so inclined. Fifty ransoms is a whole lot better than one. Fifty times better, as a matter of fact. Granted, not all ransoms are equal, but it's fair to say that whoever planned this picked a perfect place to throw his net."

Kai stood and began swinging his shoulder, ostensibly to work out a kink. "So you don't think it's related to Governor Rickman?"

"I considered that. But if it was about one person, the

kidnapping would have been more surgical, don't you think?"

Kai didn't appear convinced. "Bear in mind that we're not actually kids. We can pay our own ransoms. Your theory neglects the simple fact that no one has asked us for money —and it's been two days. Whoever did this surely wants to cash out and escape as soon as possible."

Achilles slowed the treadmill to a brisk walking speed. "In my experience, two days is about what it takes to soften people up. After sucking on silence for forty-eight hours, the paranoia really kicks into gear. People start speculating well beyond the bounds of rational thinking. They come up with crazy conjecture like organ harvesting and snuff films. They also become more pliable. More desperate to do what they're told."

"So the silence is just psychological warfare?"

"Not solely. There's also a practical reason for the delay."

"And what's that?"

"We were kidnapped on a Friday night, Kai. The banks have been closed."

Kai raised his eyebrows, acknowledging the insight. Then he nodded at the obvious corollary. "So the excitement starts tomorrow."

18
Rule One

Western Nevada

IT WAS 1:00 on Monday morning in Nevada when Danica brewed the day's first two cups of coffee. She handed one to her husband before taking the seat beside him at the big desk that was serving as their command center.

They'd spent two days preparing for this moment. They had refined operational plans and performed tactical preparations. They'd shifted their bodies to an earlier schedule and stocked up on sleep. Danica couldn't confirm feeling either completely confident or fully rested, but she wasn't overly stressed either. Their plan was relatively simple and, by her best calculations, they had everything important under control.

On the card tables behind them, back near the open bookcase, forty-eight piles of personal belongings lay neatly arranged. One for each kidnappee.

On the desk before them were two laptops, hers to the left, his to the right. In the middle was the intercom's parent module. Bruce had it connected to several components, including a large monitor. Danica expected to see it displaying a live video of the bunker below, transmitted in high resolution from the intercom, but the monitor was black.

"What's up with the screen?" she asked.

"Wi-Fi's off, remember?"

"Of course," she said, standing.

One of the brilliant fail-safes Bruce had dreamed up was relocating the bunker's Wi-Fi extender to the freight elevator. That way they could cut off the signal below while maintaining it above by cutting power to the elevator. This simple trick, Bruce explained, would allow them to sleep, leave or otherwise become preoccupied without worrying that someone would somehow hack the system and send out a message.

Bruce had stopped the elevator when it was about two-thirds of the way down. Then he'd removed the control panel up top as well. With the circuit disrupted that way, Webb explained, even an electrician couldn't get the elevator working from below. Danica found that precaution a bit excessive, but acknowledged that it was better to be overly cautious than underprepared.

She crossed the oak floor to the elevator bank, which now lay exposed at the back of the library, the massive bookcase having been swung aside. Only when she found herself staring at the ruined call box did she recall that the circuit breaker was in the laundry room. With a shrug she course-corrected.

By the time Danica was back at the desk, the Wi-Fi had connected and the entire main room of the bunker was clearly in view, complements of a high-resolution camera. While most were undoubtedly asleep in the bedrooms at that hour, she counted twelve active captives. Eight playing cards at a round table and four more reading books.

After studying the scene for a second, she picked up her coffee cup and took that first sweet sip. "Is it time?"

"Cue the music," Bruce replied. "Let's wake 'em up and set the mood."

Set the mood was right, Danica mused. For fifty years, Hollywood producers had been using the Rolling Stones' "Paint it Black" as the musical backdrop on darker productions, including *Full Metal Jacket*, *The Devil's Advocate*, *Tour of Duty*, and more recently *Westworld*.

She hit PLAY on an iPhone connected to the intercom, and the opening guitar solo began blaring from the theretofore silent speaker fifty feet below. The drums started up a few seconds later, then Mick Jagger chimed in. Danica did not hear it directly, but rather via the intercom microphone. Although typically a push-to-talk device, Bruce had set it to *vigilant* mode, so sound was always transmitting.

The two of them watched with shared satisfaction as the dozen active occupants all jolted upright in their chairs and turned toward the intercom. Seconds later, both bathroom doors flew open and the bedrooms began to empty. Danica and Bruce sipped coffee and sat in silence until all forty-eight of their meal tickets and both their spies had congregated before the intercom as if praying to a god.

"They seem to have figured out the significance of the red box," Bruce noted. "They're gathered around it, but no one is standing in it."

"It's a smart crowd. Should I put the song on repeat?" Danica asked.

"No, once will do it this first time. We'll get to the repeat phase soon enough."

Bruce waited while the song's entire taunting tail played out and faded to silence before he hit the TALK button on the sound distortion console. When he spoke, his voice echoed in the same cold robotic tone often heard in action movies. "Rule One: No questions."

"What do you want with us?" came the immediate response. It was Webb, shouting on cue.

Bruce didn't reply, of course. That was the point. That was the plan.

Beyond the never-to-be-mentioned Uber driver, whose death Danica had mentally filed away as a tragic traffic accident, they'd only suffered one significant deviation from plan. An unfortunate coincidence.

In an attempt to stop a group of angry bankers from lynching the Maltese couple, a do-gooder hostage had inadvertently forced Seb and Webb to ditch their ear mics, lest they be discovered in the proposed search for spies.

The mics Seb and Webb had worn were more a precaution than an operational necessity, but losing that verbal feedback loop had put a chink in her team's armor.

Danica watched the crowd react with the intense interest of a researcher observing an experiment. Her medical specialty was anesthesiology, not clinical psychology, but she found the situation fascinating nonetheless. Four dozen people, detained, disoriented, endangered and deprived of information for more than two days are suddenly offered a ray of sunshine, only to see one of their own immediately extinguish it with his incompetence. The networks had never broadcast a drama so compelling.

Danica found that watching the events unfold on a screen that might otherwise be showing a sitcom or movie somehow made the experience seem normal, even though this was by far the most devious, dangerous and unusual thing she'd ever done.

About half the crowd either dipped their heads in defeat or rolled their eyes in frustration at Webb's blunder. A quarter just looked confused. The remainder became belligerent, confronting and cursing the man they knew as Webster Gold. Trey even grabbed him by the shirt collar as he'd done the first day with Oz, but apparently remembering how that had turned out, released his grip almost as quickly.

Had real violence broken out, Bruce would have intervened. Demanded a stop. But fortunately it didn't, so the scenario played out as planned.

"I'm sorry," Webb said, both to his peers and to the intercom. "I got excited. I wasn't thinking."

Bruce did not key the microphone. He would say nothing —for two hours. Instead, he put "Paint it Black" on repeat.

Danica spoke, but not into the microphone. "It just occurred to me, reflecting on what we've seen the past two days, that we've done something historic."

"What's that?" Bruce asked, turning from the monitor to face her.

"We've confirmed the Stanford prison experiment."

Bruce crinkled his brow, then took a sip of coffee. "The one where they arbitrarily split students into either prisoners or guards?"

Danica nodded. "And each student seamlessly assumed his or her assigned role—to the point where the guards were enforcing authoritarian measures and subjecting their fellow students to psychological torture."

Bruce set his mug down. "I never considered doing anything remotely like this before. My whole life, I played by the rules. But now that I'm here, I don't feel bad about it. To be honest, I'm feeling pretty good. We're fighting them the way they fought us. Cleverly and covertly."

Danica saw a fire ignite in his eyes, cathartic and intense. She let it burn.

"The big bankers and blue-chip CEOs in the bunker didn't build their careers without creating casualties and then climbing over the bodies. Sitting safely in their glass skyscrapers, those hotshots constantly lied, cheated, stole, bribed, cajoled and conned their way out of trouble and into riches while the rest of us suckers slaved away. For once and for all, you and I are going to beat them at their own game. They aren't victims, they're predators—and turnabout is fair play."

Danica considered mentioning the dolphins who'd be netted with the sharks, but thought better of it. There was a term for that unfortunate but unavoidable circumstance, one acknowledged and embraced by law enforcement organizations worldwide. *Collateral damage.*

19
Direct Address

Western Nevada

WHEN THE ROBOTIC VOICE WENT QUIET, I bet myself there would be two hours of silence before it came back on. Long enough to inflict terror, short enough to fit nicely within a daily plan. I had no way to measure those 120 minutes, but enjoyed the speculation nonetheless.

In no time, some of my fellow prisoners began letting anxiety get the best of them. The music didn't help. While I practiced memorizing playing cards, attempting to get through a deck in under a minute, and Katya immersed herself in Ken Follett's *Pillars of the Earth*, Trey went looking for trouble. No surprise where.

This time the obnoxious banker had seven sycophants in tow. Apparently, the diners from another table had joined him. It shocked me, the poor judgment that otherwise intelligent people sometimes showed when picking a leader, yet it happened all the time.

Like hyenas targeting a wounded caribou, the gang surrounded the small table where Oz and Sabrina were playing chess.

I stayed seated.

Trey put his hands on the back of Sabrina's chair so Oz couldn't ignore him.

The room went quiet.

Trey leaned forward. "I'm not feeling particularly politically correct at the moment, so I'll skip the sweet talk and get straight to the point. It's going to get ugly if you don't tell us what you know."

Katya looked up from her book, then over at me.

I stayed seated.

Oz looked up from the chessboard and met Trey's eye. Although we didn't discuss it, I knew he'd spent the past two days replaying his initial confrontation with the bigot in his mind. Oz had a tell. He kept a golden trinket in his pocket, a coin or token that he rubbed to vent nervous energy.

"You want to know what I know?" Oz asked.

"I insist."

"Very well. I know bullies act because deep down, they're intolerably insecure. They sense their own inferiority, and it bothers them incessantly. Their brutish behavior is an uninspired attempt to convince themselves that they're not second-rate. But no matter how many pigtails they pull or sucker punches they throw, the itch never fades for long, because the reality is—they *are* lacking."

Trey turned red and his face contorted this way and that, but his mouth couldn't muster a comeback. After a short silence taut enough to crack glass, he nodded toward the pair poised behind Oz.

They lifted their suspect by both armpits while a third pulled his chair aside.

Trey walked around the table to stand toe-to-toe with his victim. He made a fist and cocked his arm. "Last chance."

"It's a reasonable tactic," I said. "Threatening your suspect in front of the camera. Waiting to see if our captors intervene. But there's a downside in it for you."

Trey clearly wanted to ignore me, but when everyone else turned in my direction he didn't have a choice. "Oh, really?" was his clever comeback.

There was nothing to be gained by pummeling Trey and his foolish followers. Escaping our shared cage would likely require cooperation. But I couldn't permit any silliness in the meantime. Not if it meant watching innocents get hurt.

As with many professions, rock climbers acquire skills that appear miraculous to outsiders. That's because the onlooker sees the end result without having observed the thousands of practice hours and countless repetitions required to make it possible.

I rose and walked in Trey's direction, causing every onlooker to momentarily stop breathing. Then I brushed past him and walked a couple of yards further to the side of the staircase. Without so much as a glance back in Trey's direction, I grabbed one of the aluminum balusters with both hands, one at shoulder level, the other up over my head. Zoning out everything around, the way I did when climbing at breakneck heights without a rope, I slowly made my lower body rigid and then lifted my legs off the floor. I pivoted them out until I was hanging horizontally, like a flag flying at head height. I rested there for a few seconds, still and perpendicular, before continuing upward until I'd swung a full 180-degrees from where I'd started.

While gasps erupted around the room, I moved one hand atop the handrail, then the other, at which point I began an inverted climb up the stairs on my hands. My feet eventually hit the ceiling, but I kept walking the handrail, up to the walkway and then along it until I was above the middle of the room.

"The downside is that whatever tactic you try on Oz, I'm going to employ on you, given that there's no more evidence of his guilt than yours." With that, I swung my feet around and down, releasing my grip on the handrail once everything was right-side up again. This landed me squarely inside the red box. Fortunately, my feet stuck.

Looking up at the camera, I spoke loud enough to be heard over the incessant Stones' song. "You've clearly got us sufficiently riled up. Why not save us all a bit of time and get started?"

20
Reality TV

Western Nevada

BRUCE STUDIED the confrontational scene on his screen with the intensity of an air traffic controller. Flight operations wasn't an unfitting analogy, he mused. His goal was to bring all that precious cargo home without incident. The gymnast now talking to the camera was like a brewing storm.

"Are you going to work with him or ignore him?" Danica asked.

It was a good question. "Who is he?"

Danica sorted through her files, the photo gallery that contained a snapshot of each guest's driver's license and business card. "Name's Kyle Achilles. He didn't have a card. He lives in Palo Alto."

"So he's a local. Google him. Let's find out who we're dealing with."

Bruce kept his eyes on the screen while Danica typed. Achilles was already back in his seat, flipping playing cards as if fascinated by the pictures. Leaving the red box rather than standing there like a schoolboy waiting for a reply was a savvy move. His second of the morning. Achilles had also averted the lynching. The Maltese man and his wife had slipped away somewhere off camera while Achilles was doing his circus performance.

"That explains it," Danica said, reading from her computer. "Kyle Achilles was an Olympic biathlete, but now he's a rock climber. His specialty is free solo climbing, whatever that means."

"So he's not with the healthcare conference, but he likely has sponsorship dollars. That's good to know. And if he's an Olympian, then he's tough, determined and capable. That's even better to know. Who is he with?"

"She has a business card. Katya Kozara is an Assistant Professor of Mathematics at Stanford."

"So she might be part of the conference. Investment banks like using prestige professors as consultants. Makes for a good name drop, especially when they can't point to their own pedigree."

"So are you going to work with him? Show our guests that you can be reasonable?"

"It's not time to be reasonable yet. And I don't want to empower anybody who's capable. Let's stick to the plan and let them stew another hour. Should be amusing to watch."

Danica pulled her computer into her lap and put her feet up on the desk. "You do the watching. I'm going to keep googling our guests."

Bruce studied the drama sixty feet below while Danica typed away. He couldn't see nearly as much as he wanted to and cursed himself for the shortsightedness that left him with just one camera—albeit a very good one, equipped with battery backup and infrared.

During his preparation, he'd reasoned that with no way to escape, it didn't matter what people did. They were essentially locked in a box. Plus he had spies. Two sets of eyes. So why bother watching? Add to that the fact that his to-do list had been packed, and he never seriously considered adding all the cameras required to put electronic eyes on every room.

Then Seb and Webb were forced to ditch their ear mics. That wasn't really a problem. They were still there, still acting as his eyes, still able to intervene and capable of alerting him to anything serious using the intercom. It was just annoying.

Bruce chuckled at the irony of his own circumstance. Like his guests, he was craving information.

Sometime later, Danica broke his concentration with a sudden question. "What would we do if the police showed up right now?"

Reflexively, he looked toward the tables containing the forty-eight piles of personal property. "We'd throw all those bags in the gun room with the AcotocA headsets and swing the bookcase shut. Then we'd click our computers over to email and answer the door with friendly expressions."

"What if they want to come in?"

"We'd offer them a cup of coffee. With the bookcase closed, there's nothing for them to see. If we don't act suspicious, they won't become suspicious. We're just guests of Kai's, up for the weekend."

The timer on Bruce's watch began vibrating. Two hours had elapsed since Webb broke Rule One. Time to talk to their captives again.

Danica looked over with an appreciative expression as he silenced the alarm. "Ready to reengage?"

"Let's see if they learned anything." He keyed the mic. "Does everyone understand Rule One?"

The crowd jolted at the sudden sound. All eyes turned his way. Everyone except Achilles, whose focus remained on his deck of cards. Bruce had determined that the athlete was memorizing them. He'd flip through the deck, methodically and rhythmically, studying each card for about a second. Then he'd turn the deck over and flip back through, pausing on occasion, presumably at the points where his memory faultered. It was an impressive but worthless skill. Nonetheless, Bruce appreciated the discipline and focus.

While everybody who wasn't in the main room returned in haste, nobody answered his question. Bruce repeated it with more bark in his robotic voice. "Does everyone understand Rule One: No questions?"

"Yes!" The reply came in chorus, but not everyone joined the choir. The cabal of bankers stayed silent.

Bruce refused to ask the question a third time. He wasn't a fitness instructor or cheerleader. And as it turned out, a bit of disobedience would work in his favor. "Good. Welcome to the third day of your kidnapping."

He paused there to let those two bits of information sink in, knowing they were dying to ask questions. Biting your lip at a time like this would be incredibly frustrating for anyone, much less an alpha male accustomed to having servants, subordinates and sycophants at his command. Fortunately, frustrated was exactly the kind of captive Bruce wanted.

"You're enjoying this, aren't you?" Danica asked.

"More than I'd expected. How many years have we been kissing up to the likes of these guys hoping to curry their favor?"

"Too many."

"Well we're done with that, baby."

Bruce returned to the microphone. "Everyone stand."

There weren't fifty seats in the big room, so a good portion of the guests were already on their feet, as were several of those whose chairs faced away from the camera. Most of the captives complied, including Achilles and Katya, but the belligerent bankers did not.

The eight of them were seated around the dining table, talking in hushed tones among themselves.

Bruce said nothing. He watched and waited.

"Come on, guys!" someone called from the crowd.

The other bankers all turned toward Trey, who mumbled something but didn't move.

"It's just as you predicted," Danica said. "How did you know?"

"These guys fancy themselves to be big time negotiators and they're playing by that handbook. They're hoping to gain some power and land a concession. Thing is, they have no power. They literally can't walk away. Their stubborn adherence to habitual tactics demonstrates their lack of lateral thinking. It's a good sign for us. And, of course, it gives me the perfect opportunity to demonstrate the depth of the hole they're in."

Bruce waited through a few more pointless pleas, noting that Achilles didn't step in. He didn't react in any way. In fact, he looked completely relaxed. Bored even. Like a skilled chess player waiting for his amateur opponent to make the next move.

A bit concerned by that implication but still satisfied with the overall situation, Bruce walked to the utility room, opened the circuit breaker panel, and cut all power to the bunker.

21
Escape Clause

Western Nevada

KATYA EXPECTED the bankers' disobedience to provoke some kind of a reaction, but she wasn't prepared for what happened. Judging by the cries and gasps erupting all around her, nobody else was either.

The bunker went black. Not lights-out black. Not midnight black. It went completely black. Zero-light black. Buried coffin black.

It also went still. Still as a grave. Not the people, but the place. The people continued fidgeting. Rustling. Breathing. But the space they were in seemed to die. There was no background hum, no ozone disturbance, no air flow. It was shocking, disorienting and eerie.

Achilles immediately reached for her hand. Then he wrapped his arm around her waist and whispered lightly in her ear, "This is nothing but a negotiation strategy. A game. Don't let it rattle you."

Katya knew that remaining unfazed was the rational response, given the information at hand. It wasn't like an earthquake or an explosion had sealed them in. They were where their captors wanted them, experiencing what their captors intended. But the chasm between knowledge and emotion was deep and wide. At least in her mind—as she was reminded every time the waiter presented a dessert cart.

Achilles, on the other hand, had a near robotic ability in that regard. He could close the chasm. Use logic to conquer irrational fear.

Katya would never forget the first time she saw him walk

right up to the edge of Yosemite's Half Dome and look over. From a dozen safe feet away, she asked, "How can you do that?"

His reply stuck with her. "How often do you fall when walking? And given that, what are the odds you'd fall now?"

As she parsed the statistics of hypothetical falls, a volley of vitriolic comments brought Katya's attention back to their present predicament. "Just stand up!" "Please do what they say." "Don't play with our lives!" Three different voices, three different tones.

Neither Trey nor any of his banking buddies replied, but Katya heard chairs scraping the floor. First one, then a bunch more.

Everyone stood in silence, afraid to speak, afraid to move.

"Any second now," Achilles breathed into her ear.

Katya began counting seconds. She had nothing else to do and her mind needed the distraction. Seventeen passed before the lights came on and the refrigerator resumed its hum. The bankers were all standing. Apparently the camera had its own power supply and enhanced imaging. Either that or the person at the other end was a master of human psychology.

She sucked in a deep lungful of circulating air and turned toward the camera to wait.

Achilles continued to hold her tight.

"Don't make me do that again," the robotic voice commanded.

"We're not afraid of the dark," Trey said, his volume less than full-throated, his chest turned away from the camera.

"Yes, we are," Webster said. "He doesn't speak for us."

"You're a fool, Trey," the robot said. "Tell him why, Kai."

All eyes turned toward the bunker's owner.

"Cutting the power kills more than the lights. It shuts down the fans. No fans means no fresh air." The charismatic captain of industry began shaking his shaved head. "With fifty people turning oxygen into carbon dioxide, we'll suffocate in a matter of hours."

All eyes pivoted to Trey, who reddened but stayed silent.

"Now back to business," the robot continued. "I want

you to line up in front of the camera. Five rows of ten. Nice and neat like a military parade. Take all the time you want. I don't need to go anywhere."

The last comment left Katya favoring the *master of human psychology* explanation for the timing of the lights coming on.

The captives made relatively quick work of arranging themselves as instructed, although the final formation was more elementary school than military academy, by her estimation.

"Good. Now put yourselves in alphabetical order by last name."

Disturbed by this development, Katya looked at Achilles. As a Kozara, she would no longer be by his side.

"I'll be one step away," he said with a reassuring smile. "This isn't going anywhere. They're just conditioning us to follow instructions."

Achilles appeared to be appraising their situation with the same deft insight and decisive familiarity that she would apply to a calculus equation. Was it possible that hostage taking had the equivalent of a mathematical order of operations? In retrospect, that made sense, but it wasn't something she would have anticipated. In any case, Katya found it comforting that Achilles both knew what was coming and appeared unconcerned.

The queuing process reminded her of the Southwest Airlines boarding procedure, except people were comparing letters rather than numbers. It only took a minute. As a K for Kozara, Katya was 11/26 or 42 percent of the way through the alphabet, which landed her in the third row. Fate gave with one hand and took away with the other, putting her in the same column as Achilles, meaning there was just one person between them, but she was also directly beside Trey, whose last name was Huxley.

Sabrina wasn't so lucky. She was at the other end of the fourth row, about as far from Oz as possible. Katya wondered if they weren't married either or if Sabrina had just kept her maiden name.

The eye in the sky chimed back in. "When I call your name, repeat it and recite your Social Security number clearly and accurately. Then sit down. Jeremy Ziegler, Executive Director, Morgan Stanley."

Ziegler complied, sounding to Katya like a military cadet.

"Ryan Williams, Senior Vice President, Pfizer."

Williams also reeled off his SSN, then sat.

"Kurtis Westland, Principal, East-West Capital Partners."

As the robot read the names and titles, Katya found herself impressed with the caliber of her fellow captives. Or at least their titles. Sabrina Saida turned out to be the CFO of a company called Personal Propulsion Systems. Katya wondered if PPS made skateboards or something more sophisticated.

Given her own start in a modest family many thousands of miles away, Katya felt a swell of pride when the robot announced "Katya Kozara, Assistant Professor of Mathematics, Stanford University." As her breast warmed, she wondered if invoking that emotion was the point of the exercise. Priming the pump, so to speak.

The voice answered her unstated question when it designated Kyle Achilles as an Olympian rather than a rock climber. While that revelation evoked a few nods, the recitation of Oz's given name seconds later caused a much less positive and more widespread reaction. "Osama Abdilla, CEO, Personal Propulsion Systems."

Katya could feel Trey swelling with a sense of vindication beside her. Although as Shakespeare so famously pointed out, the name didn't mean anything, the optics couldn't have been worse. The fact that "Osama" was followed by "No Social Security number," didn't help.

The voice left them no time to dwell on the news, supplanting it with a much more momentous reveal. "Quite a distinguished crowd, to be sure. Your ransom is two million dollars. Each. Figure out how you're going to get it to me—without involving anyone who's not with you in the bunker."

22
The News

Western Nevada

BRUCE AWOKE FEELING REFRESHED. He'd really needed the nap. He hadn't slept much for days, given the whirlwind of preparation required and the stress associated with pulling it off. Fortunately, it had all been worthwhile. You couldn't ask for a better catch than what shook out of the Cinquante Bouches net. The decision to hit it during conference week was inspired.

Although the distortion software made his voice sound sinister, he'd smiled his way through the reading of all fifty business cards. The forty-eight genuine ones, and Seb and Webb's fakes.

While Danica slept on, Bruce returned to their command center and opened the laptop. He typed in abc7news.com and found the story within minutes: "Big Mystery Above Napa Valley."

It was business as usual at Michelin Three-Star restaurant Cinquante Bouches Friday night, until it wasn't. With no recollection of anything that happened after serving the appetizer course to the fifty diners who each prepaid four hundred dollars for a nine-course meal, the twenty-four members of the restaurant staff all awoke on the kitchen floor around 2:00 a.m. "No one was injured and nothing was missing," Maître d' George DuChamp told ABC 7 reporter, Tanya Stewart. "The guests were gone, but the food remained. No one has any idea what happened."

Bruce skimmed ahead until his attention snagged on the word "police."

"Napa Valley Police and paramedics responded to a 911 call placed at 1:53 a.m. They searched the premises while paramedics tended to the victims…. Although the investigation remains open, the only physical evidence that a crime was committed is the single needle mark on the left arm of each employee…. No less mysterious is the fate of the diners, who have yet to be identified…."

Satisfied by his quick scan that the complete text contained nothing of concern, Bruce settled back to watch the accompanying video at his leisure—feet up, sipping coffee.

~ ~ ~

A hundred miles from Bruce's laptop, FBI Assistant Special Agent-in-Charge Vic Link was watching the story live. It began playing on the screen in Pequeño Pecado as the counter attendant handed him his breakfast burrito. Vic had planned on dining in the car while driving up to Incline Village, but ended up eating on his feet in the diner's lobby instead.

The case on the northeast shore of Lake Tahoe was better than some. The latest in a series of home invasions. But the one in Napa might be a dream.

Napa had once been Vic's territory, back when he worked out of Sacramento. Two years ago, promotion to Assistant Special Agent-in-Charge, ASAC, had brought him to Nevada. It had looked like a good move, and had set him up for his ultimate goal, SAC of a field office. But his new boss had promptly posted him to Reno, where he ran a much smaller operation. This looked logical enough on paper given Reno's status as Nevada's second city, but Vic quickly divined the truth. His boss had minimized any threat to his authority by vanquishing an ambitious deputy to the Little League. Now Vic's only short-term hope for promotion was landing a case that caught national attention.

Alas, the Napa case wouldn't be it. He was stuck on the wrong side of the state line. Nonetheless, the thought prompted Vic to call his buddy Peter back in Sacramento. It never hurt to check in.

23
New Information

Western Nevada

WITH ACHILLES to her left and Sabrina and Oz to her right, Katya leaned against the walkway railing and studied the scene below. The mood in the bunker had evolved rapidly and radically after the announcement of the ransom demand, and she was glad to be up out of the fray.

Achilles looked her way and asked a characteristically open-ended question. "What do you see?"

She loved the way their brains aligned even though their native perspectives were very different. She was a Moscow native and mathematician. He was an accomplished athlete and former clandestine operative. Beyond their age, bilingual ability and recent experience, their biographies had little in common—but they always clicked.

"I see two categories of people: the *relaxed* and the *anxious*." Fortunately, the majority fit into the former category. Unfortunately, she wasn't one of them.

"How do you account for the split?"

Obviously interested in her answer, Sabrina and Oz cocked their ears. "It comes down to cash. Who has access to two million dollars, and how difficult it will be to part with it. Two hours ago, everyone was staring blindly into the abyss. Now everyone knows just how deep a hole they're in."

"At least they think they know," Achilles clarified. "Pretty soon, I suspect the rich will start to realize that payment doesn't guarantee freedom."

"What about those of us who don't have two million at

their disposal?" Sabrina asked, preempting Katya's own question.

As a college professor just two years out of graduate school, Katya had nowhere close to two million dollars. She could scrape together twenty thousand dollars if pressed, but two million was way out of reach. She gathered that Sabrina and Oz had similar circumstances.

"I'm sure the mastermind up above has made contingencies for that." As she spoke, Katya realized that Achilles was right, of course. The people behind this had clearly planned with great attention to detail, and getting paid would have been second on their list of concerns—right after avoiding capture.

While Katya mulled that over, Kai Basher came up to join them. Although he looked like a drill sergeant, he acted more like a politician, ever mingling, engaging and moving on. Katya saw it as his means of burning off tension. Ironically, the real politician, Governor Rickman, tended to keep quietly to himself.

Achilles took advantage of Kai's arrival. After the perfunctory, "How you doing?" "How do you think?" exchange, he said, "Tell me about the manual elevator."

"What about it?"

"What's the weight limit?"

"Two hundred and fifty pounds."

"Is that strict?"

Kai gave Achilles an odd look, but he answered the question. "There's a mechanical stop that kicks in if it's overloaded."

"Is there a crank inside so you can raise and lower yourself?"

"Yes, but it's not a hand crank. It's a foot crank, and it's a lot slower."

"How does it work?"

"There are pedals built into the floor. You shift your weight from left to right like on a step trainer."

"Who is ready to pay?" the robotic voice interrupted.

Everyone turned toward the bankers.

After a bit of commotion, one of Trey's allies rose to his

feet. Wesley had Scandinavian blond hair, light blue eyes, and a physique that made Katya think he'd played football in college, but never since.

He walked to the red box and looked up at the camera. "I'm ready to pay."

"Wesley Van Sise," the robot said, pronouncing *Sise* like *sissy*. "Very good to see you outperforming your name."

"It's *Sise*, rhymes with *nice*."

"Well, Wesley, I thank you for being the first to step up and for bringing your laptop to the restaurant. What's the password?"

The question hit Sise like a kick to the crotch. He tried to control it, but his face contorted nonetheless. "I thought you were going to bring me up to make the transfer?"

"That sounds a lot like a question, Wesley."

Sise stood still as a deer in the headlights, frozen and frightened.

"Your password," the robot repeated.

Sabrina leaned in and whispered, "Why is he hesitating?"

"He's just realized that he won't be the one making the transfer," Katya said.

"What's it matter?"

"Once he logs them into his account, he can't stop them from taking everything," Oz said, answering his wife's question.

"Of course," Sabrina said. "I'm not thinking straight."

"None of us are," Katya said. *Except Achilles.*

Sise coughed his dry throat into action. "I guess I'm not ready after all."

"Are you saying you lied to me?" the voice asked.

"I changed my mind in light of new information."

"I see. Well then, allow me to further increase your knowledge base."

The power went out. The lights. The appliances. The air.

"Let me know when you've changed it back again."

24
Power Cycle

Western Nevada

DANICA FOUND HERSELF drawn to the drama playing out on the screen with the same intensity of a television series finale. She couldn't look away.

As it was with TV shows, she thought she knew where it was going but couldn't be sure. And the more she watched, the stronger the pull.

Bruce picked up on her mood. "Fascinating, isn't it?"

"It's better than the best show I've ever seen," she agreed.

"Even with bad picture and sound."

They had audio and infrared video—but neither was ideal. With only one microphone, they heard closer voices better than farther ones. And it was difficult to physically identify the orange-red silhouettes on screen. But like a whisper, the imperfection had the effect of leaning them in, both physically and emotionally.

"It's the characters," Danica added. "They're real, and we're getting to know them."

She watched her husband's expression change from jovial to concerned. "Which means we're starting to root for some and against others," he said, slowly. "I hadn't thought of that. We should stop watching."

"What?!"

Bruce muted the volume. "We shouldn't get emotionally involved. Emotions force errors—and we can't afford any of those."

"We can't afford not to watch them either."

"I'm not suggesting that we turn off the screen. I'm

saying we need to back away far enough to maintain emotional distance."

The implications of her husband's words hit Danica like a runaway truck. Stopped her in her tracks. One second she was skipping along the Yellow Brick Road, the next she felt like she'd been smeared across it. "In case we need to … hurt someone? What are you saying? Who are you becoming?"

Bruce raised both palms. "I'm looking out for us."

Danica felt tears begin to well. She didn't know what to say and was afraid to speak. Both of them were operating on emotional overload.

They stared at each other for a few silent seconds, faces twitching, throats closing, eyes blinking. Then Bruce spoke. "I suppose it's okay to watch the bankers. No chance we'll develop affection for any of them."

"And Kai," Danica added. "He'll keep us in the right state of mind."

"I love you."

"I love you, too."

Bruce unmuted the speaker, and Trey's voice immediately came through loud and clear. "—to pay."

They'd missed the crucial first part of the sentence.

"Is he telling us he's ready to pay?" Danica asked.

"Either that or he's bragging that he's not going to pay. I can't tell if he's in the box talking to us or outside among his coterie. I can't see his expression either."

Since the box was just tape, it gave off no heat and thus was invisible to the infrared. Another situation Bruce had failed to foresee.

After a short pause, the orange profile they now knew to be Trey began waving his arms like a runway lineman. "I'm ready to pay."

"He's got a phone but no laptop," Danica told Bruce, answering the unasked question while reaching for Trey's cell. She'd been in charge of cataloging the captured equipment.

Bruce grabbed the microphone. "Mr. Huxley, how nice to hear from you. What's the password on your phone?"

"It's 244364."

Danica typed the code and was rewarded.

"Why 244364?" Bruce asked, while accepting the phone.

"It's random," Trey replied, his voice slightly elevated.

Kai had numericized part of his favorite phrase to create the cabin's door and alarm codes. Apparently, Bruce was assuming that Trey had done the same, and was using that bit of insight to exert his authority. To smush the little bug firmly into place.

"Don't lie to me, Trey. Don't you dare ever lie to me."

The orange head dropped, then looked up again. "It spells *big dog* if you type it on a phone."

"Thank you. Which banking app should I open?"

Danica busied herself studying the other captives as Trey walked Bruce through the process of making a transfer. Her husband would drain Trey's account, of course, converting everything to anonymous cryptocurrency.

The fifty captives were grouped in clusters, not unlike the way they'd been arranged at Cinquante Bouches. Some were seated on the floor, others on the limited furniture provided. A few were pacing at the perimeter. Danica tried to tune in one of several muffled conversations taking place on the sidelines, but couldn't lock in on it the way she could have if she had been in the room.

She was particularly interested in what the two women were saying, not for any tactical reason. Just because she empathized with them. Both came across as educated, worldly and intelligent. Thus they served as proxies for how she'd act in their unprecedented situation, which was something Danica found herself thinking about.

During the *reality TV show*, she'd noted that while the two couples tended to stick together, the women talked far more than the men. Apparently typical gender behavior wasn't limited to social situations.

Bruce extended the phone in her direction so she could read the screen. It showed a balance of 2.2 million.

"I bet Trey's little cabal identified the account with the balance closest to two million to use as a test case," she said.

"No doubt."

"By that logic, this should get better every time."

"Not necessarily," Bruce said. "My guess is that they'll be combining selected bank accounts to pay off multiple ransoms at once."

"Of course," Danica agreed.

Bruce again keyed the mic. "Very good, Mr. Huxley. Your ransom is paid. We've got forty-nine to go. Who's next?"

Nobody reacted.

Bruce repeated the question, slowly this time. "Who is next?"

Nobody spoke. Nobody moved.

Bruce killed the power.

25
Housing Crisis

Western Nevada

KATYA PUT HER LIPS to my ear and whispered, "What are you thinking about?"

Her hair tickled my nose as I answered honestly. "I'm thinking about our captors and their brilliant plan."

"Is that admiration I hear in your voice?"

"Their scheme is simple, yet foolproof. An easy means of extracting millions with minimal risk and maximum control. I'm wondering why it hasn't been used before."

Katya didn't reply immediately.

I couldn't see her expression, but I knew she was putting my conclusion through her analytical wringer. That was one of the things I loved about her. She didn't parrot or spout. She thought for herself.

"Kidnapping rich individuals is common enough. There's also plenty of precedent for taking groups of people hostage, although that's usually by the bus or plane load, and almost always overseas. Our captors just slapped the two tactics together and added a twist."

I assumed a lighter tone for my reply, since Katya couldn't see the admiration on my face. "You could say the same about Facebook. All they did was combine the internet with an address book and add a twist."

"You think we're up against Mark Zuckerberg?"

"Someone of similar caliber."

"Like Ivan the Ghost, may he forever rot in a dark, damp cell," Katya said, referencing a former nemesis.

Happy to be brainstorming with my better half, I pressed

on. "Think about it: Cinquante Bouches was the perfect place for that kind of trap, elite and isolated. But I bet nobody ever looked at the restaurant that way before. Likewise, prepper bunkers make ideal hostage holding facilities, but again, as far as I know, this is a first. Add to those astonishing insights the fact that we have not, and likely will not ever see our captors, and this comes close to the perfect crime."

"Not really."

"What do you mean?"

"They got you."

"So far, that hasn't made a whit of difference."

"Sure it has. You crippled their spies. Very cleverly, I might add."

Although it was tactically important to hide the fact that I'd identified Sebastian and Webster as spies, I'd confided in Katya. I didn't want her inadvertently revealing anything important if they engaged her in seemingly casual conversation.

"Have you figured out how we can use them to escape?" Katya asked.

"I doubt there is a way. Anyone smart enough to concoct this plan isn't going to expose himself in such a foreseeable way. He'll sacrifice his spies if need be."

"Still, something might arise or be provoked," Katya pressed.

Smart woman.

As our conversation waned, I tuned into a discussion that was heating up across the room. The utter absence of light amplified my other senses, hearing chief among them. Alas, the dominant voice was the one that now grated my nerves like fingernails on a chalkboard. "They were supposed to let me go. But they didn't. And of course I can't ask why not, or when they plan to, because asking questions breaks their precious Rule One."

"So what? Break it. What can they really do to us? They need our money," Sise replied. No doubt he gestured as he spoke, but of course nobody could see it.

"Good point," Trey said.

I thought it was a pretty stupid point. This was nothing. We were warm and dry with food and companionship. It was true that our captors weren't actually going to suffocate us—not before they got their money in any case. But on the other hand, if Trey became bothersome they could trick him into the manual elevator with the promise of freedom and then strand him there in solitary confinement. Or they could bring him up and put a bullet in his brain or take a sledgehammer to his knees.

Katya leaned back in. "What do you think they'll do with people who can't pay?"

"Don't worry. If worse comes to worst, we could probably get four million for the house." I had inherited a nice home in Palo Alto, where four million dollars got you what cost less than four hundred thousand almost anywhere else.

"I don't see how that's possible. It would take time and require a lot of signatures. You can't sell it by phone."

I was about to explain how I saw the scenario playing out when the robot beat me to it. The intercom bellowed forth from the dark. "It's time I made something clear. Nobody leaves until everyone's ransom is paid. When I've got my hundred million dollars, I'll unblock the manual lift and everyone will be free to go. Whether that happens ten minutes or ten months from now is entirely up to you."

26
Hyenas

Western Nevada

KATYA FELT her shoulder muscles relax when the power came back on. Despite Achilles' assurances and his rock-solid logic, she hadn't been able to ignore the fear that sprang from knowing that every exhale reduced the amount of breathable air.

The robotic voice boomed back in almost immediately, disrupting her short reprieve. "Let me know when you're ready with the remaining ninety-eight million. Until that time, I don't want to see anyone in the box."

Once it became clear that was the final word, the room began buzzing with conversation.

"Is this what you expected?" she asked Achilles.

"It was inevitable. As is the next step."

"What next step?"

"Who are we in here with?" Achilles asked. He had a thing for the Socratic method. His brother Colin had been the same way. She wondered if that was the result of growing up with a father who'd taken the Hippocratic oath.

"Primarily rich people," Katya replied.

"Professionally speaking," Achilles clarified.

"Pharmaceutical executives and *bankers*. We're here with bankers. That robot is one smart son of a gun," she said with a shake of her head.

"We're about to discover what our cellmates are made of —as if there's any doubt. Let's go back upstairs to watch."

They ascended the stairs and leaned against the railing near the center of the walkway. Most of the captives were standing in tight circles, conversing in low tones. Circumstances were forcing people to reveal their cards. Their hidden secrets. The lies usually camouflaged by credit card balances and second mortgages. There was no wiggle room here. Bluffs and bluster wouldn't produce the only thing that mattered—a two million dollar transfer to the robot's bank.

Trey and his team had taken over the long dining table. They were punching numbers into calculators and passing scribbled notes around. The longer they worked, the louder they got.

Katya's eyes fell on the safe. It wasn't remarkable in its own right. It was a typical heavy metal cube opened with a digital keypad. But the fact that it wasn't Kai Basher's made it interesting. "What's your theory on the safe?" she asked Achilles.

"Like any other safe, it's there to limit access to valuables —and to keep them hidden from sight."

"I get that, but what's actually in there? Besides the spies' ear mics. Do you think it contains the proverbial key? The one they'll give us when the ransom is paid?"

"That may well be. The elevator control panel is a good guess. But I suspect there's more in there than that. I think the safe is also the equivalent of a gun under the pillow. A fallback option kept handy in case something unforeseen happens. Perhaps an actual gun. Perhaps something else."

Katya was about to ask Achilles to clarify when Sabrina and Oz joined them on the walkway. Oz seemed keen on keeping close to Achilles—no surprise there—and Sabrina made for her natural pair, being the only other captive woman.

The two women didn't have much in common beyond basic demographics and being international transplants, but Sabrina was nice enough, and Katya found her British accent pleasant.

Sabrina seemed primed to speak when Trey addressed the crowd. Katya looked down to see that he'd climbed atop the dining table. "Let's get this hammered out so that we can get out of here. I want to start by splitting the room into two halves so we can literally see where we stand." He gestured with his arms. "If you're able to pay your ransom directly, please make yourself comfortable on the lounge side of the room. If you need banking services, please join us on the kitchen side. So it's *have money*—lounge. *Need money*—kitchen."

Katya watched as people slowly started sorting themselves. She couldn't help but think of the Titanic during its final minutes, when the upper class cabins were allocated lifeboats and the steerage passengers were left to drown. Or perhaps swim with the sharks was more like it, she corrected, looking down at the bankers with their calculators and notepads.

Glancing at Achilles, Katya saw that his face had flushed, either from embarrassment or anger. She had a pretty good idea which. "You're thinking about your inheritance, aren't you?"

He turned to meet her eye. "You know me too well."

Achilles had inherited ten million dollars from his father but then lost it to a legal technicality. He could have fought the seizure in court. He could have called in a favor from a very influential friend. But he had wanted to be done with the whole situation more than he wanted the money, and besides he was an *eat what you kill* kind of guy. Living off inherited stock-option proceeds just wasn't his style.

"You could probably still get it back, if you made the call."

"Probably, but they're clearly not going to let me make that call. No worries, though. Whatever arrangement we end up with here will only be temporary." As Achilles spoke, Katya saw steel in his eyes. She knew then and there that her captors were doomed.

Rather than dwell on that, Katya turned her attention to the actions transpiring below. The apparent tally was neither disastrous nor encouraging. Of the fifty captives, twenty-eight indicated they had ready access to two million dollars, and twenty-two did not, assuming Oz and Sabrina were among the have-nots.

"Come on, people!" Trey said. "Who spends four

hundred dollars a plate on dinner without having money in the bank? Seriously, half of you can't be that irresponsible."

Nobody moved.

Trey threw up his arms, then hopped off the table.

With their mission stated and their objectives clear, the bankers began to block and tackle. The eight of them dispersed like airplanes from a hub, each targeting a different group—but none ascending the stairs.

Sabrina leaned in Katya's direction. "It was a gift. Our dinner. We flew to San Francisco for a business consultation. Then the man we were supposed to meet had to cancel his trip. He gave us his prepaid dinner as an apology."

"It was my birthday," Katya said. "Kyle brought me there to propose. We never eat at places like Cinquante Bouches."

Sabrina said, "Congratulations!"

Katya spread her arms and smiled. "Yes, this is quite the bridal shower."

They giggled, hugged and shook their heads.

Once the moment of levity passed, Katya returned her attention to the drama down below. She watched as her fellow captives interviewed and argued, always in hushed tones. They'd cringe through the terms and calculations while the bankers browbeat them with ballpoint pens and crocodile smiles.

Each confrontation ended in one of two ways. Either with the client relocating to the *have* side of the room and the banker returning to the table, signed paper in hand, or with a stalemate that was temporarily set aside.

When the eighth banker finished his assigned round, he returned to the kitchen but didn't take a seat. The other seven stood instead. They then split up, four by four, and began mounting the stairs. The pack was coming for them from both flanks.

27
Alternatives

Western Nevada

I'M NOT USUALLY one to suffer from mixed emotions, but this was no usual circumstance. Not by a long shot.

Since the days when we lived in caves, our species has reacted to danger in one of two basic ways. When the saber-tooth tiger approaches, some select *flight*, while others choose to *fight*. Like every other trait, this diversity has helped the collective survive—despite the individual sacrifices made along the way.

For most, the reaction to any particular situation will depend on the specific circumstance. My genetic coding, however, comes down heavy on the fight side of the spectrum. It's more like a big iron bolt stiffening my spine than a logical calculation. It just happens. The threat presents, the bolt slides into place, then my feet test their grounding, my fists flex and my chest leans in.

All automatic.

All guaranteed.

In this case, someone wanted to take my house. The home my father had left me. The bedroom where I loved my future wife and the kitchen where we ate. *You want to take that from me? You and what army?*

The problem was the alternative.

I wasn't just a stand-my-ground kind of guy. I was a self-sufficiency fanatic. That was the real reason I hadn't chased my inheritance a couple of years back. I didn't want to be given a lifestyle, I wanted to earn it. Where's the pride in a fast car that drops into your lap from a benevolent sky?

Where's the satisfaction in a fancy meal you didn't earn?

If I said "Hell no!" to selling the house, someone else was going to have to step in. To pay my freight. They would be the one saving my woman. And as petty and bullheaded as that might sound—even to me—I couldn't live with that.

So I was stuck—between a rock and a cliff face.

Fortunately, I'm adept at dealing with both. Accustomed to creating third options.

But before going that route, I decided to listen to what Trey and company had to say. Perhaps they would surprise me.

The original four from Trey's table approached me, while the four add-ons surrounded Oz. Sise was the first to speak. "You ready to work this out?"

"Sure. I'm a reasonable guy," I said.

"Let's start with your liquid assets. Checking, savings, stocks, bonds, 401k, IRA. What are we looking at?"

"Not enough."

"Can you be more specific?"

"Not nearly enough."

"Well, surely you've got significant household income given where you were dining?"

"Special occasion."

Sise shook his head in concert with his three colleagues. Their judgmental attitudes made me want to knock the smug expressions off their faces, but I kept myself in check. This was an exasperating situation all around, and it wasn't their fault.

"How about non-liquid assets? Do you own property?"

"I have a house."

This perked Sise up. "Where?"

"Palo Alto."

"Is it worth four million?"

"Probably."

"Well, all right then. We would be willing to cash it out for you."

"Would you now?"

"Obviously, any excess over the ransom requirement would be immediately refunded."

"So if it sold for five million, I'd get a million back?"

"Well, yes. Less interest and fees, of course."

"Interest and fees?"

"You know, closing costs. Realtor commissions."

"And interest?"

"Prime plus two percent, paid on the four million for the duration of the loan. It's quite reasonable. Everyone's been agreeable so far."

"Have they, now?"

"Yes." All four nodded.

"I'm going to see if I can do better."

"What?"

I grabbed the pen from Sise's hand. "I'll seek competitive bids."

Sise looked at his empty hand, then back at me, his puzzlement showing. "What competitive bids? Where?"

"Off you go," I said, taking a half step forward while making a sweeping motion with the back of my free hand.

Sise backed up and looked at his friends. Trey rolled his eyes and the others shrugged. Then they turned and headed for the stairs.

Katya put a hand on my shoulder.

I put my arm around her and walked back to the railing to check the scoreboard. There were still eight people on the have-not side. With Katya and me, that made ten which equated to a twenty percent ransom shortfall. Twenty-four percent if Oz and Sabrina hadn't come to an agreement either.

"What now?" Katya asked.

I turned to my love and said, "Time to take matters into my own hands."

28
Drop Out

Western Nevada

I ENTERED the bedroom behind me and opened the wardrobe. It was packed with the clothes people had worn to dinner. Clothes far less suited for prison life than the medical scrubs they now wore. Mixed in with the wooden hangers were a few from a dry cleaner. The thin white metal kind. I freed one up and tucked it into the back of my waistband.

My next stop was the bathroom. I locked myself in a stall and went to work.

There are two nondestructive ways to open an elevator door. The first and far most common involves using a button either on the call panel or within the elevator itself. The second is the one used by emergency response and maintenance personnel, typically when the elevator is powered off. They have a tool called a drop key, which is inserted into the often-overlooked hole present high up on all elevator doors. It manually disengages the latch holding the door shut, allowing it to be opened by hand.

The drop key gets its name from its mechanism of action. Since you don't want unauthorized people exposing elevator shafts, engineers came up with a clever design that's been adopted as the industry standard.

Drop keys consist of a simple metal rod that has a handle at one end and a two-inch hinged tongue at the other. When the key is inserted far enough into an elevator keyhole, the tongue will drop down perpendicular to the floor, effectively creating a ninety-degree angle. If rotated counterclockwise, the tongue will press against the latching mechanism, causing it to disengage and allowing the elevator doors to be manually slid open.

To create my own drop key, I began by unwrapping the hanger and straightening it out. I then folded it in half to create a double wire. After measuring off a two-inch tongue, I wrapped each trailing strand tightly around the pen for one and three-quarter revolutions, leaving the tongue at a springy ninety-degree angle from the body.

To create its handle, I measured back six inches and then wrapped the loose ends around the pen. Satisfied with the overall result, I flexed the excess wires until they broke, dropped the discarded ends into the toilet tank, secreted my new tool in the small of my back and left the restroom in search of Oz.

I found Katya and Sabrina huddled in tight discussion right where I'd left them, but Oz was neither on the walkway nor in sight below. As I walked toward the girls, Katya warned me off with a quick glance.

Wondering what that was about but certain I'd learn soon enough, I ducked into an empty bedroom and pocketed two pairs of white cotton socks. For many years now I'd only worn two kinds of shoes: climbing shoes while climbing, and approach shoes everywhere else. Approach shoes are a hybrid between climbing shoes and hiking shoes. They're soled with sticky rubber and work fine on basic rock climbs or any parkour-type activity.

Heading downstairs, I found that people were no longer adhering to the this-side/that-side groupings Trey had orchestrated. There was no need. I was certain everyone had memorized exactly who was standing between them and their freedom.

I found Oz in the gym, running at what I'd call a frustration pace. I'd used it myself for a million miles, mostly after the accident that took me out of Olympic contention, but on plenty of other occasions as well. I took this as a sign that he hadn't reached an acceptable banking arrangement.

Oz was alone in the room. He smiled when I came in.

"Bankers are bastards," he said, slowing his pace to lower the noise.

"In my experience, most professions have good and bad players, although the wily ones do tend to end up on top."

Oz threw up both hands. "I just don't have that kind of money. I run a startup, not a mature corporation. But rather than paying my portion with their pocket change, these guys are pushing me to mortgage the rest of my life."

"They can't force you. You can hold out. Four million means more to you than to them, so you'll win."

"*You* might win. They were prepared to lynch *me* even before affixing the freeloader label to my forehead. I don't suppose you're planning to hold out?"

British accent or not, I recognized the inflection of desperation in Oz's voice. I stepped closer and he stopped running. "I'm planning to take things into my own hands, but I need your help with that."

Oz raised his brows, expressing both curiosity and hope. "Do tell."

"I'm afraid you're not going to like it."

29
Shafted

Western Nevada

ANYONE WHO HAS WORKED in extreme situations knows there are two kinds of people: those who fold under pressure and those who focus. Unfortunately, there's no way to tell for certain which a person is in advance. You can't tell about yourself, and you can't tell about others.

If the military could divine the answer, they'd save the billions that are regularly wasted on training people who ultimately can't handle combat. Likewise, if individuals could, they'd save the years that are often wasted pursuing unsuitable professions.

I didn't know if Oz had what it took to do what I needed, but I was about to find out.

I'd considered asking Katya to help me instead, since I knew for certain that she was tougher than a three-armed ape. Putting her in the spotlight, however, would highlight the fact that I wasn't at her side.

So Oz it was.

At the moment, the bankers were busy acting like timeshare salesmen, putting pressure on the holdouts with this tactic and that, garnering guilt and playing on pride. None had gathered the gumption to hit me up again, but it was only a question of time. Meanwhile, Sise was busy taking a second pass at Oz.

From my seat on the floor in front of the elevator doors, I kept an eye on the argumentative pair as I flipped through my deck of cards. Oz made it through the first couple of minutes with snorts and shakes of his head. Then Sise leaned in so they were practically nose-to-nose. Oz reacted by throwing up his arms. He pushed past Sise and marched straight to the red box.

Turning his gaze toward the camera while raising both hands, Oz shouted, "Be reasonable. I don't have four million dollars. Like most people, I can't get four million dollars. There are plenty of whales in your net, why don't you leave us minnows alone?"

Nothing happened.

That was the problem with my plan. It would only work if our captors were watching, and as we learned the last time the lights went out, they weren't always watching.

Oz undoubtedly expected his initial outburst to be sufficient. A few critical words should have earned a reprimand. But his challenge garnered no reaction, so he had to improvise.

Once again, focus or fold became the question.

Once again, Oz came through.

"Instead of having these bankers do your dirty work, why don't you simply up the demand on them? Five million from each banker will get you where you need to be in no time."

By this point, everyone was staring wide-eyed at Oz, and all the bankers were on their feet. They were turning toward Trey for guidance, but he appeared clueless as a newborn foal.

"Well?" Oz said, shaking his fists at the sky. "Talk to me."

The lights went out.

But Oz didn't stop talking. "What are you, a toddler? Don't get your way so you make a big fuss?"

I turned my attention to the elevator door the instant it was dark, knowing that for one reason or another, Oz wouldn't be able to provide acoustical cover for long. Having mapped out my moves in advance, I had my makeshift drop key poised at the access port within a second.

Unlike a normal elevator keyhole, this one had a swinging cover similar to what you saw over some door peepholes. Installed as part of the hermetic seal, I was sure. Fortunately, it slid silently aside. The fit of my makeshift key was tight, almost too tight, but I forced it in. I felt the tongue spring free when it was about five inches in and began twisting it counterclockwise. The resistance kicked in and a second later the latch clicked.

Quickly but carefully, I pulled the elevator door open and leaned in enough to recompress the key and pull it back out. In the pitch dark, I couldn't tell if the elevator was there or I was stepping into an open shaft. I probed with my foot and didn't find a floor, so I balanced on the inside lip of the doorsill and then pulled the doors closed while listening for the latch to click.

Oz was still talking, bless his heart, but I tuned him out. The task at hand deserved my full focus and, in any case, he was on his own.

As was I.

I decided to climb down before up, figuring the floor couldn't be far and reasoning that it would be easier to analyze the ascent options from firm footing. The pit turned out to be just five feet deep. I found a buffer spring on either side of the center, the cable pulleys and the guide rails. What I didn't find was a ladder.

That was surprising. I was no expert, but I'd been through enough covert ops to see a few elevator shafts and they always had a ladder bolted to the wall. Ladders were integral to maintenance and troubleshooting.

I raised an arm overhead and felt along the entire perimeter just to be sure but found nothing. Perhaps they only installed ladders when the elevator accessed multiple floors.

Fortunately, I knew how to cope with situations like these.

30
Senseless

Western Nevada

THE FACT that the elevator shaft was completely dark, rather than just 99.9% dark, was somehow liberating. With no chance of getting any information from my eyes, I was able to ignore them.

My sense of touch took over, which was tactically advantageous. Touch was literally where the rubber met the road. Or the wall, in my case.

On the downside, the utter lack of directional reference was dangerous. It impacted both my balance and my split-second decision making, skills which were mission critical.

I knew the shaft was a double, servicing both electric and hand-cranked elevators, but little more. I hadn't seen inside. So I set about exploring the shaft's perimeter, using touch and my knowledge of what would typically be there.

Neither elevator was currently at basement level, but the weight stack for the manual elevator was, meaning the car was up top. Both the electric elevator and its counterbalance were somewhere in the middle of the shaft.

I inspected the manual counterbalance and found it to be about the same size as the stack on a gym machine. That fit with the two hundred fifty-pound weight limit Kai had mentioned.

Moving on to the rest of the shaft, I found engineering at basement level to be bare bones, once I got past the gearing and greasy chain that drove the manual lift. No ladder, no framework, no electronic equipment. Just clean concrete walls with big fat springs at the bottom and supporting rails on two sides.

Elevator rails are the rough equivalent of railroad tracks, only instead of guiding a train from below, they keep an elevator on course from the sides. Since the shaft serviced two cars, it required a rail running down the center like a fire pole.

I could climb poles almost as easily as ladders, especially ones like this that required side supports every ten feet or so. But as I approached the center of the shaft, my nose and feet warned me away. This pole had been greased heavily enough to create a slick pool in the center of the floor.

That was an eerily insightful act of sabotage, undoubtedly perpetrated by my captors specifically to prevent climbing.

Friction is the climber's friend, grease his archenemy. I'd need to avoid the pole like poison ivy.

With the ladder missing and the rails off limits, I had to explore other options. After carefully cleaning the soles of my shoes with spit and the legs of my pants, I paced out the size of the shaft. It was six feet deep and ten feet wide, with the central rail at the six-and-a-half foot point. Those dimensions indicated that the electric elevator was six-by-six, and the hand-cranked one was phone booth size. Probably felt like a coffin, given the lack of windows.

I wasn't a big fan of coffins. Whether polished mahogany or painted steel, they were one of the very few things that gave me the willies.

The dimensions of the shaft itself gave me an idea.

Rock climbers cling to the irregularities in cliff faces, the indentations and protrusions. Whereas many are measured in millimeters, some occupy the other end of the spectrum. I was standing in one of those.

In climbers' lingo, an elevator shaft is considered a *chimney*. In essence, it's two rock faces a climber can wedge himself between. Chimneys make for comfortable climbs when the span is between two and four feet. Less becomes cramped, more is a stretch.

Determined to figure out just how much of a stretch, I walked to the back wall, held my arms over my head in stick-'em-up position, went rigid, and fell forward. Kind of like one of those trust-building exercises, except that my partner was the wall.

I'm six-foot-two and my arms are disproportionately long, so I can put my palms against a seven-and-a-half foot ceiling with my feet flat on the floor. According to Pythagoras, that meant I'd be hitting the opposite wall when my hands were four and a half feet from the floor.

I took the plunge without falling flat on my face, and thanked my geometry teacher.

From that hypotenuse, I worked my way into a tented position resembling yoga's Downward Dog, then tested the grips of my feet and hands with a trial climb. It was easy enough for the first few feet, but it was clear that another fifty-seven would be terribly taxing.

Fortunately, I'd figured out another option. I hoped.

I felt my way back to the manual elevator's weight stack. Standing before it, I slipped a sock over each hand. The skin on my palms was tough as alligator hide, but given the sliding nature of the climb I was about to attempt, and my lack of sweat-absorbing climber's chalk, I figured the makeshift gloves were a good idea.

Once you overcome the mental hurdle at the core of climbing, the fear of knowing that you're only a few scant seconds and a single slip-up from death, the key to success is friction. My approach shoes maximized part of the equation, but unfortunately the wall supplied the remaining chunk. It was poured, hardened concrete. Seamless for eight-foot spans. Much worse than brick. And of course, it was completely vertical, so I got no help there. The only way I could generate enough friction to support my two hundred pounds was through the steady exertion of significant force.

I wrapped both hands around the cable that connected the counterbalance with the car and tested its tension by pulling with one foot against the wall. The cable moved more than I would have liked. On the big elevator, it would be bowstring tight, since the tension is driven by the countervailing weights.

But the manual lift wasn't very heavy.

I brought my other foot up so both my legs were parallel to the floor, putting me in the position I'd use for climbing. The cable gave even more.

That was not good.

But neither was the situation on the other side of the wall. There, Katya and I risked suffocation and the loss of our home.

I began climbing, hand over hand, foot over foot, up into a darkness so absolute it could have been outer space. The higher I got, the more the cable bowed. The more it bowed, the more awkward my climb became. The insurmountable problem was Newton's third law of motion. The cable received as much force as the wall.

Before long, the iron strands were digging into my crotch. I was still well below the thirty vertical feet that would mark the midpoint of my climb and the apex of the cable's arc. I considered repositioning the cable to my side and continuing onward, but that would be difficult and dangerous on several dimensions, including gripping the cable, applying sufficient force, and maintaining balance.

Frustrated but not defeated, I prepared to switch to plan B.

31
Off the Rails

Western Nevada

GIVEN THE NEED for speed inherent in avoiding detection, I decided to start my plan B with a Superman move rather than descend to begin the climb anew. Superman referencing the action rather than the actor, whose sanity I was currently questioning as I often did when up on *the wall*.

I'd recently seen a video of a kid who simultaneously solved three Rubik's cubes while juggling them. Looks impossible. Sounds impossible. But it's really just a question of practice.

I was clueless with Rubik's cubes, but I could climb. I could pull off feats of strength and gymnastic stunts that looked no less likely than that juggling act. The big difference, of course, was the room for error. His was infinite. Mine infinitesimal.

But I wasn't complaining.

In fact, I felt blessed.

I rehearsed the Superman move a few times in my mind while removing my makeshift gloves, then brought my thoughts to a near-meditative state. Satisfied that my muscles were programmed to react, I counted down. *Three ... two ...* on *one* I released the cable and threw my arms over my head while straightening out and springing back in an arcing motion. Although that inverted pounce lasted no longer than a single second, it felt like forever before my palms hit the opposite wall and my body locked rigid as a doorway arch.

At that point, I was exactly where I wanted to be—except upside down and with the cable between my legs. Again, I visualized the sequence of moves required to relocate. Whereas my last stunt had demanded perfect positioning during a coordinated muscular explosion, this one stipulated steady balance and unfaltering friction while flipping over like a half-cooked pancake.

After a few mental dry runs, I slowly released my left arm, followed by my left leg, and then rotated them up and over until I was facing the floor with both hands and feet in place and my backside tented toward the sky.

Relieved to have reestablished four points of contact, I let out a long, slow exhale. Then started inching skyward for the third time.

Unlike the cable climb, this was one of those gymnastic feats that you'd be very hard pressed to do without previous conditioning. It was just too specialized. The stress on the wrists and palms was tremendous, and the unrelenting strain was immensely fatiguing. But I'd been climbing rocks for years. My muscles, tendons, bones and joints were accustomed to supporting my body weight for long intervals at odd angles.

Again, it was the utter darkness that got to me. Since I was unable to see the tip of my nose or significantly change my body position, a coffinlike claustrophobia kicked in. I couldn't power past the fear with logic either, because my true position was actually more precarious than my imagined one. If I slid, slipped or fumbled, I'd likely fall to my death.

I focused on measuring my progress instead. To do that, I swept my right hand to the side after every few feet of vertical movement, feeling for a center rail support. One of the crossbeams required to keep the rail rigid over a seventy-foot rise.

The first time I found one, I didn't know if I was thirty feet up or forty. I wanted to rest, to use the two-inch beam like a shelf, but I couldn't spare the time. If my absence was discovered, it could get ugly. For me and for Katya.

Odds were that I was above the main elevator at this

point, but I still didn't see any light spilling in from the keyhole above. That was concerning. I was counting on it to serve as a peephole. I supposed it could be covered like the one below, but that didn't seem likely. There was no need for a hermetic seal up top.

The lack of light wasn't my only concern. Despite my conditioning, my shoulders and knees were starting to fatigue. It was the unrelenting pressure.

When climbing cliffs, you're constantly alternating muscles and grips. A hand, a toe, two feet, a fist. Having to push hard against both sides of the shaft without respite or reprieve, I found myself tenting my back up and then rounding it down to allow blood back into strangled tissue.

Pressing on with the stoic and stolid determination soldiers had used for centuries, I lost all track of time. Somehow that seemed related to the darkness, although my mind didn't grasp an inherent connection.

My nose was the first sensory organ to provide positive feedback, an indication that I was closing in on target. It registered a whiff of cigar smoke.

My ears contributed a few feet later when they registered the faint hint of a muffled discussion. It faded almost instantly, like a car radio station going out of range. Were it not for the cigar, I'd have been second-guessing my own ears.

I twisted my neck and strained to see the faint stream of light that should be coming through the keyhole. There was none.

Despite that disappointment, my glands rewarded me with a delicious drop of adrenaline. This caused me to quicken my pace and I soon bumped into the bottom of the manual lift. I was prepared for that eventuality, so fortunately it didn't dislodge me.

I shifted my grip from the wall to the elevator frame and worked myself around. A minute later, after feeling my way onto the doorsill, I put my eye to the small circular opening of the keyhole.

32
The Right Squeeze

Western Nevada

DANICA was keeping busy by studying the infrared images on the surveillance monitor while Bruce worked the computer. With so many guests initially unable or unwilling to pay, he was doing additional research. Attempting to determine who should be spared and who should be squeezed.

Wanting a break from the screen, she set down her coffee cup and turned his way. "We never discussed the details of reaching a hundred million, beyond the basic math. How do you expect it to play out with those who can't afford to pay?"

Bruce wheeled back from the monitor, but instead of turning to her, he reached for his bag. A black Briggs & Riley backpack. After a few seconds of fumbling, he pulled out a black leather pouch and held it up.

Recognizing it, Danica rolled her eyes but smiled. What's that saying about successful marriages? Something about learning to love your spouse for his faults.

Bruce extracted a long cigar and went to work with trimmer and torch. To his credit, her husband smoked only on rare occasion. Usually while releasing pent-up steam.

She watched him get the tip of his Dominican glowing just right and then contentedly put his feet up on the desk before answering her question. "We didn't discuss the details because we're counting on the magic of a diversified portfolio. I have no doubt that there's a hundred million in that crowd. Where it comes from doesn't matter."

"So why one hundred million? Why not two hundred million? Why cap it at all? We could simply demand that everyone open up their bank accounts and take it all."

Bruce savored a couple of long puffs before replying. "Two reasons. The first is *time*. We want to be out of here today. The odds we'll be caught increase with every hour. Most of those guys can write a two-million-dollar check without changing their lifestyle. They routinely throw thousands at airlines to rent a few hours of extra leg and elbow room. They're not going to suffer the psychological stress of being buried in a bunker for something they'll never miss. On the other hand, if we threaten to take *all* their money away, to make them ordinary, well, then we'll have a serious fight on our hands. A long and dangerous fight."

"And the second reason?" Danica asked.

"The second is *discipline*. I picked a number that gives us all the money we'll ever need. Our share as two of the four team members will be fifty million dollars. Would our lifestyle really change if it were a hundred million?"

"Not in any meaningful way."

"So why risk prison? We keep it simple; we keep it safe."

"And we let them figure out the details," Danica said, appreciating her husband's wisdom. "No need to get extreme."

"Exactly." Bruce set his cigar aside, balanced on the corner of the table, and returned his feet to the ground. "What's going on below?"

Danica turned back to the screen. "Oz is still off camera —hiding, no doubt."

"How can you tell which orange glow is his?"

"I'm just guessing. I know he's one of the smaller ones, and I'm assuming he's with Sabrina. She's not in the main room. Neither of the women are. They are easy to identify."

"I'm not surprised that Oz cracked. Between the racial profiling, the physical assault and an inability to pay, I might have blown a gasket myself." Bruce canted his head. "What have you learned about their financial situation?"

"Not much. Neither Oz nor Sabrina has a social security

number, so my ability to background check them is limited. His company is just a startup. No revenue yet, so they're probably strapped."

Bruce shook his head. "If they're pinching pennies, what were they doing at Cinquante Bouches?"

"You know what the J.P. Morgan conference is like. It's full of people putting on airs and praying for the big score." Danica nodded toward the cigar. "Your ash is about to drop."

She watched her husband maneuver an empty coffee mug under his stogie and give it a tap. As he picked it back up, Danica asked a question that had been rolling around the back of her mind. "Why doesn't one of the rich guys just offer to cover the whole check?"

Bruce enjoyed a pensive puff before answering. "Rich people tend to get that way by treating their assets like children. They shelter, nurture and grow their money, then defend it like a lioness would her cubs. My guess is they're all waiting for someone else to pay."

"Plus they're bankers," Danica said with an appreciative nod. "Professional exploiters of other people's money."

"Exactly."

As Danica pictured the captives down there in the dark, a new concern struck. "It's utterly dark in the bunker when the power is off, right?"

Bruce nodded. "They might as well be blind."

"And with the appliances and air-handling system off, there's no background noise."

"There's fifty people in the room with beating hearts and breathing lungs, many of whom chatter nervously. Why are you asking?"

"I'm just wondering, given their heightened senses and the extreme circumstances, if they could hear us talking?"

Bruce went rigid, as though the thought produced a physical shock. "I suppose it's possible."

"Perhaps we better close the bookcase."

Bruce rose. "Couldn't hurt."

Danica had played with the secret door earlier. It was an engineering marvel. The hidden hinges were so perfectly aligned that, despite the size and contents on its shelves, the bookcase moved with the ease of an ordinary door. There was no lock, no hidden button. Neither was required. Why would anyone ever attempt to yank a big built-in bookcase from the wall?

When Bruce was back in his seat, she hit him with her next big question. "So how does this end? What happens when everyone pays?"

"We do exactly what we'd have done without this little weekend excursion. We return to AcotocA, wind it down in the wake of our regulatory defeat, then quietly move on, the way startup people do every day."

"Except instead of heading for Arizona or Florida, we're moving to a Caribbean island," Danica said, immediately taking to the plan.

"I'm thinking Saint Kitts."

"But what about the people down below?"

The feet went back up on the desk. "That's the true beauty of the plan. Because we've made our ask modest and the procedure painless—a bit of fright aside—our *big dog* guests can quickly return to their lives. In no time they'll be wrapped back up in the daily affairs of mastering financial markets and running corporations. The bunker experience will be reduced to a story they'll tell time and again over dinners like the one we disrupted. It will become a source of pride. Given the adventure and implicit heroism, some might secretly consider it the highlight of their lives."

Danica wasn't quite so optimistic, but she admired her husband's positive perspective. "So what exactly happens once they've paid in full?"

"We clean everything up. Wipe everything down. Load the car. Then summon Seb, Webb and Trey to the manual lift. In that order."

"Why Trey?"

"Camouflage. We don't actually bring him up. We raise him halfway then leave. By the time he and the others figure out that they're free to go, we'll be long gone."

"If everything goes according to plan."

Bruce leaned back and blew a ring of smoke. "We're up

here with all the power. They're down there with all the fear. I don't see how it could go any other way."

33
Bounce

Western Nevada

I SAW NOTHING through the elevator keyhole. Nothing at all. In fact, the only way I could tell that I had my eye in the right place was by feel.

This was not what I expected. It was certainly not good news.

Having left the elevator drop key at the bottom of the shaft, I had nothing with which to probe the socket. No way to verify if it was simply covered on the other side. No way to look before I leapt.

Clinging to the inside of the elevator's double doors like a barnacle on a boat, I felt for the latch that kept them closed. The same construction I'd unlocked below with my makeshift key. I found it after a few sweeps and lifted slowly with a steady force. Once it disengaged, I used my fingertips to put a crack between the doors.

I pressed my eye against it—and saw nothing.

I widened the crack—and saw next to nothing. Were it not for the absolute darkness, I'd never have detected the few photons that found their way through a minuscule ceiling gap.

Something was covering the elevator. Concealing it, most

likely. I widened the gap enough to fit my hand through. The surface I contacted was hard and smooth. Given the temperature I determined it was wood. The bookcase that Kai mentioned, no doubt.

Not good news. I hadn't expected it to be closed.

I widened the gap enough to put my ear to the wood—and barely made out muffled speech. Two distinct voices, one higher than the other. Neither intelligible. Both close by.

I began searching the paneling by feel, hoping to find a door handle of sorts.

I did.

It was right where you'd expect it to be, around waist level at one side. The handle was a simple piece of metal screwed into the wood. It wasn't attached to a latch or lever, it was just something to tug on. A means of pulling the bookcase closed behind you, concealing your retreat. Something the prepper mind would undoubtedly consider important.

I braced myself and pressed lightly against the wood with a controlled movement. My fingers compressed without effect. I repositioned my hands and pressed again with more leverage. This time the panel yielded. Just a couple of millimeters, but enough to offer hope. I pressed a bit more and it continued to give. Cumulatively, I'd moved it a centimeter. That exceeded the slack on any typical latching mechanism and led me to believe that the bookcase wasn't locked shut. I could push through.

When a SWAT team breaches a door, they assemble in a formation known as a stack. A role-designated line. The point person is the *commander*. The decision maker. The first to put eyes and a weapon on the scene. Second is the *breacher*. The man swinging the battering ram, positioned to step quickly aside. Behind the breacher is a second *gun*, followed by a *mule* carrying extra equipment, and so on.

I didn't appear to need a breaching device, but I also didn't have a firearm or any other weapon for that matter. I had no backup either. Worst of all, I had no way of knowing what resistance I'd encounter once I pushed the bookcase aside.

Put in this solitary position under ideal circumstances, I'd use a hand drill and fiber-optic camera to see what was waiting in the other room. As it was, I'd be going in blind. And blinded. My eyes were accustomed to absolute dark. The battle might be over before my pupils could constrict, with me on the losing side.

The conclusion was clear but depressing. I had to regroup. I had to go back down.

Frustrated but not defeated, I pulled the bookcase back to flush, and slid the elevator door closed. After taking a second to ponder the best means of descent, I pulled the second pair of socks from my pocket and put them on like protective gloves.

Still clinging to the doorsill, I reached into the black void until I found the cables that ran between the roof of the shaft and the top of the main elevator. They were considerably thicker than the one used to support the manual lift. No doubt specified for a much greater weight.

I paused to adjust my grip so the socks wouldn't slip, then released my legs and slid down. After a few seconds of semi-controlled slide, I hit the top of the elevator car with a louder than optimal thud. Fortunately, a minute of silence convinced me that I alone had heard the noise.

By my calculation, I was two-thirds of the way down. That left twenty feet to go.

The cable had undoubtedly put a black streak on my scrubs, but there were plenty of clean ones in the bunker. Feeling freed by the fact that I was already messy, I rolled over the top of the cab, hung from its edge, and moved hand over hand to the greasy pole. I slid my way to the next crossbeam, worked around it, and a second later was on the ground. From there, all I had to do was rejoin my fellow captives and change my clothes without being observed.

In the past, whenever our captors had extinguished the lights, they'd left them off for hours. I couldn't verify if that pattern held, because the keyhole was covered. If the pattern had changed and the lights were now on, it could get ugly fast.

I pocketed my drop key, then manually released the door latch. Cracking it a tad, I confirmed that my fellow captives were still in the dark. With a sigh of relief, I slowly and silently slid into the room.

Quite a few people were sleeping through this phase of the crisis, as evidenced by snoring. Others were talking in hushed tones.

Walking slowly and listening intently so as not to stumble over anyone, I made my way to the gym. The mats were a good meeting place, suitable for both meditation and slumber. At the moment, the love of my life was doing neither. She was in an animated but muted conversation with someone on the mathematics of blackjack. "Katya."

"Achilles!"

"Who else is here?"

"Sabrina and Oz."

"Anybody else?" As I uttered those words, the lights came back on. Everyone reflexively covered their eyes while their pupils contracted.

"What happened to your clothes?" Katya asked.

"Long story. Oz, would you mind running next door and grabbing me some clean scrubs? I'd just as soon nobody saw me this way."

"Be right back."

While Oz ran the short errand, I gave Katya a long kiss. It might have been rude with Sabrina watching, but given what had transpired and all that was yet to come, I sided with the poet Robert Herrick and gathered a rosebud.

Oz returned in haste and tossed me the clean clothes. As I turned my back to make the change, Katya asked, "What did you learn?"

"The top is blocked by the bookshelf Kai mentioned. I couldn't see anything, and it would have been foolish to go in alone and blind."

"So?"

"So I decided to come back for Oz."

"For Oz?" Katya said.

"What can I do?" Oz asked, sounding surprised.

"Be a second set of hands. Help me with a bit of shock and awe." I motioned him closer and the four of us sat in a circle.

While I laid out my plan, I was pleased to see Oz grow a look of determination in his eyes. Once I finished, he said, "I'm in."

As I prepared to rise, Katya reached out to hold me down. With her hand on my arm she turned to Sabrina and spoke excitedly, "Tell them what you told me."

Oz and I looked at them and then each other in surprise.

Sabrina blushed. "I saw something. Something I shouldn't have."

34
Game Changer

Western Nevada

KATYA had wanted to go with Achilles on his first trip up top, and now she wanted to go with him on the second. She wasn't the passive sort. But she understood the logic he'd exercised in leaving her behind. As one of only two female prisoners, her absence would be conspicuous.

Skewed though they were, the demographics of the captives weren't unusual. Ninety-six percent male. Ninety-eight percent white. One hundred percent stressed. That also described most corporate boardrooms.

The unusual aspect was that the men all seemed keen to avoid her. For Katya's entire adult life, men had maneuvered to come close. They'd change direction or offer a hand or invite her to join this and attend that. She attributed the current reticence to Achilles' display of extreme athletic prowess and an unwritten yet intuitive rule of the jungle. *If you're locked in a cage, don't upset the gorilla.*

The Maltese couple, on the other hand, wouldn't leave her side. Part of that was probably the impulse to stick with the only other mixed pair, but most of it was motivated by the same jungle logic, no doubt.

Katya could tell by body language and verbal cues that Sabrina's relationship with Oz was very different from what she enjoyed with Achilles. It wasn't necessarily less loving, she told herself, but it was clearly more hierarchical. As fit, clever and beautiful as Sabrina was, Oz clearly held all the power.

Katya didn't sense that Sabrina felt suppressed, so it was a harmonious imbalance. As much give as take. And Katya recognized that male dominance was more the norm than not, particularly if you considered not just modern wealthy societies, but the whole history of the world. Nonetheless, because of their fundamental difference in perspective, she knew that Sabrina would never become a best friend.

Fortunately, they were close enough that Sabrina had confided in her, even when she hadn't in Oz. Now that both men were back and the four were alone, she put her fellow female on the spot. "Tell them what you told me."

Sabrina blushed. "I saw something. Something I shouldn't have."

If Oz was offended that his wife hadn't told him first, he didn't show it.

"Go on," Katya said, making her tone soft and encouraging.

"Back in the restaurant, Cinquante Bouches, when we were led into the other room and told to turn around, I slipped. I landed hard and startled—in a puddle of someone's urine. As I looked up, I saw one of our black-clad captors slip a big pair of headphones over my husband's ears." Sabrina looked at Achilles as she spoke.

"What happened next?" he asked.

"Oz collapsed into the waiting arms of the second captor. He just dropped like he'd been shot the instant the headphones went on. Then the first gunman grabbed an identical pair, spread them with both hands and raised them in my direction. That's all I remember seeing."

"They knocked us out with some newfangled device," Katya couldn't help but blurt. "And that's why we don't remember."

Achilles and Oz both stared with rapt expressions. Katya recognized their contemplative countenances as the universal look of boys with new toys. Granted, these were mental explorations, but then both were the intellectual type.

"Are you sure you're not just remembering a vivid dream?" Achilles asked. "That seems like the kind of subconscious scenario my mind might use to fill a void."

"I asked myself the same question," Sabrina said. "But it was easy to dismiss."

"The urine on your dress," Achilles said, answering his own question.

"Exactly."

Everyone instinctively turned toward Oz, who maintained a deeply thoughtful expression. After it continued for several seconds, Katya asked him, "Did that trigger your memory? Are you remembering the headsets as well?"

Oz closed his eyes and slowly raised a finger.

Achilles took advantage of the opportunity to ask a delicate question. "Why didn't you mention this earlier?"

Sabrina blushed once more. "I'm not sure, exactly. It felt like forbidden wisdom, if that makes sense."

Katya knew exactly what she meant, having once walked in on her parents' lovemaking. She also noted the religious subtext in Sabrina's phraseology and wondered if that was why Sabrina had not taken it to Oz. It hadn't worked out well for Eve—or Adam.

Oz mumbled "Excuse me," and left the room.

35
Compromises

Western Nevada

I FOUND the headphone aspect of our kidnapping intriguing. From a tactical perspective, it was irrelevant to the task at hand. But strategically, it escalated the importance of my escape plan.

The possession of a unique technology was a potential means of identifying our otherwise anonymous assailants. So much so that I'd have wondered why they used it were I not familiar with the limitations of conventional anesthetics.

I knew from my spy days that drugs like ketamine and propofol have very limited durations. They only knock you out for minutes. That's why they're administered via IV rather than injection during surgical procedures, to hit you with a steady drip.

Theoretically, an earphone anesthetic would make it possible for a small number of people to manage a large number of prisoners for an extended period of time outside the confines of a hospital. Oz, as a technical guy, seemed to be fascinated by this advancement—the way victims often are.

But curiosity couldn't be our guide.

We had bigger fish to fry.

Sharks you might say.

First on that list was the lights. Getting them turned off a second time was going to require a bit more finesse than the first time.

I considered throwing a towel over the camera. The sudden blindness would surely provoke a reaction that would likely include lights out. But it might well lead to a subsequent line-up, prison headcount style, during which Oz and I would be missed.

My next thought was to ask the governor for help. He was a politician, and as such would love to be able to talk of heroic efforts to aid our escape. But I couldn't think of anything for him to say that wouldn't put him in personal danger. He was maintaining an exceptionally low profile, and he was probably smart to do so. If the police showed up at the cabin door, he'd be the hostage our captors would threaten with a gun to the head.

After discarding several other alternatives on account of their anticipated side effects, I decided to suck it up and talk to Trey. He was already working with the robot.

I found the banker at the dining table with his coterie. They appeared to be busy drafting uniform loan agreements with pen and paper. The sight made me want to punch him in the face, repeatedly, but I spoke quietly in his ear instead. "We should talk. In private."

He looked over his shoulder at me with a quizzical expression. Judging my intention to be sincere, he rose and led me to the empty garden which they'd been using as a negotiation room.

I expected a smarmy remark about my success obtaining a competitive bid, but he wisely waited for me to open. I said, "There's a good chance we won't be freed—even if we pay. You realize that, right?"

He replied with a single slow nod.

"They'll cut the power—as they've already done several times—then just walk away. Within a few hours, all their problems will vanish."

"I get it. What's your point?"

"I'm working to gain us the upper hand, and I need some help."

"What kind of help?"

"I need the lights turned off for a while. How much ransom have you raised?"

To Trey's credit, he let me get away with the subject change. "The current total is eighty-eight million dollars, of which we've already paid eighty million."

"Good. Go to the box and ask them to settle for that amount."

"They won't take it."

"How do you know?"

"They know they can get a hundred million. They've done the research."

"What research?"

"Your house, for example. Zillow values it at 4.2 million."

I just stared at Trey.

He stared back.

"Is that a no?"

"It's an opening to compromise. A bit of quid pro quo."

"Why do I get the feeling the quid is all going to be mine?"

Trey didn't smile at my pun, which was probably smart. One flash of those bleached teeth and I might lose control of my fist. "We'll loan you the money, interest free. You just have to put it on the market and accept any offer that nets you four million or more. You agree to do that, and I'll ask them to settle for ninety-two million."

36
Repeat Performance

Western Nevada

OZ WAS RUBBING his lucky coin, and I was mentally rehearsing the mechanics of our upcoming climb, when Trey began arguing with the robotic voice. By that point, the two had spoken multiple times, typically with the banker transferring funds and our captor supplying intel on hostage assets.

But this wasn't a typical transaction.

The hostage was taking a stand, trying to lower the total ask by eight million dollars.

As the negotiation grew contentious and everyone's attention turned toward the rebellious banker, Oz and I moved to the blind spot beneath the camera beside the big elevator's door.

We were both wearing two sets of scrubs. I also had a wide strip of sheet wrapped around my waist and small dumbbell plates strapped under my arms. The combination was a bit clunky, but nobody was watching me.

We slid into the elevator shaft the instant the power died, using the groans and sighs of others to camouflage our noise. Before the initial commotion died, I lowered Oz to the floor and dropped beside him.

Working silently from our script, we shed our outer scrubs and left them on the floor to facilitate a clean return if one became required. Then I set about turning the sheet into a rope by rolling it up and knotting the ends.

"Put all your focus into balance and feel and you'll be fine," I whispered in Oz's ear. "Make the darkness your friend."

Oz said nothing.

I positioned him in the right place along the back wall and repeated my climb up to the first crossbeam, which was made from two-inch angle iron. When coming down, I'd calculated that there were six crossbeams in total, located at ten, twenty, thirty, forty, fifty and sixty feet. We'd be using them like ladder rungs.

To kick off what was essentially a traditional assisted climb, I crouched atop the first crossbeam with my left shoulder brushing the wall and my feet firmly planted shoulder width apart. Confident in my balance, I got a good grip on one end of the rope and dangled the other end between my legs. Then I squatted, lowering the rope into Oz's upraised hands.

My partner began wrapping the rope around his wrists, securing his grip while removing all slack. Once the rope was taut and Oz was still, I straightened up.

The classic deadlift move elevated Oz's uplifted hands by about a yard. That put them just high enough to grasp the section of crossbeam between my feet. I moved aside once his grip took the pressure off the rope, then I braced my left hand on the wall and used my right to help him join me atop the beam.

"That wasn't so bad," he said, still breathing heavily.

I didn't bother to point out that he was only a few feet off the floor. It was a whole different ballgame when you were fifty feet up. Fortunately, the dark would help with that. And it wasn't like he could chicken out. At that point he wouldn't be able to descend on his own, given that he was unaware of the central rail and unlikely to find it in the dark.

"The next step puts us atop the elevator," I said.

"Whenever you're ready."

I checked the knots at both ends of the sheet. They hadn't migrated or loosened. With the rope squared away, the weakest link in our crane was my balance. If I felt myself slipping, I would force myself to fall backwards, looping the rope over the rail and leaving us dangling face-to-face.

Fortunately, that didn't happen.

And so it went, lift by lift, rung by rung.

We completed the remaining four crossbeam moves and a fifth onto the doorsill in a similar fashion and without incident.

If Oz panicked at any point during the blind sixty-foot ascent, he didn't show it. Then again, this was the easy part. The isolated, controlled, predictable part. Our next move would be none of those.

I handed him one of my makeshift weapons, which consisted of a four-foot strip of sheet looped through a small dumbbell plate. I didn't know if the resultant device was technically a bludgeon, club, flail or sling, but I was certain that it could wreak havoc in close-quarters combat—and soon would.

37
Misgivings

Western Nevada

BRUCE POUNDED the desk with his fist, startling his wife. Everything had started out fine, more or less, but instinct told him their situation was about to go south. Something wasn't right. He knew it, but he couldn't put a pin in it. The uncertainty was unbearably frustrating.

"What is it?" she asked.

He stood and started to pace. "The banks close in an hour, and we're not there yet."

Danica rolled her chair around to intercept him. She took his hands in hers and met his eye. "We've got ninety-two million dollars. Isn't that enough?"

Bruce had no doubt that it was enough. He had made the plans and done the math. He had the beach house, yacht and money manager picked out.

But he wasn't ready to calm down yet. Mentally or physically. He could feel his muscles twitching and his emotions boiling. The unrelenting stream of adrenaline and caffeine were taking a toll.

He pulled his hands back from hers. "The plan is one hundred million dollars. Weren't you just arguing that it should be two hundred million or more?"

"You were very convincing," she said with a soothing smile. "But seriously, I don't see the problem. Seb and Webb say everything is fine."

The engineers had retrieved their earpieces from the safe at the start of this latest blackout and were back in radio contact. Per their reports, nerves were on edge but nothing was awry.

Bruce gestured toward the front door. "Just because things are running under control in here doesn't mean they're going according to plan out there."

Danica didn't waiver. "You've seen the news reports. The police are clueless."

"Just because they say they're clueless, that doesn't mean they actually are."

"They're not here, so obviously they don't know where we are. Our original trail is now stone cold, and there's no new trail to follow."

"Maybe they've figured out *who* we are."

"You're just tired, and that's understandable. We've been at this for three days with lots of pressure and little sleep."

"So I should just take a nap?"

"Why don't you get on the microphone and warn our prisoners that the banks are closing. Let them know that they'll be in for another night if they don't pay the other eight million immediately. You don't even have to turn the lights on. Talk to them in the dark. Maybe play the song first."

"The song, now that's a good idea. Cue the music and put it on repeat this time. Let's see if a few rounds of "Paint it Black" makes them crack. If not, I'll give them the now-or-never warning."

Bruce sat back down, then immediately wheeled over and kissed his wife. He turned toward the screen as she hit PLAY. None of the prisoners jumped outright as the eerie guitar solo kicked in, but most started fidgeting. Everyone's image began to glow brighter, their heads and chests transforming from dark yellow to white as pulses pounded and thoughts raced.

Island life was going to be a shock after years of Silicon Valley stress and a culminating experience like this. He didn't know if the thrill of properly putting a little white ball or hooking a big blue fish would serve as acceptable substitutes, but he was more than ready to try. If those hobbies didn't prove sufficiently stimulating, he could always crank it up a notch. Perhaps a bit of polo or a poker club? Then there was mountain biking, rock climbing, scuba diving and sailing. Most importantly, he'd never again have to deal with the likes of Kai Basher.

He had earned his retirement.

Almost.

He was almost there.

What were those little yellow figures thinking?

Riveted though he was by the monitor's display and the cacophony of panicked subterranean conversations, Bruce's heightened senses flashed a sudden warning. Something was awry.

As if directed by a divine hand, he turned around—just in time.

38
Pounce

Western Nevada

IT WAS GAME TIME. The crux of our captivity. Do or die. If Oz and I managed to move the bookcase without attracting attention, we'd have a fair chance of taking down our antagonists without a protracted fight. On the other hand, if one of them saw the bookcase shift, we'd be sitting ducks. Although slings could be devastating in close quarters combat, they were useless at a distance and hopeless against guns.

The pivotal question confronting us was how best to open the door. Very slowly, hoping to avoid the attention that perceptible motion would cause, or very quickly, seizing the advantages of shock and speed.

While climbing the shaft, I'd concocted a plan that covered most contingencies. Unfortunately, it required putting Oz on point. My ego wasn't comfortable with that arrangement, but I let logic rule.

As I whispered, "You ready?" to Oz, music began playing in the room beyond the bookcase. It was the same song they'd played days ago to wake us up and set the mood. The Rolling Stones, "Paint it Black."

Something was happening. The right kind of something. A distraction. "This is good for us," I said.

Oz had his sling wrapped for action, but held the dumbbell plate in his hand so it wouldn't clunk around. "I'm ready," he replied.

I did my stiffen and fall forward trick, catching the far side of the shaft. Even with my experience and training, it was a frightful experience, allowing myself to fall in that way, face forward into complete darkness, knowing the ground was a breakneck distance down.

But, of course, I hit the opposite wall. It hadn't moved in the dark.

I climbed up until my butt touched the ceiling of the shaft, at which point I began feeling around, knowing there had to be a pulley assembly up there, and most likely an accompanying motor. Objects to which I could cling and hide. I found more or less what I'd expected and quickly wedged myself into position.

"I'm ready," I whispered.

Oz began moving the bookcase, millimeter by millimeter, using the hand-bracing technique I'd shown him. After a few seconds, light started streaming through. I watched as he slowly wedged himself into the crack and crept toward the opening edge.

This was it, the moment of truth. If he was seen, he'd surrender. Then it would be up to me to swoop in to the rescue with my best Batman impression. If not, I'd join him on the doorsill and we'd both breach the room, either hard and fast or sneaky and slow, depending on what he saw.

I got the signal. A finger beckon.

A few seconds later, I dropped silently to his side.

He whispered, "A man and a woman at a desk about fifteen feet from the bookcase. They're facing the other direction."

"See any guns?"

"No."

"We take it slow until we're clear of the door, then we rush. I'll take the man. You take the woman. Remember to swing for the stomach or a joint—a shoulder, knee or elbow."

"Roger that."

"Three, two, one." We slipped free of the door and charged.

Engrossed though they were in the monitor and despite having their backs to us, the man turned as we pounced. He met my eye, then his hands began to move. Was he going for a gun? An alarm? No. His eyes held too much panic, sorrow and fear.

He couldn't get out of his chair.

I couldn't get past his sorrow.

He raised his arms.

I adjusted my swing, slowing the acceleration and shortening the angle. The kilogram of chromium steel cruised beneath his upheld hands and crashed into his gut, expelling air and interrupting all neurological function without puncturing flesh or pulverizing rib.

As he doubled over and toppled out of his chair, the gruesome crunch of cracking bone coming from behind caused me to turn my head. I caught sight of the woman clutching her elbow as she wailed in agony and rolled onto the floor.

I gave the room a quick 360-degree inspection to see if anyone was responding to the noise.

Nobody appeared, but that didn't mean nobody was there. Between the screaming and the song it was hard to hear.

Where were the weapons? The H&K MP7s they'd used in the restaurant? Had they stashed them out of sight or gotten rid of the evidence? "Keep an eye on these two," I told Oz. "They need to be facedown on the floor. I'm going to check the house."

Oz reached for the iPod playing *Paint it Black* on repeat.

"Leave it on for now," I cautioned him. "We don't want to do anything to raise suspicion below."

Oz gave me an odd look, but withdrew his hand.

I cleared the first floor quickly, noting the location of the circuit breaker panel and picking up a couple of kitchen knives along the way. Bladed instruments have always fascinated me. They somehow resonate with the warrior in my soul. They are, in my opinion, the proper replacement for the teeth and claws that evolution has systematically phased out of our biology. Despite that affinity, and even though I knew a circus-style trick or two, I didn't relish the idea of taking one to a gun fight.

Having seen no cars outdoors on the drive, I checked the

garage before ascending the stairs. Just a single sedan, a black Dodge Charger, and two dusty cross-country motorbikes, both red and white. The kind with knobby tires and hand guards. That indicated four people, max. It was a good sign, but I saw an even better one.

The area closest to the door was piled high with electronics, guns and ammunition. Handguns, long guns, submachine guns, and four fully automatic .50 caliber machine guns complete with tripods. One for each corner of the house, no doubt. I'd probably find corresponding hardened positions if I looked upstairs.

The nearest weapons were two H&K MP7s. Presumably the ones that had been used at the restaurant. I grabbed one and popped the magazine to be sure I wouldn't come up empty. What I saw shocked me. It was loaded with blank rounds. They'd deliver bang, but no bullet. I checked the other gun and found the same setup. That was something worth contemplating, but later.

Setting the MP7s aside, I picked a Glock 19 from the pile, popped the magazine, and quickly pumped in fifteen 9mm rounds. I racked the slide, then grabbed a thick roll of duct tape off a pegboard rack. Since I didn't have a suitable pocket, I hung it around my waist on an improvised duct tape belt.

Feeling fully capable of dealing with whatever came my way, I left the garage and crept upstairs.

The bedrooms and bathrooms all looked empty and felt empty.

Returning to the study on the first floor, I found that Oz had the scene under complete control. Both prisoners were still on their bellies, but the woman now appeared unconscious. She had a set of big white headphones over her ears.

I caught the tail end of the man's sentence. "—usually just a few minutes."

Oz glanced over as I walked in. "We were just discussing the knockout system he used on us. No side effects beyond a few minutes of memory loss. I put a pair on the woman and she went out like a light."

The lack of side effects was good to know, but not my immediate concern. "Who else is here?" I asked the man.

"My wife needs a hospital," he said.

"Answer his question," Oz said.

I tucked the Glock into the small of my back and pulled the duct tape off my makeshift belt.

"It's just us," the man replied.

The lie stopped me in my tracks and prompted me to take another precaution. I found the bone conduction microphone console on the desk and pulled the plug in front of our captive's face. "I know you're lying. Do that again, and this could get ugly."

"Up here, it's just us. I swear."

I bound his wrists behind his back, then moved on to tape her ankles.

39
Ninety-Eight Percent

Western Nevada

WITH THE CABIN SECURE and our captors bound, I wanted to rejoice. I wanted to pound my chest and shout at the sky, but we weren't out of the woods yet. Katya, Sabrina and forty-six other innocents were still locked in a cell with two spies and, presumably, their guns. Guns with real bullets. If I didn't play this right, we'd be trading a kidnapping scenario for a hostage crisis.

Worst of all, the spies would know they could get whatever they wanted by threatening Katya and Sabrina.

"How long will she be unconscious?" I asked, referencing the woman.

"Until the headphones are removed or the battery dies in about eight hours."

Satisfied that I had full command of the threat, I grabbed an iPhone off the desk. It was plugged in but powered off. Our captors didn't want their location tracked. I held the power button and then, in a supremely satisfying reversal of roles, asked the man for his password.

"2-4-6-8-10," he replied.

The phone awoke. I handed it to Oz. "Call 911. Give them our map coordinates. You'll find them in the *Maps* app."

He studied the screen. "One bar. I'll see if there's a better signal outside."

While Oz called the cavalry, I turned my attention back to our captive. "What's your name?"

"Bruce Devlin. I run the company that invented the

anesthetic device you see on my wife's ears. Kai Basher, the bunker's owner, sabotaged our commercialization effort. This is payback. I'm sorry you got caught up in the crossfire."

The need to be understood is one of those odd, universal human traits that strikes hard in situations like these. It's why so many captured criminals confess. The police interrogation handbook is full of tactics for evoking the reflex. But I couldn't care less about my captor's cathartic needs or his legal status for that matter. My driving concern was rescuing Katya. "What's in the safe downstairs?"

Bruce blinked a few times while his mind shifted gears. "Two handguns and a large supply of ketamine."

That made sense.

"How did you know I had spies with bone-mics?" Bruce asked.

Although anxious to move on, I knew it would be wise to spend sixty seconds establishing rapport. "That's just what you do in such situations—if you're smart. As anyone who did what you did would have to be."

His face grew even more miserable. "You played us. You got my guys to remove their mics so they wouldn't be discovered. But then you didn't attempt to find them..." He was talking to himself, thinking out loud. "Which means you already knew who they were."

"I knew any spies would be disguised so we couldn't later identify them. So all I had to do was look for altered appearances."

Bruce shook his head. "Was I stupid or unlucky?"

"Your plan worked with forty-nine out of fifty." Technically it was forty-seven out of forty-eight, but that didn't have the same ring to it. "That's a ninety-eight percent success rate."

"And a two percent failure rate," Bruce said, still shaking his head. Then he stopped and looked up. "But only if all people are created equal, which of course they're not. I snared an Olympian."

"And a governor. And a couple of dozen multimillionaires. It was a good plan. Don't beat yourself up."

"Why are you being nice?"

"Trey used up all my venom. How do I enable the elevator?"

"He is a real prick, isn't he? You don't enable the elevator, not unless you're also an electrician. I pulled the circuit boards on both ends. None too gently. The manual lift is the only way to go. Speaking of which, how did you ascend?"

"I climbed."

"Climbed what? I greased the rail and there was nothing else to grip."

"I'll refer you to my previous answer about forty-nine out of fifty."

Oz returned wearing a satisfied smile. "They're on the way. Police and paramedics."

I gave him a thumbs-up but kept my eyes on Bruce. "Where's the money?"

"It's in cryptocurrency on the red flash drive."

I'd suspected as much. "What's the password?"

"Payback$100MM, capital P, capital Ms."

40
Cranking Away

Western Nevada

I WANTED to get Sabrina and Katya out of the bunker before the police arrived, on the off-chance that the officer in charge would be a moron. From what Kai had told me about our location in relation to Reno, I figured that gave me about twenty minutes.

Oz clearly had the same idea. "We should get the women out now."

"Agreed."

"Should we turn the power on?"

"No. Our concern is the spies. With the lights off, they're less likely to act."

I turned to our conscious captive. "Bruce, how do I talk to the bunker in the robot voice?"

He didn't respond right away. He was off in his own deep thoughts.

"Bruce! How do I talk to the bunker in the robot voice?"

"It's automatic. Just press the TALK button on the screen and speak through the computer microphone."

The videophone console on the desk was connected to a dedicated laptop that displayed a live, infrared fisheye view of the bunker along with a digital version of the console control panel. While I composed my thoughts, searching for a scenario that wouldn't provoke an unwanted reaction from the spies, Oz grabbed the mouse, pressed the button and spoke. "We need the women, and only the women, to approach the manual lift."

After a second of silence, a torrent of quiet conversation

broke out below. While most were leaning into their circles, three began moving slowly through the dark. Two smaller figures appeared to be feeling their way toward the hand-cranked elevator while a larger one approached the camera. He began repeating the same phrase, which became clearer the closer he got. "I wish I knew what was going on. I wish I knew what was going on…" One of the spies was talking to Bruce.

I had no right to reprimand Oz, despite the fact that he'd given the spies reason to believe that something was amiss. The best move was to roll with it as quickly as possible and hope for the best.

I ran back to the open bookcase where the manual lift was located. The crank itself was identical to the one below. A handled lever about two-and-a-half feet long that rotated around a shaft which disappeared into the wall. This one, however, was blocked by an iron bar that protruded from a hole in the floor. The placement kept the crank from rotating clockwise while the ratchet prevented counterclockwise motion.

I pulled the bar from the hole, tossed it aside with a clatter, and began cranking. "How do I know when the elevator reaches the bottom?" I yelled over my shoulder.

"When the cabin moves into alignment with a doorway, it triggers a mechanical bell both above and below. The bell also tinkles when weight is placed on the floor."

I cranked away at the wheel like a caffeinated hamster. I knew that elevators were weighted to offset the mass of the cab plus a typical load, so the gearing wasn't extreme. I figured it was about four-to-one, meaning that moving the two-and-a-half-foot crank through its five-foot-diameter circle would raise or lower the lift one-fourth of the circumference or about four feet. If that was correct, then fifteen revolutions would move it the required sixty feet.

The bell in the back of my mind rang about the same time as the one above my head. It was on the other side of the wall—a concession to the camouflage I assumed—but easy enough to hear.

"What's happening?" I called back to Oz, who was still

standing before the screen.

"The women have opened the door and ... both are now inside ... and the door is closed." The bell tinkled again as he spoke.

I began turning the crank but it quickly caught. I put on more pressure, but that didn't help. "The elevator won't budge. They're too heavy."

"Try harder," Oz said.

"It's not a strength issue. The elevator locks if it's over the limit."

"They appear to have figured that out. One of the women just exited."

I put pressure on the crank and this time it moved. As I sweated my way through fifteen fast and furious revolutions with the ratchet rattling away like a scared snake, I couldn't help hoping that Katya was the one who remained aboard.

Oz walked over to join me, leaving our captives unattended.

"Wait for the bell. Meanwhile, please stand guard."

Oz disappeared but only momentarily. "Please, Oz. Let's not blow this at the ninety-yard line."

"No worries. I just placed a pair of those earphones on his head."

Why hadn't I thought of that? Probably because I'd wanted him awake for interrogation. "Good thinking."

Before he could reply, the bell dinged.

41
The Downside

A Few Minutes Earlier
Western Nevada

SEB found himself growing accustomed to the absolute darkness. There was something peaceful about it, given the knowledge that it would only be temporary.

"You know," Webb whispered, leaning close. "This is the last day we'll have to work for the rest of our lives."

"I was just thinking that. It's mind-boggling in the very best way."

"What are you going to do?"

"This has all happened so fast that I haven't had a second to plan the specifics. But I'm sure it will involve a foreign, warm-weather, beachfront location where I can hire servants for next to nothing."

"Me too. I'll have a cook, a maid and an administrative assistant to manage all the pesky paperwork life tends to cough up."

"But no chauffeur," Seb said. "I want to drive my own Ferrari."

The first couple of times the lights went out, the two spies had spent their time slowly wandering around, listening in on conversations. People tended to whisper in the dark, so that made overhearing difficult, but more often than not Seb caught the gist.

Initially, the talk was all speculation. Who had done this and why? When that became clear it turned to money. When that grew old people reverted to the same small talk you could overhear in any coffee shop. Discussions of sports, politics and television programs. The one thing Seb and Webb never heard was the only thing they cared about: plans to escape. That was the genius of including Kai in the mix. He deftly explained the hopelessness of their situation.

The Olympian had pushed him on this and that, exploring various avenues, but everything was a dead end. That was the brilliance of Bruce's plan. They were in the underground version of Alcatraz.

The excitement did kick up a notch when Oz freaked out, but his wife quickly and wisely got him under control. The man had started out on thin ice and continued to skate. If he hadn't been in the net, the whole operation would have run on rails. But Seb wasn't going to curse fate. One out of forty-eight wasn't bad.

Then communication with the cabin went off-line.

As an engineer, Seb and his partner in crime knew that there were lots of reasons for technical glitches. For starters, none of them had worked with bone mics before. They didn't know how fragile they were. Anything from a weak battery to a loose wire to an inadvertently flipped switch could be behind the silence. Of course, as nervous undercover agents, Seb and Webb worried there was more to it than that.

"Maybe we should do what Trey asked, and agree that ninety-two million dollars is enough," Webb said.

They were speaking in the utility room, which was their rendezvous point. As engineers and apparent lovers, they could justify the odd behavior easily enough.

"Are you nuts. Do the math!"

"I have. My share of ninety-two million is twenty-three million. Sounds like about twenty million more than I'll ever really need—especially once I leave California with its ridiculous real estate prices and outrageous taxes."

"Not that math, the stay-or-go math. We'll have the full hundred million in less than twenty-four hours. For simplicity's sake, let's say it takes twenty hours to secure the remaining eight million. Your cut of the incremental income works out to a hundred thousand dollars an hour." Seb couldn't see Webb's face, but he was certain it was contorting.

"Yeah, you're right. I'd end up kicking myself for walking away from that."

"I've been thinking about the whole big-net kidnapping thing."

"Genius, right? I wonder why nobody else has thought of it?"

"Actually, I was thinking about the downside."

"What downside?" Webb whispered.

"When you toss a big net, you risk catching a shark."

"Oz turned out to be tame enough."

Actually, Seb blamed Trey for the issues, but that wasn't his point. "Yes, but we could have snagged a soldier or a mobster or a gun nut."

"At Cinquante Bouches? Maybe a mobster, but how probable is that?"

"What I'm saying is there's a risk in going big. The more times you roll the dice, the greater the odds you crap out."

"You can't win big if you don't play big."

"I hear you. I'm just glad we won't ever have to do this again." Seb gestured with his head even though Webb couldn't see it. "We should get back to the big room."

"Right behind you."

They were near the door that led from the garden to the main room when Bruce's distorted voice came over the intercom. "We need the women, and only the women, to approach the manual lift."

"What's that about?" Webb whispered. "We never discussed letting the women go early."

"I don't know. I don't like it. It's not like Bruce is planning to have his way with them. Maybe he really wants us. Maybe it's a coded message."

"So what do we do?"

"I think it's time we grab the guns."

42
Just One Kiss

Western Nevada

SELFISH THOUGH IT WAS, I couldn't fight the feeling of intense disappointment I experienced when Sabrina opened the elevator. I wasn't the least bit surprised that Katya had selflessly stepped aside, and I was happy for Oz, but my stomach dropped nonetheless.

As Sabrina fell into Oz's arms, I shut the door and, despite my fatigue, began cranking like I was trying to whip cream into butter.

Back in my Olympic training days, it wasn't unusual for me to build up lactic acid faster than I could burn it, causing the cramps and nausea that accompanied lactic acidosis. Then, as now, I pushed through knowing that a respite was coming.

Behind me, Oz had Sabrina in a bear hug. He was busy whispering what I assumed was a combination of sweet talk and a situational debriefing. Soon I'd be doing the same.

Meanwhile, I was fully focused on cranking as quickly and efficiently as possible. Sending the elevator back down.

When circumstances were suspicious, like the situation we'd created by calling for the women, the best move was to seek safety before your opponents worked up the gumption to take action. In this case, that meant getting Katya on the elevator before Sebastian and Webster grabbed their guns.

I was counting revolutions in my head the same way I did repetitions in the gym. The bell chimed at the peak of my fifteenth turn, and I stopped on a dime. The tinkle followed an eternity later. I gave Katya a second to shut the door, then started hauling her up. The gears cooperated, but the cramps and nausea quickly returned.

I tried forcing myself to slow down, to catch my breath. I told myself that if my sweetie was aboard, she was safe. If she wasn't, if one of the spies had grabbed a gun and was coming up to investigate, then I needed to be ready to react.

Oz showed himself to be on the same wavelength. Without my asking, he moved into backup position.

Despite decreasing my speed, my shoulders were burning like phosphorus grenades when the bell rewarded my efforts. I wouldn't be much of a hugger. Still, the soldier in me refused to stand down. I pulled the Glock from my waistband and held it behind the door.

I needn't have worried.

The elevator opened and Katya was there, dumbbell poised for action. Upon seeing my face she dropped it to the floor and flew into my arms, which of course summoned the strength required to reciprocate. "You've got a bloody lip. What happened?"

"Let me tell you about that later," she said.

"Is it okay to kiss you?"

"It's mandatory."

As I crushed my lips to hers with all the hunger and passion of a wedding day, the world went black.

43
Weight Problem

A Few Minutes Earlier
Western Nevada

KATYA found herself feeling calmer than the circumstances warranted—although anything less than hysterical would clear that bar. She was locked up sixty-feet underground. Only her fellow captives knew her location. She was mere hours from suffocating to death in what would become a mass grave. Her boyfriend was single-handedly attempting to turn the tables on an unknown quantity of ingenious foes. And it was so dark she might as well have been blind.

Speaking of blind, she was getting used to doing yoga in the dark. It was more difficult at first with no visual cues to aid her balance. But after a bit of practice she found that the blindness put her in better touch with her body. She suspected that her postures were actually improving.

Sabrina reported a similar experience.

Katya noted that her fellow female prisoner had her emotions under control better than many of the men. Although she was a bit too deferential to her husband for Katya's taste, when Sabrina spoke freely her questions were insightful and her observations thoughtful. This contrasted starkly with some of the bankers and executives, the so-called alpha males, some of whom could be heard sobbing in the dark. Fortunately, their annoying lamentations blended into the backdrop of quiet conversations and were easily ignored.

Transitioning through vinyasa into extended child's pose,

Katya wondered if this was what it felt like to be at war. Not the *our country is fighting overseas* kind of war, but the *our city is under siege* variety. In any case, she was determined to join her man as part of the resistance if and when the opportunity arose.

Sabrina slid closer on the mat and whispered, "How long has Achilles been a rock climber?"

Even though the nervous question was clearly prompted by the ongoing escape attempt, the topic wasn't a dangerous one. The discussion would sound casual enough if overheard by a spy. Still, Achilles' warning regarding Sebastian and Webster kept the two cautiously quiet while conversing in the dark.

Before Katya could answer, the robotic voice came over the intercom. "We need the women, and only the women, to approach the manual lift."

The two clutched each other.

"This has to be good news, right?" Sabrina asked.

Katya hoped so. "If it is, then the announcement will have surprised the spies as much as us. They may take action."

"What do we do?"

"We scramble onto the elevator as soon as it arrives and immediately shut the door."

"If you say so."

They rose and made their way out of the gym hand in hand, as people did to remain together in the dark. Katya stopped as a thought struck. "Just a second."

She felt her way back to the dumbbell rack and grabbed a five pounder. It wasn't the adjustable kind like the larger ones but rather a single piece of iron that had been dipped in pink vinyl. Keeping it in her right hand, she found Sabrina with her left. "Let's go."

Normally they navigated the room by sticking to the perimeter, but since the elevators were directly across from the gym, the two women fumbled their way through the crowd. Katya found it interesting that almost everyone remained in the main room when not sleeping. She attributed it to the attraction of camaraderie and the calming vibe of a big room with a high ceiling.

A bell jingled once as they drew close. They hadn't heard it before, but given the context it was instantly recognizable as an elevator chime.

The room fell silent in response.

They found the door and swung it open. The floor reacted to Sabrina's weight as she stepped inside, dropping a tad and ringing the bell again. Katya quickly followed and closed the door.

Someone called, "Good luck," and Katya exhaled in relief. Then—nothing happened. There were a few mechanical clinks but no motion. That couldn't be a good sign. Surely Achilles would be quick on the crank.

"Is the door closed all the way?" Sabrina asked.

Katya opened it an inch and pulled it tight. She heard it click. Still, nothing happened.

"You can't both go at once. You're too heavy."

Katya recognized Kai's voice. "I'll be right behind you," she said, and stepped out of the lift.

The instant the door clicked shut, she heard the elevator start to move. As she stood there listening to it fade, her ears registered something much less pleasant occurring just a few feet away. The subdued snicks and thunks and sucking sounds of someone opening and closing the safe. Plus the telltale scrape of someone removing a weighty object made of metal.

44
Transformations

Western Nevada

WHILE SITTING IN THE DARK on the yoga mat practicing poses beside Katya, Sabrina had felt certain that the nightmare was about to end—one way or the other. And what a nightmare it had been. As bad as the other captives had it, she had it worse.

Only she and her husband had to deal with both internal and external threats. And as far as Sabrina knew, only they had a serious secret to hide. Internally from their fellow captives, and externally from their captors and the police.

The racism wasn't new to them, nor were the violent outbursts from insecure pigs. Everyone with dark skin encountered those on a near-daily basis in parts of the United States and Europe. But when you added in the stress of being kidnapped and buried alive, then topped it off with the humiliation of relative poverty, their situation was practically intolerable.

Still, she and Oz had kept stiff upper lips, as their classmates back at Oxford liked to say. The two of them drew on their conditioning to remain calm, then found a couple of friends and clung tight.

But what would happen to her if Oz and Achilles didn't come back? She'd be one of two unprotected women locked in a room with dozens of frustrated men. Potentially for days. Weeks even. It took every ounce of willpower she had to keep certain images from infesting her mind.

Achilles hadn't helped when he pressed one of the small dumbbells into each of their hands prior to leaving, and advised them to "Stay in the gym and keep this close."

Fortunately, the call summoning her and Katya to the elevator came well before self-defense was required. Despite being delivered by a robotic voice, the words swelled her heart like a party balloon.

Then the elevator refused to work.

Sabrina found herself crying when Katya slipped back out of the cab, allowing her to go first. To escape. To finally be safe. But those tears dried up like a morning rain as she rose out of the dark pit and up toward Oz.

Seconds later, the bell chimed and the elevator door opened and Oz was there. She fell into his arms and relaxed into his embrace—until the words he whispered in her ear turned her stomach to ice.

Sabrina trusted her husband, respected her husband, and deferred to her husband. They had committed themselves not only to each other, but also to the same driving cause. Nonetheless, she was hesitant to blindly take such rash and repulsive action mere seconds after emerging from her dark ordeal—especially since it was Katya and Achilles who protected and then freed her.

"Do as I say, my virtuous princess," Oz said, calling her by the Arabic translation of her name. "There's no time to explain now, but I assure you that all will become clear soon enough and you will be forever grateful that we were so quick to act."

While Achilles cranked away with the speed of a spinning top, spraying sweat and spreading heat, Sabrina accepted the headset Oz pressed into the hand behind her back. Somehow this whole unbelievable, unexpected, unprecedented experience had come full circle. For the life of her, she couldn't understand why.

But she would do as she was told.

When Achilles bear-hugged Katya in a repeat performance of what Oz had done when she stepped from the lift a mere two minutes earlier, Sabrina and her husband slipped anesthetic headsets over their unsuspecting, unprotected ears.

Their two heroic friends slumped to the floor like robots

unplugged with Achilles somehow still clutching Katya in his arms.

Sabrina stared at them for a few seconds, absorbing the second half of the show she'd seen start three days back. It was disconcerting, observing people she knew to be so animated instantly rendered so helpless. "What is this all about, Lion of God?" she asked, using the Arabic translation of his name.

Oz held up a finger. "Please don't interrupt me now. I need to focus."

"Can I help?"

Oz transformed the finger into the halt sign while turning his gaze away and down. It was a move he used to convey that he was concentrating. He stayed that way for a dozen of her rapid heartbeats, then walked around the bookcase and out of sight into the room.

Sabrina gave the sleeping couple another glance. The sight made her heart heavy, but she hardened it and turned to follow her husband.

45
Oops

Western Nevada

THE ROOM Sabrina followed Oz into was obviously the study of a man who put a premium on having a grand place to work. Floor-to-high-ceiling bookcases and windows. An enormous matching oak desk. Classic oil paintings. It looked more like a gentlemen's club than a mountain lodge.

Oz was already at the desk, clicking away at a laptop, doing something in the settings. At one point, he raised a fist in triumph, then pulled a red flash drive from its USB port and slipped it into his pocket. He shut the lid, pulled the power cord and set the assembly off to the side.

Looking over at her with triumph in his eyes, he asked, "Will you move the rest of this equipment into the cubby where we got the headsets while I make a call? I need to close down the office and get Omar and Shakira to Vegas."

Sabrina understood the need to abandon their office, but she had no idea how Las Vegas figured into things. Certain that information would be forthcoming, she turned her attention to the remaining equipment.

It was fascinating.

The big monitor displayed an infrared image of the main room below. The people were pulsating silhouettes of red, orange, yellow and white, while the rest of the room was largely black. Mere minutes ago, she'd been one of those heat signatures.

It looked like everyone was crowding around the manual elevator, but as she studied the scene, enough people moved that she reassessed. They were gathered around a body on the floor. A motionless red and orange figure.

Did the lack of yellow and white mean he was dead? What had happened? Who was down? Had he collapsed—or been attacked?

Her ears tuned into the talk coming over the speaker just before Oz unplugged it. She'd grown so accustomed to the background chatter over the preceding days that her brain automatically filtered it out if she didn't focus. She didn't catch any words, but she grasped the tone, and it was panicked.

Oz yanked the cord and other plugs from the big screen and lifted it off the table. Sabrina grabbed a few of the smaller pieces and followed in a daze. *Were they stealing the money? Could that be it? Was Oz so upset with the bankers that he was going to turn the tables on them?* She wanted to ask but bit her lip. He would only get upset and snap without answering the question. Not because he was a cruel person, but because he got that way under pressure. She would know soon enough, anyway. She was, if nothing else, a patient person.

Oz set the equipment down in the hidden closet with all the grace he'd use depositing garbage by the curb. He then pointed to the dozens of white kitchen trash bags lined up neatly on card tables off to the side. "Find our belongings and set them over with the laptop. They're going with us. The rest of the bags go into the closet."

"All right." That was an activity she understood.

"But don't turn on your phone," he added.

She was less clear about that, but would do as he asked.

Oz left the room and a second later Sabrina heard a door open and close. She went to work finding their stuff. It didn't take long, in part because his phone was in the same bag as her purse. As she checked the contents, she heard a car start up followed by a quick engine rev. Then it turned off again.

Oz returned a few minutes later and helped her hide the last few bags. "Please finish up with the stuff on the desk while I deal with the card tables."

She wasn't sure why the card tables needed dealing with,

but didn't dwell on it.

Oz walked over to the big elevator and pulled what looked like a bent piece of wire from his back pocket. He slipped it through the hole at the top of the elevator door and began playing with it. "Achilles told me how these work, but I've never actually done it and—" Oz trailed off and then triumphantly pulled the elevator door aside. "There you have it."

He also opened the second door.

Sabrina found it kind of creepy seeing that big black hole, knowing it led down to the cell where they might well have died. Where forty-six people were still waiting to be rescued.

Oz peered down into the gloom and muttered, "Far enough."

She was about to ask him to clarify when he said, "Would you mind going to the kitchen to grab me a glass of water, with ice please?"

"Sure." She could use a drink herself.

Sabrina filled two big artisan cups, the kind with tiny air bubbles trapped in the glass. As she entered the study, she caught sight of Oz pushing something across the floor. Had her eyes played a trick? She hurried around the bookcase in time to see him push it over the edge of the elevator shaft. Correction, push *a woman* over the edge.

A second later, Sabrina heard a terrible thud accompanied by a sickening crack. She brought both hands to her mouth as her knees went weak. "What did you just do?"

"Forget about it."

"What did you just do?"

"I solved a problem."

"You just killed our captors in cold blood. They were helpless. Completely in our control."

"I'll explain later."

"You'll explain now."

Her husband almost snapped. She saw it in his eyes. But the anger faded as quickly as it rose. "Nobody can ever know about this place. Therefore, they need to be with the others."

"What? But—" her eyes went to Katya and Achilles.

"No!"

Oz grabbed Achilles by the heels.

"No, Oz! I forbid it!"

The thunderous look returned.

She moved to stand between Achilles and the open elevator shaft. Braced by nothing with her back to the abyss, a single step from the end of her life, Sabrina was scared. Even more scared than she'd been down below.

But she wasn't going to move.

Oz read the determination on her face. "All right. All right. We'll stash him in the manual lift. Grab the door."

She gave her husband a sideways glance.

"We'll leave him alive. I promise."

She walked over and opened the smaller door.

Oz grabbed Achilles by the ankles and dragged him inside, causing the bell to tinkle. Her husband struggled, given Achilles' large size, but he eventually managed to stuff the former Olympian all the way into the tight space, albeit upside down.

"You'll never get Katya in. Wait! You're not going to—"

"No, I'm not," Oz interjected.

He shut the elevator door and began turning the crank, counting off each revolution. At seven he stopped. He positioned the crank at the bottom of its rotation and abutted it with a metal rod that nested into the floor. To Sabrina's relief, he then closed the freight elevator doors.

"What about Katya?" Sabrina asked, fearing the answer but needing to know.

"She's coming with us."

They were a half hour down the road with the bookcase closed and the front door locked before Sabrina realized what they'd done.

Or rather hadn't.

The revelation sliced down the length of her spine like an icy sword.

Back in the house, she'd been completely caught up in the mystery of Oz's actions. Then in the car, she'd been wholly absorbed by the implications of his revelation. Until that very second, her overtaxed mind hadn't found the wherewithal to ponder anything that wasn't right there in front of her face.

She turned to Oz and forced sound from her throat. "You didn't forget. It was part of your plan."

"Forget what?"

His tone told the tale but she spoke the words anyway. "To turn on the bunker's power."

Chapter 46: *Stuck*

Location: Unknown

WHEN I REACHED for my neck in a subconscious attempt to ease the throbbing pain, the motion flipped some neural switch that brought the rest of my mind online. Consciousness then kicked in with the force of an electric chair. Memories and circumstances collided like troops combatting on an open field.

I had escaped captivity—but was back in the dark.

I had called the police—but was alone.

I was unbound—but upside down.

I knew what had happened—but had no memory of it. Somehow, our captors had regained control. They'd once again put their earphones on my head, thereby erasing my memory of the fight. But they hadn't put me back in the bunker. At least not on the floor.

My legs were haphazardly propped up on one wall and my head was abutting another. It was akin to being in a vertical coffin. But of course, it wasn't a coffin. And the contraption beneath one shoulder told me it wasn't a closet either. It was the manual elevator.

I constricted myself like a cannonball and then rocked upright. The process caused something to scrape across the floor. I guessed what it was before my fingers closed around the spongy set of hemispheres. An anesthetizing headset.

The fact that it was there on the floor rather than wrapped around my head was a stroke of good fortune. *Great* fortune. Whether the headset had come off as my limp body slumped or was knocked off by some subconscious flailing, I'd never know. But the serendipitous shift had probably saved my life.

Or at least postponed my death.

I traced my hands around the two rectangular grooves in the floor, the manual pedals that confirmed my exact location. They were fixed in place. Just part of the floor.

I took a deep breath and began feeling around. Finding the lever didn't take long. It was on the floor in the center of one side. I pushed it through its arc, then hopped atop the pedals. They moved—but not through a full rotation.

The gears were locked.

The steel bar was clearly back in place.

I considered crying out, but only for a second. Surprise might be my only advantage. Giving it away would be foolish. Besides, if anyone were able and inclined to help me, they'd be doing so already. Katya would see to that.

Katya…. Where was Katya? The last thing I remembered was turning the crank of this very lift. Sending it down to pick up the women. Somehow, while Oz and I were thus distracted, the villains had turned the tables. There must have been another man—or six.

I just couldn't remember.

I began to study my would-be coffin. It was essentially five wooden panels—three walls with a ceiling and floor—attached to a steel frame. That frame was held adjacent to the concrete wall of the elevator shaft by steel rails that ran along two sides. The concrete that formed the fourth wall disappeared when the car aligned with either the upper or lower doorway. The whole construction was suspended by a counterweighted cable and raised or lowered by a chain attached to cranks and gears.

With that picture in mind, I asked myself the big question. The Houdini question. How to escape?

I inspected the crack between the edge of the car and the side of the shaft wall. The gap was only pinkie-finger thick.

I ran my hands over the walls as I tried to recall the image of the wood. I'd only glimpsed it briefly before sending it down for my sweetie. At the time, it didn't strike me as anything fancy. It wasn't polished hardwood like in an old hotel. My fingers completed the picture. It was plywood, sanded and stained. That was bad news. Plywood was tough stuff.

Since the surface of the shaft was undoubtedly the toughest sidewall, and the opposite side the only one that wasn't braced by supporting rails, my first move was obvious. I braced my back on the concrete, lifted my legs parallel to the floor, and pressed.

Although I no longer cross-country ski competitively, my quadriceps remain overdeveloped from my Olympic training. Back in the day, on a seated leg press configured similarly to the way I was now, I worked out with a thousand pounds. I pictured Katya, worried and waiting, and pressed with everything I had. The metal creaked and the plywood flexed but nothing broke. My feet didn't punch through the wood and the cab didn't come off the rails.

I adjusted my position.

Since the depth of the box was too shallow to let my legs press with full force, I slid to the ground. There, I was able to get my knees right, but then the force vector didn't hit the wood at a ninety-degree angle. I was applying more pressure, but less efficiently. The net result was a wash. It gained me nothing.

Despite all evidence, I was confident that I could defeat that wall if there proved to be no other way out. I simply would not be bested by a piece of plank. But I would likely blow a knee or disc in the process. Since I would be needing those parts after escaping, I sought an alternative.

In the dark.

A few deep breaths brought me to the conclusion that the floor was the weak link. Although I couldn't think of another setting where that would be the case, it almost certainly applied here.

As any accomplished martial artist is well aware, the weak links on the human body are our joints. Our elbows, knees, wrists and especially our neck. Joints have lots of little parts and are much more susceptible to stress than larger, less-sophisticated anatomies.

The elevator had an equivalent construction. The pedals

in the floor.

When one raised, the other lowered, as pedals always do. I moved them as far as possible and began a tactile exploration. Each pedal was surfaced with the same type of wood used in the rest of the box and measured about ten-by-twenty inches. Combined, they occupied a space of twenty inches square, big enough to accommodate two large feet spread shoulder distance apart. If I could remove both pedals along with the accompanying framework, I'd have a hole I could squeeze through.

My first impulse was to rip the pedals off their frames, but that wouldn't get me anywhere. The frames themselves would block me. So I went to work feeling for the fasteners that held the system together. The good news was nuts and bolts appeared to be used in all the crucial places. The bad news was I had no tools.

I figured that if I could remove one piece, I might be able to use it as a tool. I just needed a bit of luck—and a weak link.

I didn't find it.

Everything was too tight for soft flesh to budge. Even fingertips trained to grip rocks.

"Think, Achilles. Think!"

47
Unlocked and Loaded

Western Nevada

THE ANSWER to my tool problem was literally at my fingertips. The headset. If I was right, the instrument that imprisoned me would also set me free.

I needed metal, preferably stiff but bendable. With the aid of my teeth, I found exactly that beneath the foam and fabric padding of the headband.

I don't know how long it took me to remove the bolts from the left side of the pedal assembly. So completely absorbed was I in the minute mechanics of the disassembly process, that it was like entering a temporal rift. The absolute darkness undoubtedly contributed to the effect that psychologists call *flow*.

Once I set the fourth and final nut aside, I rose and put my full weight on the mechanism.

It tilted.

I began bouncing with increasing force until the right half gave. Not completely, but hopefully enough for a highly motivated climber.

A few scrapes later, I wriggled past and ended up dangling from the distorted assembly. I had no idea how high up the shaft I was, but suspected it was somewhere in the middle. That would be the intuitive choice for stranding someone.

I climbed around to the far side of the central rail and began a controlled slide. I hit the top of the freight elevator a few feet later. As my second foot came to rest atop the cabin, it brushed against something soft and limp. Something that hadn't been there during my initial climb.

Something that sent a shiver down my spine.

My nose went to work along with my hands, cataloguing blood, sweat, soap and scented shampoo. *Not Katya's!*

The shoe at the end of the leg I'd grazed told me the victim was male. No surprise there. But his pants material was unexpected. It wasn't the thin, tough cotton of surgical scrubs. Therefore, he probably wasn't one of my fellow prisoners.

How long had I been unconscious? Apparently, long enough for a third party to become involved. Was this a cop? That seemed the most logical conclusion, but my continued probing quickly dissuaded me of that idea. He wasn't wearing a uniform, and he wasn't alone. He was with a woman.

She had somehow landed with one leg draped over the cable pulley. She also had a badly damaged elbow.

A badly damaged elbow. These weren't cops or fellow prisoners. They were our captors. The two Oz and I had apprehended.

I went back over their bodies with their pictures in mind and became convinced. I also discovered their cause of death. One suffered severe head trauma, the other a broken neck. I inspected the rest of the elevator roof, expecting to find Oz but coming up blank.

Perhaps he'd fallen all the way down.

I had a decision to make. Which direction to climb? The decision driver was caring for Katya. Not just finding her, but saving her. She was likely in the bunker, but there was nothing down there I could use to help her. My mind's eye flashed to the stockpile of guns in the garage.

I went up.

I reached the keyhole quickly and found myself facing the same dilemma I'd encountered during the first round. Again I was blind and unarmed and facing an unknown opposing force as I put my palms to the back of the bookcase. At least this time I knew what lay on the opposite side—if not who.

Taking it slow and steady, I inched the concealing wall away. As I moved toward the corner I passed the hidden closet. With what little light filtered through I could see that it was now stuffed with kitchen trash bags. Most likely the ones that had been laid out on card tables.

Curious, but unwilling to delay my incursion now that the bookcase was noticeably out of place, I continued on and peered into the study.

It looked abandoned.

I crept quietly around the corner and pushed the bookcase back into place. The element of surprise appeared to be on my side. I walked directly to the garage and peered inside.

The rolling door was open, the black Dodge Charger gone. The stack of weapons remained intact except for two H&K MP7s. The ones I'd discovered to be loaded with blanks. Both were missing.

I filled two twenty-round magazines with some very serious 4.6 x 30 mm ammunition. I slapped one into a remaining MP7 and slid the spare into my back pocket. Then I loaded a Glock 19 with 115 grain FMJ 9mm Parabellums. It went into a shoulder holster which I strapped into place. I wasn't planning a Lara Croft-style twin-handgun firefight. The G19 was for Katya.

Feeling infinitely more confident than I had seconds earlier, I stepped back into the cabin. I took my time clearing it, room by room. Someone had somehow surprised me the last time, and I wasn't about to let that happen again. But the further I got, the clearer the obvious conclusion became.

The circus had left town.

I considered calling the police, but it occurred to me that the earlier call might have been the mistake that put me back in the dark. Either due to corrupt cops or someone powerful intercepting the police band. A dirty FBI agent or local sheriff perhaps.

I returned to the garage in search of rope—lots of rope. I didn't find any. Not so much as a clothesline. But I did find an acceptable substitute. One hundred feet of garden hose, coiled around a wheeling caddy. I took the hose, but left the caddy. I also pulled a drill off the rack along with a

1.5-inch wood-boring bit, and grabbed a weapon sling.

I used the bit to drill a hole near the bottom of the back of the bookcase directly opposite the big elevator. Then I ran the hose nozzle through, knotted it off, and tossed the coil into the shaft. Last but not least, I pulled the big metal pin from the ground, freeing the manual lift. Rather than simply toss the bar aside, I stashed it behind a row of books. An ounce of prevention.

Noting that my makeshift drop key had been left in the elevator lock, I retrieved and pocketed it. Just in case.

Satisfied with my prep work, I walked to the laundry room, opened the breaker box, and flipped the big unlabeled switch.

48
Thin Air

Western Nevada

MY HEART was in my mouth as I descended the hose. Given all the curve balls I'd encountered in the past few days, I was far from clear on what to expect. All I knew for certain was that I wouldn't stop until Katya was safe at my side.

Within seconds, I reached the bottom of the shaft.

I put my ear to the door, but heard nothing. Given the armor plating and hermetic seal, that wasn't too surprising. I released the latch, opened it a crack, and peered inside. With one exception, everyone visible appeared to be sleeping. The man closest to the elevator doors was clearly dead. It was Webster. He had a massive hematoma on the left side of his head and a deadeye stare. The bruise told his tragic tale. It was shaped like the side of a dumbbell. *Good girl!*

Among the unconscious, the interesting one was Kai. He was seated in an armchair that he'd moved to face the manual elevator. He held a Glock 19 in his limp hand.

The stillness of the scene perplexed and frightened me until I remembered that I'd just turned on the power. That recognition sparked the revelation that explained the rest of the picture and moved the panic deep into my bones. They'd been in the dark long enough to suck all the oxygen from the still air.

How long was the gap between unconsciousness and death when the heart was pumping useless gas to the brain? It probably wasn't more than a few minutes, and no doubt depended on the individual's health.

Fighting the urge to rush inside, I widened the gap and

slipped through the doors. With my MP7 ready, I crept to Kai and plucked the Glock from his hand. After wedging it beside its twin beneath my shoulder holster, I felt for his carotid pulse—and found it! Strong and steady. The bunker's owner stirred at my touch but didn't waken.

Katya wasn't in the main room, but then neither were most people. Had they escaped? Or spread out in search of air?

I glanced into both downstairs bedrooms and saw that most beds were occupied. The explanation was obvious. Growing weak and wanting to conserve both oxygen and energy, they'd lain down.

Katya was not among them.

She wasn't in the gym or restroom either.

The pantry had a few occupants, as did both the garden and the utility room. All were flat on their back in what yogis would call *shavasana* position. As I watched, a few started stirring.

Katya wasn't among them.

It occurred to me that I also hadn't spotted Sabrina or Oz.

Sebastian was on a couch in the main room, not far from his fallen fellow spy. I found a second Glock wedged between his sofa cushions.

He awoke while I was wresting it free.

I jammed the barrel of my MP7 into his mouth.

As his eyes went wide, I raised his Glock to my lips in the hush sign. "Roll over. I want you kissing cushion," I whispered. "If I see your eyes, I'll shut them with a bullet. If I hear your voice, I'll silence it with a bullet."

Sebastian rolled over without a sound.

Carrying three Glocks in addition to my MP7 was overly awkward, so I popped the magazines and ejected the chambered rounds from the two I'd just seized.

That noise garnered a few reactions around the room. More people were waking up.

I squeezed the magazines into elastic slots on my holster. Then I quietly slid the neutered Glocks under the couch, and hurried upstairs. It took me less than a minute to check all four rooms. By the end, my heart felt like it was full of rocks. Katya was not in the bunker.

49
Blank Stare

Western Nevada

SINCE KATYA WASN'T IN THE BUNKER, it was painful for me to be there. I knew that pain wouldn't stop until I found her safe and sound. In the meantime, the only thing I could do to assuage my anguish was to constantly keep moving in her direction.

Wherever that was.

But first, I had to see forty-five other souls to safety. And one to jail.

I ran around checking the pulse of anyone not stirring. Thankfully, mercifully, Webster was the only casualty. I wondered if anyone else knew who had killed him, given that Katya had done the deed in the dark.

The fact that I was armed drew mixed reactions. Some people shrank back, others asked questions. I ignored them all. This was a triage situation with no time for distraction. If CPR was required, seconds mattered.

Satisfied that no lives were in immediate danger, I returned to the main room. Despite all that had transpired, I figured I'd emerged from the shaft less than five minutes earlier.

I walked behind the couch on which Sebastian was obediently kissing cushion and turned toward the rapidly gathering crowd. Some were shouting questions at me, others were reacting to the sight of Webster's dead body. I snugged the muzzle of the MP7 into the back of Sebastian's neck. While the crowd cowered, I asked him, "How many of you are there?"

"Four," he said, his face buried in fright, his voice muffled.

"In addition to you and Webster?"

"Including us."

"Are you sure?"

"Of course."

Knowing that good interrogation technique involves shaking things up to keep the subject off-balance, I bent close enough to whisper menacingly in his ear. "Willing to bet your life on it?"

"Yes. Just us four. I swear."

I believed him, but I kept the menace in my tone and the muzzle pressed tight. He and his colleagues had threatened Katya's life and tried to steal our home. "Describe the other two."

"A man and a woman, both fifty years old." Sebastian went on to characterize the couple Oz and I had attacked upstairs. The couple I was all but certain were now dead in the elevator shaft.

"You received no outside assistance?"

"None."

I pressed the muzzle further into his flesh. "Employed no consultants, informants or snitches?"

"No."

I had what I needed for now. It was time to address the crowd. They had all backed away and many had sought partial cover behind walls. "It's safe to leave. The electric elevator isn't working, but with the hand-cranked lift we can evacuate one person at a time."

Expressions immediately softened. One of the CEOs ran to the manual lift and tried to open the door while a dozen others hurled questions at me. Kai's was the most commanding. He was standing next to Governor Rickman. "Where did you get the submachine gun?"

"You have to crank the lift down to the bottom before the door will open," I called to the CEO. "Be careful getting in; I had to dismantle the floor."

Turning towards Kai and the governor, I said. "I got it from your garage after climbing the elevator shaft."

"How did you get into the elevator shaft? The doors are locked and bulletproof."

"I fabricated a drop key from a coat hanger." I pulled the crude instrument from my back pocket and tossed it to Kai.

"Who's upstairs?" the CEO asked, pausing in the doorway.

"Nobody. One of our kidnappers is here on the couch. One is there." I used the H&K to gesture toward Webster's body. As I did so, Sebastian popped his head up, spotted his colleague and cried out in anguish.

I pushed him down into the couch and turned back to Kai. "The other two are in the elevator shaft, also dead. Whoever does the cranking is the next to go up."

Sebastian's cry turned into a wail and he began writhing on the couch.

I paid him no heed.

"How do I use this?" Kai asked, holding up the drop key.

I told him.

Everyone but the guy cranking the manual lift watched Kai work the lock. It took a few tries, but he got it. "Well, I'll be."

He pulled the doors aside. "I don't see any bodies. What's with the hose?"

"The bodies are higher up. I couldn't find rope."

"Why can't we use the electric elevator?" Governor Rickman asked.

I flashed on the image of two corpses getting tangled and mangled by pulleys and cables. Perhaps even leaking on the riders. "They ripped out the panel upstairs as well."

"I'm an electrical engineer," a member of the crowd volunteered. "I might be able to repair it one way or another."

"Great. You head up next."

I pulled a Glock from beneath the couch and turned to

my favorite banker. It was best to keep the troublemakers busy at times like these. "Trey, I need your help keeping Sebastian covered. He should be the last to come up." I extended the gun, butt first.

Trey didn't take it. He chose to give me a defiant look instead. "Which means I'll be next-to-last?"

"Think of it as women and children first."

"Why don't *you* stay?"

"Because Katya is missing and I need to find her."

"It's not just Katya that's missing. Your Muslim friends are gone too. Why is that?" Trey asked, as his cabal gathered around.

"I don't know. That's what I plan to investigate."

"The women were called upstairs by the kidnappers. Why was that?" Trey pressed.

I didn't like where this was going. Nor did I care to defend myself to a jackass I was trying to help. "That was Oz. He was using the kidnapper's microphone. We wanted to get the women out of the reach of the real spies."

"The women, but not the rest of us?"

"Perhaps you've noticed that I'm freeing you right now."

"You, but not Oz. How did he get upstairs? Is he a climber too? Is he up there with a gun right now? Picking people off, one at a time, while you distract me by offering a gun with no ammunition?"

50
Double Jeopardy

Western Nevada

I DIDN'T HAVE THE STOMACH for more from Trey, and Katya didn't have the time. "I'm leaving. I suggest someone keep an eye on Sebastian."

Trey crossed his arms and nodded knowingly. Kai and Rickman didn't look particularly pleased either.

I took a quick detour into the bedroom to change into my own clothes. They were nothing special, but Katya's ring was in the pocket of my jeans. No way would I lose that again.

Kai and Rickman intercepted me a minute later on the way to the elevator shaft. Kai spoke softly. "I'll take the Glock."

I pressed the gun into his outstretched hand, then slipped him a loaded magazine.

"Thanks."

Climbing the garden hose proved to be a breeze. It was actually quite grippy. I had to time my move around the electric elevator to avoid being hit by the hand-cranked lift, which was running nonstop, but that was no big deal.

With the doors open below and the bookshelf swung wide above, I had enough light to visually confirm that it was the corpses of our captors atop the electric elevator. I was about to move on when it struck me that they might prevent the lift from docking up above—assuming the electrical engineer could get it working.

The fix was obvious but gruesome. Drop them into the pit.

I did the math. With forty people to go and the manual

lift requiring two-plus minutes per person, it would take an hour and a half to get everyone out. Not long in the grand scheme of things, but given my own experience disembarking planes after long flights, I knew it would be tremendously frustrating. Deciding that the living had to take precedence over the dead, I did the deed.

Crunch, crunch.

The first thing I saw up top was the electrical engineer working the elevator panel. That helped allay the uneasy feeling over what I'd just done.

The next thing I saw was people searching the pile of kitchen bags for their belongings while others talked on their repossessed phones. That gave me an idea.

I dragged all the remaining bags out into the study where I could systematically inspect them. It didn't take long to find the bag with my phone, wallet and Katya's purse. While it felt good to slide my belongings back into my pockets, they weren't my end goal. I was looking for the little leather café au lait purse with a gold buckle and chain that matched Sabrina's dress.

I didn't find it.

I made a second pass of the kitchen bags, this time inspecting the IDs in purses and wallets. No Sabrina, no Oz. Three people were gone, but only two sets of identification were missing.

Chewing on that, I returned to the hidden closet. It also contained the computer equipment which, like the kitchen bags, had been in the study when Oz and I stormed in. The big monitor was there, as was the bone-mic console and the video intercom. Notably missing were the laptop computer and the red flash drive. The one with the cryptocurrency, including the four million dollars I'd borrowed.

Combining all that with the other facts yielded a virtually inescapable conclusion. A sad and scary conclusion. Oz had hijacked the robbery.

He'd seen the opportunity to co-opt the perfect crime and had seized upon it. That disappointed me on many levels, despite being understandable. It was, after all, ninety-two million dollars. Many if not most men would at least be tempted.

But why take Katya? Why not stuff her in the lift with me? An answer came quickly. She'd have put it overweight, making it impossible to strand me in the suspended coffin. Although sufficient, that explanation felt slim. Especially since he'd shoved the kidnappers to their deaths and left the rest of us to suffocate. So why take her?

No other explanation leapt to mind, but a practical consideration did. I looked around and found another item missing. The duct tape.

As I fought to suppress the image of Katya brutally bound, a secondary conclusion struck. A most unwelcome one. Trey had been right about Oz. He was everything the blowhard banker had said—if only opportunistically.

They say it's better to let one hundred guilty men go free than send one innocent man to prison. While I still embraced that central tenet of the United States justice system, I had to say that it felt pretty crappy becoming a victim of one of those hundred.

While that bitter pill went down, two significant things happened simultaneously. The combination was both unfortunate and disconcerting. Police sirens became audible in the distance, and Harold Herbert Huxley III emerged from the elevator gripping a gun. I couldn't tell if the Glock held a magazine or chambered round, but there was no mistaking Trey's target. He was aiming at my heart.

51
Backed Up

Western Nevada

I MET TREY'S EYE. He was a good twenty feet away and standing more like an archer than a shooter, with a side profile and a rigid right arm extended straight from the shoulder. He looked like a movie poster. Given his poor choice of grip, I checked his other hand. It held a rolled up sheaf of papers. The loan notes. Bastard.

"What are you doing?" I asked.

"Ensuring that you don't leave."

"Why would that concern you in the least, much less enough to draw a gun?"

As I spoke, it struck me that I hadn't heard one word of thanks. There had been no grateful smiles or pats on the back either. I hadn't been looking for any of those, so their absence hadn't register—until now.

At first, the lack of gratitude seemed natural enough. People had much more pressing matters on their minds. Things like seeing sunlight and phoning family. But on second thought, I realized that I wasn't getting a grateful vibe from the growing crowd. The body language exhibited by my fellow captives indicated that they remained wary. Again, the reaction seemed to fit the circumstance, especially since I was toting a submachine gun, but that conclusion also paled under scrutiny.

Trey didn't answer my question. He issued a command instead. "Drop your weapons."

It only took a blink to play out the proposed scenario in my mind. I could swallow my pride, put down my guns, and wait for the police to arrive. Given the sound of the sirens, that discomfort would only last about two minutes. Or I could tell Trey to pound sand and ignore him. In either case, the police would immediately disarm everyone.

But then what?

There would be interviews, and apparently accusations. Did Trey genuinely suspect me of being one of the kidnappers? Or was he just seizing an opportunity to salve his wounded ego? More importantly, could he twist the facts to present a compelling case?

My problem, I immediately recognized, was the dark. Nothing I'd done in the dark had been seen or heard. When the lights came on, I was there, armed to the teeth. Webster was dead and Sebastian subdued, but nobody outside my little circle knew to view that scene with the knowledge that they were spies. I had freed everybody, but that was what they expected the captors to do.

The truly damning evidence, I decided, was that the other three members of my group were all gone. As the captors would be.

The police would have Sebastian, so the truth would eventually come out. And they also— I stopped myself. The headsets were missing. There had been a bag full of them in the hidden closet.

"Put it down, Achilles!" Trey repeated.

The investigation would take more than a few hours. It would take days. Days during which Katya would be twisting in the wind. And if things didn't go my way, if there was any kind of blip, days would drag into weeks. The justice system was more backed up than the plumbing at a sausage plant.

Ignoring Trey, who had obviously never fired a weapon, I picked up Katya's purse and walked to the garage. Once on the other side of the door, I ran to the cross-country motorbikes.

Trey wouldn't follow. Not immediately. Not ever. Not knowing that I could be waiting.

He'd defer to the cops.

They were my concern.

Two motorcycle keys were hanging from coat hooks on a

rack full of matching gear. I helped myself to a red and white helmet, jacket and gloves before sticking one key in my pocket and palming the other. I gave the first bike a shake, then the second, listening for gas. Near as I could tell, both were topped off. I found the one that responded to the key in my hand.

Shaking my head at the stupid banker, I hopped on, revved the engine, and headed for the hills.

52
First Steps

Western Nevada

PULLING OUT OF THE GARAGE, I saw the police approaching from the east. The squad of sedans and SUVs was hard to miss with its flashing lights and blaring sirens. I turned to put the cabin between us before taking a broad cross-country loop that would put me back on the road they'd come in on. Hopefully I hadn't been spotted, but it really didn't matter if I had. They couldn't follow me on four wheels. My immediate mission was to be impossibly far away before anyone considered pursuing me on two.

Or from above.

As I dodged tree trunks and boulders, my mind kept toggling between thoughts of *this is crazy* and *no other option*. It was a predicament with which I had considerable experience.

The further I moved from the scene of the crime, the more my ultimate move crystalized. Once Katya was safe, I would ask forgiveness. Remotely and through lawyers—if required.

Hopefully, it wouldn't be.

If the lead detective was any good, he or she should quickly come to the correct conclusion.

I ended up on Forest Highway 100 heading downhill into Reno, which was vastly preferable to I-80 given both the traffic volume and the ease of escaping into the woods if required.

It wasn't required.

Before my mind fully caught up with my body, I found myself on the outskirts of Nevada's second most famous city. I was sweaty, shaken and speckled with road grime, but still without a tail. Still breathing free air.

Knowing it wouldn't be wise to enter a populated area with a submachine gun slung around my neck, I stashed it in the trash can of a cabin close to town. Unloaded, of course. If I didn't retrieve the H&K, it would almost certainly find its way to the city dump. I considered carrying the Glock in the shoulder holster under my shirt, but decided that would add pointless risk, so it too went in the trash. As did Katya's emptied purse.

I continued moving quickly. A window of opportunity existed before the electronic law enforcement net would eliminate my ability to use plastic. I intended to slip through it.

The first thing I did upon entering the city proper was pull up to an ATM—of which there are a million in Reno—and withdraw the daily maximum on Katya's card and my own. That put two thousand dollars in my pocket.

Then I hit a Walgreens in search of a Vanilla Visa.

Vanilla Visas require no identification to purchase or register. They are essentially money-laundering mechanisms hiding in plain sight wherever gift cards are sold. This Walgreens had only one left. I loaded it to the maximum and walked out of the store with five hundred dollars worth of anonymous debit card spending power that I could use anywhere in the US—or online.

Taking advantage of being off the bike, I asked a passerby where I might find a major shopping center. He directed me to the Meadowood Mall, which was near where the 589 ring road crossed I-580. An easy fifteen-minute ride.

I needed two new smart phones, two new SIM cards, a backpack and spray paint. The mall quickly yielded them all. I had the backpack salesman staple my receipt to the tag; then I straightened the staple in the men's room and used it to pop the SIM cards on both my old phone and Katya's. I'd destroy and dispose of the old components after transferring the data to my new devices.

Returning to my stolen motorcycle was risky business. It was distinctive, and the police officers at the cabin would likely have issued a BOLO for it. With that in mind, I'd parked in the shadow of a white Ford Bronco at the outskirts of the lot and left the helmet, jacket and gloves with the bike.

I approached it indirectly, beginning from a distant mall entrance and twice walking as if heading to different cars. When nothing caused concern, I decided to apply the flat black paint right there on the pavement.

I used a plastic shopping bag to mask the helmet visor, then went to work with the can. Within three minutes, the bike, helmet, jacket and gloves were all black. The leather was ruined and the coverage sloppy, but I'd effectively pulled the plug on the police radar.

I went for a walk around the parking lot to toss the can, clear my head and give the paint time to dry. The drying would be near-immediate in the hot Nevada sun, but the clearing might take a while.

It appeared that Oz and Sabrina had betrayed Katya and me in extreme fashion. We weren't old friends or even new ones in the sense that our relationship would have continued after release, but we had banded together in a foxhole. Shared stress and shared time.

During that time, I had misjudged their characters, and ultimately I had enabled them to do what they'd done. It was going to take considerable effort to work my head around and past that failing.

If they killed Katya, I never would.

In one of our earlier conversations, once we'd adapted to our circumstance and were stuck making small talk in the dark, Oz told me they'd come to San Francisco to see the Bay Area and meet with an advisor. A wealthy Maltese who was flying in for the conference. He'd canceled his trip at the last minute and given them his prepaid dinner reservation at Cinquante Bouches in apology.

I'd believed him then and decided that I still did.

At least the advisor part.

In this new light, I was beginning to question Oz's Maltese origin. Lots of Americans claimed to be Canadian when traveling abroad for simplicity and security reasons.

Canadians didn't tend to be the targets of animus the way Americans did. It stood to reason that other nationalities might do the same. For a Middle Easterner, claiming to be Maltese would be a savvy move. The citizens of that particular EU nation exhibited a Middle Eastern skin tone and even spoke a similar-sounding language.

Regardless of that potential white lie, I wondered if the canceled advisor meeting he referenced was the key. Had it made Oz desperate enough to resort to murder?

Crazy as that sounded, the startup world had set plenty of precedent. From personal experience, I knew why. The incessant stream of glitz and pressure stoked greed while it warped values.

Some got swept over the edge.

Just the other day, Silicon Valley had been shocked when news broke that the CEO of one red-hot medical startup had systematically fabricated everything. She'd raised billions from Wall Street by peddling a breakthrough diagnostic that she knew didn't really work—and she'd sold thousands of patients life-threatening test results in the process.

She'd essentially committed mass murder for money. It was a story fit for a major movie, and in fact one was in the works.

I would mull over that angle later. At the moment I had to tackle a couple of much more pressing questions. Why had Oz taken Katya? More importantly, where had he taken her?

I pulled out one of my fresh phones. "Siri, what's the address for Personal Propulsion Systems?"

While Siri thought, I prayed I was remembering the name right. The robot read Oz's title off a second after revealing that his given name was Osama, so I'd been a bit distracted. Still, the name had enough of a ring that it stuck. I hoped.

"There's a Personal Propulsion Systems in Melbourne, Florida. Is that the one you want?"

It was. I remembered overhearing Sabrina mention *Melbourne* to Katya and thinking *Australia*.

As I turned from my head-clearing walk back toward the bike, a CVS pharmacy caught my eye. I decided to risk a quick visit. Three minutes later I walked out of the store with an additional thousand dollars of anonymous online spending power. Just in case.

Knowing I'd pressed my luck with that last electronic transaction, I ran for the motorcycle. I threw on my freshly painted outfit and keyed the ignition. As the motor roared to life, I kicked the stand, twisted the throttle and shot off like a swarm of black killer bees.

My first stop would be the cabin with the trash can. My second the airport—but not to catch a flight. Couldn't risk that. With a three thousand-mile drive ahead of me, I had a car to steal.

53
Working the System

Western Nevada

I HAD NO IDEA where Katya was or whether she was even alive. I didn't feel the transcendental tear in my soul that I was certain would accompany her passing, but I heard that people rarely did.

Factoring in the gravity of the scene behind me, which included two confirmed kills and another forty-seven attempted murders, I knew the odds that she was alive were slim. When I found her, it would likely be in a ditch. But I would never stop looking.

The question was *where? Where to look?*

I had painfully few clues. The best I could do was triangulate from *who*. The couple who had taken Katya claimed to call Melbourne, Florida, home. The man ran a business called *Personal Propulsion Systems*. The woman was its CFO. At least according to the business cards our captors had read aloud.

I hadn't asked Osama Abdilla about his business. I'd been focused on saving our lives. The niceties of polite social interaction had been far from my mind.

Now I wished I had asked. Finding Katya amounted to tracking them, and their business was the obvious place to start.

Siri showed Melbourne to be on Florida's Space Coast, the midsection of Atlantic coastline that housed NASA's Kennedy Space Center, America's gateway to space. My goal was getting there ASAP.

I couldn't fly. Not as a wanted man. Trains would be too slow and also required ID. That left cars. Since renting was out, my options were *buy*, *borrow* or *steal*. I wouldn't trust anything I could afford, and knew no one nearby from whom I could borrow, so I was left with theft.

I didn't like the idea of stealing, of dealing an innocent person a potentially crippling blow, so I went to the airport. I left the bike in long-term parking, with the jacket and gloves stuffed into the helmet, then headed for the rental car section of the parking garage.

Reno wasn't Vegas, but it was still a good-sized airport. One thing those all have in common is an atmosphere of coordinated chaos. With pricing pressures forcing transportation providers to watch every dime, you end up with lots of lines. Lines to obtain boarding passes, lines to check bags, lines to pick up rental cars and lines to return them. In this case, and for the first time, a line was my friend.

I cruised the parking garage searching for the car company with the worst staff-to-volume ratio. On that day at that time, with plenty of planes going out and just as many coming in, I couldn't go wrong. But there was a standout. A very active operation manned by a single haggard soul.

His circumstances begged for heroic effort, for him to rise to the occasion and overcome with quick, efficient service and a reassuring smile.

He wasn't having any of that.

No doubt, he'd decided long ago to give his employer exactly what it paid for.

I picked my car and waited for my moment. The former was a full-size sedan, checked in but not blocked in. The latter was a customer frustrated by a contentious bill.

My appropriated vehicle was a white Ford Fusion, about as anonymous as cars come. The only things missing were a full tank of gas and a large cup of coffee. Twenty minutes and twenty miles out of the airport, I hit a gas station with an eye on obtaining both.

Filling up after prepaying forty dollars in cash, I caught sight of something that made me rethink the coffee. A hitchhiker with a Vegas sign.

He looked more like a college kid than a hippie. Decent haircut, clean clothes and a backpack that was stuffed but not stained. The Vegas sign was in his left hand. His right held a Bible.

I looked at the navigation app on my phone. Las Vegas was 440 miles southeast along what promised to be a very desolate stretch of highway. It would take me six hours. Hours much better spent sleeping.

I didn't know whether the Bible was a prop, profession or lifeline. But I decided to find out.

54
Silent Witness

Western Nevada

VIC was once again on the way to Incline Village when a call from Sacramento lit up his phone. It was Peter. "Hey, what's up?"

"Your lucky day, my friend. That case we were talking about, the Napa restaurant."

"Yes?"

"They just found the victims up near Lake Tahoe—on the Nevada side."

"Dead or alive?"

"Alive."

"Where, exactly?"

"An isolated cabin not far from Crystal Bay. I'm sending you the map coordinates."

"How long ago were they discovered?"

"Minutes."

"You're the best, Peter. I owe you big time."

Vic pulled to the side of the road, punched the coordinates into his navigation app, and hit the gas. He didn't call his boss, but he did leave word with his office, both to put a stake in the ground and to cover his ass. It would be just like his boss to nudge him aside for a protocol violation.

The scene was swarming when Vic reached the top of the long and winding wooded drive. Ambulances, paramedics, firemen and police. Lots of police. But Vic appeared to be the first federal agent.

The cabin was made of logs, but it resembled President Lincoln's childhood home about as much as President

Washington's Delaware-crossing boat resembled a modern motor yacht. From the doorway, the interior looked like a five-star hotel, less the reception counter. High ceilings and fine furnishings focused and enhanced magnificent views.

No one was paying the finery any heed. All the action was off to the side in an enormous study that boasted floor-to-ceiling windows and bookshelves. One large section of shelving had been swung aside to reveal two open elevator doorways and a closet. There was a lot of action around it. In fact, there was a lot of action everywhere. There had to be close to a hundred people, between the medical and law enforcement personnel and the victims.

Vic quickly spotted the RPD officer who was likely in charge of the scene. Lieutenant Marty Acevedo, who of course went by Ace, was busy talking to a group of victims. They were dressed like doctors, but then so was every victim at the scene.

Vic walked up and stood next to his city counterpart without interrupting.

"Then we heard two sickening thuds coming from the elevator shaft. We looked inside and saw two bodies. A man and a woman." The speaker was a big blond fellow with over-bleached teeth. He had a New York accent and emitted an arrogant air despite his demeaned position.

"And you think it was this Achilles fellow who did it?" Ace spotted Vic as he spoke, causing a telltale shadow to flash across his face like a flying bird.

The two had worked a few cases together, always pleasantly enough, so Vic knew the slip didn't reflect personal animosity. Ace was reacting like anyone would when his winning hand got trumped.

"Nobody else was in the shaft. It had to be him," Blondie replied.

"And then he fled on a motorcycle?" Ace asked.

"One of those cross-country types with a big suspension and knobby tires. I ordered him to stop, even raised a gun, but he ignored me."

"Where did you get a gun?"

"From under a couch."

"Down in the bunker?"

"That's right. Achilles left it there."

"I'm confused. He left you a gun?"

"It wasn't loaded. That was part of his trick."

"Yet you're surprised that he ignored you when you raised it at him?"

"He didn't know it was empty. He gave Kai an identical gun that was loaded."

"Why would he do that, if he was one of the kidnappers?"

"To make us think he wasn't, obviously."

"But then he ran?"

"Right. Once I made it clear we were on to him."

Ace put his hands on his hips. "We're going to need to continue this discussion downtown. You'll be more comfortable there."

Vic noted that Ace didn't indicate whose downtown office he was referencing.

Blondie crossed his arms. "We're not going anywhere but to the airport. We need to get back to New York. My bank has chartered a plane."

"This is a complicated case. We still have a lot of questions."

"My colleagues and I only have one. Where's our money? Collectively, we're out forty-eight million dollars. You know who took it. You have their names right there on your pad. You should be looking for the four of them, not sitting in a *comfortable office* with us."

"Please calm down. There's a process to these things."

"Don't tell us what to do or lecture us on process. We're not ignorant hicks. And don't you dare try to pull any of that obstruction of justice crap. We're happy to provide any information you may require by telephone, from New York. Or did you bring a subpoena?"

Vic chose that moment to step forward—not on Ace's toes. More like a dance move. "Vic Link, FBI. I missed the first part of your discussion. Do I understand correctly that you believe one of the victims was really a kidnapper?"

"Six of them, actually. Four got away with the money.

One is dead, another is still in the bunker."

"So you believe six of the fifty were in on it?"

"How many times do I have to repeat myself with you people? This is why we're going to New York and not downtown."

Vic ignored the rebuke and addressed the rest of Blondie's coterie. "Do you all agree with that? Some of the victims were in on the abduction?"

A few bankers said, "Yes." The rest nodded.

"They were undercover, so to speak? Masquerading as fellow prisoners before double-crossing their partners upstairs?"

"Exactly. You have their names," Blondie said, pointing to Ace's notepad.

Vic turned to Ace. "Did you hear that?"

Ace kept a straight face, but his eyes smiled. "I did."

"What?" Blondie asked.

"With eight eyewitnesses claiming that there are perpetrators hiding among the victims, all the victims have to be treated as suspects—and detained."

Vic watched with some satisfaction as the arrogant banker puckered like a fish, but it didn't last. "Nice try, but no dice. All you have to do is interrogate Sebastian. He can confirm who his accomplices were, here and now."

"I'm afraid that's not an option." The gravelly voice emanated from somewhere behind Vic's left shoulder. He turned to see a fit sixty-something male with a shaved head and piercing eyes standing beside the governor of Florida.

"Why not?" Blondie asked with a tinge of panic.

"Sebastian is dead. He committed suicide."

55
Bad Ride

Location: Unknown

KATYA OPENED HER EYES to pain and blackness. Her first thought was that she was back in the bunker, but that oddly appealing idea evaporated like a desert mirage. She was moving.

Also, the dark wasn't absolute. She couldn't see any source of light, but there seemed to be a few photons bouncing around. More like midnight in the woods than an underground cave.

The conclusion came quickly. She was in the trunk of a car.

The lack of light wasn't her primary concern at that moment. It wasn't even in the top five. For starters, she really needed a bathroom. Not that she could actually make use of one. Her wrists were bound behind her back and her ankles were also taped. This arrangement had her lying on her chest with her face in fuzzy flooring.

The carpeting seemed to be inducing an allergic reaction, because her eyes were itchy and her nose was clogged. The latter was particularly concerning because her mouth was taped shut. She was having trouble breathing.

Had the owners kept cats in the trunk?

Katya attempted to dislodge her gag by opening her jaw as wide as possible. This had the unexpected result of putting pressure on her ears. Ears that were covered.

She was wearing a headset. One of the big pairs like you used to protect your ears on a firing range. It must have been duct taped in place. Wrapped vertically around her jaw. Was that to prevent her from overhearing something? What could they not want her to hear? A secret plan? Achilles calling her name? No, she realized. That wasn't it at all. It was likely one of the anesthetic headsets that Sabrina saw at Cinquante Bouches.

So why wasn't she unconscious? Katya pondered that for a minute, for a mile, all the while struggling to take her mind off her exploding bladder. She concluded that the batteries had died.

How much longer could she hold it? How much longer would she have to? Which would give out first—her bladder or her nose?

Rather than dwell on those unpleasant details, Katya attempted to analyze her situation, beginning with a timeline.

What was the last thing she remembered?

The shock of that answer hit her hard.

She'd heard the sounds that Achilles primed her for—the clicks and whooshes of an opening and closing safe. Seconds later, she'd been grabbed by the arm and quietly threatened not to speak or move. She'd responded by swinging the small dumbbell fast and hard at the side of her assailant's head. He—Sebastian or Webster, she wasn't sure which—had collapsed at her feet. Miraculously, he hadn't shouted, and she hadn't screamed.

Had she killed him? Or just knocked him out? Katya didn't know. But she'd made it onto the elevator. Her last memory was stepping aboard.

Was that it? The reason for her cruel confinement? Revenge for killing one of the kidnappers' spies? No way to tell.

Given what she knew about the memory loss associated with headphone use, Katya concluded that she'd been ambushed as she exited the elevator. Sabrina was likely in another trunk. Hopefully Achilles and Oz were too.

That was the best-case scenario, she realized. Achilles would never permit her to be taken. His assault on the cabin had obviously failed.

The idea that Achilles could come up short in something so important, something so close to his core competence, was more frightening than any of the physical threats to Katya's health. She simply couldn't turn her mind's eye in that direction.

She decided to focus on saving herself. Getting the duct tape off her mouth was top of that priority list. Katya figured that she could use the carpeting to catch the edge and peel it off. But the edge didn't seem to be exposed.

The headset would have to come off first. No easy task given that it too was taped.

She began rubbing the side of her head against the floor like an affectionate cat. A few passes were enough to realize that dislodging it would be a challenge. The tape was tightly wrapped.

She repositioned herself to gain better leverage, moving into something resembling Child's Pose, facing downward and bent double with her knees to her chest. The yoga position smashed her back against the roof of the trunk, but it gave her a good angle. A few seconds later, she almost wished it hadn't. The duct tape wasn't just stuck to her chin, the earphones and headband. It also clung to her hair.

Katya wanted to rip it off quickly, like a Band-Aid. But she didn't have the range of motion. She had to twist it millimeter by millimeter and endure the pain of each follicle pulling free. It felt like the world's worst bikini wax—but higher.

The end result yielded good news and bad. The good news was that when the headset peeled off, it took the gag with it. The bad news was that the sticky wad of tape remained tangled in her hair.

Best to ignore it. To focus on the positive. *One problem down. Make that the start of a trend.*

Katya decided her next move would be to free her hands. Although a less painful undertaking, it promised to be more difficult. It felt as if her wrists had been wrapped a dozen times. She pictured the kind of overkill an exuberant kid would use on an art project. But that image quickly fled her mind.

The surface beneath the tires changed and the car began to slow. What would her captors do when they saw what she'd done? How much more duct tape would they use the next time?

56
About Face

Western Nevada

WHILE WAITING for permission to enter, Vic reflected that his boss had a proper office. A corner suite in a dedicated, modern building. Although not quite as impressive as the shining blue glass and white stone in Sacramento, the Las Vegas field office was both comfortable and stately. A source of employee pride.

Vic's satellite office in Reno, by contrast, was a generic rental space. One was more likely to associate it with a startup commercial operation than the point of the Justice Department's spear. He found the disparity motivating. One more reason to keep clawing his way up the lofty ladder.

"Mr. Brick will see you now," his administrative assistant announced, rising and coming around her desk. She always escorted visitors to the door. *Boss's orders*, Vic had heard. *A pet peeve. Part of his persona.*

"Thank you, Melanie."

Brick was reading when Vic entered. That was what he went by, Brick or Mr. Brick. Take your pick. If you asked for his first name he'd say "Special Agent-in-Charge." Heaven help the underling who addressed him as Percy.

Vic sat opposite the big desk and waited for his boss to look up.

Brick didn't. He kept his eyes glued to his laptop screen. "Special Agent Link, have you found the money?"

The money was the ninety-two million in ransom payments collected from forty-six hostages and converted into cryptocurrency. Forty-six very influential, now former hostages. Bankers and executives who were now using their apparently limitless supply of political connections to rain pressure from above. The torrent flowed downward, of course, leaving Vic and his career drowning in the gutter.

Despite that unpleasant circumstance, Vic found the cold reception puzzling. Brick was habitually and intentionally one of those *everybody's best friend* guys. He was always slapping your back with one hand even when stabbing it with the other.

"The money can't be tracked directly," Vic said, struggling to maintain a positive tone. "That's the point of cryptocurrency. To retrieve it, we have to find the people who control it."

"And you've made no progress there?"

"They, like the money, have gone off-grid."

"The two Maltese, the Russian and the American?" Brick clarified.

"Actually, the two may not have been Maltese."

That got Brick to look up. "Pardon me?"

"They may have been Middle Eastern."

"But they received ESTA approval. Their passports had to be valid," Brick noted, referencing the visa program that allowed EU citizens to enter the United States for up to two years as long as they didn't stay for more than ninety days at a time.

"Their Maltese passports are valid, but the government can't find the documents used to obtain them."

"Which means some government clerical worker probably sold them," Brick said.

"That's the most-likely scenario," Vic agreed.

"So now we believe they're from the Middle East. You'd think the State Department might have gotten a clue from their names."

"Actually, although Arabic in origin, Abdilla and Saida are

among the most common Maltese names. There's a lot of Middle Eastern blood in the Mediterranean."

Brick grunted, then cocked his chin. "If the passports are fake, what makes you think the names are real?"

"They have a history. I've confirmed what they claimed while challenged in the bunker. Both did study at Oxford. If you think about it, it's relatively easy to create a false background if all you have to change is nationality."

"Were they Maltese at Oxford?"

"The university confirms it."

"So they come from powerful families," Brick said, probably thinking of the other Osama. "Parents who wanted more opportunities for their children than they were likely to get at home."

"Or at least parents who wanted to cover all the bases. They probably retained their native citizenship as well."

"Not that the suspect countries would ever let us check their records."

Vic confirmed his boss's assumption with a somber nod. "I'm afraid there's more."

Brick pursed his lips. "Why am I not surprised about that either?"

"I just learned that Abdilla and Saida flew from Las Vegas to London while we were still investigating the site."

Brick banged the table. "How on earth did they get past the TSA?"

"The detain order didn't make it into the system until they were already through security, and they landed before the system synchronized with historical data."

"Historical data? They were in flight."

"But past the checkpoint."

"Just them? Not the Russian or the American."

"It appears so. We're still combing through flight records at McCarran and other airports they could have reached before the curtain came down, but no hits so far."

"So in any case they've split up and we can assume half the money is now overseas," Brick said with a shake of the head.

Vic didn't comment.

"How did the four ever get together in the first place?" Brick asked. "The American used to be one of us."

"We're still looking into that."

"Look faster. We need to find them before they make the money vanish."

They've already done that, Vic thought. "Will do."

Brick returned his attention to his laptop screen.

Vic saw himself out, forcing his pointy titanium pen through the bottom of his pants pocket as he walked, then letting it slide down his leg and onto the floor while closing Brick's office door.

"Thank you, Melanie."

"Have a good flight."

Vic walked to the elevator and pushed the button before doing an about-face and returning to Brick's office suite.

Melanie looked up with surprise as he walked in.

Vic mouthed, "Lost my pen," with a shrug of his shoulders while glancing around. He spotted it in the gap between Brick's door and the floor. He pointed while moving in, ears peaked and properly tuned.

"—in any case we've got our fall guy," Brick said.

57
Into the Woods

Location: Unknown

KATYA couldn't help but tense up as the car finally came to a stop. They'd left the highway about three minutes earlier and made several turns. More than it would take to reach the typical highway exit gas station or diner. It didn't feel like they pulled into a parking space either. They just stopped.

Was that good or bad?

She rolled onto her side to enable a clear view of the action if the trunk opened. Whatever her fate, she wouldn't shirk. She'd face it head-on.

Two doors opened. One closed. The passenger door.

Two people approached, one from each side.

The trunk popped and she saw no one. Just green trees and blue sky. Then Oz peeked around the corner on the driver's side.

Katya felt a warm wave of relief run down her body. "Oz! Thank goodness. What happened? Where's Achilles?"

His expression went the wrong direction. His eyes and lips narrowed.

He moved around to the back of the vehicle and she saw that he was holding a submachine gun. The same brand she'd seen at Cinquante Bouches. Probably the same gun.

"Get out," he said in a flat monotone.

Katya was all too happy to leave the trunk behind. She'd rehearsed the move in her mind a dozen times. Roll onto her back, swing her legs up over the sill, then inch her way out until her waist was on the edge and let gravity take over while ducking her head. However, she found it hard to accomplish with her mind reeling from the revelation that Oz was now her captor.

Her extraction technique proved to be quite clumsy in practice, but it got her feet on the ground. The worst part was the headset, which was dangling from the duct tape still stuck to her hair. Ignoring it, she turned to her left and saw Sabrina.

Holding a handgun.

Tough as it was not to look at the ugly instrument of death, Katya met her friend's eyes. Sabrina's expression wasn't as hard as her husband's. In fact, Katya was sure she saw compassion. But there was also an unsettling intensity in her expression. Almost like her face had a split personality. "Sabrina, what's going on?"

As Katya spoke, Oz yanked the earphones away from her head, pulling a wig's worth of hair with it. "Ouch!" She couldn't help but shout.

Katya resisted the urge to turn to Oz. She wanted Sabrina's answer.

But Oz didn't stop there. He crouched and sliced through the duct tape binding her ankles with a box-cutter blade. As Katya shook her legs out and lifted her wrists in his direction, Oz shut the trunk.

He handed Sabrina the box cutter, then returned to the driver's seat without saying a word. He shut his door, started the engine and reversed the black car back out the way he'd driven in.

She and Sabrina were left standing on a dirt road in a forest. Katya couldn't see anything more than that. The road itself had weeds growing in the center. Clearly, it was low traffic.

They watched Oz disappear around a bend. Then they heard his engine alter its tone and accelerate.

Katya turned to her former friend. "What are we doing here, Sabrina?"

Sabrina appeared about to speak, but after a second she just pocketed the box cutter and used her gun to point into the woods.

"What's in there?"

Sabrina didn't answer. After a few extremely strained seconds, she raised her slumping hand, reaffirming the initial gesture with a quivering barrel.

Katya stared, trying to talk her friend down with her eyes.

It didn't work. Sabrina's expression grew more resolute.

Katya began to walk.

Tears streamed down her cheeks. All she wanted was to hold Achilles' hand. But his hand wasn't there.

With each step, Katya became ever more aware of her surroundings. The smells began to overwhelm her. The pollens, the saps, the decaying leaves. She felt the air as it entered her lungs and every twig as it pressed flat beneath her shoes. She reveled in nature's symphony. A distant stream. The wind on the trees and the rodents in the leaves. Even the songs of bugs and flights of birds.

Above it all, she could hear her own heart beating fast and strong. Full of love and life.

The world was so beautiful.

58
Bad Conclusion

Near Dallas, Texas

I OPENED MY EYES as a firm hand squeezed my thigh. I'd been out cold. Not drugged, just depleted. Apparently, despite the emotional strain and physical circumstances, I'd managed to score some solid slumber.

"Dude, this is my stop," the man in the driver's seat said.

The car wasn't moving, the sun was on the brink of rising, and I was where? "Where are we?"

"Dallas outer loop. Service station at the junction of I-635 and US-80."

I remembered. My latest hitchhiker was going from Amarillo to Houston, but Florida was east out of Dallas rather than south, so I was only able to take him halfway. About 375 miles. Actually, *take him* wasn't entirely accurate. The deal was he drove, I slept. "Thank you. Good luck."

"You need gas," he said.

We hadn't negotiated gas. Apparently, he didn't feel inclined to chip in. That was okay, the sleep was good as gold.

He popped the trunk and got out. I'd made him put his Army duffel in the trunk, whereas I'd kept my own modest backpack on the floor at my feet. A simple safety precaution. "And a car wash," he added as I walked around to the driver's door. "There's crap all over the trunk."

The *crap* was actually mustard, and I'd squeezed an entire big bottle onto the back of the car myself. It was a security precaution. Twenty-eight ounces of prevention.

These days the cops used ANPR to scan passing cars. The mustard would confound the automatic number-plate recognition technology with what would look to human eyes like hooliganism rather than criminal intent.

I was now more than halfway to my destination, which seemed odd. With all its western connotation, you'd think Dallas, Texas would be closer to Reno, Nevada than Melbourne, Florida. But it wasn't.

Although the hitchhiker/driver thing was working out great, I decided to take the next stretch alone. I had a call to make using a burner app. One that I didn't want overheard.

Disposable phones weren't required to make untraceable calls anymore. You could just use a specialized phone app. Progress. I rented ten *Mini Burner* numbers at burnerapp.com for a mere two dollars each. The numbers were good for two weeks or twenty minutes of talk time, after which they'd automatically be recycled.

Turning the car toward Shreveport, Louisiana, I took a while to compose my thoughts, then called a number I'd looked up many miles earlier. When the operator answered, I asked for a name I'd found on the same website.

"Who's calling, please?"

Knowing the safe side of the legal line was already in my rearview mirror, I said, "Detective Dallas, with the Dallas PD."

She didn't comment on the coincidence. Count on the FBI to stick to the script. "He's not in the office, detective. I'm putting you through to his cell."

Despite the early hour, the ASAC assigned to the Reno satellite office picked up almost immediately. "Special Agent Link."

"Good morning. Did I catch you at home?" It sounded like he was in the car, but best to clarify.

"No, I'm driving. How can I help you, detective?"

"Have you found Katya Kozara?"

"No. Do you have information as to her whereabouts?"

I slapped the steering wheel, but didn't deviate from my plan. "What's your direct number? I got to you through the switchboard."

He balked for a second, but then recited the ten digits.

"Thank you, Special Agent Link. This is actually Kyle

Achilles calling."

Silence. Then, "I'm glad you called. I need to inform you that there's a warrant for your arrest and you should turn yourself in immediately." He knew there was no chance I would do that, but he had to put the advisory on the record.

I bounded past his request and dove right in. "I want to apologize for not sticking around the cabin until you arrived. Given the circumstances, I couldn't afford the delay. The indefinite delay."

"That might be considered reasonable. Depending on the circumstances," Link said.

I was certain that the special agent had studied my FBI file, and was therefore familiar with my biography and service record. I could skip the intro. "Obviously, I don't have a lot of time, so I'll keep it brief. I broke out of the bunker with the assistance of Osama Abdilla. Together, we disarmed and disabled two of our captors, a husband and wife team. Because we were worried that our significant others would be leveraged against us if the spies down below learned of our coup, we ordered them up using the captors' voice disguising software. That is the last thing I remember before waking up in the manual elevator with no idea how I got there or where Katya was. Do you follow so far?"

"Keep talking."

"I broke out of the elevator, in the dark. Found the bodies of the two captors we'd disabled, atop the main elevator. Climbed upstairs and found the house abandoned. Grabbed guns and a makeshift rope from the garage, then switched on the power to the bunker. Went down and found one of the undercover captors dead. Disarmed the other while he and the rest of the captives were still waking.

"Katya wasn't there. Panicked, I returned upstairs to look for her. When Trey made it clear that he misunderstood my role and I realized the extent to which that misunderstanding might impede my search for Katya, I decided to postpone our discussion until it couldn't interfere."

"That might be considered reasonable," Vic said again.

"On the other hand, so is double-crossing half your team in order to double your take."

So the FBI was seriously considering that scenario. I was disappointed, but didn't have time to worry about that now.

Tracing a phone call doesn't take minutes like they show in the movies. It's virtually instantaneous. But, you need to be connected to the right equipment. Given that Vic was in his car, he almost certainly was not. He'd be able to figure out where I was later, based on the progression of cell phone towers connecting our call, but I'd be long gone by then on a highway that branched off.

Even if he could identify the cell tower my phone was currently using, closing down a major highway in a different state and funneling everyone through a roadblock wouldn't happen for anything short of someone shooting the president.

So I was safe.

For the moment.

But I was no closer to finding Katya. Not yet.

"Do you have any information regarding Katya's whereabouts?" I asked.

"There's a warrant out for her arrest as well. Until this call I thought she was with you."

"I wouldn't have run if she were."

"Does that mean you'll turn yourself in when you find her?"

"Of course. But by then, you'll likely have learned enough to have lost interest in me. Speaking of which, any luck locating Osama or Sabrina?"

Vic's response came slowly. "In a manner of speaking."

I waited for more. Vic was clearly weighing how much to tell me. Per protocol, he shouldn't say anything. But he wanted to keep me talking and it served his interests to build a bond.

I decided to nudge him in my direction. "You're familiar with my service record, and you have a feel for my loyalties and capabilities. Why not use those to your advantage? Keep the dialogue active?"

Nothing.

"You met Trey Huxley, I'm sure. Compare that impression to what you know about me. Surely you—"

"They left the country," Vic said, cutting me off.

"Mexico or Canada?"

A long pause. "Neither."

"Neither? But—" I stopped myself and took a second to think. They had money. Nearly a hundred million dollars. "Did they charter a plane?"

"They flew commercial. They beat the TSA BOLO."

"How did they get Katya on a commercial flight?"

"They didn't."

My blood froze in my veins and my heart seemed to stop pumping. If Katya was still missing, but no longer their prisoner, then she was most likely dead.

Vic drew the same obvious conclusion. "If you've been honest with me, it's time to turn yourself in."

59
Diamondbacks

Someplace Hot

KATYA didn't hear the ugly gun bark. She didn't feel a bullet blast through her back. She got a command instead. "Hold up your wrists."

Katya raised her arms behind her back. She was pretty flexible and managed to get them nearly parallel with the ground.

Something snicked, then Sabrina sliced the tape. It took a few passes on the first side, then Sabrina made a clean cut on the second. As Katya rubbed her wrists, Sabrina tipped her hand. "Don't peel it off. We'll just be putting more back on."

So they weren't going to kill her. Not yet, anyway. "What do you want with me?"

"This is your chance to use the toilet. I suggest you take advantage of it."

For a non-answer, Sabrina's reply was full of welcome information. First and foremost the stated opportunity. But also the implication that Oz was coming back. That they'd be driving onward. Perhaps he wanted her out of the trunk while he went for gas, lest she begin banging away.

Katya began processing the new information while taking care of business, but didn't get far. Sabrina hadn't offered supplies. Katya interrupted her analysis to scavenge some of the leaves with which she had a newfound affinity.

When all was done, Sabrina motioned back toward the dirt road. She didn't speak. She didn't smile. She just pointed with the gun.

Oz was slowly backing around the bend as they arrived at

the drop-off spot.

Katya took the opportunity to ask her burning question. "Where is Achilles?"

Sabrina looked away.

The car came closer.

"Where is Achilles?" Katya repeated.

"He won't come for you."

"Of course he will. He'll never stop coming. He—" Katya cut herself off as the obvious conclusion turned her lungs to lead.

"Everyone thinks you're dead," Sabrina clarified.

Once Katya regained her ability to breathe, she asked, "Why?"

"Because they think Oz and I flew to Europe—and you weren't with us."

Katya felt the tears flowing again. She didn't bother blinking them away.

She was suddenly very thirsty. Her overloaded bladder had somehow suppressed that impulse, but now it came crashing back. Katya wondered if her body was attempting to create a distraction.

Oz put the car in park and popped the trunk. He got out holding a roll of duct tape and a plastic bag. He pulled a bottle of water from the bag and held it out. "Drink."

She took the bottle and twisted the cap. It resisted until the tiny plastic tabs gave. A good sign. She downed half, then put the cap back on, intending to ration it out.

While she was drinking, Oz pulled a gray sweatshirt from the bag and began stuffing it into its own sleeve. She caught the words Arizona Diamondbacks written on it in large letters surrounding a big "A." When he finished, he tossed it in the trunk. It took her a second to recognize that it was a makeshift pillow.

Oz proceeded to hold up the tape. "I suggest you finish the water. In a minute you won't have the use of your hands."

She did. Then she extended her hands out in front of her waist.

Oz grabbed one and used it to turn her around.

As he clasped her wrists together behind her back, she asked, "Where's Achilles?"

The only answer she got was the screech of duct tape.

She climbed into the trunk as soon as Oz finished, hoping he'd forget to do her feet. In a single seamless move, she turned around and tucked her feet out of sight.

Oz reached back into the bag and pulled out a sleeve of Fig Newtons. He tore it open and set it down before her face. As she pictured what would come next, Katya couldn't help but notice that the packaging configuration resembled a trough. With that thought, the trunk slammed shut and she saw nothing more.

Oz spoke to her through the lid. "I left your mouth untaped so you can eat. If you make any noise the next time we stop, it's going back on. Then you won't get anything to eat or drink for days."

For days, Katya repeated to herself. Suddenly the pillow didn't seem particularly kind.

She reflected on the sweatshirt insignia. Where, exactly was Arizona? In the Southwest, that was for sure. Did it border with Nevada? That sounded right. They were both big and hot and *yes!* they did. The Grand Canyon was in Arizona but could be reached from Las Vegas. But whereas Reno was way up north, Vegas was way down south. And it was a long state. Not California long, but longer than San Francisco to Los Angeles, and that was a five-hour drive.

Due south. Like Reno to Vegas.

As the car picked up speed, Katya was hit with the realization that there was something else due south. Something that fit with the fugitive scenario. Mexico.

60
Buzzards

I-20, Eastbound

I FOUND MYSELF driving way too fast in reaction to Vic's revelation. Not too fast for my physical safety. Speed limits, like all precautionary measures, are designed with the weakest links in mind. The oldest cars coupled with the slowest reflexes. I was nowhere near either lower limit. But I was driving too fast for legal safety. Well above what it would take to attract a highway patrol officer.

I activated the cruise control, but ironically that proved to be less safe. Without the engagement that accompanied passing other cars, without the constant subliminal mathematical calculations involved in piloting around and between other moving objects, my mind continually wandered off the road.

Knowing that there was no safe option given the combination of my current mental state and my need to keep moving, I took a rest stop turnout—and got lucky.

The hitchhiker didn't have a sign. She didn't have a thumb out. I knew who she was by the big backpack at her feet, and the bulge in her jeans near the ankle.

She was standing near the start of the parking lot, presumably studying a map but really observing the occupants of parking cars. It was dangerous for anyone to hitchhike, but especially so for women. This brave or desperate soul had adopted a savvy tactic to eliminate that risk.

The percentage of the population at large that would do harm to a hitchhiker is very small. Call it two percent. By contrast, consider the people who might be inclined to take advantage of a helpless woman. The odds that they would stop to pick such a hitchhiker up are quite high. Probably above fifty percent. By selecting her driver rather than the other way around, the twenty-something Latina could virtually assure herself a safe ride.

The trick to recruiting her to do my driving would be getting her to trust me. I'm a big guy who's visibly powerful. The knife she had concealed wouldn't make a whit of difference if I put my mind to harming her. She'd sense that fact. Our brains are hardwired for such calculations. They have been since day one.

Deception is another thing we're adept at registering on a subconscious level, so I decided on the direct approach. I parked as near to her as I could get, then walked straight over. I dangled my keys and opened with a line from an old Burt Reynolds movie. "I've got a long way to go, and a short time to get there. Need some help with the driving. You up for it?"

"Just you?" she asked, buying time. I was sure that she'd seen me alone in the car.

"Just me." You might think that mentioning my credentials or using a religious reference would buttress my case, make her more inclined to trust me. But oddly enough, studies well regarded by the law enforcement community show that people who do either of those are more likely to be lying than people who don't. So I gave her a sincere smile and left it at that.

"No, thanks. I'm actually waiting for someone."

Her reply was obviously a lie, but I didn't challenge it. "Have a nice day."

I took advantage of the facilities, both out of need and on a hunch. But she was still at her post when I came out a minute later. It wasn't until I keyed the ignition that she came running. "Where are you headed?"

Despite Vic's revelation, I was still heading straight for the city where Oz and Sabrina worked. I literally had no place else to search for clues. But I wasn't headed there directly. "The airport in Orlando, Florida."

Unlike the earlier hitchhikers, I let my new traveling

companion keep her backpack on the rear seat. Same logic she was applying, but in reverse. I told her my name was Kyle and she introduced herself as Lily. We discussed the route, which took us southeast across Mississippi to Mobile, Alabama, then east across the Florida Panhandle before breaking south toward Orlando. I told her I needed to get some sleep and we left it at that.

I reclined the passenger seat and shut my eyes, but didn't attempt to sleep. That would be an exercise in futility and I had some serious thinking to do. Obviously, I hadn't turned myself in. Not because I faulted Vic's logic, but because I hadn't done a thorough analysis of the new data.

Being honest with myself, I knew I wouldn't consider my analysis thorough until it yielded a conclusion that left Katya alive. I wasn't sure if that was a strength or a weakness. Probably both. In any case, I knew I'd stick with it until the day I died.

The question I couldn't get past was why Oz and Sabrina had initially taken Katya with them. Had the flight been a change of plan? If so, then she would likely turn up someplace between Reno and Vegas. Given the BOLO, Vic would be informed almost immediately, so clearly that hadn't happened yet.

Despite my optimistic resolve, I couldn't help picturing Katya's body on the side of a desolate, sun-drenched road, with buzzards circling about. If I closed my eyes, I saw buzzards. If I opened my eyes, I pictured buzzards. I didn't believe that she'd really been killed because I couldn't feel a knife in my heart, but the morbid imagery was distressing nonetheless.

To get the bloody birds out of my mind, I changed the channel. I pulled out my iPhone with its fresh SIM card and began researching Personal Propulsion Systems.

I was expecting to find a scooter company. One of those trendy, battery-powered skateboard or Segway-like rolling transporters used in place of walking. What I found was something entirely more audacious.

PPS was developing a jetpack. An actual jetpack. One of those James Bond, Buck Rogers, Rocket Man-style engines you strapped to your back and flew with. I supposed the Space Coast location should have been a tipoff, but I missed that clue.

The PPS website was just a Work In Progress placeholder, but I did find a few other companies in the niche, and one had a very impressive video. It showed a man flying over rivers and lakes using a device that looked exactly like what the comic books predicted. At first I thought it was faked, but it proved to be real. *USA Today* confirmed it in a front page story on November 11, 2015 titled "Man on jetpack flies around Statue of Liberty."

That meant the core *Iron Man* technology had existed for years. If a fatal flaw hadn't been found, it would now be in the refinement and regulatory approval stage. It occurred to me that between jetpacks and drones and hover boards and self-driving cars, the Department of Transportation had to be hopelessly swamped.

The world was evolving at an incredible pace. It was no wonder that so many people were so scared.

Turning back to PPS, I found very little online beyond a basic description and a few dates. One notation in a business database got me thinking. A year ago, PPS had changed hands. Neither the former nor current owners were listed, but the sale indicated that Oz had acquired the company, rather than founding it. That surprised me.

Having spent quite a while in Silicon Valley, I knew that the inventors of breakthrough technologies clung to their virtual babies like genuine mothers. They were loath to let go while life remained. This implied that Oz had purchased a dead company.

Why do that?

Usually, such buyouts were made to acquire an asset, rather than a product line. A patent, a piece of real estate, a name.

I didn't know what assets Personal Propulsion Systems had, and I wouldn't until I was there on the ground. For the moment, I had far more questions than answers. But I was grateful to have them. Anything but buzzards.

61
A Few Words

Location: Unknown

KATYA LOST all sense of time in the trunk. She had trouble telling if minutes or hours had passed since she last wondered how long she'd been there. There just weren't many pegs to hang memories on, and the constant back and forth between wakefulness and furtive sleep spoiled the few clues she had.

Why her captors didn't listen to the radio was beyond her. Katya was most interested in the news, but would have been happy to hear music. Any music. Well, almost. Some styles got pretty monotonous.

She could hear Oz and Sabrina speaking, although they did precious little of that. And when they did it wasn't the Queen's English they'd used in the bunker. It was Maltese. At least in theory. It sounded very Middle Eastern to her. Then again, perhaps Maltese did.

When the couple did talk, Katya listened intently. Hoping to hear her name or Achilles'. Preferably in some context, but just the tone would do. So far, she'd learned nothing beyond the fact that the couple currently wasn't big on communicating.

Either their relationship had degraded since the bunker or stress was keeping them silent.

For her own part, Katya tried to take inspiration from what Achilles had told her about his months in jail. He'd staved off melancholy by focusing on improving body and mind.

Her body improvement options were limited, given the fact that she was locked in a box. She estimated the trunk to be about five feet wide over the rear bumper tapering to three feet where it backed the seats. The depth was a bit over three feet. The height about eighteen inches. Not bad as cars went, but pretty crappy for a bed.

One thing was for sure, she'd never complain about the economy seat on an airplane again.

To help pass her waking hours, Katya constructed a mental blueprint of the trunk and then invented yoga poses it would accommodate. Attempting to act them out stretched her muscles and calmed her mind.

Her greatest triumph was freeing her hands. She stumbled into the opportunity accidentally during one of her innovative yoga postures. The end of the tape caught on a cutout in the trunk lid. Leveraging it to work the tape around, given the gymnastics that required, probably took the better part of an hour. But it was good to have a goal and ultimately worth it.

The first thing she did with her hands was prepare the torn-off tape so that it could quickly be reapplied. It would be a shoddy job, but if she was lucky it would just appear to have come loose with wear.

The second task she gave her freshly freed hands was to search the trunk for an emergency release. Some button or lever or pull the automaker installed in case you happened to lock yourself in the trunk. If there was one, Oz had yanked it out. Just like the elevator control panel.

It shocked, surprised and distressed her to no end that they'd been the spies all along. She and Achilles had both swallowed that hook. To make matters worse, Trey had been right.

While Katya sucked on that sour nugget, the car pulled off the highway and up a ramp. It stopped a minute later, probably to get gas. She could hear the radio blaring in a nearby car and the starting of a diesel engine. Then Oz's British accent reached her ears. "Given the ease with which my voice can travel through the seats, imagine what a bullet could do."

The radio came on a second later, blaring loudly from speakers just above her head.

Katya felt the driver and the passenger exit. She felt the opening and closing of both doors. Her hopes started to soar but quickly crashed. She heard the gas cap coming off and felt the fuel start flowing. One of them was right there, inches from her head.

She went to work smoothing the wrist tape back into place. It was impossible to inspect her work, but it probably wouldn't matter. They weren't going to have her step out into the parking lot. If they opened the trunk at all, it would likely be to stuff some food in.

She heard the gas pump kick to a stop, and somebody closing the cap. But nothing after that. A few minutes later, both doors opened and closed. The ignition cranked and they began to move. No food. No water. No toilet.

The radio was switched off and the car stopped shortly thereafter. It remained in idle. The passenger door opened, the trunk popped, and Oz dropped a plastic bag before her inquisitive eyes. He made no reference to what was inside, but he did tell her one thing. "Plan to pee on the floor."

That wasn't a good sign, she decided. He was dehumanizing her in his mind.

As they merged onto the highway, Oz and Sabrina began an animated conversation that led Katya to believe they'd received some interesting information. Either from a news program or a telephone call. Although they were rambling in an incoherent language, Katya recognized a word that made her blood run cold. An Arabic word. The only one she knew. *Inshallah*. God willing.

Later during the heated discussion, she also picked out two English words. Both spoken with emphasis, both repeated a couple of times. One was *serenity*, the other *tranquility*. Although she was all for both of those, given the context, Katya didn't get a warm and fuzzy feeling. In fact, she couldn't help but repeat two words of her own. Words that popped up in free association: *suicide* and *bomber*.

62
Realignment

Florida

LILY AND I were approaching Gainesville, nearing the home stretch, when mental lightning struck. It was one of those connections that comes because you aren't actively grasping for it.

Fatigued but unable to sleep and tired of spinning my mental tires, I'd just broken part of the implied contract my hitchhiker and I had adhered to for nearly 800 miles. The no-chitchat proviso. Speaking loud enough to be heard over whatever she was listening to, I said, "What takes you to Florida?"

Lily looked over and studied my expression for a bit longer than road safety rules allow. She followed it with a one-word answer, but pulled out her earbuds. "Work."

"Whereabouts?" She knew I was headed for the airport in Orlando, but had given no indication whether she'd be getting out prior or continuing on after our ride concluded.

"A nice town on the beach."

"Florida has a lot of those."

"I know."

"Which one?"

She glanced my way again, but for a safer interval this time. "Don't know yet."

That answer fit the hitchhiker mold, but it didn't fully square with the thoughtful nature I'd observed at the rest stop. I decided to press on. "How will you know when to stop moving?"

Lily didn't answer immediately. We had plenty of time, and since neither of us was predisposed to idle banter, I figured she was taking the question seriously. Answering it for herself. Using me as a peripheral tool, like a classroom whiteboard.

"I've been waitressing in a small Texas town for five years. Like the work well enough. The people, the atmosphere, the predictability. Those all suit me. But life's about more than work, you know?"

"Sure," I said, supplying just enough feedback to keep her going.

"I kept dreaming about Hawaii. Began saving for my grand vacation. Instead of indulging when a big tipper came along, I put the extra money in a shoe box I'd decorated with magazine cutouts. Palm trees and beaches."

"Sounds smart."

"No. Actually, it was stupid."

"How so?" I asked, guessing that someone stole her shoebox.

"Because instead of saving for a dream vacation to the beach, I could just move to the beach and make every day a vacation. Why waitress in Texas when you can waitress in Florida?"

"I thought your dream was Hawaii?"

"Florida gives me easy access to almost everything I want. And it's a lot cheaper. Plus you can't hitchhike to Hawaii," she added before going on to describe the benefits of waitressing on the beach.

I'd stopped listening by then because an idea had ignited my brain. A flash sparked by seven insightful words. *Easy access to almost everything I want.*

My mind kept racing after she stopped talking and I realized I was being rude. "Congratulations on figuring things out while you're young. Few people are so insightful or fortunate."

That won me the kind of smile that earned big tips in her profession.

I pulled up the burner number app on my phone and said, "I need to make a call."

Lily nodded and popped her earphones back in. She was still wearing a grin.

"Special Agent Link."

"It's Kyle Achilles. Do you have any news for me?"

"Do I have news for you? Who do you think I am?"

"I think you're the person second most interested in solving this case."

Vic scoffed, but played along. "Katya has not turned up. Nor have you, I note."

Judging by my change in shoulder tension, I decided that counted as good news. The buzzards really had me worried. Ignoring his second comment, I asked. "What about Osama and Sabrina?"

"They disappeared at Heathrow."

"Identity switch?" I guessed.

Rather than exiting through passport control, international passengers could continue on to another international flight. That transit created a gap during which it was possible to swap to a second set of papers using one of several tricks. That wasn't a knock against Heathrow. It simply wasn't possible to create an airtight system when inputs were required from all over the world.

"That's the working assumption," Vic said.

"So there's no definitive photographic evidence of their UK arrival? Or their US departure, for that matter?"

"We have exit footage from McCarran," Vic said, referencing the airport in Vegas.

"Good footage?" I asked.

Vic hesitated. "You think they faked their exit?"

"I do."

"Is that because it's the only scenario that makes Katya likely to be alive?"

"Maybe. But it also fits. Otherwise, why bother to take her in the first place?"

"I don't know. But you know as well as I that escape and evasion scenarios are very fluid. They can and often do change minute to minute."

He was right. They did. "What about their home and office?"

"Both abandoned. They left nothing significant behind at either location."

Vic's tone didn't blip but that bit of intel sent my heart racing. Not wanting to show my excitement, I asked a camouflaging question. "What was the kidnappers' connection to Kai Basher?"

"As if you don't know."

"Humor me."

"Why do you ask?" Vic persisted.

"I haven't had much time to watch the news."

"Seriously."

"I'm working a puzzle here, and from what I saw they don't fit the typical criminal mastermind mold."

Vic took a swallow of something before answering. "Mr. Basher believes it was about remuneration and revenge. He knew the couple you encountered upstairs, first as the man's boss, then as their competitor. Basher recently beat them in a battle worth billions."

"So they considered themselves victims? Decided that a second wrong could put things right?"

Vic didn't comment.

I made a mental note to look into the couple once this was over. Their situation was sad but not uncommon. Their actions, by contrast, were extraordinary. I found the psychology fascinating.

"I have a request," I said.

"Me too. Do you want to go first or shall I?"

"I trust you've pulled Personal Propulsion Systems' financial records. Specifically their purchase history. I'd like to see it, along with your forensic analysis."

"What are you looking for?" Vic asked.

"It's a *know it when I see it* kind of thing."

"I'm going to need more than that."

"I don't think you are. Can you send it right now? Text it to this number?"

"I can't share materials from an ongoing investigation with an outsider."

"Sure you can. Make me a consultant."

"You're a suspect, Achilles. Not a consultant."

"Who says I can't be both? Sounds to me like a smart tactic on your part. Keep your friends close and your enemies closer. If you can't beat 'em, join 'em. Two heads are better than one. Pick your favorite proverb and show yourself to be a wise man."

"What makes you think I need help?"

"If you're sure you can solve this without me, go right ahead. I'm all for that. I'll hang up and you'll never hear from me again."

Vic sighed. "The report's not ready yet."

63
More Heat

Western Nevada

VIC WOULD HAVE LIKED to order a beer with his lunch but resisted the urge. He wasn't really a drinker, and that would be a legitimate firing offense. Unlike the illegitimate one on his horizon, he noted with a shake of his head.

The bastards on the upper floors of the Hoover Building weren't just setting him up to be a scapegoat. They were working him hard first. He felt like an ox who was plowing a field knowing that he'd end the day as dinner.

Unless he solved the case.

The waitress brought his burrito and Vic immediately began basting it with hot sauce. Every exposed bit of tortilla and cheese got a good shellacking.

Vic had always enjoyed a bit of spice, but the new job in Nevada had upped his consumption considerably. It clearly stimulated the same part of his brain that many tickled with chocolate. Unfortunately, his chosen emotional fix also aggravated his stomach. Still, Vic couldn't resist. He kept bottles of both hot sauce and antacid in his car. The fire and the extinguisher.

As he picked up his fork, Peter Olivo slid into the booth across from him.

"Hey, you made it after all. Sorry, I went ahead." Vic gestured toward the burrito.

"No worries. I don't have time to eat. You sounded like you were in desperate need of some release, so I violated a few speed limits. Why don't you unload as much as you can in ten minutes?"

Peter was a buddy from the Sacramento office. A Hazardous Materials Expert rather than a Special Agent, he was visiting to consult on a Reno case.

Vic pushed his plate aside. He'd have the waitress reheat it once his colleague left. "I'm about to get fired."

"The mass kidnap case?"

"Right. It's likely to take months if not years to solve. But I'll burn up within a week."

"Burn up?"

"From all the heat. Forty people are out a couple of million each. Most are New York big shots. One is the fricking governor of Florida."

"Yeah, I've seen him on the news. He's doing a good job leveraging both the anti-crime and the heroic victim angles." Peter was studying Vic's plate as he spoke. "You aiming to go out on a disability discharge?"

Vic smiled despite himself. "I like this kind of heat."

"Good luck with that."

Vic shrugged.

"So what's a win?" Peter asked. "What makes you a bull rather than a scapegoat?"

"Finding the money. In public the victims all talk about justice, but in private they're all fuming over the financial loss. Can't say that I blame them. Someone took two million dollars of my money, I'd be all over it."

"So find the money."

Vic fought back a smart-aleck retort. Peter was there to help, and it was a reasonable if unsophisticated suggestion. "You ever try to track cryptocurrency?"

"Not my shtick."

"The short of it is, you can't."

Peter leaned back and frowned. "How's that possible, given all the subpoena and computing power at our command?"

"I asked the same question. Franklin in cybercrimes gave me this analogy. He said we have the power to observe the cryptocurrency universe, but only at the macro level. He likened it to looking at a piggy bank that's always shaking. We can see coins going in, and coins coming out, but connecting the two is impossible."

"Because it's an enormous piggy bank."

"Exactly."

"What about the human aspect?"

"Of the eight suspects, four are dead and two disappeared at Heathrow. Probably."

"Probably?"

"We're not entirely sure it was them rather than another couple pretending to be them. The video is inconclusive."

"In any case, that still leaves two of the eight alive and in the U.S., right?"

"Yeah, a man and a woman. But I'm not convinced they were in on it. I've been in contact with him, and he—"

"What? Why didn't you start with that?" Peter interjected.

"He says the other two kidnapped her, so he's tracking her down."

"I'm confused. Why is it unclear if they were in on it?"

"That's a longer story than you have time for. In a word: conflicting testimony."

"But he's your only real lead?"

"My only short-term lead. And he's ex-CIA."

"And you're current FBI. If you want to stay that way, focus on him. Make him your win."

"That's what the Hoover Building has in mind. But it probably doesn't get the money back or render justice."

"Still, it saves your career, right? You don't need an actual victory. Just something that looks enough like one to move the mass kidnap case off the front burner."

"You sound like my boss would if he ever said what was really on his mind."

"Good. If I've got the two of you aligned, I'll consider my job done. Gotta run."

Peter slid out of the booth but looked back at the table. "Seriously. That hot sauce. I don't know."

64
Sandcastle

Florida

UNFORTUNATELY, the Beachline Expressway, which ran past Orlando International Airport and eastward to the Space Coast, didn't have rest stops. Since Lily preferred to stay on the highway, I dropped her at the airport exit with thanks and best wishes. Given the volume of rush-hour traffic, we were confident that she could easily find a safe ride. "What do I owe you for gas?" she asked.

"Gas is on me, but if you could spare a few hairpins I'd be obliged."

She gave me an uncomfortable look.

"It's not a fetish. Just something I need for an upcoming project."

Her face rebounded a bit, but retained a skeptical tinge. Nonetheless, she pulled two bobby pins from a side pocket on her pack. I tucked them away, and we said our goodbyes.

Before pulling back onto the highway, I opened the glovebox and slipped three hundred dollars into the envelope containing the rental agreement for my appropriated ride.

My foray into Orlando International Airport was fruitful and quick. I hopped into an almost-returned Ford Focus and pulled away within seconds of putting my Ford Fusion in park.

The point of the switcheroo was to put a few more days on the clock. The rental agency was likely tracking the Fusion by then. Probably as much from confusion as concern. In either case, neither they nor the police would go out after a moving vehicle. Not a rental Ford, anyway.

They'd wait until it was parked, which of course it hadn't been until now. Hopefully the money I left in the glovebox would square things away. No harm, no foul.

Merging back onto the highway a few minutes later, I thought about the obstacles that lay ahead. I'd tipped my hand to Special Agent Link when inquiring about Personal Propulsion Systems. As a result, he might well have arranged to put surveillance on Oz's home and office.

Going there now would be a calculated risk. But not going also came with a cost. A steep price. It would delay or perhaps even stall my investigation. Since Katya was almost certainly suffering every minute of captivity, I had to gamble.

To improve my odds, I would assume that there were stakeouts and then find my way around them. During that last hour of my marathon cross-country drive, I figured out how.

I decided to hit the house first, then the office.

I knew how to find where Oz and Sabrina lived because it had been a point of contention in their loan discussions with Trey. The banker had asked about size and location and had gotten excited by both answers. The couple lived in a huge place on the beach.

Oz had gone on to dash Trey's hopes, explaining that their residence was an architectural oddity. A literal castle on the sand that had once belonged to a German brewer and Oxford classmate who had it custom-built as a modern homage to the ancestral home pictured on his beer bottles.

The brewer died in a boating accident shortly before Oz was scheduled to move across the pond. At the funeral, Oz agreed to buy the pink elephant from the estate for a song. Then, rather than use the architectural oddity strictly as his home, he turned the castle into a corporate residence. A home for all the startup's employees. A salary saver and tax write-off. It was perfect for his purposes, but worthless for Trey's.

I didn't have the castle's address, but figured it couldn't be hard to find. Rather than drive State Road A1A with my eyes peeled, hoping to get lucky before dark, I inquired at a gas station. "About three miles down on the left, just past the golf course."

Because of the guns and badges and radios, the laws and procedures and uniforms, law enforcement agencies tend to be fundamentally misunderstood. People forget that police stations are essentially the same as every other organization. They're staffed with officers and administrators who face dozens of competing professional priorities and plenty of complicating personal issues. Too much work, too little time.

If an FBI office in Nevada asks a Florida police precinct to watch a house or office as part of a robbery investigation, they will likely comply. In a routine way. As time permits. And not with their best guy. This isn't disrespect, it's human nature.

The castle house was on the barrier island that protected most of the eastern coast of Florida. The PPS office was on the mainland, across the Intracoastal Waterway, in a commercial zone closer to Cape Canaveral. I'd driven past it earlier without stopping or slowing, taking mental pictures for future reference and comparison. I hadn't detected a surveillance operation, but that didn't mean one wasn't there.

I got the same initial impression of the castle. It almost certainly was not being watched. At least not effectively with a routine operation. The location was too isolated to accommodate anything routine, and the priority was too low for anything extreme. No chance of agents in ghillie suits with night vision goggles and sniper scopes.

The architectural footprint resembled four classic castle turrets all shoved together to create a shape a bit like butterfly wings. The street side of the house had a big central door designed to resemble a drawbridge, and the only windows facing that way were tall and thin, like archer slits. While far from conventional, I thought it was pretty cool.

The castle was three stories tall.

The city provided public beach access parking half a mile down the road. I aimed for it.

Although I doubted that the big bureaucratic wheels at the rental car company had churned through enough checks to spit out a stolen car alert, I decided to err on the side of caution and assume my ride might be towed.

After parking in the darkest available spot, I slipped the Glock into a shoulder holster worn beneath my shirt. During the day it would be obvious, but at night it would pass a casual glance.

I put the car key in my backpack with the MP7 and hid it in the mangroves of a restricted access sand dune. Nobody would be looking that way, much less walking back there at night.

I trotted toward the castle using the firmer sand down by the water as joggers tend to do. Most of the bordering beachfront homes were lit only by the moon. They were probably second or third homes, used by their elite owners only when St. Barts and Saint-Tropez weren't calling.

The castle came into view—a dark silhouette faintly outlined by the moon. The facade was more or less square in that it was as tall as it was wide. Aside from the fact that there were large cylindrical faux turrets on the left and right, the brewer-built beach house appeared typical on its ocean-facing side. Lots of glass and plenty of balcony. Like the adjacent homes, the castle connected with the beach via an elevated, gated walkway that protected the precious vegetation. Also like its neighbors, it showed no signs of life.

I jogged past without slowing and continued another quarter mile before circling back, as joggers do. This time, I ran along the top edge of the beach, where the sand morphed into sand dune and the mangroves sprouted. I stayed close to them, keeping our shadows and silhouettes intertwined.

When I neared the castle walkway, I tripped intentionally and dropped to the ground.

65
A Bigger Plan

Florida

I HAD ENJOYED the second epiphany of my investigation shortly after my talk with Vic. Or maybe it was a delusion. When you were thick in the weeds—or mangroves—it was hard to tell.

At the time, I had tried to stifle my enthusiasm. To keep my hopes from reaching breakneck height. But as I climbed the underside of the castle's elevated walkway, I found myself buoyed by bulletproof logic.

The sequence went like this.

Oz and Sabrina had taken Katya with them. That was risky. Taking a hostage increased the odds of getting caught.

Several hours later, Oz and Sabrina flew from Vegas to London and disappeared. That was also risky. Lots of pinch points involved.

Two risky moves that are entirely unnecessary—if your goal is to escape abroad and you've got ninety-two million dollars at your disposal.

Why not simply charter a private plane? That would be faster, safer and easier.

Passport control for private jets is a joke. People with that kind of money don't play by ordinary rules. They pay for privileges. And, of course, the private aviation facilities that count on those exceptionally demanding jet-set consumers have obsequious behavior built into their business models. They bend over backwards to accommodate, then charge through the nose.

So I didn't believe that Katya had been kidnapped and discarded. And I didn't believe that Oz and Sabrina had fled the country on a commercial jet. They had a bigger plan in play. I didn't know *what*, but I knew *where*—if not at present then at least in the past.

But I was alone in my thinking.

Oz's ruse had worked.

I was also alone in my positioning, which at that moment was on the verge of investigating the house where Katya's kidnappers had lived and schemed.

Vic told me that Oz and Sabrina "left nothing of interest at either location." I considered that to be a huge clue. A big blinking neon sign. But I had a different perspective from Vic.

Vic assumed that Oz and Sabrina had been in on the kidnap and ransom all along. Under that scenario, of course they would have gotten their affairs in order at home before leaving for good.

But I knew they hadn't been in cahoots with our kidnappers.

I knew they had simply reacted to an opportunistic score.

And yet they'd cleaned up.

They'd "left nothing of interest at either location."

How was that possible? And why bother? If you had just stolen ninety-two million dollars, why concern yourself with any of your old stuff—a few prized possessions and pictures aside? You wouldn't care about your old clothes. You wouldn't give two shakes about your struggling startup's modest office. You'd just run far and fast to your new life in the lap of luxury.

But they hadn't.

They'd grabbed Katya. And they'd made cleanup arrangements. Two very distinct and incongruent acts.

My assumption was that Oz had called home when he was pretending to call 911. He'd ordered the house and office abandoned and arranged the phony Vegas to London flight. Why?

There was one obvious explanation. A simple answer that checked both boxes. Concealment.

But what were they concealing? Not the theft of ninety-two million. That was out in the open. They had to be concealing something else. Something whose value was great enough to keep it at the forefront of their minds even immediately after a vast unplanned fortune fell into their hands.

As I worked my way from the underside of the walkway to the underside of the castle's big front deck, I didn't have a detailed hypothesis as to what that competing priority might be. But I had a general idea. And I had hope that I would soon learn more.

My optimism sprang from knowledge that Vic didn't possess. Knowledge based on my personal experience rather than his bad assumption. I knew that the home and office cleanup had been quick and cursory, because Oz ordered them at the last minute. As everyone knows, when you rush, things get missed. Little things perhaps, but hopefully enough in this case to indicate intention, direction or destination.

Despite doubting that the house was under surveillance, I didn't risk going onto the castle's main deck, which branched out above the mangroves from the second floor. For the same reason, I ignored the balconies attached to the third. I climbed straight to the roof.

If a serious surveillance op was underway, I figured I'd find someone there. So I kept quiet and timed my noisier moves to coincide with the crashing waves.

Nobody was there.

The rooftop was big and flat and presumably leveraged for both private sunbathing and upscale entertaining. Perhaps during rocket launches from the nearby Cape. Given all that, I knew it would be equipped with an access point. An entrance to the castle.

Scrambling over the ledge after an uneventful climb, I quickly spotted a hatch that also served as a skylight—one secondary to a large central glass dome. Sized roughly the same as a conventional door laid flat, the hatch bubbled outward to keep debris from settling.

I crept to the rim and peered inside. Even cupping my hands, I couldn't see much more than a few stairs. I had a flashlight on my phone, but wasn't about to employ it.

The hatch lock appeared typical for a house door, except that it wasn't attached to an external handle. From the outside, it appeared that you simply lifted the door by its rim. Presumably with the assistance of concealed springs.

I was prepared to go to work on the lock with Lily's bobby pins, but a trial tug eliminated the need. The hatch wasn't locked. Easy to overlook when you were in a hurry, I assumed. Come to think of it, why would you bother locking up at all if you were leaving for good? Of course it was the police who had been there last. The officer probably left it as he found it.

I raised the skylight just enough to roll over the edge and slip inside. Quietly bracing myself, I settled it back into closed position. Then I palmed my Glock and crept down the stairs.

66
For the Birds

Location: Unknown

KATYA WAS ASLEEP when the Charger finally came to a stop. Sound asleep. After thousands of fitful miles—hungry, thirsty, cramped and callous miles—her body finally overrode the feelings of discomfort and fear and dropped her deep into slumber's forest.

The car's decreasing speed and opening doors didn't rouse her, but the blast of light from the popping trunk broke through the fog. Before Katya could think, she used her hands to shield her eyes, exposing the fact that she'd broken her bonds.

Nobody spoke.

Katya's ears immediately alerted her to an alien environment. A strange sound emanated from all around. It resembled a 17-year cicada hatching, but was more earthly. A soft soprano peeping rather than an eerie insect hum.

Oz appeared beside the bumper with a gun in his hand. "Get out."

Katya wriggled from the trunk and into a surreal setting. "Where are we?"

A gleam entered her captor's eyes. "Rule One: No questions."

Katya didn't actually require his reply. Her location wasn't that difficult to define, even when seeing it for the first time. She was in a huge tubular hangar fashioned from corrugated steel. It measured well over a football field in length and was about twenty yards wide. In addition to barn-sized doors, the semicircular ends each housed multiple wall fans. Instruments undoubtedly designed and regulated to keep the temperature under control.

A makeshift wire fence cordoned off the twenty-yard end section where Katya, Oz, Sabrina and two other people now stood. The strangers both wore protective coveralls, clear goggles and white filter masks. One also wore a shower cap. They were toying with a tool Katya couldn't identify but which, to her great relief, was definitely not a chainsaw.

The remaining eighty percent of the hangar housed birds. Fluffy yellow birds. She was looking at a literal sea of chicks. Tens of thousands of peeping baby chickens.

Under normal circumstances, Katya would have been delighted and fascinated. She'd have scooped a few up and buried her face in the soft yellow fluff. But her thoughts didn't go there. Given the context, stories of Sicilians feeding their rivals to wild pigs jumped unbidden into her mind. There was no better way to utterly and completely dispose of a body. Was she about to become chicken feed? Shot in the head and left to be picked clean?

No.

Surely they wouldn't have gone to all the fuss of bringing her here just for that? Unless.... Could Achilles have somehow offended them so profoundly that this was to be their revenge? Some vendetta? Was there an Arabic proverb about feeding your enemies to the chickens?

Sabrina broke Katya's nightmarish trance. "Come with me."

This time, her former friend wasn't holding a gun.

The car that had presumably transported Katya from an underground bunker in Nevada to a chicken farm in Mexico was parked in a corner of the hangar. Sabrina led her toward the opposite side, giving her a chance to study the reappropriated part of her surroundings.

The first thing she noticed was the floor, which was covered in something that resembled tiny wood chips, but wasn't. Given that it extended into the chicken-covered section, she assumed it was the functional equivalent of kitty litter.

"It's ground corncob," Sabrina said, answering her unasked question. "Cheap, clean, organic and effective.

When the chickens are grown, the farmer will have about three times the volume he started with, transformed from agricultural waste into fertilizer."

Despite her curious nature, Katya really wasn't in the mood to learn about farming. She was, however, quite keen to uncover what she could about her captors and their activities. Clearly they were living in this big barn, if that's what you called it. There were four folding cots over in the corner, topped with pillows and sleeping bags. Next to them, four short-legged folding beach chairs were situated in a circle around a teapot, which rested on a portable camping stove. Four midsized suitcases rested against the back wall—two upscale, two clearly economy.

Katya was the fifth wheel.

The middle of the freed-up end of the barn was occupied by dozens of big folding tables. A whole field of them. The kind you'd use at an outdoor wedding banquet, if they weren't so old and worn and irregularly covered with what looked like sprayed black rubber. Beneath each table were crates of something Katya couldn't see.

The two people wearing protective clothing were busy at a central table. One was male, the other female. Both had complexions matching her captors'. Their size and shape resembled Sabrina's and Oz's as well

The table they stood beside held five-gallon buckets and bits of hardware Katya couldn't identify but which she figured were power sprayers, given the context. Both remained focused on their work as she walked past.

Beyond them was a forklift, a stack of pallets, and one of those huge rolls of plastic wrap you sometimes saw in airports for wrapping luggage destined for airports where pilfering was common. The roll was big enough to wrap a person, Katya realized. What a horrible way to go. Suffocating with your arms strapped to your sides and your eyes wide open.

Fortunately, that vision didn't last. Sabrina appeared to be headed for a structure in the corner, if that was the right word. It looked as if boxes had been stacked like bricks to form an L-shaped wall about eight feet high, then covered with blue tarps. Where the makeshift structure met the barn's curving wall, there was a quarter-round opening one would have to duck to get through.

Sabrina gestured her inside, then followed.

Katya began to cry the moment she laid eyes on what lay beyond. The tears just started flowing. It wasn't because she was the weepy type. Quite the opposite. She'd kept it together in the trunk. Through the cramps, hunger and thirst. Through the days and nights of darkness and depressing uncertainty. While each minute took her a mile farther from Achilles, she maintained emotional control. Mental control. Spiritual control. Up until that minute, hope and faith remained foremost in her heart, like twin battlements on a castle.

After all that, this was too much. Too unjust. Too unfair. Standing there before that corncob and crap-covered floor, staring at a rusty chain, hefty padlock and empty bucket, Katya felt the bricks of her psychological foundation begin to slip.

67
The Remains

Florida

THE INTERIOR of the castle was as remarkable as its exterior. At its heart, a central courtyard rose from the ground-level garage to the soaring skylight three floors above, adding space and light. Wrapping the courtyard's perimeter, a circular staircase lifted eyes skyward like the rockets that blasted-off nearby. One couldn't help but think that King Arthur would have been proud to own this place.

Despite its size, the castle didn't take me long to clear. No doors were closed, and navigation was made easy by moonlight streaming through glass. The rock-solid structure also worked to my advantage, allowing me to walk without making a sound.

That was the good news.

The bad news was what I found inside. Or rather, didn't.

The house did not seem to have been hastily abandoned. Nothing of value had been left inside. The remaining kitchen equipment looked old and cheap. The forsaken sticks of furniture were far from special—more like the sentimental stuff you'd bring from your old house than what you'd buy for your new. The residual clothes clearly weren't worth packing.

Everything I found, all the physical evidence, supported Vic's point of view. The departure had been planned.

Discouraged, I suddenly found myself scared and weary.

If Vic was right and I was wrong, if Oz and Sabrina had been in on the kidnapping all along, then Katya was probably dead. I couldn't accept that, but couldn't efficiently fight it either. Not in my current state.

I set the alarm on my phone for 2:30 a.m. and lay down for a restorative nap. It was a tactical move, one that I hoped would set my mind and body right.

I chose the room closest to the skylight stairway, in case an emergency escape became required. I passed out quickly, but didn't make it to the alarm. At 2:20, I bolted upright in my borrowed bed feeling better in more ways than one. I had the answer.

Or at least an encouraging idea.

Suppose Vic and I had begun with a bad assumption. Suppose Oz and Sabrina and their PPS employees hadn't just left the dregs of their existence behind. Suppose they had actually left everything behind.

Vic and I both subconsciously assumed that the tenants would match the residence. We assumed that when people bought a house they did so with long-term intentions. We also assumed that houses match their owners' lifestyles. Both assumptions were strongly backed by statistics, and supplementarily backed by Oz's and Sabrina's business cards. Those of a CEO and a CFO.

But they could be wrong.

The house might have been bought as camouflage. If so, it had certainly proved effective. Take that one piece of data out of the equation, that Potemkin facade, and the remaining evidence sketches a very different story.

I began counting out facts on my fingers. *Thumb*—two Middle Easterners. *Index*—trying to blend into the upper strata of the U.S. population. *Middle*—want the authorities to believe they've left the country. *Ring*—but actually stay despite the danger. *Pinkie*—after coming into a lot of money. *Thumb two*—committing multiple murders. *Index two* —and kidnapping a woman.

I ran back through the facts a few times, continuing to throw fingers like a kid who couldn't quite count. Despite the repetition, a new picture failed to form. I'd erased the old one, but kept drawing a blank. Oddly enough, I kept getting hung up on the money. The same money that was driving the FBI's conclusion.

If it wasn't about the money, then it had to be about

something else. Something more important to Sabrina and Oz than ninety-two million dollars. That had to be terrorism, right? But terrorists depend on secrecy. So why would Sabrina and Oz draw attention to themselves by usurping the kidnappers' plot? Why not just go home along with everyone else?

If it wasn't about the money.

I didn't know. But as I sat there in the dark in the house where Oz, Sabrina and their colleagues had lived, I sensed that the answer to that question was the key to finding Katya.

I saved that as the go-to puzzle I'd work whenever circumstances permitted. For the moment I had physical evidence to gather.

I grabbed a couple of sturdy wire hangars from a closet, then exited the castle the way I'd come in—via the roof in the dead of night.

Emerging into the fresh ocean air beneath the blanket of stars, I wondered where Katya was at that moment and what she was seeing. The likely options chilled my heart.

I glanced over the rooftop toward the business district a few miles northwest, setting my sights. It was time for the day's second illegal investigation. Time to visit Personal Propulsion Systems.

68
Not the Gulag

Location: Unknown

KATYA DID NOT SLIP INTO DESPAIR. She did not slide into insanity. She held on—with tooth and nail. Wit and wile. Hope and faith.

The ground wasn't really all that bad. Much softer than the trunk.

The chain was tough. More psychologically than physically. Knowing that human history's darkest days had been punctuated by placing people in chains, it was difficult not to see the device as more than a restraint. Hard not to hear the taunts of a million ghosts. Depressing to picture how her life might end.

But she battled the blues and fought back the fear.

Time and again, she told herself that this was nothing, not when compared to the gulag or the galley of a slave ship. And in contrast to history's forsaken souls, she had Achilles.

But not at the moment. Then and there, she had to go it alone.

Her wits and wiles had thus far failed to connect *serenity* and *tranquility* with the events she'd witnessed since leaving the trunk. But she had learned a thing or two about farming chickens.

The gap at the end of her cell was literally a window into that world. A completely automated world. Gone were the days of Old MacDonald. The birds were watered and fed through dispenser troughs that ran the length of the hangar. Those troughs were hung on thin cables that allowed them to be raised as the chicks matured. Also attached to the dangling troughs were perches and colorful plastic appendages. The former allowing the birds to rest their feet, the latter, Katya finally figured, serving as toys.

That was their world. Their entire lifespan. Food, water, perches and plastic toys. That and companionship.

She could do with a bit of that right now. Someone to whisper and stroke her hair. Oddly enough, in addition to Achilles, she missed Sabrina. The previous version—before she turned traitor.

Katya spent much of her time attempting to figure out what Sabrina and company were up to. The chain gave Katya seven feet of freedom. Not quite enough—no matter how she stretched and strained—to see around the edge of her makeshift partition into the portion of the room that hosted human activity. She could only imagine what was going on there.

Well, that wasn't entirely true. The chain didn't restrict her nose and ears. She could hear and she could smell.

A bit.

Precious little could be heard over the peeping chicks and churning fans. Only the occasional word or phrase—which she was now convinced were Arabic—and the comings and goings of the car.

It was her nose that clued Katya in on the interesting activity. Even with the fans blowing twenty-four hours a day, fortunately in her direction rather than the chicks', she detected the smell of paint. That and cigarette smoke.

The paint fumes weren't like a passing whiff of perfume either. Rather than a spritz or two, the activity seemed to be constant as a water sprinkler—interrupted by meal and sleep breaks.

She wanted to know what they were painting, and why. Surely that activity was somehow linked to her fate. *No, not her fate.* Her future had yet to be written. *Their plan for her.*

One of the things Katya did to fight the boredom was count chickens. Obviously that was impossible, but she busied her mind by counting the chicks within a projected grid square and then multiplying it out. Her calculation yielded a staggering fifty thousand birds.

Katya also counted 300 boxes in her wall. That too was an estimate, given that they were hidden beneath tarps, but she could see enough corner bumps to guess. Her hungry mathematical mind continued to play, calculating that 300 was enough to fill twelve pallets if stacked three-by-two-by-four.

Was that a lot? Depended on what the boxes were filled with. If gold, diamonds or uranium, it was a fantastic supply. If chicken feed, it wouldn't satisfy her neighbors for a day.

Maybe that was why they were using the tarps?

Probably not.

Katya was trying to figure out how to create an undetectable ground-level gap she could peer through when a woman ducked into her cell. A strange woman carrying some curious equipment.

Florida

I DROVE PAST the Personal Propulsion Systems office and parked at an apartment complex a half-mile closer to the beach. No sense tempting fate by leaving a car where a patrolling cop might investigate it, given the suspicious hour.

While there, I took the opportunity to do a license plate swap. Fortunately Florida, like Arizona, only required rear plates. In order to avoid adding grief to an innocent's life, I picked a car with the bumper sticker: *Lost your cat? Try looking under my tires.*

The PPS building was a generic standalone box, undoubtedly leased, with white walls and a door plaque for signage. Personal Propulsion Systems. No hours, no phone number, no welcome mat. A typical manufacturing startup.

The glass front door exposed a modest lobby and a reception counter. Its lock was a typical cylindrical deadbolt. Easy pickings, so to speak. But I went around back instead. Less exposure. Again, why tempt fate?

The backside stank of spoiled food and was lit by an overhead light on the fritz. Its flickers revealed a leaky dumpster and two entry points. The first potential entrance was a gray metal fire door equipped with a standard lever lock, the second a delivery bay with a rolling garage door. Both made me smile.

Most homeowners are unaware of the security flaw built into their garages. That's because it's disguised as a safety feature.

The emergency door release is a plastic handle attached to

a string that's tethered to a toothed latch. It's often red but sometimes black. When you pull the string, it levers the tooth free from the drive chain, thereby freeing the door to manual movement. This allows the garage to be opened in the case of equipment failure or an electrical outage. It also gives burglars an easy way in.

I chose to exploit that weakness because garage doors are rarely alarmed.

I began by shoving one of my borrowed wire hangers between the garage door and the weatherstripping seal at the top. Then I twisted the hanger ninety degrees, turning it into a wedge. Satisfied that I'd created a usable gap, I unwound and straightened the second hanger, leaving the hook at the end. I fed the hook through the gap and guided it to the emergency release lever with the aid of my phone's flashlight.

It hooked.

I pulled.

The door released.

The whole procedure took me about two minutes. A burglar who knows his craft and comes with his tools prepared can pull it off as fast as you or I could use a key. Knowing that, I'd locked the release on my home garage with a cable tie. Of course, that garage would soon be forfeited to Trey's bank if I didn't recover the stolen funds.

I slid the door up a couple of feet, rolled under, then settled it back into place. I spent the next minute allowing my senses to adapt to the new environment while listening for a telltale beep and scanning the walls for a blinking red light.

Nothing triggered a warning.

After confirming that there were no external windows, I turned on the production bay lights. The big room contained nothing but a few wooden forklift pallets and about forty linear feet of empty metal storage racks. The bare concrete floor had a bit of a shine, as though it had recently been washed.

The remaining interior of Personal Propulsion Systems was no less generic than its exterior. Aside from the big bay

I'd entered, it contained five offices, a set of restrooms, a conference room and a kitchen. The furniture was solid but probably a decade old. Sun-bleached gray laminate and stained navy fabric. Looked like it had come with the building. No paperwork, no electronics. Not a calendar on the wall, not a fan in the corner.

I took pictures of everything, and then made a video circuit.

Only two of the offices felt like they'd been used, or rather, recently cleaned out. The two smaller ones. The other three had the look of rooms still staged by the leasing agent.

Both the used offices were interior facing, with windows onto the production floor rather than the street. *Was that a sign of something to hide or just efficiency trumping ego?*

Normally I would bounce that question off Katya. She had both an acutely analytical mind and elevated interpersonal intuition. A rare combination that made her superior at sussing the meaning out of certain situations, especially when the driving motivation was more complex than one of the seven deadly sins.

I missed her so.

I gave the offices another run-through, looking behind bookcases for lost papers and beneath desk drawers. I found nothing.

Nothing in the house. Nothing in the office. Just as Vic had said. Had he been right about the rest?

Was my charter plane hypothesis hooey?

Was Katya dead?

No. I didn't believe that. I wouldn't believe that. I couldn't believe that.

What was I missing?

I turned off the light, sat down in the middle of the production floor, crossed my legs and tried to absorb everything. I attempted to calm and quiet my cerebral cortex while allowing the back of my brain to dwell on the myriad subtleties that suffused the ground, the walls and the air. I began to listen, intently. To feel, acutely. To breathe, deeply.

The stench of spoiled food intervened.

The leaky dumpster.

It hadn't bothered me until I attempted to focus. It was like trying to take a critical test with someone sniffling in the background. I struggled to ignore it, but the stink overwhelmed my other senses, pushing them off balance and out of kilter.

My thoughts turned to the big rubbish bin. I highly doubted that my clever nemesis had suffered the judgment lapse that would be required to leave a smoking gun in the trash. A sales receipt. A napkin sketch. The cardboard backing of a used up notepad. But I had nowhere else to turn at that moment.

I would reinspect both premises during the day. Assume the added risk in exchange for improved lighting. But I wasn't especially hopeful.

I raised the garage door and rolled back under.

My focus now on the dumpster, I detected the buzzing of flies. Lots of flies. Lovely.

The stinky receptacle was a big gray contraption. Old metal, dented and scratched. I lifted the lid and peered inside as the streetlight flickered and the insects buzzed.

The source of the stench was immediately evident, but it took a few blinks to identify, so odd was the sight.

The flies didn't help.

I used the flashlight on my phone, just to be certain. Even took a photo. No mistake about it. The dumpster was piled high with two types of food. Food now rotting in the Florida heat. A boatload of potatoes and a sea of eggs.

70
Accessorizing

Location: Unknown

WERE IT NOT for the cigarette dangling from her lips, Katya might have mistaken the woman entering her cell for Sabrina dressed in work clothes. The two women shared the same build and patrician bearing. Their faces had similar features, accented by lustrous black hair and plump lips. But as she got closer, Katya saw that the woman before her was older than Sabrina. Probably by ten years, but maybe less given the cigarette use.

Fearing the worst, Katya fixed her gaze on the intruder's dark eyes. They appeared intelligent, but telegraphed no emotion. Her facial expression was also frustratingly neutral. Like someone showing up for a routine job.

Or a sociopath.

Katya's eyes moved on to the woman's hands. Her left held a canvas bag. Her right a thick strap made of the same khaki material. It had wires coming out of both ends and a chrome keyhole exposed in the middle. One of those circular keyholes, like on bicycle locks and vending machines.

The intruder stopped and studied Katya in the dim light.

Katya finally caught on. "You're Sabrina's sister."

"I'm Shakira. Please raise your shirt." Shakira didn't acknowledge the relationship, but the erudite intonation of her words resembled Sabrina's. There was a coldness coming off her, however, that Katya had never sensed from Sabrina. Even when her former friend was holding a gun.

As Shakira demonstrated what she wanted by exposing her own toned midriff, Katya corrected an earlier assessment. Shakira wasn't holding a strap. It was a belt. A buckle-less belt with wires protruding from both ends and a cigarette-pack sized object in the center.

Katya began to shiver. "What is that?"

"Raise your shirt!"

Suddenly, gulags and galleys didn't look so bad. Katya considered resisting, but her inner logician quickly concluded that would not end well. She was chained to a wall. Shakira was clearly committed to a plan. Best to get to the other side of that bridge without cigarette burns and bruises.

Katya lifted the top of her scrubs, exposing a few inches of skin but no more. *Please, no more.*

Shakira tossed her cigarette to the ground, then wrapped the belt about Katya's waist. She cinched it tight with a big binder clip, ensuring that the box snugged tight against Katya's lumbar spine.

Shakira then pulled a soldering iron from her bag and went to work attaching the taut wires to a tiny plastic device. While Katya watched in horror, it began emitting a dot of red light.

Katya's shaking grew worse.

Continuing with the calm of a battlefield surgeon, Shakira covered the connection with burlap and began to sew the belt shut. She used thick black upholstery string and a menacing needle. The tools were crude, but her fingers quick. She finished before Katya stopped shaking.

The clip disappeared into the canvas bag only to be replaced by a big pair of scissors. Shakira used them to snip the thread and excess cloth.

Katya thought that was it, but the sadist wasn't done yet. After Shakira's cool hands confirmed that the box was centered on Katya's spine and the diode aligned with her bellybutton, she reached back into her bag and extracted a familiar household item.

"No," Katya pleaded, half to Shakira, half to God.

Shakira looked up at her. "Yes."

The evil sister opened her superglue multipack and punctured the tips of all four tubes. Then, one by one, she squeezed them out, cementing the belt to Katya's waist.

When Shakira finally finished, Katya looked down at her new wardrobe item with its shiny keyhole in back and demonic red dot up front. It was too small and light to be a suicide belt. Those were packed with explosives and shrapnel. Bolts and ball bearings and nails. This weighed less than half a pound. Was it some kind of electronic leash? A shock collar? A tracking bracelet?

Shakira clearly wasn't going to say.

But she did surprise Katya. She pulled a small brass key from her pants pocket and raised it in display.

Katya found herself swallowing dry.

Instead of inserting the key into the box on the belt, Shakira used it to remove the padlock from Katya's chain.

Katya said, "Thank you," without thinking. Shakira's actions had likely made her situation worse, not better. The question was, *How much worse?*

Shakira picked up her bag and walked back toward the exit. Before ducking through the makeshift doorway, she turned and beckoned.

How much worse? Katya was about to find out.

71
Permission Slip

Western Nevada

VIC HIT *ANSWER* without checking the phone's screen. He was running late for his boss's staff meeting and gunning the gas to make a light. "Special Agent Link."

"It's your special assistant calling."

Vic made the light then glanced at his phone. A Texas area code. Another burner number, no doubt. "Good to hear from you, Achilles. Not a great time, though."

"Did you seriously just tell me that it's not a good time for you?"

Vic started to retort, but stopped himself as the comment sank in. He hadn't thought about it until that very moment, but his personal situation really wasn't that bad. Not in the grand scheme of things. Yes, his career was off track. Yes, he was working for a dishonorable man. But he hadn't been crippled or diagnosed with cancer. And the woman he loved was neither dead nor being held hostage.

Vic pushed his own problems aside and focused on the present opportunity—beginning with a self-assessment. He didn't believe Achilles. He didn't disbelieve him either. Vic was exactly where the judicial system wanted him to be, doing exactly what it required of all Americans. He was presuming innocence until guilt was proven. Vic would also be doing precisely what the Justice Department required of him in particular, and enforcing its duly-issued arrest warrant.

But that opportunity would come later—if ever. At that moment, he had to pick between conflicting priorities. Either looking good before his boss or solving his case.

"I'm rushing to a meeting. Do you have an update for me?"

"I might. Depends on what you have for me."

"This isn't a negotiation, Achilles. Either we help each other or we don't."

"I'm not trying to negotiate. I need your puzzle piece to see if mine fits. And don't think I don't know you'd arrest me if you could, regardless."

Vic took a deep breath, then uncapped the pink bottle and downed a swallow of antacid. "Hold on. I'll pull over."

"Thank you."

Vic opened his laptop and called up the report he'd compiled on Personal Propulsion Systems. "PPS was acquired twelve months ago in a private transaction for an undisclosed price. The deal included all intellectual property, inventory and equipment. It included the assumption of a lease. It did not lock down any employees."

"So they assumed all the obligations and bought all the assets except the people?" Achilles clarified.

"That appears to be the case."

"The old owners basically just cashed out and walked away?"

"For an undisclosed sum."

"How many people did the rebooted company employ?"

"Just four."

"That seems low. Most serious tech startups have three to four times that number. Are they all Maltese?"

Vic hesitated. He wasn't comfortable exposing that aspect of the investigation. But Achilles' tone implied skepticism, and it might be helpful to learn what he knew. "According to their passports."

"Are they really Middle Eastern?"

"We're not sure. But it does appear that all four are related. Two brothers married to two sisters. Oz and Sabrina are younger; Omar and Shakira are older."

Achilles remained quiet long enough that Vic began to wonder if the call had dropped. He was checking the screen when Achilles said, "So it's now a family business—Maltese or otherwise. That's good to know. What purchases has PPS made since the acquisition?"

"They appear to have run everything, personal and professional, through a single business credit card account. You interested in their production-related purchases?"

"That's right."

"Early on, it was mostly chemicals, raw materials and laboratory supplies. Some mold-making equipment. Exactly what you'd expect from a jetpack manufacturer."

"What chemicals?"

"The ones used to make rocket fuel. I checked. There's aluminum powder, iron oxide, white fuming nitric acid, white phosphorus, ammonium perchlorate, and a few others I'd be hard pressed to properly pronounce."

"All in large quantities?"

"Yes."

"Will you text the list to me?"

The request surprised Vic, given the implication. "Are you going to leave your phone on?"

"Perhaps you could do it while we speak. Just copy and paste the whole spreadsheet, business and personal purchases." Before Vic could respond, Achilles added, "What were their more recent purchases?"

Vic readied the text, but didn't hit SEND. "There's nothing since the day you escaped the bunker. Clearly, they're staying off the grid. A few weeks back they bought a used forklift and a bunch of shrink wrap."

"No eggs or potatoes?"

Vic wasn't sure he'd heard that right. He'd been distracted by preparing the text. "Say again?"

"Did they buy pallet loads of eggs and potatoes?"

"No. Is that surprising?"

"A little bit."

"Why?"

Achilles hesitated.

Vic could guess why. He'd found something. Most likely at the PPS offices. Vic was essentially asking Achilles to confirm his location. Vic had already sent all the law enforcement agencies around Cape Canaveral a BOLO. Surely Achilles had anticipated that. This wouldn't actually change anything. It was more a test of their partnership.

"I found large quantities of both products in the dumpster behind their office."

"Did you now? Thank you for saying so."

"Can I get the list?"

"I'm texting you their purchase history now. But just so you know, people often dump trash in other organizations' dumpsters. Ironically, it's a form of theft. Stealing dumpster space."

Achilles didn't respond.

Vic jumped into the gap. "At the beginning of our call, you said you might have something for me. You said it depended on what I had for you. Do you have something now?"

"I have a thought."

"I hope it's enough to assuage my boss for being late to his staff meeting."

"Your text hasn't come through yet."

Vic pressed SEND. His screen confirmed delivery.

A few seconds later, Achilles said, "Thank you. Here's my thought. What if Oz didn't buy PPS to make jetpacks?"

Vic hadn't seen that coming. Given the source, he took the question at face value and thought out loud. "Was there some asset he wanted? The intellectual property? The building lease?"

"In a matter of speaking, yes. What if he wanted their permit?"

"Their permit for what? To fly in restricted airspace?" That was an interesting angle. Had nothing to do with kidnapping people in California, but it was worth exploring.

"Their permit to buy rocket fuel ingredients," Achilles said.

Vic's hopes dropped. "What's so special about that?"

"Many of those chemicals are controlled substances. And for good reason."

"What reason is that?"

"They're not just used to formulate rocket fuel. They're also used to make explosives. The serious stuff. Military grade."

72
Willie Pete

Florida

I NEEDED an expert in explosives. A chemist. Someone whose knowledge far exceeded my own.

Google served up a potentially perfect solution.

The University of Central Florida was home to the National Center for Forensic Science, whose mission is to provide professional training in the areas of fire debris and explosives.

Excited by the serendipitous discovery, I copied the faculty list off their website onto my phone, then drove an hour west to Orlando. The NCFS was a modern-looking white building with blue glass. I mused that it would work well playing itself in a television show.

So would the professor I encountered while approaching the front door.

Dr. Emile Wisecock looked exactly like his online faculty photo, which in turn looked exactly like a proper British chemist—from a hundred years ago. He had a neatly clipped strawberry blond mustache that matched the rest of his properly combed hair, but it was the armless round wire-framed eyeglasses clinging to his nose that did the trick. That and the aged leather briefcase he toted. The modern coffee cup in his other hand spoiled the image a bit, but I was willing to bet there was tea with milk beneath the plastic lid.

"Excuse me, Professor Wisecock. Do you have a minute?"

"Yes, yes," he said.

Apparently, I looked like a student. I supposed the NCFS

would do a lot of seminars for mid-career active duty military and law enforcement.

I followed him to his office, which was neat around the edges but cluttered near the desk. The shelves with their books and baubles—a pan balance, an antique microscope, a brass apparatus I didn't recognize—appeared to be strictly for show, whereas the old oak table was clearly where the action happened.

Wisecock gestured me toward a well-worn wooden chair and took his own behind the desk. He enjoyed a sip of his hot beverage, then asked, "How may I help you?"

"I have a puzzle for you, Professor."

The strawberry blond eyebrows raised.

"How do you make a bomb out of potatoes and eggs?"

"That sounds more like a knock-knock joke."

"I know. But it's a serious question. I'm assisting the FBI in an investigation where terrorists are working with eggs and potatoes."

Wisecock's expression changed to that of a man who'd answered the phone only to find himself talking to a telemarketer. He didn't ask about the case. He didn't ask if I was a chemist. He clearly had all the information he wanted. "Bret Dinkins? Did he send you to me?"

"No. I'm working with ASAC Vic Link."

"Don't know him. But he sounds like a Dinkins clone."

As I waited for Wisecock to continue, I kept expecting him to reach for his glasses. I'd have thought they'd require constant adjusting, but they clung to his nose like a one-legged bird.

The professor watched me wait a bit before bowing his head in defeat. "Tell the FBI that you can get a stink bomb from an egg if you leave it out in the sun long enough. And a potato will break a window if you throw it hard enough. But otherwise the country is safe from your produce-packing terrorists."

"So there's no special chemical you can derive from them?" I offered.

Wisecock shook his head.

"No connection at all between eggs, potatoes and

armaments?"

"Not chemically. Not in any practical sense. Though they are both good for pelting protestors."

"Thank you for your time, Professor."

I spent the drive back to Cape Canaveral reflecting on what I'd learned and working out what to do next. Wisecock's references to throwing eggs and potatoes made me think of hand grenades. Oz had also bought white phosphorus, which was frequently used in those.

Willie Pete, as it was nicknamed, was pyrophoric, meaning self-igniting. That made it great for lighting fires pretty much anywhere. Since that combustion produced lots of dense smoke, white phosphorus grenades were often used to create camouflaging smokescreens that even infrared couldn't penetrate. Interesting though that was, it didn't provide a solid, sensible link back to the produce I'd found.

Perhaps Vic had been right. Perhaps someone with a ton of rotting trash had spotted an available dumpster and opted to save a hundred bucks.

I decided to drive by the restaurants within a mile or so of PPS to see what their dumpsters contained. Or rather, behind those restaurants.

The closest major intersection had a shopping center that housed the usual burger and coffee franchises, plus an independent pizza place and a Chinese restaurant. I bypassed the storefronts and hit the alley.

Back home in California, I frequently utilized a similar passage near my house as part of a shortcut. But I had never really studied it. Driving slowly through this one now, I came to understand that there was a lot more going on in alleys than I'd realized.

The dumpsters were corralled in yards. This created a clean and orderly appearance, although now that I thought about it, preventing scrounging was probably job one. The homeless were bad for business.

The emptied cardboard boxes were kept in a separate section. They were flattened and baled, and obviously bound for—

I hit the brake.

What had happened to the egg and potato boxes? And not just the boxes but also the individual cartons and sacks?

I put the car in park, right there in the middle of the alley, and pulled out my phone. I found the dumpster photo and confirmed my mental image. There was nothing but the produce itself in the trash. It was like a big vat of egg and potato soup.

Suppose Oz wasn't using the eggs and potatoes to make explosives? Suppose he was using the packaging to conceal explosives?

My spine prickled as I pondered the possibilities. I was deep into some pretty horrible imagery when red and blue lights began flashing right behind me.

73
Oh, Brother

Location: Unknown

FREED FROM HER IRON SHACKLE, Katya followed Shakira into the greater hangar. The furniture arrangement had changed during her imprisonment. The tools were all gone, and only two tables remained standing. The rest of the stuff she'd seen was stacked against the far wall.

Shakira walked toward the man Katya hadn't met. Seated behind one of the tables, he too was now dressed in casual clothes. He too looked familiar. But instead of resembling Sabrina, he took after Oz. *An older brother?* Katya wondered.

Before him on the table were a stuffed ashtray and a black box roughly the size of a card deck—with a diode that glowed red. Instead of a keyhole, it had a simple red rocker switch.

As she approached his table, Katya saw that the man's hands and forearms were oddly scarred with round splotches. Looked like he had been splashed with acid many years back. A workplace accident, she guessed, reflecting on the paint fumes.

The sight made her think of Chemical Ali, Saddam Hussein's intelligence chief. His *executed* intelligence chief. Executed was just what this one would be, once Achilles got hold of him.

Unaware of his pending fate, the fourth member of Oz's team remained seated. While she approached, he studied her from the comfort of his folding chair.

Hoping to bond a bit with the man who appeared to literally hold her fate in his hands, Katya said, "You must be Osama's brother. I'm Katya."

He tilted his head as if amused and said, "Omar."

He continued to study her for a few seconds, then turned to Shakira and spoke something in Arabic, exposing nicotine stained teeth.

Shakira lifted Katya's shirt from behind, showing off her handiwork.

Omar nodded, then rose. He stuck a hand in the right front pocket of his pants. Frowning, he then checked the left. Disappointed again, he said something in Arabic.

Shakira patted her own pockets then answered, "*Laa,*" which Katya assumed meant "No."

During the ensuing dialogue, Shakira found a pack of cigarettes over by the teapot. She extracted one, passed the pack to Omar, then took a seat behind the second table.

Katya hadn't been able to follow the conversation despite the context, although she heard both of her captors say "Osama." This made her assume that Oz figured in somehow. Whether he was the concern or the solution, she couldn't tell. Given his apparent position at the top of their limited hierarchy, perhaps he was both.

The two came to agreement.

Omar looked at her and said, "Sit."

There were no chairs left. Katya considered sitting on a table, but opted for the floor to be further away. Like her cell and the rest of the hangar, it was covered in cushioning corncob chips and chicken crap.

As she adjusted her legs, Katya noted that the mixture didn't look quite the same as the stuff on her floor. At first she thought it might be the lighting, which was brighter here. But a quick experiment with shadows convinced her that wasn't it.

She picked up a few kernels as her captors lit cigarettes. They weren't as uniform in color as those on her floor. These had been misted on several sides with paint. A white enamel and a flat beige, close inspection revealed. There were also globules of black rubber mixed in and partially painted over. The stuff she'd seen coating the card tables. Whatever they'd painted, it had first been rubberized.

The smokers seemed indifferent to her inquisitive

activities. They treated her like a familiar dog. Given the "collar" around her waist and her position on the floor, that was almost understandable.

When he finished his cigarette, Omar checked his watch and stood. He came around to her side of the table and leaned his backside against the edge while looking down at her.

Katya considered standing up so they could talk face-to-face, but didn't think that would go over too well with a man who probably valued women somewhere between cows and sheep. Best to let discretion be the better part of valor.

Still, she met his eye.

Omar reached around and grabbed the black box from the table. He held it up, like a lawyer presenting Exhibit A. Then he surprised her by speaking solid English. Accented, but educated. Refined even. "Do you know what this does?"

Not *is*, she noted. *Does.*

She rose to her feet. "Please tell me."

74
Pretty Face

Florida

MY CORTISOL LEVEL always spikes at the unexpected sight of red and blue lights in my rearview mirror. The unpleasant jolt is a side effect of my driving style—and the resultant fear of tickets.

I drive fast because the idea of wasting precious minutes of life getting from point A to point B irritates me at the molecular level. Plus, as an American and an Olympian, I'm inherently competitive. So conditioned to working to get ahead that I'm uncomfortable ever being behind.

But at that moment, I wasn't speeding. I wasn't even driving. I was parked. Unfortunately, I was also the subject of a nationwide BOLO alert.

On the hope that the officer was just prompting me to move along, I set down my phone, put the car in drive and hit the gas.

In response, I got nothing. No siren blip. No loudspeaker announcement. Nothing.

I drove away.

If they're not busy with an active call or headed someplace specific, police officers will leverage opportunities like my alley encounter to run spot checks. Either that officer hadn't, or my plate was still considered clean. Either way, I'd gotten lucky. Very lucky.

I berated myself for the careless behavior that almost put me in jail. Even though it wasn't rational, I believed Katya could feel me coming for her. Even though it was egotistical, I felt that gave her hope. Even though I had no concrete lead, I knew I could save her.

If I stayed out of jail.

So where to next? Literally and figuratively.

I needed to do some deep thinking so I drove toward the castle, searching for a beachfront motel. One where an absentee owner paid minimum wage and the included breakfast came from a self-service microwave.

The Seaside Escape fit the profile and my mood. Plus it had free Wi-Fi and a beachfront pool. All for seventy dollars, according to the vacancy sign. Turned out the seventy bucks excluded Florida's substantial hotel tax and the two hundred dollar deposit required of people paying cash, but I wasn't complaining. It was still cheap compared to California.

A neighboring shop sold me a twenty dollar swimsuit that was comfortable but ugly. I changed in my seventy dollar room then headed out for a hard run and a deep think.

The beach was beautiful. Sugary sand and warm blue water, topped with sunshine and treated to a cooling breeze. I felt guilty for being in such a pleasant place, knowing that Katya was likely in a cage.

I ran harder.

I put my arms and legs on autopilot as I'd done so often during my Olympic training years. Then, with the blood flowing and the endorphins building, I put my mind to work.

What did I have?

I began throwing fingers as I ran. One: I probably had four Middle Easterners in the US using false passports, one of whom was a chemist.

Two: The four certainly had large quantities of chemicals that could be used to make rocket fuel—or explosives.

Three: They also had jetpack technology.

Four: They were located near NASA headquarters.

Five: They had an unlimited supply of cryptocurrency.

Six: They may have bought large quantities of eggs and potatoes for the packaging.

Seven: They were holding Katya.

What else? I had the feeling my list was missing something important. Whatever it was, it eluded me. I kept running, hoping it would come.

When it didn't come for several miles, I doubled back. I didn't want to get too far from my hotel in case insight struck.

With the sun now more to my back than my front, I began to analyze my list. Which of the seven factors were relevant, and which were distractions? It didn't take much distance to decide that there was no way to know without forming a composite picture.

I began building that picture around Katya, because I needed her to be part of it. What purpose could she serve? She was Russian. Could she be a scapegoat? Wouldn't that be ironic? Katya and I both scapegoated as part of the same conspiracy for different reasons. That was a possibility, although she was a weak choice, being a prominent and gainfully employed mathematician rather than a chemist.

Could it be her mathematics expertise they were after? Also possible but improbable. Her abilities weren't so unique that you'd need to commit a complicated crime to acquire them.

A solid answer hit me as I hurdled a sandcastle. *Katya looked innocent.*

In this day and age, the one thing terrorists needed most was white skin. Throw in blonde hair and good looks and you were golden.

The conclusion resonated with my experience, my spy sense as it were. Oz had taken Katya for her face.

75
Adding Up

Western Nevada

VIC LOOKED at his phone and felt his spirits drop. Some people say the way to know if your marriage is happy is to note how you feel when you arrive home. *Are you happier when your spouse's vehicle is there or when it's not.* Vic didn't buy the so-called *Garage Test.* Sometimes you want company, sometimes you want to be alone. But he did subscribe to the *Telephone Test*, at least as it applied to your job. Were you happy to see the boss's name or not?

He definitely wasn't feeling the joy as *Brick* flashed on his phone. Especially after the disastrous staff meeting Achilles made him late for. "No discernible progress" was how Brick had summarized Vic's report for the record and in front of his peers.

"Special Agent Link."

"Do you know who I just got off the phone with?" his boss asked.

"No, sir."

"Director Brix."

Brick liked the fact that his name was so similar to the big man's. Sitting in his boss's lobby, listening to Melanie answer the phone, "Mr. Brick's office," Vic could tell that people often worried they'd been transferred to the wrong extension. He also heard her leveraging the fact when making requests. "Mr. Brick's instructions are" or "Brick said you should" were frequent refrains.

Vic didn't relish what was coming, but he played along. "What did the director want?"

"He wants his phone to stop ringing. Governor Rickman

is a personal friend of his, you know. Their wives were sorority sisters at Vanderbilt. I know you're not married, so let me tell you. When your wife has a priority, you have a priority. A persistent, nagging, relentless priority.

"And the bankers. They've got their lawyers set up on rotation. Not a single hour goes by without one of them calling to check in and throw a few threats around.

"So he has a question for me, and now I have a question for you. How close are you to solving this thing?"

Vic couldn't help but smile at the news. Not from a sadistic impulse, but from relief. If Brix was getting hourly calls from high-priced lawyers at work, and his wife was constantly pestering him at home, then scapegoating the Reno ASAC no longer made sense. Firing Vic wouldn't fix the director's problems. Neither would jailing Achilles. The only cure for those symptoms was getting the victims' money back.

Or giving Brix a victory so grand it made him bulletproof.

Vic weighed his words. "Sounds like solving the crime isn't the issue."

"What?"

"Jailing the thieves isn't going to keep the director's phone from ringing. Only recovering the money will do that."

Brick took a few seconds to chew and swallow. "What's your point?"

"If this was a simple robbery, a well-planned, well-executed robbery that began with a brilliant idea and ended with a double-cross, then the odds of our catching the criminals are very low. They have unlimited financial resources and a big head start. We don't even know what continent they're on."

"What do you mean, *if?*" Brick asked, picking up on the salient detail. "*If* this was a simple robbery."

"Suppose the money wasn't the end goal. Suppose the robbery was a means to achieving another end."

Brick scoffed. "We already know what their goal was. Kai Basher explained it perfectly. Money plus revenge. Money they felt they would have earned if their product hadn't failed, and revenge against the people they blame for its failure."

"That only explains the four AcotocA employees. The dead people."

"Dead people with no criminal or clandestine experience. Dead people who obviously contracted out for assistance and then got double-crossed."

Vic had considered and rejected the contractor scenario. "If it really was a team of eight—four executives plus four experts—why have six in the bunker and just two above?"

"Because the plan only required two above."

Brick was technically right, but the balance made no operational sense. "Why would the four AcotocA executives allow themselves to all be put at the mercy of two contractors?"

"Because they were amateurs."

This wasn't going anywhere. Vic had let it get off course. He attempted to put it back on. "I've been looking into the activity of the company owned by the pseudo-Maltese."

"Personal Propulsion Systems? The failed jetpack company?"

"Right. The bulk of their purchases were chemicals. Chemicals used to make rocket fuel."

"You find that surprising?"

"There wasn't much in the way of other material purchases. The components used to assemble the jetpacks themselves."

"Maybe that all came with the company when they acquired it. Maybe the fuel was the toughest nut to crack. Have you asked the former owners?"

"They confirmed that there were a lot of components and prototypes. Extending flight time through fuel optimization and motor construction was one major hurdle, but not the biggest one."

"No? What was—the heat?"

"Actually, it was the whole safety-regulatory issue. They concluded that they'd never be able to sell a jetpack in the U.S. regardless of price or performance because they're inherently too dangerous. They were thrilled to get a buyer."

"Why are you bringing this up?" Brick asked, his tone curt but tinged with curiosity.

"Because the same controlled chemicals used to make rocket fuel are also used to manufacture military-grade explosives, like RDX."

That got a long pause. "What are you saying?"

"I'm saying I want to go to Florida. I'm saying the missing money might not be Brix's biggest problem, but rather what the missing Middle Easterners are planning to do with it."

"With it and a ton of RDX," Brick added, his tone now more base than acidic.

76
Insufficient

Florida

THE MORE I EXAMINED the angle of *Katya as the face of a forthcoming crime*, the better it fit the facts. The explanation snapped in place like a custom-made part.

It felt great to have both a working hypothesis and the accompanying ray of hope. Nonetheless, the specific question of why she had been taken remained. *Taken to do what?*

To get the answer, I kept working my list of Oz's seven core assets. And I kept running. So buoyed was I by my breakthrough that my feet barely touched the hot sand.

I decided to tackle the *Jetpack Technology* asset next and found that I wasn't sure what to make of it. Presumably, it included compact propulsion and guidance capabilities, but I didn't know what that gave a terrorist that he couldn't get from a drone.

Other than the obvious ability to put a person in a place that might otherwise be unreachable.

Or get him out of a place that might otherwise be unescapable.

But neither could be accomplished without generating tremendous heat and noise. Or attracting a lot of attention. Whatever characteristics first-generation jetpacks might have, *stealth* would almost certainly not be among them.

For the moment, I tabled *product usage* as the driver behind the company acquisition. I'd stick with *chemical purchase permits* for now.

I moved on to the fourth item on my asset list. Location. NASA headquarters was clearly a high-value terrorist target.

Doing something there would be a huge coup, given that the space program was a symbol of American superiority and military might. It was a site that captured American hearts and minds like few others.

I stopped running.

The same could be said of Disney World. And it was only an hour away. Could that be it? Were they looking to blow up Mickey Mouse's house? It was one of the most crowded places in the States. And unlike the World Trade Center, it was packed with a complete cross-section of American life. It was the perfect terrorist target.

As I ran back to the Seaside Escape, I tried to calculate how many omelets and french fries were consumed every day at The Happiest Place on Earth. My analysis quickly reached the point where accuracy didn't matter. The answer was undoubtedly *enough*. Tons.

With that box checked, I found myself picturing Katya delivering a truckload of eggs and potatoes. She couldn't drive a truck, but she could be taught. In theory, all she'd have to do was get past the gate and then accelerate.

What kind of security did Disney have in place? I was certain it was extensive. Invisible, but expansive. It was probably better than most military installations, given the money involved and the need to maintain a pristine reputation. But would those measures extend to somehow sniffing produce? And if so, how vigilant would the guards be, given that they likely hadn't ever experienced a genuine threat. Not once while screening tens of thousands of trucks.

Furthermore, to the best of my knowledge, the state-of-the-art system was still a dog. Literally a trained canine.

And then there was the money. The cryptocurrency. Could that be intended as a bribe? How hard could it be to find a gate guard who would take five million dollars to look the other way for five minutes? That was almost certainly possible. But how would you find an amenable guard without getting arrested first?

You'd use Katya.

Whereas Middle Eastern male faces raise defenses,

beautiful blonde women lower them. Getting past a Disney gate probably wouldn't be too difficult for Katya.

I got back to my room and hit the shower.

As I soaped up, I knew I was on to something and nothing at the same time. The broad strokes fit the puzzle pieces, but the picture they formed was too fuzzy. The Disney truck example fit, but so might a Washington-bound train. Or a Miami plane. Or a Cape Canaveral rocket. *Something and nothing at the same time.*

I grabbed the lone, thin towel and began to dry off. I wasn't sure what to do next.

I had nothing I could act on.

Nothing to call Vic with.

I needed more.

77
Little Slips

Location: Unknown

OMAR SMILED at Katya's request for information on the little black box in his hand, exposing the teeth that ruined his otherwise handsome face. "This box senses the one in your belt. They are married, you see. Part of a pair. An electronic couple. The one here in my hand, is the male. The master. The one in your belt is the female. The servant. Do you follow?"

Katya wasn't sure that she did, but still she said, "Yes."

"Good. Now, you will note that both display a red light at present. That means that they are engaged, but not yet married. Both are technically free to roam. But—" he raised the box for emphasis "—once we consummate the marriage with a key, their lights will turn green. From that moment on, she cannot live without having him near."

"How near?" Katya asked, her predicament now crystal clear despite the allegorical explanation.

"The answer is one of signal strength, not distance."

"Approximately?"

"About one hundred meters across an empty field. Much less when obstructions are involved. Walls and windows and trees. Metal is particularly bad. Entering a bank safe would definitely be a bad idea, no matter how close her master is." Omar finished speaking, then just sat there waiting. He knew what the next question would be.

Katya couldn't help but ask. "What happens if she goes too far?"

"The same thing that happens if the belt is removed, the box is tampered with, or the battery dies. The signal keeping the connection open gets cut, causing an electronic bridge to close. Then the female box explodes.

"It won't be a big explosion. Nothing like a suicide vest. But it will blast you in half. Your spinal discs will shred everything between your hips and ribs."

Katya fought back the shivers and sobs, but couldn't restrain her tears. It was his shift from the generic *her* to the specific *your* that did it. That and the demonic dot winking up from her waist.

"No need to get upset. You'll get a warning. If the signal strength drops to ten percent, the box will beep and the light will turn yellow."

Katya didn't find that particularly reassuring. Suddenly, she could no longer cling to logic. Her brain struggled as if starved of breath. Horrible images burst through her natural defenses, flooding her mind and depriving it of oxygen.

Both captors seemed content to sit silently and watch her suffer. Omar even lit a second cigarette.

Katya focused on breathing deeply, then forced her analytical mind to reengage. Sticking with his analogy, she asked, "What about divorce?"

Omar nodded, approvingly. "Yes, that is permitted. Once the woman has served her purpose."

"And what purpose is that?"

"You'll know soon enough."

As Omar spoke those words, Katya heard a car approaching. She recognized the beefy engine. So did Shakira.

Omar rose and walked to the barn entrance. They'd covered the glass square in the pedestrian door with a piece of cardboard, but had punched a peephole into it. He peered through, then wheeled the big door aside.

The black Charger rolled in.

Katya couldn't see who was behind the wheel because the front windows had been tinted dark. Either that or they'd swapped one black Dodge for another. That seemed unlikely. She checked the license plate just in case. It no longer displayed the blue mountains and yellow sky of

Nevada. Instead she saw two oranges flanked by green letters.

A Florida plate.

Florida, not Mexico. Arizona, California or Texas she would understand. You'd want to switch plates before crossing the border in a stolen car. But Florida didn't border on Mexico.

She turned to Shakira. "We're in Florida? Not Mexico?"

Shakira crinkled her mouth. "What would we want with Mexico?"

"What do you want with Florida?"

Before she could answer, an Arabic command interrupted. Katya looked back to see that Oz had exited the car.

Shakira froze.

Oz walked toward them, looking first at Katya then back at Shakira. He wasn't happy. He launched into angry Arabic.

Shakira and Omar both responded apologetically.

When they finished, Oz reached into his pocket. Still mumbling, he whipped out a key. Not the brass padlock key. A round-nosed silver key. While he was extracting it, an object fell from his pocket and landed amidst the corncobs and crap at his feet.

He didn't notice.

Omar didn't notice.

Shakira didn't notice.

Katya did. It was his gold trinket. The one he kept kissing in the bunker. Katya didn't know what made the coin-sized object so special, but it clearly held value for him.

She threw herself at his feet.

78
The Missing Ingredient

Florida

I CALLED THE FRONT DESK and offered the clerk five dollars to print out a personal email. He was happy to do it for ten.

I put my swimsuit back on, grabbed my damp towel and a ten-dollar bill, then headed for the pool via the front office.

The printout was the PPS purchase history Vic had texted. I'd expected the equivalent of an annual credit card statement, but the FBI had gone the extra mile. They'd converted the codes and abbreviations into full descriptions. The list included product name, price, quantity, vendor and date. They'd also separated out the production-related purchases from the personal and operational expenses.

I saw what Vic meant about chemicals that were hard to pronounce. Hexamethylenetetramine. Polybutadiene acrylonitrile. Bisphenol-A diglycidyl ether epoxy resin. I read it all through twice, then began swimming laps. Swimming could be even better than running for thinking because the scenery wasn't the least bit distracting.

My plan was to keep reading through the lists until things started to click. Credit card purchases are windows into people's lives. They track movements, meals and interests. Pictures and patterns emerge.

Aside from the California trip and another to New York, the purchase history showed that Oz and Sabrina had stayed in the central and southern Florida area. Primarily along the eastern coast, with only a few flight-related purchases in Orlando. That moved Cape Canaveral back to the center of my geographical focus.

I looked at the items Vic had classified as Operational Expenses. There wasn't much beyond utilities. Some stationery. A few standard office and cleaning supplies. No bills above a hundred dollars. The first notable was forty gallons of house paint. Eight five-gallon buckets. Six enamel, two flat. Colors not listed. That caught my eye only because I'd seen nothing to indicate that Oz and Sabrina cared one whit about the walls in either their home or office. They certainly hadn't repainted. And there were no paint brushes listed either.

But that wasn't much of a lead.

The only other noteworthy item was a thousand dollars' worth of Flex Seal. But I didn't know what to do with that information either.

I filed both oddities away for later consideration.

Then the absence of paint brushes made me think about the missing egg and potato receipts. I double checked to see if Vic had missed them, perhaps due to a misclassification.

He had a section titled Personal Purchases which included food and very little else. That mirrored what I'd seen in the castle and reiterated the transient tone of their lifestyle. As for food, the receipts indicated that they cooked at home far more often than they ate out.

I found nothing in the production products that might have been pallets of eggs and potatoes. But there were two paint sprayers. That explained the missing brushes, but not the plain walls.

Again, I filed the information for future reference.

I decided to dedicate the next few laps to thinking about the produce. It was just such an odd find, a dumpster full of raw potatoes and eggs. Given that the purchase wasn't on the credit card, either it wasn't their trash or they'd gone to some effort to conceal the acquisition with theft or cash.

The *not their trash* option seemed more likely. If you weren't hiding the purchase of large quantities of volatile chemicals, why hide pallets of produce?

There was one obvious answer. Concealing that link was somehow mission critical. Obfuscating the purchase made perfect sense if the eggs were ultimately going to explode when cracked, or the potatoes when put in a fryer.

But overall it made more sense that the eggs and potatoes were someone else's trash. When you hear hoofbeats, assume horses, not zebras.

This line of thought was taking me in figurative circles and literal laps, but it eventually gave me another idea.

I returned to the edge of the pool. Dried my face and hands, then read through the production purchases again. After three passes, I dove back into the pool and pondered what wasn't there.

I didn't know enough about chemistry to do a chemical analysis. Or about production to analyze that aspect of the PPS operation either. So instead of bottom-up, I tried performing a top-down analysis.

Suppose Oz was planning to explode NASA's next rocket. Access aside, did PPS have everything required?

They had the chemicals. They had plenty of mixing and measuring equipment, plus heating and cooling apparatuses. They'd also purchased mold-making equipment. In short, as far as I could tell, the answer was *yes*. They could manufacture military-grade bombs. Perhaps even crude missiles using modified jetpacks.

Now that was a scary thought.

No, wait! I corrected myself. They had everything they needed to create *explosives*. They did not have the electronics required to transform their explosives into missiles or bombs. Specifically, they didn't have the detonators. There was no reason a jetpack company needed those. And therefore, they had no permit to purchase them either.

79
Red Light, Green Light

Florida

KATYA didn't have to work hard to appear sincere while begging Oz not to key the box. If forced to choose between that act and another more common violation, she'd need time to think about it.

But she didn't think about it.

Instead, she focused on the gold trinket now pressed beneath her palm. She wriggled her hand to work it in tight between the base of her pinkie and thumb. She was no magician, but she didn't need to perform a trick, to pull it from a nose or ear. She just had to slip it into her pocket as she rose.

Omar picked her up off the ground by hauling on the back of her shirt. He just grabbed a fistful and yanked. Oz's older brother proved surprisingly strong for his size and weight. So sudden was his move that she nearly dropped the precious object. With a clumsy but plausible fumble, she managed to smack it against her chest in a move somewhere between *I'm choking* and *Oh, gracious!*

As Omar let go, she bent over coughing, then slid it into her bra. The precious object wasn't a coin, she realized as it went in. Much too jagged and rough.

What was it then?

She couldn't look now.

"I see my brother has explained his special construction to you," Oz said.

Ignoring her condition, he stepped forward and placed one hand on the side of her waist, like he was about to lead her in a dance. But instead of taking her hand in his, he reached his other hand around to the small of her back and thrust the key into the black box. While she gasped, he twisted.

The box beeped and the diode's color changed from red to green.

That was it.

She was *married*.

Not to Colin. Not to Achilles. To a vile man with scarred hands and nicotine stained teeth.

"Would you like to test it out?" Omar asked. "See how far you can walk before you get the yellow light?"

Katya knew she should. It would give her valuable information. A statistic that might soon save her life. But she didn't think she could handle the additional emotional strain. Not right then. Not right there. Not with three heartless monsters watching. Where was Sabrina? she wondered. "Maybe later."

Omar grinned at her answer. It was a smug expression, like you'd see on someone making a winning chess move.

"Very well then," he replied, pulling out the brass key.

Katya knew what that meant. Despite the electronic leash, she was to be shackled in her cell again. Locked up like a bad dog.

She dropped her gaze so he wouldn't see that she welcomed the opportunity. She welcomed it because she wanted to be alone, to reflect on what had transpired—and examine her prize.

Katya wasn't sure why she cared so much about Oz's silly trinket. But she knew that he valued it. Highly. The fact that she had taken his treasure from him gave her hope. Hope that there just might be greater things to come.

"Remember what I said about the signal," Omar said as he snugged and locked the chain just below the explosive belt. "It's the only thing preventing detonation. See that you don't do anything to disrupt it."

"When do we leave on our mission?" she asked.

Omar said nothing.

Katya figured he still stung from his brother's earlier rebuke.

"Has to be soon, right?" she pressed. "Otherwise you would have waited with the belt. You don't want an accident either."

"You would be wise to spend your time getting right with God, rather than guessing about things that really don't matter." Omar said. He left her there with that lovely thought.

She didn't take his advice.

She sat cross-legged with her back to the opening and listened. Over the peeping chicks and blowing fans, she heard a bit of Arabic banter followed by car doors opening and closing. Seconds later, the mighty engine roared to life and two of her captors departed.

Katya waited patiently for a few minutes to be sure the remaining terrorist didn't plan to join her, then she pulled the golden object from her bra.

Although sized like a large coin, it clearly wasn't. Oz's good luck charm resembled a flower with alternating gold and white leaves. Real gold and porcelain, she believed. The intricate seven-sided design also had accents of translucent emerald green. Crystal, she supposed. In the center, surrounded by a ring, was Arabic text. She couldn't read it, of course. To her, it looked like so many squiggles. But surely it was a pithy phrase. Words of wisdom, praise, or a Koran verse.

While the back was flat and plain, except for what appeared to be a serial number, the front was textured. Her first thought was a brooch, perhaps for a queen or other office holder. Then she discovered irregularities on the edge of one of the petals and changed her mind. They were something she recognized from her own jewelry. The remnants of a broken off attachment ring. But not for a pendant. She was holding a medal.

Had Oz been preemptively awarded some great honor in anticipation of completing his current assignment? That might make sense if it was a suicide mission. The thought chilled her until she realized it made no sense. If the medal was a recent award, the clip wouldn't be broken.

It had to be something historical. Something deeply

meaningful to Oz—or his family. Perhaps it had belonged to his father or grandfather. A symbol of glory days now past. Or perhaps, days he hoped to recapture.

That felt right.

Katya returned the medal to her bra with a sense of accomplishment. Despite being chained to a wall and strapped with explosive, she'd scored both a physical and a mental victory.

With that thought, she decided to attempt sleep. Whatever was coming, she wanted to confront it at her best.

An odd rumble roused her some time later. She wasn't sure how long. Minutes? Hours? Naps could be difficult to judge, particularly those fueled by extreme stress and exhaustion.

As she shook off the shroud of sleep, her ears identified the sound. A truck had rumbled past the barn. She heard the big door slide aside, then the shrill beeping of a backup warning. The truck maneuvered inside, followed by the Charger.

Katya heard doors opening and closing, and the scrunch of approaching footsteps. She rose to face the person ducking into her cell.

It was Sabrina. The evil sister was holding two objects. One was a handgun, the other a set of headphones.

80
Just One

Florida

THERE ARE only a few civilian uses for detonators, the biggies being building demolition and rock quarrying. As a result, there are only two detonator suppliers in east central Florida. Just enough to keep each other honest. One appeared to be both a manufacturer and a supplier of demolition products, the other was a specialty supply company servicing construction contractors.

I drove to the closest, which was an hour up the coast in Titusville. Barnes and Baker Demolition Supply sat on cheap land near the intersection of 528, the Beachline Expressway, and I-95. Bold blue lettering on the fading white warehouse made it easy to spot. It looked like the founders had begun their manufacturing and warehousing in a big older building, then bumped out a storefront adjacent to the parking lot once they moved into retail.

I counted four well-used utility vehicles, all off to the far side. Looked like I'd be the only customer. That suited me just fine.

The storefront that greeted me consisted of a long counter with a cash register at one end, a computer at the other, and a ring-for-service doorbell on the wall. No product posters or displays. Just a few legal notices. Apparently, if you came to B&BDS, you knew what you wanted.

I rang the bell.

A good sixty seconds later, a man emerged rubbing a shop rag between his hands. His scalp was bald, his eyes blue, and his welcoming smile peeked through a casually kept gray mustache and beard. He looked a bit surprised to see me. "Help you?"

I held out my hand. "I'm Kyle."

He put the towel on the counter. "Barry. What can I do you for?"

Based on name alliteration, his age and the intelligence in his eyes, I sized Barry up as a founding co-owner of B&BDS and decided he'd appreciate a direct approach. "I consult with the FBI. Have a few questions if you can spare a second?"

His smile disappeared. His lips said, "Sure," but his tone said maybe.

I stuck with direct. "Have you recently sold any blasting caps or other detonating equipment to a person who appeared Middle Eastern? May have spoken with a British accent?"

"Is this a joke?"

"No, Barry. It most certainly isn't."

"That happens, we're going to let ATF know. I mean, there's racial profiling and then there's common sense, you know?"

"Even if the person has a permit?"

"Permits are required, but are easy enough to fake."

"What do they look like?"

Barry pointed to one of the certificates on the wall. It looked like a Federal Firearms License or auto registration, a half-sheet printout in black and white. "Title 18 of the United States Code, Chapter 40," he said, reciting the wording along the top.

"Do you make a record of each purchase?"

"Got to. That's Title 27, Part 555."

"Good to hear. Have you sold any detonators lately?"

"Plenty. But only to regular customers. There are storage regulations, so users tend to buy them as needed."

"So no unusual orders? Walk-ins that surprised you?"

"What's this about?"

I pulled out my phone and called up a photo of Katya. No easier way to lighten a conversation between men than to interject a pretty woman. "Have you seen her?"

Barry took my phone and studied the image attentively, using zoom. "No. I'd remember her. That's for sure. She's about the 180-degree opposite of our usual customer."

"Would you call ATF if she came in looking for detonators?"

Barry's expression changed. He got it. "No, I wouldn't."

I pulled five crisp twenty-dollar bills from my wallet and laid them on the counter in a fan. Then I picked a business card off the counter, flipped it over and began to write my phone number with a borrowed pen. I had to stop and check the number in the burner app, as I'd gone through so many in my calls with Vic. "Do me a favor and call this number immediately if either she or a Middle Easterner comes in. While they're still at the counter. All you have to say is 'Please hold,' and I'll know." I put the card on the lip of the register. "Will you do that for me, Barry?"

"Sure. Why don't you email me that picture for reference." He handed me a fresh business card. "Address is right there."

I headed south on I-95, past Melbourne toward the Treasure Coast and Rebound Construction Supply. According to their website, they offered everything required to get wind and water-damaged commercial and residential property ready for reconstruction, including demolishing unstable structures.

I wasn't sure whether it was good news or bad that Oz hadn't been to Barry's store. On the one hand, it left me with only one more good chance of confirming my hypothesis and getting back on track to finding Katya. On the other hand, it meant there was a chance of catching Oz in the act.

If Barry called.

And I was close by.

I spent the drive south thinking about exploding produce. Terrorists would go with one of two tactics. Either get the eggs and potatoes widely distributed, aiming for hundreds of individual explosions, or use them as a single stealth bomb.

The trick with the individual scenario would be timing.

How would you time the individual explosions? You'd want them to go off all at once and with people nearby. That seemed a tough nut to crack. If it were, say, candy specially labeled for a movie premiere, that might work. But eggs and potatoes were everyday items.

The stealth bomb scenario would be much simpler. But you'd want something high profile. Something akin to what The World Trade Center had been for New York City. It was a symbol. It was an economic engine. And by involving aircraft, it touched every American's life.

I started thinking about prime targets. Economic engines that attracted large crowds. Preferably affluent but diverse ones. By the time I neared my destination, I'd moved on from fixed places to major cultural events, things like championship ball games, celebrated music concerts, and presidential state dinners. Any one of them might make a good target—although major league sports and arena concerts didn't typically have eggs on the menu.

I needed to spend some time on Google, and resolved to do that next. If I didn't get lucky at the second store.

Rebound Construction Supply looked only slightly busier than B&BDS. There was just one car in the customer part of the lot. A black Dodge Charger.

Florida

KATYA JOLTED AWAKE beneath a barrage of cool water. It wasn't from a glass or even a bucket. She was being sprayed. Her first thought was of the belt. Would the water short circuit it? Was it about to explode. She looked down and saw the diode blinking red.

Behind her a woman spoke. "Time to wash up."

It was Shakira, holding a hose.

"Don't look at me. Wash up," Shakira said, directing the spray full on her face. "There's soap and shampoo in the pail."

Katya looked and saw there was indeed one of those bare metal pails beside her on the corncob and crap floor. She was still in her corner of the chicken barn, but the glance back had shown that something had changed. The boxes that fenced her in had been removed.

Katya stood.

The spray moved with her.

Since there was soap, Katya assumed she was to strip. She immediately thought of the stolen medal hidden in her now-soaked bra. Could she move it to a new natural hiding place with Shakira standing right behind her?

She'd have to try. The movements would appear innocent enough, given that she was washing.

Hopefully, clean clothes and a towel would be forthcoming. And a change of venue. The floor was becoming nasty as it got wet.

Despite the rude awakening and crude circumstances, Katya welcomed the opportunity to wash. It had been days, many of them sweaty, since the last time her skin had seen soap. She'd spent every intervening second confined to a car trunk or a barnyard floor. At this point, her scent would probably curl wallpaper and her hug leave a permanent stain. Katya didn't expect her next stop to be a pleasant one, but at least she'd face it clean. *Positive attitude, Katya. Positive attitude.*

Each time she turned to wash her front side, Shakira focused the flow on her eyes. Message delivered. Katya began directing the water with her hands. The conditioning shampoo took forever to rinse, but she'd have used it twice if Shakira hadn't turned off the hose.

As Katya squeezed out her hair, a towel landed on her shoulder. She dried off, then wrapped herself with it, soggy belt and all, but didn't turn around.

While attempting to fall asleep some hours back, Katya figured out why Omar glued the belt in place. It wasn't to prevent her from taking it off. The booby trap and stitching took care of that. It was to prevent her from rotating it around. From placing the bomb in front—and giving her captor a hug.

Shakira placed a big tooth comb in her hand.

Katya went to work battling the tangled mess. Usually, she'd be seated before her vanity on a cushioned stool. She'd have spa music playing or perhaps some Spanish guitar. This would be a meditative, relaxing chore. Today she felt like she was preparing for her own hanging.

When she finished, Katya just stood there holding the comb down at her side, staring at the curved slope of the corrugated steel wall, listening to fifty thousand chickens. Each of them was destined to be eaten. Did she make it fifty thousand and one?

She sensed movement behind her, then felt the headphones slip over her ears.

~ ~ ~

When Katya awoke, she was no longer wearing the towel.

She wasn't at the farm or in the trunk of a car. She was in the back seat of the Charger, beside Sabrina.

Katya could feel the explosive belt around her waist, but she couldn't see the glow of its light. A momentary surge of hope flooded her veins, but a quick inspection revealed that the diode had been duct taped over.

The shirt she now wore was a gray polo. Not at all her style. A green logo on the breast read Clean Cut Quarries. Interesting. Beneath the shirt she saw blue jeans and buckskin work boots.

The thought of someone dressing her unconscious body gave Katya an odd, uncomfortable feeling. It made her cringe until she remembered Oz's medal, and where she'd hidden it. Her deception remained undetected, her little victory intact.

"You're going to be making a purchase for Kurt Valenta at Clean Cut Quarries," Sabrina said, handing Katya two pieces of paper and a stack of twenty-dollar bills. "You're his new assistant, just relocated from California. You're to give the impression that you and Kurt are close."

Sabrina, dressed in flattering white shorts and a tight cleavage-exposing shirt, went on to describe Kurt. Then she explained what Katya was to buy and where it was located. The first half-sheet of paper made note of this. She was to charge the blasting caps to the company account or pay cash and get a receipt. The second half-sheet of paper was a copy of Clean Cut's purchase permit. It was essentially her identification. Katya got the impression that Sabrina herself had gotten close to Kurt.

The two former friends role-played while Oz drove them south. Sabrina acted the part of an experienced store clerk, Katya that of a friendly buyer.

They were, indeed, in Florida. The highway signs declared as much. When one of them announced an upcoming rest stop, it gave Katya an idea. "I really need to use the bathroom."

Sabrina said nothing.

Oz said, "We'll stop. It will be a good practice run."

Katya wasn't sure what he meant, but was glad for the

response.

Oz parked at the picnic end of the rest stop, fifty yards beyond the building, where there were no other cars.

Sabrina pulled a phone from her purse and initiated a video call with Oz. Then she switched her input to transmit from the main camera. "Put this in the front left pocket of your jeans. We've sewn it to hold the camera in the proper position. We can see what you see. Hear what you hear. Hear what you say. Do anything stupid or suspicious, and Oz will blow the belt. Block the camera, and Oz will blow the belt. Get the picture?"

"I get it."

"You're replaceable," Oz added.

"I get it," Katya said. She definitely did.

82
Mixed Messages

Florida

BLACK DODGE CHARGERS are common enough cars, and this one had a Florida plate. It also had darkly tinted windows, which I didn't remember seeing back at the bunker. Nonetheless, my pulse rate rocketed. You expect to see pickups at construction supply stores, not sports cars.

And neither discrepancy was disqualifying. In fact, if thinking about it, I'd have anticipated both.

I parked at the back of the lot, putting the Charger between me and the main door. I struggled to see if the car was occupied, but between the tinting and the lighting it was impossible to tell without walking up and putting my face to the glass.

The left end of the store had a portico positioned above barn-sized doors for loading pickups in the rain. The main entrance was a sliding glass door on the right. Given their sun-eschewing reflective coatings, I couldn't see inside them either.

I glanced around to be sure I hadn't become so focused on the car as to miss something critical. Nothing caught my eye.

It was easy to imagine trucks lining the drive in the days and weeks following a hurricane, but at the moment Rebound Construction Supply looked like a Christmas store in July. Perhaps the midday hour had something to do with it. In my experience, such stores were busiest in the early and late hours, as crews drove to and from worksites.

So what now? If I got out of the car, I exposed myself—and potentially lost the element of surprise. But staying there was suspicious as well. If Katya was inside, and someone was waiting in the car, they'd be nervously watching anyone entering the lot. Plus sitting there would delay my reaction if Katya were to walk out. And it wasn't like I could call the cops.

I slipped the Glock into the small of my back and slowly stepped out of the car. My sunglasses were a decent disguise, given that a steady flow of casually-clothed guys was expected, and I was not.

I started walking toward the entrance with my face looking down at my phone but my eyes focused on the familiar Dodge. This could be it. Right here, right now.

Scenarios played out in my mind. I pictured the doors sliding open and Katya walking out with a box of blasting caps in her hands. Sabrina would be right behind her, hand in purse, finger on trigger. A smiling but silent companion. Katya would spot me, but I'd ignore her. I'd keep walking as casual as could be, then I'd swat the purse and slam Sabrina to the ground. Oz would walk out a few seconds later, having pretended to be an unassociated party. I'd shoot him on the spot. Except, it wouldn't go like that. Because of the reflecting door glass, he'd see me before I saw him. Then what? Would he open fire through the door? No chance of that. He'd run to the cargo-loading exit and try to flank me. I'd have to get Katya and Sabrina out of sight before he could. Would I have time?

I passed the Charger.

No activity.

I put my phone in selfie mode and angled the screen toward the windshield, giving myself a rearview mirror. Someone was behind the wheel. Someone dark skinned with black hair. It was Oz!

I turned to confirm.

Our eyes met.

His grew wide.

I heard the store's doors swish open as I reached for my gun.

I stole a glance and saw Katya. Katya! She was alive! My Katya was alive!

She looked healthy enough, but was oddly dressed. She wore jeans and work boots and a polo shirt with a corporate logo on the pocket. Under her right arm was a white box the size of a small microwave oven.

Her face lit up when our eyes met, but then filled with fear.

Where was Sabrina? I'd expected to see her on Katya's tail.

Oz opened his door.

I turned his way and raised my gun.

Katya yelled, "Achilles, don't shoot!"

83
So Close

Florida

KATYA had endured a lot of emotional whipsawing in her life, but the past few minutes broke the record. The first lash came at the checkout counter. She had hoped to pen a note while signing the receipt, but Sabrina had been too clever. She stood just a few feet away, pretending to inspect the offerings of a battery display rack while her gestures and charms kept the clerk preoccupied.

Katya had no doubt that Oz would detonate the belt if she made any overt plea for help. Her only question was whether he planned to detonate it in any case. For all Katya knew, this was her last act. Supplying terrorists with explosive equipment. In five minutes, she might be dead in the trunk of a stolen car.

Her hope was that they needed her for many more such acts. As nerve-racking as they would be, each would leave crumbs for Achilles to find. She prayed he'd catch up before the errands ran out.

Heading for the door, her purchase complete, Katya was surprised that Sabrina didn't immediately follow. She hung back. Probably to ensure that Katya hadn't left clues behind, and the clerk didn't pick up the phone.

Then she saw him. Achilles was right there in front of her, separated by just twenty feet of gravel parking lot. He wasn't dead!

Her heart flooded with joy, but the warmth only lasted a second before a cold wave of fear crashed. Oz was getting out of the car. The black box was in his hand.

"Achilles, don't shoot!" she screamed.

Oz raised the black box to show that his thumb was on the red rocker switch. "Put the gun down before anybody sees you, Achilles. Don't force me into a corner."

"Do it, Kyle," Katya said. She used her left hand to lift her shirt, exposing the beige canvas belt while silently cursing Oz for being so diabolically clever. Achilles couldn't make a move without sacrificing his queen. Checkmate.

Or was it?

Could she act? What could she do? Should she sacrifice herself? They were very likely going to kill her anyway. At least this way, Achilles would kill them too. And stop whatever it was they were plotting. But what was that? Beyond *serenity*, *tranquility* and an Arabic medal, she didn't have much in the way of clues.

Achilles didn't drop the Glock. He returned it to his waistband.

"Put it on the ground!" Oz commanded. "Use your shoe to cover it with gravel, then walk back to your car."

Katya hated to see Achilles disarmed, although that beat being shot. She knew that Oz had two guns with him, even though he'd flashed neither. He obviously wanted to avoid attention.

But what was his next move?

Was he going to lock Achilles in the trunk of his own car? Or would he have Sabrina drive him someplace? No, Oz wouldn't split his team up that way, Katya decided. And he didn't need to. As long as Oz held her hostage, Achilles was neutralized.

Achilles appeared to come to the same conclusion.

He went along.

He used his shoe to swipe a swath of gravel aside, then laid his gun on the bare patch. This gave Katya an idea. She angled her body so that the right side was toward Oz, then quickly ran her left hand up the inside of her shirt, grabbed the medal, and brought her hand back to her side. While Achilles kicked gravel over his Glock, she dropped the medal by her foot then stepped on it.

Just then, Sabrina walked outside. Had she seen the secretive move? Katya didn't know. She'd been focused on

Achilles and Oz.

"We're okay," Sabrina said. "I knocked over a display and kept them distracted."

Katya took that as a no. Now she just had to make Achilles aware of the medal without alerting her captors.

"I love you, Achilles," Katya said.

He met her eye. "I love you, too."

She flicked her eyes toward the ground. Just two quick moves. Then she ground her left foot a few times and blew him a kiss.

Achilles turned to Oz. "I'm not leaving without her. And you're not leaving with her."

"Wrong on both counts. But you'll be together again soon enough, if you both behave. What's your phone number?"

Achilles recited a number that Katya didn't recognize, but she immediately memorized. If there was one thing she was good at, it was numbers.

Oz typed as Achilles talked, then Achilles' phone rang. "It's a video call. Answer it with video."

Achilles did.

"Now here's what you're going to do," Oz said, live and on the small screen. "You're going to go sit in the back seat of your car, and you're going to stare into the camera. You're not going to look anywhere but into the camera until I hang up. If your eyes wander, the next thing you'll see is Katya exploding from the inside out. Are we clear?"

"How do I know you won't kill her anyway?" Achilles asked.

"Because despite some evidence to the contrary, Sabrina and I like the two of you. This affair isn't personal, it's business. We proved that when we spared your lives back in Nevada.

"Once I hang up the phone you're going to go to a hotel on the beach, one with room service. You're going to sit in your room and watch the waves. You're going to wait for me to call and tell you where to pick up Katya.

"While you wait, I'm going to be watching your phone's location. It better be in such a room an hour from now, otherwise, you lose. If I call and you don't answer the phone, you lose. Are were clear?"

"We're clear."

"Do we have an agreement?"

"We do."

"Good. Now, go get in the back seat of your car, and know that while I watch your face on my phone, Sabrina is going to be listening to the police band. We'll be listening in until our work is done. And just to avoid another stupid but deadly mistake, you should know we have a friend, a good friend, a close friend, high up in the FBI."

84
Picture Perfect

Florida

I HAD NEVER been more pained or frustrated in my life than I was while sitting there watching Oz and Sabrina drive Katya away. I'd been outplayed. Outmaneuvered. Blocked from taking any assisting action.

"Keep your eyes on the phone and don't say a word," Oz said after unmuting. "I'm not going to warn you again."

I felt like a schoolboy made to stand in the corner during a championship game. Every fiber in my body was screaming at me to act, but I was forced to remain completely passive. Forced to focus on the face of the man I wanted to rip limb from limb, but for whom I was afraid to show even a hint of disdain.

Had Oz spoken the truth about sparing our lives? It wasn't likely, but it was possible. Anyone driven to fulfill fanatical acts of terror had to possess an exceptionally strong sense of allegiance.

And I had earned his allegiance.

Back at the bunker, I had probably saved his life, and Sabrina's, more than once.

So I struggled to appear amiable.

Although my face remained directed at the phone, my mind's eye wandered twenty yards across the parking lot. What had Katya buried? A slip of paper probably. A receipt from a takeout food place, perhaps? Someplace they regularly patronized.

Oz spoke again, disrupting my thoughts. "Go straight to a beachfront hotel and wait by your phone. I'm sending you the link to a geo location app. You have thirty minutes to be in your room with the app installed. Select the option that allows anyone with your number to track it."

Before I could reply, Oz hung up. The bastard had really thought things through.

I bolted from the car and ran to the spot where Katya had been standing. Oz hadn't ventured that way when he retrieved my buried gun. Nor had anyone else. Not a single customer had come or gone since our Mexican standoff. I wondered how the place stayed in business. In any case, their misfortune was my good luck. The gravel had not been disturbed.

I spotted Katya's buried treasure right away because it wasn't a crumpled piece of paper. It was something shiny. Sized like a large coin but not perfectly round. It resembled a lapel pin with a serial number. The back was all gold but the front also had petals of white with green accents. And in the center—Arabic writing.

I had no time for further study. I shoved the trinket in my pocket and ran back to my car.

After two failed attempts, I found a motel a quarter mile from a large shopping center that took cash and had an available room with the right kind of window. With only seconds on the clock, the clerk told me I could get just about any food I wanted from a third-party delivery service. He gave me a flyer.

I ran to my room, installed the required app and adjusted the settings as Oz instructed. Once I was certain he could track the location of that phone, I plugged it in and got down to business.

First on my list was forwarding all calls from the tracked phone to my spare. I configured the app to make the handoff seamless. There would be no audible clue what was happening. In the virtual world, I would appear to be right there in that room. Oz could see and talk to me there—no matter where I really was.

I ordered fuel in the form of a pizza and then set about identifying the golden trinket Katya had left me. An object I now recalled seeing Oz kiss in the bunker.

I began by laying it before the window atop a piece of

white note paper and taking a close-up photo. Then I copied the photo into an image search.

Google found no matches. Its *Best guess* was a *Window*. That puzzled me until I scrolled down and saw the *Visually similar images*, which were stained glass windows of the same shape. The algorithm hadn't taken size into account.

I repeated the exercise with a dollar bill in the picture for scale, but that didn't help. Google focused on the money and assumed the trinket was a coin.

I considered attempting to translate the Arabic script in the center, but the artistic arrangement was such a spaghetti jumble that I decided to make that my last resort.

The pizza arrived and I tore in. As the inviting scent of baked bread and melted cheese tickled my nose, I tried not to think about what Katya was or was not eating. She hadn't looked malnourished. People hiding out tended to subsist off fast food or packaged food. Katya would usually choose hunger over either option, but that was for short periods of time. Hopefully Sabrina was similarly finicky.

After a second slice, I held the object against my chest like a brooch and took a selfie in an attempt to prompt Google to find similar headshots. It worked! One of the best guesses was a man holding up an award and wearing a similar object.

I clicked the link to visit the page and discovered that I was likely holding The Order of Abdulaziz Al Saud, which was awarded for meritorious service to the Kingdom of Saudi Arabia.

The design in the photo was a bit different, with silver instead of gold and text that didn't quite match mine. It also had an appendage with crossed sabers and palm leaves that connected it to a ribbon. My object was missing that element. But Wikipedia informed me that there were four classes of the esteemed prize, thereby explaining the minor differences.

I inspected the artifact again and found imperfections where the attachments had broken off. It was a medal. A revered award. That explained Oz's affection.

There was no doubt now. This was The Order of

Abdulaziz Al Saud.
    Oz was a Saudi.
    Just like bin Laden.

85
Fall From Grace

Florida

OZ ENJOYED an endorphin boost as he carried the box of detonators back into the barn. Encountering Achilles had been a surprise and a setback, but he had prevailed through superior planning coupled with calm execution.

He handed the box off to Omar, who tossed his cigarette in order to receive the precious package with both hands.

"How long?" Oz asked.

"Just a few hours. Where's the girl?"

"In the back seat, wearing headphones."

Oz turned to Shakira. "Put her in the trunk."

"Not the barn?"

"I don't want her to see what Omar is up to. Besides, the barn's wet."

"What does it matter if she sees? I mean…" Shakira shrugged.

"Probably nothing. But I can't foresee everything. Can you?"

"No, I cannot. Thank you for reminding me."

"See to the girl."

Oz entered the chicken barn and slumped into a folding beach chair. The farm was an ideal working and hiding place, and he would forever be grateful to the distant relative who allowed them to use it. But Oz would also be happy to leave it behind. There was only so much cheeping one could take.

Sabrina sat down beside him and ignited the butane burner to heat the teapot. "You did well today, my lion."

"We did well, my virtuous princess."

It was true.

Their long struggle to restore the Abdilla and Saida families to positions of honor within the kingdom was nearly complete. Ninety-five percent of the hard work was behind them. Soon King Salman would see that his son had been wrong to shun their families and imprison their patriarchs. Soon he would restore their status and their fortunes.

So long as they did the damage without leaving any proof. As bin Laden had before them.

Oz pulled his father's medal from his pocket and pressed it to his lips. Except, he didn't.

"What is it?" Sabrina asked.

Oz rechecked his left pocket.

The Order of Abdulaziz Al Saud wasn't there.

Surely he wouldn't have put it in his right? Away from his heart?

He checked anyway.

It wasn't there, either.

"My father's medal. I can't find it."

"Did you check all your pockets?"

Oz stood and performed a thorough pat down.

"When did you last kiss it?"

Not *see it*, Oz noted. His wife was wise to make him recall the act. He had to think. He had definitely kissed it in the bunker. And up top. When the house was cleaned up and the woman was in the trunk. "Right before we left the cabin."

"Back in Nevada? No, you kissed it before bed our first night on the cots." Sabrina gestured behind them to the beds.

"You're right. I did."

Oz walked over to his cot and carefully checked the sleeping bag. No medal. He checked underneath. Nothing. As he searched the other beds, Omar and Shakira walked over. "What's going on?" Omar asked.

"Oz can't find your father's medal," Sabrina said.

"Where did you last see it?" Shakira asked.

"We've been through that," Oz snapped. "Before bed,

our first night here."

The four all looked at the floor. The vast expanse of corncob and crap-covered ground.

"I'll go buy a metal detector," Omar said.

"Better get two," Sabrina said.

Oz liked the idea. But he might have a better one. "When something valuable is missing, the wise move is to consider both options."

"Both options?" Shakira repeated in a questioning tone.

"Either it was lost or it was stolen."

Three sets of eyebrows raised, then all turned toward the Charger.

Oz popped the trunk using the button beside the steering wheel. As it whooshed open, he went around back and yanked the earphones off Katya's head.

She didn't stir.

He picked up a bottle of water and began pouring it into her nose.

She bolted upright, snorting and coughing, eyes wide, face frightened.

Oz instantly regretted acting rashly. He'd let panic get the better of him. He took a few deep breaths while Katya caught her own, then composed his words. "Sorry about that rude awakening."

She didn't reply.

He handed her the bottle. It was still two-thirds full.

She took a drink.

When she finished, he took back the bottle and studied her face while he screwed on the cap. Her composure was returning to normal. "I have a very important question for you. A very serious question. Do you understand?"

Katya nodded.

"Do you understand?" he repeated, slower this time.

"I understand," she said, her voice calm and cool.

"Good. Now, please tell me. What did you do with my father's medal?"

Recognition flashed across her face. Just a split-second's worth, but enough.

86
The Setup

Florida

KATYA KNEW she'd blown it by the change in Oz's eyes. Her reaction had given her secret away.

She'd have kicked herself, were she not in a trunk.

If she hadn't just woken up to waterboarding, or if she'd been given a minute to prepare, to compose herself and her thoughts, then she probably could have convincingly feigned complete ignorance. *What medal? I never met your father. You've had me chained up in a barn or locked in a trunk.*

But it was too late.

"If you give it to me, Omar won't have to go looking for it," Oz said, his tone brittle as lightbulb glass.

"I don't have it."

"If you give it to me, Omar won't have to go looking for it," Oz repeated.

Was there any reason not to tell him the truth? Katya wished she had time to think through that critical question, but she clearly didn't. The fuse feeding the powder keg of his rage was already lit. "Achilles has it. I gave it to him at the store."

"You never got within fifteen feet of him. I was there, watching most attentively."

"Watching him, not me. I slipped it from my bra to my hand, then dropped it to the ground and stepped on it while you had him burying his gun."

"You stepped on it?" he said, his tone rising.

"I meant no disrespect."

Oz studied her face.

She held his eyes, which seemed to soften a smidge.

"Did Achilles see you drop it?"

"I'm not sure."

"Did you signal?"

"Yes."

"Do you know if he got it?"

"I can't be sure."

"You better hope he got it. If somebody else did. If I can't get it back … I'm going to be very upset with you."

Katya had no doubt what that meant. Fortunately, she could answer honestly. "I think he got it. He's a very good investigator. As you've seen."

Oz pulled out his phone. He started to dial then stopped. She saw him begin working different scenarios in his mind. After a few minutes of solo back and forth, he nodded to himself. "Do you want to live?"

Katya coughed to wet her dry throat. "Yes."

"Do you want Achilles to live?"

"Yes."

"Then you need to do exactly as I say. Exactly."

"Okay."

Oz told her what he wanted. Once, twice, three times. Then he put his phone on speaker and dialed.

Achilles answered after four rings. "Hello?"

"That took too long. Who are you with?" Oz asked.

"I'm in my room, eating pizza, alone. My mouth was full, that's all." To Katya, he sounded sincere.

"If I catch you lying, she dies."

"I understand."

Oz nodded to Katya. "Achilles, did you get the object I left you?"

He took a few seconds to answer. "I have the medal."

Katya exhaled as Oz smiled. "That's good news. Have you shown it to anybody?"

"No."

"Are you sure? It's important."

"I'm locked up in a hotel room. The only person I've seen is the pizza delivery guy."

"Have you discussed it with anybody?"

"Again, I'm locked up in a hotel room. The only person I've seen is the pizza delivery guy. The police and FBI are both after me. There's a BOLO alert and a warrant for my arrest. I'm not talking to anyone."

"That's good, because Oz will trade me for it."

"When?" Achilles asked, his voice suddenly excited.

"Tomorrow. But only if you don't tell anybody about it. He says he'll know if you do. He says he has friends in local law enforcement and the FBI."

"Well then, he's better connected than I am. Are you okay?"

Katya looked at Oz.

Oz nodded.

"I'm fine. Aside from not letting me leave, Oz and Sabrina are being very nice. It's like when we visit Colin, a bit awkward but comfy enough. Don't worry about me. Don't worry about anything. Don't talk to anyone. Just wait for Oz to call and tell you the location for the exchange. That's the best way to help me."

"I understand. I love you."

"I love you, too."

Oz ended the call.

Katya wondered if she would ever talk to Achilles again—and immediately answered her own question. Of course she would. Tomorrow, when Oz set up the exchange they both knew would be a trap.

87
Things Unsaid

Florida

I LOOKED at the phone and smiled. Despite the extremely frustrating end to our encounter, it had still made me giddy. Katya was alive! And I was on the right track. My instincts were working. Psychologists would say this just set me up for a bigger blow if something went wrong, but that was nonsensical. Losing Katya would devastate me in any case.

But nothing would go wrong.

I would not let it!

Nor would Katya.

She had come through in a bigger way than I'd initially realized. That medal of merit clearly meant a lot to Oz. I could feel his panic over the phone. Sense his intense focus in the background. It was evident in his intonation and Katya's prep. Surely sentimentality was involved, but I felt certain there was more to it than that. It had to be linked to his plan. Maybe simply as an identifier, maybe in some grander way. In any case, it gave me leverage.

The call hadn't just exposed a potential vulnerability. It gave me a timeline and an avenue of attack. I had to figure out how to exploit it. And quickly. Tomorrow was only hours away.

Katya made it clear that the exchange would be a trap. I'd have assumed so in any case, but by comparing her status to visiting my brother, she'd left no doubt. Colin was dead.

I slipped out the back window of my room, which unlike the first floor wasn't barred. I jogged to the shopping center and found a hobby shop. Florida was filled with those, given the abundance of retirees.

It took only ten minutes to top off my handbasket, thanks to the shop's efficient organization. Pleased, but far from relieved, I hustled my purchases back to the room.

I cleared everything off the modest desk, and prepared to get to work. Time to replicate a Saudi medal.

I set aside the bag containing six cans of metallic blue spray paint and a contractor pack of masking tape. From another bag, I extracted a can of gold spray paint, jars of white and emerald gloss enamel, a small tub of liquid latex mold maker and a multipack of paintbrushes. After selecting an appropriate brush, I went to work using the heavy-duty flyer from a deep sea fishing tour operator as a mat.

With the help of the hotel's hair dryer and a roll of gauze, it took me about an hour to create a latex mold thick enough to handle the quick-drying epoxy clay I'd bought. I carefully filled it halfway, then added a lead washer to give it weight before topping off the epoxy.

Satisfied with my handiwork, I set the filled mold aside. I had an important phone call to make while it dried.

In between bites of cold pizza, I used a Vanilla Visa to add another app to my portable phone. A clandestine video recording app.

After shoving the end of a slice into my mouth, I used a fresh burner number to call my old friend in Reno.

"Special Agent Link."

"Oz says he has 'a friend, a good friend, a close friend, high up in the FBI.' "

"That's quite an opener."

"I thought you should know."

"I'll keep that in mind. Anything else?"

"The bombs are real. They bought detonators this afternoon."

Vic paused. "How do you know what Oz is saying and doing?"

"I caught up to them. They're holding Katya hostage. Using her unsuspicious face."

"Have you been shot?"

"What?"

"Do you need medical attention?"

"No. I'm fine."

"I've read your record, Achilles. Talked to people who know you. There's no way you would have let them get away with Katya if you'd actually caught up to them. Not without a very serious fight."

"You're right about that. But Oz was one step ahead of us. He's sewn an explosive belt around her waist."

Again Vic paused. "What can I do?"

"Sound the alarm. Put Florida on high alert. The governor is part of this, right? I bet he calls your boss on a regular basis."

"What do I tell him?"

"You tell him you have a credible threat."

"And then what? He shuts down Disney World? Closes Cape Canaveral? Evacuates Miami? You're talking like a civilian, Achilles. You know there's no magic wand. No team of stormtroopers standing by ready to swoop in and save the day. What we have are FBI, ATF and local law enforcement officers who already have burgeoning backlogs and grumbling bosses."

I wanted to mention the National Guard, but thought better of it. Vic was right. And he wasn't finished.

"Do you know how many tips the FBI gets? Have you been to the call center in West Virginia?"

"No."

"Over 2,000 tips a day. Not all are credible, of course. But if just ten percent clear the hurdle, that's still over 200 a day. As the third most populous state, about seven percent of those relate to Florida. That's fourteen credible threats on Governor Rickman's plate each and every day."

I knew all that, more or less. But this wasn't just a suspicion. It was happening. I had predicted the detonators, and now I was predicting ... what? What specifically was I predicting?

"What do you have, really?" Vic asked. "You have a jetpack company that bought the chemicals used to make rocket fuel. And you claim to have the same people buying detonators. Do you know how many tons of those chemicals are sold in the US every day? How many thousands of detonators?"

I wanted to say "By Saudis?" but didn't. I only knew that because of the medal. Oz had warned me not to mention it. He said he'd know if I did. He said he had a source within the FBI. I didn't believe him, but couldn't be sure. Certainly not enough to risk Katya's life.

It wouldn't matter anyway.

Of the 9-11 hijackers, fifteen out of nineteen had been Saudi, but we hadn't so much as slapped the King's wrist. Instead, we classified the twenty-eight pages of the official report that discussed those details. Hid them away. That staggering miscarriage of justice taught federal law enforcement that going after the largest foreign petroleum producer was a fool's errand. The lobbyists and oil interests had Saudi Arabia shielded.

"So you're not going to help me stop them?" I asked.

"Actually, I'm going to do everything I can."

"What does that include?"

"I'm not sure. Let's grab a cup of coffee and brainstorm. I'm here, in Florida."

88
Looking Backward

Florida

OZ CHECKED HIS WATCH and acknowledged that he would likely get little sleep that night. Although he'd settled into his sleeping bag hours back, he was essentially just waiting for the 2:00 a.m. alarm.

His restless mind was the culprit. It was fighting nervous tension by rehashing old points of contention.

Alfred, Lord Tennyson, had famously asserted that " 'Tis better to have loved and lost than never to have loved at all." The British poet was wrong, of course. Not surprising, given that he was a Cambridge guy. Anyone who had lost something truly important knew that it doomed you to spend the rest of your life looking backward, rather than forward. And that was no way to live.

Oz hadn't lost a love. Actually, he and Sabrina were closer than ever—because they had lost everything else.

One day they, along with Omar and Shakira, were the rich offspring of two of Saudi Arabia's most celebrated families, enjoying the kingdom's wealth and privilege without having to endure its stifling climate, religion or social norms. The next day, the four were the destitute offspring of men charged with corruption. Their fathers disgraced, jailed and robbed of all possessions. Their mothers out on the streets.

They were victims of the new crown prince's purge. Mohammad Bin Salman's audacious move to boost his wealth and consolidate power under the cloak of reform.

Who knows what would have happened to the children if they had been in Riyadh at the time, rather than abroad? Many family members of other victims simply disappeared.

Either murdered or jailed—not that there was much difference in the House of Saud.

Mentally, what happened to the two sibling couples was very clear. They'd been set on a relentless course to recoup what had been lost. The power, the prestige, the fortune.

Oz and Omar's father had been one of the most celebrated businessmen in Saudi Arabia. Founder of the Al Abdilla Advisory Group, he had interests in many industries, including leisure, tourism, education, transportation, real estate and hospitality. He served on the boards of multiple multinational corporations and international associations.

All his positions and every ounce of goodwill he'd generated vanished when he was jailed. And, in the bitterest bite of irony ever tasted, so did his fortune. About six hundred million dollars, stolen by the crown prince in the name of anti-corruption.

There was no easy climb back from that fall. For him or his family.

There was no way to request a retrial. Not that there had been one in the first place.

The family of Sabrina and Shakira had suffered a similar fate. Their father jailed, their mother disgraced, their fortune stolen.

The only way to restore the families' names, status and fortunes was through royal decree. And the only way to warrant one of those, given that the crown prince had ordered the arrests, was to win over the king himself.

How do you sway a man who has everything? There's only one way. You stroke his pride. Not an easy task, given what billionaire king's consider normal. In fact, the last man to so touch a Saudi king had done it many years ago. And he had done it with one of the most memorable acts in human history. His name was Osama bin Laden.

Of course, the king had feigned disgust in public. He had even condemned the act. But in private, he couldn't have been more pleased. More proud. His David had outsmarted and slain the West's Goliath. His warrior had initiated America's demise. Forced it to begin choking off its own lifeblood, its precious freedom, its great economic base, out of paranoia.

Oz would finish the task.

Rolling from his side onto his back, Oz reflexively reached into his left pocket, only to find it empty. The medal that the king had presented to Oz's father not once, not twice, but on three separate occasions was not where it had been for the past two years. It hadn't magically reappeared.

The medal was a symbol with strong sentimental value, for sure. A link to lost pride and status. Oz would hate to lose it.

But that wasn't his concern at the moment.

The problem was that the medal identified him as Saudi. The king would not be pleased if the upcoming event was linked not just to his country but directly to his palace. That would have the opposite of Oz's intended effect. It would enrage the king. Have him cursing the Abdilla and Saida names.

Some might speculate in any case, but there would be plenty of speculation. Fact was, there were tens of thousands of Abdillas and Saidas in the Middle East, and quite a few more in Malta. Because of their legitimate Maltese passports, their true national origins would always be in doubt—if investigators didn't have the medal.

Oz would do anything to retrieve it. To keep his dream alive.

But first, he had other business. A plan to follow. A thoroughly thought-through and meticulously prepared list to finish checking off. Beginning now.

He reached over and caressed his wife's arm. "It's time. Prepare the girl."

Florida

KATYA was already awake when Sabrina slid the key into the padlock securing the chain around her waist. Not from the noise—the fans and peeps had camouflaged those—but from the nerves. Her pre-battle nerves.

Oz had told Achilles that he would call today to arrange to swap her for the medal. It was a trap, of course. She knew that. Achilles knew that. Oz knew that. But traps could work both ways. So really, it was a battle of minds. Oz versus Achilles. Or more accurately, Oz and his three accomplices against her and Achilles.

She had to find every opportunity to help him. She had to be bold and brave while appearing meek and mild. She had to be clever and cunning while coming across as clueless and incompetent.

And she had to do it with a bomb strapped to her back.

Or neither of them would live to see the next sunrise.

She would die single, thousands of miles from both her birthplace and her home, just days into her thirty-second year, after helping Middle Eastern terrorists commit a terrible crime against the adopted country she loved.

And she wouldn't die alone. Achilles would die trying to save her. She couldn't picture that. Achilles dead. He was too virile. Too grand a force of nature. Surely he would prevail. They would prevail.

During the night, she had made one small step toward justice. She'd used the corner of the padlock at her waist to scrape a K into the corrugated steel wall. Just a single initial a few inches from the ground, but enough to identify the building even after the chickens had obliterated all other evidence.

That was how you survived life's toughest times, Achilles had once told her. You claimed little victories.

Sabrina held out a handful of clothes. Literally just a handful. A red, revealing top with a pushup bra and a pair of cutoff jeans shorts. Dangling from her middle finger, almost symbolically, were a pair of high-heeled strappy sandals. "Put these on and comb your hair."

Katya's hair was already in good form. She'd attempted to calm herself to sleep by combing it for hours. Clearly Sabrina was also a bit distracted. "Do you have an overcoat? Or perhaps a sweatshirt?" she asked Sabrina.

"The car has a heater," Sabrina replied.

As she changed, Katya noted that they'd sized her outfit just right. She hoped that was due to good guesswork on Sabrina's part and not the result of an activity undertaken while she wore a headset. That was one creepy invention.

The boxes and tarps that had formed her prison wall were now rearranged atop pallets. Twelve, she noted with some satisfaction, confirming her earlier calculation. Twelve pallets of trouble.

She followed Sabrina to the Charger and was seated up front. As Oz got in behind her, he slipped a black bag over her head. Katya didn't complain. She figured it was better than the headphones. In the back of her mind, she was worried about long-term brain damage from them. Of course, in the front of her mind, she was worried about short-term brain damage from a bullet, so the drive was hardly going to be worry free.

Katya decided to change the subject. "How far are we going?"

Oz took his time responding. "Do you want to see Achilles?"

"Very much."

"I will return you to him later today, as promised, but only if you do three jobs for me first. Three acting jobs."

That explained the outfit, she thought. All except the black bag, which clashed.

"Two will be relatively simple, one considerably more complex. Can I count on you?"

"As much as I can count on you," Katya replied.

Oz didn't pause to consider her clever quip. "Good. In about an hour, we're going to arrive at our first destination." He went on to tell her exactly what the coming task entailed, leading her to believe that this was the simple job and raising her anxiety regarding the complex one.

He concluded with a question. "Do you know what will happen if you do anything to endanger the mission?"

"You'll blow the belt, and I'll die."

"No. That's what will happen if you blow the third job. If you jeopardize this one, I'll shoot the guard. I'll have my gun on him the whole time. If his face registers alarm or he starts looking around, you'll end up splattered with his blood before he can push a panic button or pick up a phone."

Katya couldn't see Oz's eyes, given the bag over her head. But she was certain that they were burning with a zealous fire.

"Why don't you lean back and take a nap. It's going to be a long day."

She did just that, and eventually drifted into a fitful, semiconscious state.

Oz eventually roused her by pulling the bag from her head. "Two minutes. Get ready."

She returned her seat to the upright position.

Oz passed her a set of the magic headphones. As intimate as she'd been with them, this was her first opportunity to inspect a pair. It reminded her of the noise-canceling headset Achilles liked to use on airplanes. It just had a few more lights and a much heftier button.

"The on/off switch is designed for safety. You have to press it down to slide it. Please practice."

Katya did, causing the lights to come alive. She noted that the green diodes flashed for five seconds after the headset was turned off. A secondary safety feature, no doubt.

"We're almost there. Put it on."

Katya confirmed that it was off, then clenched her teeth

and complied. She found that the headset muffled sounds a bit but wasn't noise canceling. Clearly this was a different technology.

Oz slid down in the back seat.

Sabrina pulled up beside the guard hut.

Katya got out—wearing the anesthetizing headset, a sexy shirt, and an explosive belt.

90
Not the Money

Florida

KATYA didn't need to do much acting during her first job. Playing a damsel-in-distress came quite naturally at that moment, and Oz had done a good job of putting fear in her eyes. In fact, had the third-shift guard been able to read her mind, the only incongruent emotion he'd have found was surprise.

When Oz first described his mission, Katya had expected the guard booth to be attached to a government office building or a high-tech corporation. Then, as they drove deeper into Florida's dark interior, she expected it to be a hidden intelligence outpost or defense research center. But the outfit located in the midst of Florida farmland appeared to be an actual farm. Not an Old MacDonald farm, but rather a modern restaurant and grocery store supply hub. The kind of place that put truth in those *farm fresh* claims.

The squinty-eyed security guard struck her as more of a night watchman. A past-his-prime former cop or military vet supplementing a paltry pension or disability payment with an easy paycheck. The kind of guy people with a lot to lose keep on hand just in case.

The light exposing the guard's face came from below rather than above. And it flickered. Not a computer monitor, a television show.

He rose as she approached, casting crumbs from his chest onto the floor.

"Oh my god! Can you protect me? Have you heard?" Katya said, delivering her line as she pulled the earphones from her head.

The guard ducked down to see who was driving the car. Sabrina hadn't pulled up to the booth as you would when entering, but rather alongside it so the passenger door was closest. The message was clear, they'd stopped for information, not admission.

Sabrina said nothing. She just shook her head and buried her face in her hands.

When he turned back to her, Katya gave the guard an imploring look.

"Protect you from what?" he asked, eyes growing wide while darting between her face and parts further down.

"You really haven't heard? Oh my god! It's terrible." She discreetly powered the headset up with her right thumb while extending it.

He exited the booth and walked her way. Two beautiful women, obviously stressed, asking for help in the middle of the night. He, the only man for miles around.

"You've got to hear it. Please!" Katya said, jiggling her hand as a fisherman would a lure.

The guard accepted the headset, slipped it over his ears and instantly dropped to the ground.

Oz bounded out of the backseat and into the hut, a submachine gun in his hand.

Sabrina made a quick phone call, then got busy doing something on the screen.

The gate began retreating.

Katya returned to the car. She got into the back seat rather than the front and began covertly feeling around. If she found the black box, she'd snatch it and run into the neighboring field. She'd run like she'd never run before. Far and fast. She'd fly over the ground.

Katya pictured the sequence as her hands silently darted this way and that. She should remove her sandals first—they were designed for a different kind of action. And run low, so the car would shield her from Oz's gun.

The box wasn't there.

At least not on the seats or floor.

Satisfied that Sabrina was still preoccupied with her phone, Katya slipped off her shoes and used her toes to feel beneath the seats. She found nothing.

Time was running out. Katya could see lights approaching in the rearview mirror and hear the sound of trucks. She slowly slid a hand into each of the seatback pockets, careful not to alert Sabrina. Nothing there either.

"It's right here," Oz said, startling her.

Katya turned to see Oz holding up the black box. As her hope evaporated, an idea struck. "It just fell into your lap, didn't it?"

Oz met her eye and Katya knew that she was right. He knew exactly what she meant. "As Seneca the Younger said, 'Luck is the point where preparation meets opportunity.' I came to the conference to brainstorm my problems with a very inventive man. He ended up canceling on me—and gave me dinner at Cinquante Bouches in apology. The solution didn't fall into my lap. I was working it. I was primed and prepared when opportunity presented."

Katya conceded the point. The Oxford scholar had connected dots that others would never have seen. But her mind immediately moved on to the corollary. "So it wasn't for the money? You turned on Achilles and kidnapped me —for the headsets?"

"The money is nice too. But the headsets will buy something that money can't."

Katya found the courage to ask. "What's that?"

Oz smiled. "Sabrina and I want the same thing you and Achilles do, Katya. We want our old lives back."

The arrival of two trucks interrupted their conversation. One was driven by Omar, the other by Shakira.

The generic white cabs with plain white trailers thundered past them through the open gate and into the yard. Oz ran off after them, leaving Katya alone with Sabrina.

Katya glanced nervously at the diode on her belt, preparing to chase him if it turned yellow.

"It's not just our lives," Sabrina said. "It's our parents, our siblings and our children for generations to come. I wouldn't do this just for myself."

Again, Katya felt compelled to ask, even though she feared the answer. "Do what, exactly?"

Sabrina grew a distant look.

Katya waited. Eventually she concluded that Sabrina wasn't going to answer, but then her captor said, "You know, for most of human history, war was fought on a much smaller scale. It wasn't country against country, it was clan against clan. People knew what they were fighting for, back then. It was their own family, their own fortune, their own land. That made sense. It was natural. Survival of the fittest."

She stopped there, so Katya asked, "And today?"

"Today, it's all politics. The soldiers and sailors don't really have a personal stake in the matter. They're paid a minimum wage to do the politicians' bidding. More often than not, they don't really know what they're fighting for. They certainly never know the truth behind why.

"The generals and politicians pretend it's about ideals. Religion or some other flavor of righteousness. *Our way of life!* they proclaim. In the UK and America you call it democracy. But really, it's the same reason every time, every place. More money for the country, more power for the politicians—along with their patronizing individuals and organizations."

"So, what you're doing, it's not jihad?"

Sabrina smirked and said, "No. But of course, that's what everyone will assume is the motive. Even you. You, who've seen how we dress. You, who haven't seen us pray once, much less five times a day. You, who have never heard us reference the Prophet, peace be upon him." She smirked again and turned back around.

Katya was happy to have the cognitive distraction. Something to mull over besides her immediate odds of survival.

Her reprieve didn't last.

The trucks, whose engines had revved this way and that back by the loading bays, began rumbling out again. Then Oz came back into view. A moment later, he slid in beside her. His gun wasn't smoking, but his words lit her up. "Time for your next act."

91
Strange Exchange

Florida

AFTER OZ SHUT the farm distribution center's gate behind the two trucks and retrieved the headphones from the snoozing guard, Katya again found herself being driven through the balmy Florida night toward an unknown destination on an unstated mission. They drove for half an hour along rural roads without passing a single car, only to pull to the side of the road in the middle of nowhere.

Oz hadn't put the bag back on her head, probably because there was nothing to see but dark fields and night sky. As soon as Sabrina stopped, he got out, gun in hand, and grabbed two things from the trunk.

One was a second MP7.

As he handed it through the window to his wife, Katya felt the tempo of her heartbeat increase from *andante* to *vivace*.

The other was a shopping bag. Oz slid back in beside Katya and put it in her lap.

She looked inside and saw a black Adidas tracksuit. By the weight she knew there was something else underneath. She peeked and discovered matching shoes. Her first thought was that this would greatly aid her escape. All she needed to do was snatch the little black box and run.

Without getting shot.

She didn't have time for a second thought before Oz said, "Put them on, now."

He watched while she donned them over her current clothes. Once she'd laced her shoes, he pulled a flash drive from his pocket and held it up. "In a minute, you're going to be making a purchase. You don't need to verify the merchandise. You don't even need to speak. All you need to do is walk up to the leader, nod and hand over this drive. He will then verify it, and leave."

She wanted to ask *What merchandise?* but thought better of it. She'd know soon enough.

Sabrina pulled back onto the road. A few miles later, their headlights illuminated the reflectors of three parked cars. The trio was waiting in a corner lot that hadn't seen commercial use in a generation. One was a black muscle car not unlike their own. The other two had bull bars. Both were black in the front and back with white middles and gold stars with SHERIFF on the doors.

Katya's heart leapt at the sight. She braced in expectation of Sabrina hitting the gas, but instead Sabrina pulled into the lot. This caused the three cars to come alive, engines and lights.

Sabrina parked perpendicular to them so that their headlights combined to form a makeshift stage of illuminated gravel. She left the Charger's engine on.

"You're working *with* the police?" Katya asked.

"I want to remind you that this acting job is a silent part," Oz replied, adding to the mystique of the moment. "If they say something, you smile or nod or hold up the drive, whatever is appropriate. I don't want to see your mouth open. Your job is to make the payment and wait for them to leave."

Katya could do that. She got out of the car and walked into the crossbeams. It was uncomfortable to look toward the light, so she used her peripheral vision while keeping her face turned to the side.

A large man with a broad jaw and a military haircut got out of the muscle car and joined her. He, too, was wearing a tracksuit. To Katya's eye, he was obviously Russian. Maybe Ukrainian or another close neighbor, but definitely Slavic.

And definitely not a cop.

Nonetheless, if it weren't for the belt, she would have said *Save me!* Instead, she kept quiet and held up the flash drive.

The man gave her a head-to-toe-to-head appraisal, then

took the drive and returned to his car.

Katya did her best to shield her eyes from the direct light while watching him. The familiar glow of a laptop illuminated his face. A few hundred of her heartbeats later, he said, *"Vcyo normalno"* into what she assumed was a hands-free speaker. *All's good*, Russian style. Katya couldn't hear him, but his lips were easy enough to read given the heightened state of her senses.

The engines and lights of both Sheriff's cars turned off, then the driver's doors of all three cars opened. While the flash drive recipient returned her way, two equally impressive men holding handguns took seats in his car. "You have 24 hours," he said in Russian, handing her an envelope. *"Ponyatno?" Understand?*

Katya nodded. She grasped the words if not their full meaning.

The Russian returned to his car and drove off with his colleagues.

Sabrina pulled the Charger up on Katya's left.

Oz got out and snatched the envelope. He checked it, then looked inside both Sheriff's cars. Apparently satisfied with what he saw, he returned to the Dodge and opened the back door. "Get in."

She did.

They drove away.

What was going on?

92
Best Face

Florida

RUSS DUNWOODIE was only five minutes into his drive when the dreaded flashing red and blue lights appeared ahead. No way to avoid the incident without a major detour. This was the only direct route to the highway.

As he drew closer, Russ saw police officers working the scene. Correction, sheriff deputies. The uniforms were dark green with gold five-pointed stars. Their cars had matching fronts and rears, although they appeared black in the pre-dawn light.

One deputy pointed a powerful flashlight at his trailer plate, then a second used her baton lights to land him on the side of the road like she was parking a plane. As he complied, Russ saw that two other trucks had also been pulled over. At least this wasn't personal.

Russ hated these surprise checkpoints on any occasion—who didn't?—but this was especially bad timing. Today, he was in a hurry. The Miami run he made every week this time of year was by far his favorite. He had a sweet little señorita down that way who liked house calls and didn't mind the fact that he couldn't stay more than forty-five minutes.

Christ, he hoped this wouldn't take long.

Two female deputies approached the passenger side of his cab, wearing the same uniform as their male counterparts. The Latino who hung back even wore the traditional broad-brimmed hat.

Russ rolled down the window but the lead deputy, a petite blonde, went ahead and opened the door.

"It's a crime that they make you wear that necktie," he

said, trying to start on a sympathetic note. It did look ridiculous on a woman. Same flat black fabric he'd worn with his Class-A uniform many years ago. Probably Army surplus.

Despite the outfit, the deputy at his door was striking. Her expression, however, looked strained. Perhaps he'd hit on a sore note. Perhaps they were investigating a particularly nasty crime. Serial killers did like Florida.

"Sir, I need you to take an impairment test."

"Was I doing something wrong, officer?"

"It's a random stop we're conducting in conjunction with the field test of new equipment. We appreciate your cooperation." She held up a big pair of headphones.

Man, she was stunning. What was she doing working as a cop? She could earn five times as much at a club near the beach. Ten if she allowed touching.

"Will it take long? I've got a hard deadline for reaching Miami."

"Just a few minutes. The sooner we start, the sooner you'll be out of here. Please put these on and follow the audio instructions."

"You mean close my eyes and touch my nose? That kind of stuff?"

"Exactly," she said, extending the headset.

He slipped it on.

~ ~ ~

Russ shook his head, feeling a bit bewildered. He'd really zoned out.

"You're all set, Mr. Dunwoodie," the beautiful deputy said. "Thanks for cooperating. Drive safely."

Russ liked the sound of that, despite the disorientation. Cooperating with what? He didn't remember. Best to get out of there before the officer sensed that all wasn't right. "Thank you, officer."

He watched her and her fellow deputy return to their car, then checked his GPS. Looked like he'd only lost fifteen minutes. Ironically, the safety stop would force him to drive faster than usual. Still, he wouldn't be late with his delivery —or miss out on a rendezvous with his sweet little señorita. Although today it wouldn't be her face he pictured in his head.

Pulling back onto the empty rural road that connected the farm with the highway, he noted that another of their trucks had also been snared. Did law enforcement really have nothing better to do?

As he upshifted, Russ smiled to himself. At least the sheriff was putting his best face forward.

93
Tricks and Trades

Florida

AS THE SECOND of the trucks pulled back onto the road, its driver oblivious to the cargo swap, Oz dropped to his knees and raised his arms toward the rising sun. It wasn't a religious move, although he was just about ready to believe.

He'd struggled for months, attempting to figure out how to make that undetected switch happen. He'd looked into making the swap in the warehouse, but the eggs and potatoes were packed just in time. Farm fresh. He had considered bribing the truck drivers, but that tactic was way too unpredictable. And it would leave a trail. Outsiders would have knowledge of a step the police could trace.

One of the ingenious elements of his plan—one which the anesthetic headsets enabled—was cloaking the cause of the explosions. The government would not know what had exploded or how the bombs were put in place. That information gap would make his masterpiece all the more terrifying and the federal efforts to prevent a repeat that much more crippling.

"You've done it, my lion of god," Sabrina said, as if to emphasize the point.

Oz rose and embraced his wife. "We've done it, my virtuous princess."

In fact, both were well aware that they had not done it yet. But the success or failure of the plan was now out of their hands. Their soon-to-be clean hands.

"Now we just need to get away with it," Oz added.

Sabrina's face darkened a shade. "She knows very little.

You've done a good job keeping things from her."

"She knows enough."

"But she has no proof. It will just be conjecture. There will be tons of conjecture. Dozens, hundreds, maybe thousands of tips. Most of them conflicting."

Oz understood his wife. She knew why it needed to be done. Attempting to convince her of that would be pointless. What she needed was justification. Something to alleviate the guilt. "You're right. I tell you what. If Achilles shows up at the meeting as instructed and hands over my father's medal without fuss, we'll let them both walk away. But if he deceives us or tries to harm us, then—"

"They get what's coming," Sabrina said. She kissed him.

"Let's get the sheriff's cars out of sight," Oz said, breaking the embrace. "Follow me."

He walked back to the car where Katya was waiting, recovering, contemplating. *Oh, the swirl of thoughts and emotions that must be bouncing off the walls of her pretty head!*

"That was the third task. Am I done?" she asked, as he slid behind the wheel.

Oz didn't turn toward her, but put levity in his tone. "You are. Thank you. You did great."

"So let's call Achilles."

"We'll do that in just a few minutes. Meanwhile, put this on and lean your seat all the way back." He pulled the black bag from his side door pocket and passed it over.

Oz could tell that Katya was both nervous and brimming with questions. To her credit, she held her tongue and complied.

He pulled onto the road and headed toward dawn as Sabrina followed a few car lengths behind. A couple of miles later he turned left on a similar stretch of paved rural grid square, then left again five miles north.

Oz had initially intended to dig a big pit on a remote and unused piece of land. Some place with easy but rarely used access. A fire road or the like. Then he saw a news story and got a much better idea. He went online and confirmed that you could in fact ask Google to find just about anything. In this case, that thing was a map of Florida sinkholes.

The one the semitrailers were backed up to had formed when the covering land collapsed into a large underground cavern whose roof was some thirty feet down. Given the circularity of the hole up top, and the sheerness of the drop, it almost looked man-made.

Oz smiled when he saw that Omar and Shakira were already hard at work with the manual forklifts they'd dropped off in advance. Between the two trucks, they had sixty pallets to dump.

Omar had cleverly devised piers for dumping the pallets into the holes. He'd simply trapped the ends of car loading ramps under the rear tires of the trucks, securing the proximal end.

The dumping would go faster if Oz and Sabrina helped, so he turned to Katya. "Stay in the car with the bag covering your eyes. Don't give me a reason to renege on my promise."

He started to exit but then thought better of the decision. He grabbed a headset from beneath his seat and placed it over Katya's bagged ears. When she went limp instead of flinching, he knew that it worked despite the intervening cloth.

The intercepted trailers were full. Loaded with thirty pallets each. Their replacements had been full too, although only forty-eight of the pallets now en route to their scheduled destinations held the genuine article. Twelve were packed with Oz's secret recipe.

It took ninety minutes of coordinated effort to unload the two swapped trailers. The women positioned pallets at the edge of the trucks for the men, who then transported them to the edge of the pier and set them down at the tipping point before quickly withdrawing the forks.

The experience was fun in a novel sort of way, given that each participant only had to do it thirty times. As teenagers, the brothers would have had a blast playing with the forklifts and watching the cargo topple and crash. Oz wasn't so sure about the sisters, although neither complained. In any case, the exercise was a much-needed tension release.

They still had a long day ahead.

Once the last pallets had toppled and crashed, they backed the trucks off the ramps and used them for their proper purpose, first to load the forklifts, then to load the sheriff's cars. It would be safer to transport them to the drop-off point that way.

The cars were real. Somehow *borrowed* for a day by industrious Russian brokers in exchange for a five-figure fee. The uniforms were similarly acquired out the back door of a uniform supply store. *You had to love the Land of Opportunity.*

The car drop-off should be a non-event, and the truck return certainly would be. The only real work that remained before the disgraced Saudi Arabian sons and daughters boarded planes in Orlando was retrieving the Order of Abdulaziz Al Saud.

That wouldn't be a problem either.

Not with his hostage wearing an explosive belt—and the clever trick Oz had planned.

KATYA FELT the world coming back into focus. Her head was bagged, her wrists bound, her body reclined on a cot. Her ears, however, were not muffled or plugged.

She almost wished they were.

Katya realized that she'd never again hear Arabic without cringing.

All four familiar voices were active. Oz, Sabrina, Omar and Shakira all sounded excited. Not panicked but celebratory!

She'd pieced together what they were celebrating—just not exactly why.

They had switched out the trailers on two of the farm's delivery trucks. Because of the headsets, the drivers were completely unaware. And because the substituted trailers were the real ones, stolen from the loading bays the night before beneath the nose of a similarly oblivious guard, there would be no lasting physical evidence of the exchange.

The intent was clear. To make an investigative trail go cold. But her captors' overall objective remained a mystery. Beyond giving the recipients some really bad produce.

As she listened to the irksome banter, a fifth voice chimed in. A new voice. One she hadn't heard before. She pictured a mature man but couldn't be sure. It was such a different language that Katya doubted her ability to decipher age cues.

Glasses clinked a second later, tea mugs she guessed, and then the new voice spoke two English words she'd heard before. *Tranquility* and *serenity*.

Why say them in English?

Surely there were Arabic words for those sentiments?

Perhaps they were Americanizing an Islamic prayer? Or custom? Or curse? Could that be what you said at a Muslim funeral?

She heard the mugs go down and the party rise. A moment later, the bag was pulled off her head.

Oz was standing over her, an open laptop in his hand. They were right outside her chicken barn, which she now saw was one of four on the farm. A few feet off to the side was the teapot-and-folding-chair arrangement that had earlier been inside. The implication was clear. All evidence of Oz's operation and her captivity had already been obliterated—by tens of thousands of chickens.

Except her scratch mark.

"Are you ready to call Achilles?" he asked.

She sat up and pivoted her feet to the ground. "Yes. Of course."

"Good." Oz pulled a phone from his back pocket and sat next to her on the cot. "Just watch what you say. It's definitely not too late for you to blow it. Or me to blow it, if you know what I mean."

She'd have grasped a much more subtle hint than that. It was difficult to think about much else when you had a bomb strapped to your back. "I understand."

Oz hit DIAL and handed her the phone as it started to ring.

"Kyle Achilles."

"It's so good to hear your voice. I'm fine. I can't wait to see you. I keep thinking about that question you almost asked me."

"Me too. I was a fool to wait so long."

"That's enough!" Oz said, taking the phone as Omar stepped up and put a gun to her head. "I trust that satisfies your need to know that she's all right. Now, if you want her to remain that way, you'll do exactly as I say. Take I-95 to 714 and head inland. Should take you about twenty minutes. Then—"

"No!"

"What did you say?"

"We're going to do the exchange on a beach. A public beach. In our bathing suits. Just the four of us."

"If you want to see—"

Achilles cut Oz off again. "If you're sincerely interested in exchanging the detonator box for the medal, then you'll have no problem with this plan. Not if you get to pick the beach. Which you do."

Katya desperately wanted to warn Achilles about Omar and Shakira, but she literally had a gun to her head.

As Oz contemplated the offer, she found herself praying that Achilles had anticipated additional team members. The possibility that after the exchange a third party would simply gun the two of them down. But even if he had, how could he stop that? Were they going to dive into the ocean?

"We don't have bathing suits," Oz said, delaying while he consulted his laptop screen. It showed a map with a blinking red dot. The location of Achilles' phone, no doubt.

Oz panned the map out.

"They sell bathing suits on every street corner around here," Achilles said. "Just be sure to grab the spandex kind. No pockets."

"If you alert law enforcement, it's over. We'll be watching and listening. I want to be very clear about that. I want to be absolutely certain that you don't underestimate my abilities in those regards."

"I'm coming alone."

"I'll call you shortly with the name of the beach. Be ready to leave." Oz hung up.

At first, Katya was encouraged that Oz agreed. It indicated that he was sincere about the trade. But then she factored in what she'd learned about him. The way he thought things through thoroughly enough to create a seamless cascade. One planned outcome following the other as if compelled by gravity. The detonator buy. The midnight truck exchange. The roadside swap. All completely undetected. And those were just the three operations she knew about.

This was a guy who had used a chicken coop for his base

of operations knowing nobody would think to look there and he'd leave no trace behind. This was a man creative enough to control his hostage with an explosive belt.

And yet he'd only spent a few seconds analyzing Achilles' offer. An offer which altered a critical element of a crucial exchange. There was just one explanation for that. He'd considered various geographies in advance and was prepared to adapt accordingly.

Her only hope was that Achilles had done the same—and then calculated one step further ahead.

95
Second Guessing

Florida

EVEN THOUGH I KNEW that second-guessing an operation after committing to it could be deadly, I found myself questioning one earlier decision. Declining Vic's offer to meet. It would have been very nice to have a wingman while heading to the beach.

I was pretty sure that I'd won Vic over. But I'd declined his offer because I was equally sure that he'd arrest me nonetheless. Bottom line: I simply couldn't risk getting locked up before Katya was safe and secure.

Still, at that moment, I'd have welcomed some backup.

As it stood, I was betting everything on my ability to outthink the competition. That wasn't purely a question of IQ, of course. It was more a combination of experience and logic. Very much like chess. Was it arrogant? Yes. Dangerous? Definitely. But I'd come closer to catching Oz and Sabrina than the FBI.

Part of the reason was that I knew my opponent. Not deeply, but intimately. We'd survived a very traumatic time together. I had a feel for how his mind worked. I knew Oz to be brave, calculating and rational, if misguided.

On that note, I still didn't know exactly what he was up to or why. I didn't believe that he and Sabrina were radicalized Islamic extremists. They just weren't religious enough. They hadn't performed *salah* once while we were locked away in the bunker. Although it was possible that Trey's accusations had deterred them, I didn't get the sense that either Oz or Sabrina felt repressed in that regard. And I wouldn't expect an extremist to cower in any case.

With religion out of contention, I was left with more traditional motives for Oz's crimes. I felt good about my ability to take logical account of those—and prepare accordingly.

My phone rang.

"Yes?"

"Stuart Beach. Got that? Stuart Beach. Should take you twenty minutes. See that it doesn't take twenty-one." Oz hung up.

I had the map ready, so I knew in an instant which way to head. And I wasn't in my room. I was poised near a set of freeway on-ramps in my now metallic-blue car. This was a risky move. Oz might continue to watch 'me' on the map and 'I' wouldn't be moving. But I figured he'd be otherwise occupied, and besides, there would be reasonable doubt that in my excitement I'd forgotten my phone.

The upside of the head start and 'forgetting my phone' was that it gave me a few minutes for reconnaissance. To get the layout, I zoomed in the satellite image while driving. The beach named after Stuart was miles long with a single, large public parking lot that was separated from the water and sand by a dense band of palm-trees and other tropical vegetation. Expensive houses rested to the north of the park proper. Hotels and condos to the south. None above five stories in height.

That was very good news. No obvious place to put a sniper or easy place to be one. I say *obvious*, bearing in mind that Oz was scrambling too. And *easy* meaning beaches were tough places for distance shots, given the shifting air currents. You needed time to study the patterns and dial them in.

Nonetheless, I prayed that a stiff but unsteady breeze would be blowing.

Driving slowly along the back row of the beach's parking lot, fifty yards from the few cars there at that off hour, I spotted a suspicious character standing in the doorway of a sun-faded BMW 5-series. His hands were hidden and he was looking toward the beach.

As I slowed, the beachgoer bounced a bit, or more

accurately shook. My spirits sunk as I recognized a move I'd seen a million times.

Once his hands freed up from his fly, the driver then used his left to shut the door and his right to lock the car. He stashed the key atop the rear tire and walked casually toward the shore.

Disappointed, I continued cruising the parking lot disguised only by sunglasses and a baseball hat, looking for a black Dodge Charger and people who didn't appear interested in improving their suntans. I spotted neither.

That surprised me a bit.

It concerned me a bit more.

This was one of those circumstances when predictability meant the difference between life and death.

Either Oz and company had switched cars or they'd parked and walked or they'd been dropped off by a driver who was waiting nearby.

My guess was the last.

To spot a driver waiting on either of the adjacent properties, I'd have to go back out onto A1A, as the park had its own exit. I didn't have time for that.

Frustrated, but not defeated, I parked for a quick exit—in case I had to race to the nearest hospital emergency room. Those, I'd already mapped out.

I hid the key between the back seat cushions, and tested to be sure that the ignition wouldn't start. Satisfied, I removed my hat and shirt, fiddled with my phone, and got out of the car.

In one hand, I held my cell phone. In the other, my replica medal. It had turned out quite nicely. All those hours spent painting model planes and soldiers as a child had finally paid off. Oz would realize my handiwork was fake once he got ahold of it, but not before.

Knowing that the parking lot would be the easiest place to take me out, I ran for the beach. Fast and hard but not so emphatically as to arrive short of breath.

I spotted my targets almost instantly. They were a couple of hundred yards to the north.

Late morning on a weekday was not a crowded time for

most local beaches, and Stuart was no exception. Up that way, near the multimillion-dollar homes, they were practically alone. Three figures. Two darker skinned and one dearly beloved.

Time for the most important meeting of my life.

96
The Unexpected

Twenty Minutes Earlier
Florida

FOR WHAT WOULD BE her last ride as a captive—come what might—Katya was back in her damsel-in-distress uniform. Sitting sandwiched between Oz and Sabrina in the back seat of the Charger, nervously stroking the explosive belt, she prayed the revealing red top would still be adjacent to her cutoff jeans in an hour.

Her captors actually did buy bathing suits, changing in the curtained corner of a surf shop while Omar and Shakira watched over her.

As Oz and Sabrina returned to the car, Katya couldn't help but note that they made a very attractive couple. So lean, fit and energetic. She with flowing dark hair and he with glowing dark eyes. What did they need that they didn't already have? What troubled them enough to kill for? After her talk with Sabrina, Katya knew it was nothing spiritual.

Up front, with an ominous big backpack snugged between them, Omar and Shakira were wearing casual clothes. Where would they be during the exchange? More importantly, what would they be doing? Katya had struggled to divine some clue to that question, to discern some hint or innuendo, but with the clock nearly run out, she had exactly nothing.

The Charger's trunk was full. Katya could tell by the way it rode. Probably not an anesthetized body this time. Probably the suitcases she'd seen in the barn. This had the feel of being their last stop.

It certainly would be hers.

They pulled into the public parking lot for Stuart Beach, a county park. Omar stopped the car at the trailhead, next to the handicapped spots.

Oz, Sabrina and Katya got out.

No one was around.

Oz hopped on the phone, presumably to call Achilles. "Stuart Beach. Got that? Stuart Beach. Should take you twenty minutes. See that it doesn't take twenty-one."

Oz hung up and spoke to Omar in Arabic through the open window. Although Katya was dying to know what they were saying, she couldn't grasp a single word.

Omar then handed Oz a black box and a silver key. The objects that had been the subjects of Katya's nightmares and dreams. At least that was a good sign.

The Charger drove off, and the three former bunker inmates started toward the sand.

Oz held a cell phone in one hand and the little black box in the other. Sabrina held nothing. Katya too, held nothing. But she was wearing the belt.

So what was Oz's plan? Katya tried to pierce the veil of the presented scenario as they walked toward the water, but couldn't come up with anything beyond the obvious. Technically, he was complying with the rules of the exchange.

Katya began to get her hopes up that he really was honorable. Misguided and extreme, but a man of his word. She desperately wanted to believe it.

There was plenty of supporting evidence. His behavior in the bunker. The fact that he hadn't been unnecessarily cruel. Their intellectual discussions.

But she didn't truly believe it.

Oz was clearly obsessed with secrecy. And both she and Achilles were loose ends.

They walked north, away from the already sparsely populated sand near the trail, toward the virtually abandoned stretch fronting lavish and widely spaced private residences.

Oz stopped at a place near no one and no structure, a blind spot as it were. The three of them turned to look back toward their tracks and waited for Achilles.

They didn't speak. They just breathed and baked and watched.

And then he came. Running.

Katya's heart filled with love and pride as she saw the athletic figure bounding effortlessly toward them across the sand. Was that his plan? Just run and tackle Oz, crushing him like a tick beneath the tire of a sports car?

"That's close enough!" Oz called, holding up the box, the key clasped between the first joints of two fingers, his thumb poised atop the red rocker.

Achilles slowed but kept walking, his eyes active as windshield wipers during a downpour. He held a cell phone in his left hand. His right fist was clenched.

"Are you okay?" he asked her, stopping just six feet out.

"Careful!" Oz warned. "Don't blow it."

"Same as last time," Katya replied.

"Show me the medal," Oz said.

Achilles raised his right hand and produced the gold bauble like a magician with a coin.

Oz smiled and handed Sabrina his cell phone, freeing a hand. "A fair exchange. My treasure for yours." He took a step forward with the box and key extended like a handshake. His thumb still on the toggle.

Achilles mirrored his pose with the medal, then closed the gap.

"First the medal," Oz said. "You're bigger than I am."

Katya expected Achilles to object, but he raised his hand like a man about to play a winning card.

Picking up on the air of confidence, Oz cautiously raised

his black box back out of reach before extending his open palm.

Achilles slapped the medal down. He left his palm atop Oz's, sandwiching the precious trinket between their grips.

He met Oz's eyes.

The two stood that way, staring silently at each other for what felt like forever, while Katya barely breathed. Then, faster than Katya could comprehend, Achilles somehow whipped Oz around. Before she knew it, Oz's back was to Achilles' chest and Achilles' back was to the ocean. Achilles had the medal-holding hands pinned between their bodies and the black box-holding hands clamped against Oz's heart.

Katya screamed.

Sabrina screamed.

Oz yelled, "What are you doing? Are you crazy?"

97
Black Box

Florida

KATYA ALMOST SHOUTED the same questions as Oz. Was Achilles crazy? Had the stress finally broken him? Had the threat to her so twisted his heart that it cut off the blood to his brain?

Surely not.

Surely he was somehow, some way, a single invisible, inconceivable, unbeatable step ahead.

If only she could rotate the belt. Then she wouldn't be stuck standing there like a dumbstruck damsel-in-distress. Then she could pounce on Sabrina and press the bomb to her spine. But in that regard, Oz was one step ahead—thanks to the superglue.

"Your plan failed," Achilles growled.

Oz said, "Release me immediately, and I'll let her live. Don't make me press the toggle. Her blood will be on your hands."

"Go ahead," Achilles said. "Expose your last card."

"No!" Katya said. "Don't! Achilles, what are you doing? I don't trust them either, but I know the box works."

Achilles didn't look at her. He kept his gaze on the bordering vegetation. "How many of them are there?"

Katya answered, "Two. Oz's brother and Sabrina's sister."

Achilles smiled, as if that made sense. As if it somehow vindicated a core conclusion. "What kind of guns do they have?"

"The kind that fit in a backpack, I think."

"You haven't seen a long gun?"

"No."

Achilles looked at Sabrina long enough to issue a command. "Call them. Tell them to come here. With their guns still in the backpack."

"Enough!" Oz said. "I'm going to count down from three, then I'm going to turn Katya's spine into shrapnel. Then my gunmen are going to come out here and escort us safely away while you wail and mourn over the two halves of her bloody corpse."

Katya couldn't believe she was actually living the nightmare. The literal countdown to the end of her life. With Achilles standing by.

He wouldn't even look at her. His eyes were back on the trees bordering the beach.

She turned toward Sabrina, who wore a similarly surprised expression. As their eyes met, Sabrina shook her head.

"Three!" Oz said.

"You were very insistent that I tell no one about the medal," Achilles said, his voice and gaze unwavering. "You had to, of course, but that was what did it."

"Did what?" Oz asked, voicing Katya's question.

"Convinced me that you'd never let me get away. There was no way I could unsee it."

Oz rolled his eyes. "It's not a question of seeing. It's a question of having. That medal has great sentimental value to my family. Receiving it was a great honor."

"All true, I'm sure. But you wouldn't risk everything to reclaim it. Unless it could ruin everything. Your whole plan."

"That's ridiculous. It's just a piece of metal. Precious metal. Symbolic metal. But metal nonetheless."

"Yes, with a serial number. A traceable history. It identifies the recipient. It also marks you as Saudi Arabian, not Maltese."

"Enough games," Oz said, turning red. "Two!"

"So I asked myself, what foolproof means could you conjure up to ensure that I died with your secret? Your first thought was probably to lure me into a trap. A kill box. The crosshairs of a sniper rifle. But you knew I'd anticipate that. And you knew Katya would try to tip me off. So what was left? What clever trick? What sneaky deception?"

"I don't know what you're talking about," Oz proclaimed.

But Katya saw that he did, and her stomach relaxed a little.

Then Achilles revealed the conclusion that made everything clear. All his actions up to that point. "The box I'm pressing against your heart. It's not *the* black box. It's a second bomb."

Katya felt the muscles around her eyes and jaw slacken. She saw that Sabrina, too, was completely surprised.

"So here's what we're going to do," Achilles continued. "Sabrina is going to call your siblings here, with their guns in their bag. They're going to set the bag down. Then Sabrina is going to remove the real black box and set it on the ground. Then one of them will take the bag to the parking lot while the other disarms the bombs. Which one is the technician?"

"The brother," Katya said.

"I think not," Oz hissed. "Best they come here with their guns in their hands. It's a bit more messy, but you still lose. You might snap my neck, you might not, but Katya will surely die."

Achilles ignored the protest. "Once the five of us are alone with no guns present, and Katya is freed from the belt, then I'll tell Sabrina where her sister can find the medal. When she reports having it in her hands, you walk away."

Katya immediately grasped the logic of splitting them up that way. It created balance. If Achilles were to attack Oz and Omar while she grappled with Sabrina, Shakira would come running with the guns. That was the Saudis' safeguard. On the other hand, if the Saudis tried to renege, she and Achilles could run away faster than Shakira could bring her guns to bear. That was their safeguard.

What Katya didn't get was the talk about finding the medal. It was in Oz's hand.

Oz smiled. He'd clearly reached the same conclusion. "Nice try, but they already know where to find the medal. They've been watching us through binoculars. They know it's in my left hand."

Achilles powered Oz's left hand around in front of his face, then slid his grip down onto Oz's wrist. "Is it?"

Oz stared at the object now exposed in his hand. "A fake!"

"Do we have a deal?"

98
Just In Time

Florida

STARING DOWN AT THE DUPLICATE, Oz almost laughed through his tears at the irony. Beaten at his own game. Outmaneuvered with a swap *he* hadn't seen coming.

Now it was Shakira running to the parking lot, rather than him and Sabrina.

Soon Omar would be disarming his little black boxes, rather than triggering them.

Then Achilles and Katya would walk away, rather than being blown away.

Was there nothing Oz could do to stop it? No trick he could pull? No force he could apply? *Think, Osama. Think!*

Omar approached, tool bag in hand, somehow looking simultaneously defiant and defeated.

"I'm in the parking lot," Shakira reported over the speaker on Sabrina's phone. "Where do I go?"

Achilles, who still had the black box pressed to Oz's chest, ignored Shakira's question. "Have Omar disarm the bombs."

Oz strained his brain in search of leverage, but found none. It wasn't just the bombs in play, it was Achilles' superior strength. Oz said, "Omar will disarm Katya's belt with the key, then you tell Shakira where the medal is. Once she has it in her hand, Omar will remove the belt without tripping the booby traps. Agreed?"

Achilles said, "Agreed."

Omar opened his bag and extracted a silver key, some wire cutters, and a big pair of scissors.

Ten minutes later, Oz and his team were back in the

Charger, with both the real and fake medals in his hands.

Oz could live with the fact that he'd lost a battle but won the war. Yes, his pride was stung and swollen from having been outmaneuvered. Yes, the fact that he would be leaving the country while Achilles and Katya were breathing was unfortunate.

But his plan would still succeed.

Unfortunately, the Americans would now know what had caused the explosions and how the bombs had been planted. That knowledge would assuage the terror and blunt the economic impact.

But the King would be thrilled.

Sensing his internal struggle, Sabrina put her hand on his leg.

"What now?" Omar asked, as they exited the guest parking lot of a neighboring condominium complex.

"No change. The airport in Orlando," Oz replied.

Omar hit the gas.

"So we're okay with them alive?" Shakira asked.

"We're fine," Oz replied. "Without the medal, Achilles has no proof. That leaves the FBI with two options. Either they choose to believe him, and in so doing, admit their own failure. Or they choose to blame him, and claim to have swiftly delivered justice. Which do you think they'll pick?"

Nobody answered aloud, but three heads nodded. They understood organizational politics.

"If they go with option one," Oz continued, "the kingdom's defenders will just go into overdrive. The lawyers and lobbyists and oil execs will work the boys' clubs and back rooms, exactly as they did the last time. Without proof, even the FBI can be drowned out."

"We learned that from 9-11," Omar added.

"Exactly."

"What about Uncle Asim?" Shakira asked.

That was a bit trickier question. A complication. On the one hand, if the farmer disappeared this very day without having made any arrangements, it would give credence to Katya's captivity story. It was what lawyers would call a strong supporting detail. That would be worse for them. On the other hand, if Asim stayed, he would now certainly be picked up. That would be worse for him. And then them— if Asim talked.

Sabrina turned and stared at Oz with fire in her eyes. "Yes, what did you have planned for Asim if we let Katya and Achilles go?"

"It's no problem," Oz said without missing a beat. "We'll have Asim meet us at the plane."

Oz had paid an old family acquaintance handsomely in cryptocurrency to use his corporate jet to fly them from Orlando to Barcelona. Oz had considered hitting the Caribbean, which was much closer, either as a stepping stone or a temporary hideout. But he decided that a half measure would be too risky. Islands were scarcely populated. Word would get around, and then they'd be easy to find.

Barcelona, by contrast, was a huge nexus. A hub for Europe, the Mediterranean, and Africa. And it was as international as cities came. They could easily blend in. And it was only an eight-hour flight away. They'd be on the ground before dawn tomorrow.

Sabrina relaxed at his reply.

As Shakira called Asim with the urgent news, Oz turned his attention to rubbing sticky gunk off his father's medal. Achilles had duct-taped it under the cover of the fuse box beneath his repainted car's hood. Oz would have liked to duct-tape Achilles to a car engine and watch him roast. Since that was now unlikely, he'd have to settle for watching thousands of other Americans burn.

Oz checked his watch. Just under four hours.

"How long to the airport?" Sabrina asked.

"Two hours," Omar and Oz replied in tandem. "We'll be airborne just in time."

99
Tight Connections

Florida

I HUGGED KATYA like no man had ever hugged a woman before. I wrapped my arms around her so completely and tightly that I half expected the water within us to merge like two pools, bringing the rest of our bodies along.

Her tears started flowing the instant the key turned in the black box, extinguishing the diode on her belt. I could only imagine what that horror had been like. Living day and night with a guillotine ever hovering over your head.

Then Oz's older brother went to work removing the belt. I had half a mind to snap every one of his fingers when I saw that he'd glued the burlap to her flesh. But I kept both my control and my focus on target.

Once all that remained on Katya's waist was a ring of coarse fabric, I had Omar disarm both bombs. He only had wire cutters and a big pair of scissors, but he made do. Clearly, the Saudi expat was good with his evil little hands.

Removing the detonators was important. I wanted the bombs as evidence, not necessarily against Oz, but in support of my story. And I didn't want to be carrying armed explosives around. I noted that the detonators were homemade. Good enough for Katya's belt, but obviously Oz hadn't considered them sufficiently sophisticated or reliable for his big project.

Whatever that was.

By my reckoning, we only had hours, maybe minutes to figure that out.

As soon as we released our embrace, I unlocked my

phone with a special triple-tap and nervously checked the clandestine recording app. Since the screen remained lifeless, there was no way to tell if it was actually recording. That was the point.

It had.

I checked the first frames. Me in the car. I checked the last frames. Me unlocking the phone, just seconds ago.

"What's that?" Katya asked.

"A video of everything that just happened. I hope." I panned through the mini display at the bottom while Katya looked over my shoulder.

"You did a good job of capturing faces, all things considered," she said. "I had no idea you were recording."

"The trick was holding the phone in the same hand I used to press the box to Oz's chest. With that setup, keeping the camera on the action was easy."

Satisfied with what I'd seen, I started the process of sending the video to the server in the cloud. That would take time, given its size.

With the upload underway, I hit Katya with the big question. "Do you know what their intentions are? What they're planning to blow up?"

She shook her head, frustration apparent. "Only bits and pieces. I've been trying to figure it out. They secretly swapped the trailers of two semitrucks. Both from some farm."

"Which farm?"

"I don't know. I only saw it from the road."

"Do you know how to get there?"

"I'm sorry. Oz kept a bag over my head."

"No need to apologize. We'll find some way to figure out where they're going."

I'd considered insisting that Oz tell me his plan, but quickly discarded the notion. Ours was already a high-wire negotiation. No sense turning it into a wrestling match as well. Since possession of the medal was what gave me balance, and the medal only mattered to Oz in conjunction with his plan, it was too big a risk. Besides, knowing what a planner he was, I had no doubt that Oz would have a convincing fake story prepared.

Katya cocked her head. "One driver mentioned he was headed to Miami."

"You spoke to the drivers?"

"On a script. Sabrina was right behind me with her face hidden beneath a hat. And Oz was listening on the phone. But one driver just happened to mention his destination because he was in a hurry and it was a ways to go."

"That's good. Did he give any indication where in Miami?"

"No. He just said, 'I've got a hard deadline for reaching Miami.'"

Katya went on to describe the roadside stop and how Oz had made use of the headphones.

"So no clues from the other driver?"

"Nothing."

"Any clues where Oz is going now?"

"They're leaving the country."

"How do you know?"

"I don't know for certain, but I believe they cleaned out their hideout and loaded their suitcases into the trunk."

That confirmed the urgency.

I checked my phone. The video upload was complete. I copied the download link and texted it to Vic. Then, while Katya and I walked the beach hand in hand, I called the FBI ASAC on the phone.

"Special Agent Link."

"Vic. It's your white knight calling. Did you get my text?"

"I saw a text from a number I didn't recognize. I'm in a meeting, so I didn't open it."

"It's a video of Oz and Sabrina and their two co-conspirators. Their siblings, Omar and Shakira. It was taken just minutes ago on Stuart Beach, Florida. I think they're on their way to an airport right now."

"Which airport?"

My phone started beeping. "My battery is dying. I don't know which airport. International for sure. Stuart Beach is midway between Cape Canaveral and Miami. Could be Miami, Fort Lauderdale or Orlando. Maybe even Tampa.

But in any case, my money is on a private flight."

"Why?"

"Because they have ninety-two million dollars, and want to fly below the radar."

"Anything else?"

"Yes. That threat you refused to prioritize, it's going to be happening today in Miami. Actually, there will be two incidents. One in Miami and one someplace else. Or maybe two in Miami. I'm going to work on figuring that out. You need to get teams in place at all of Florida's international airports, including those with puddle jumpers to the islands. The video is all the justification you'll need, and it has—" My phone died.

"—their pictures," I said to myself.

Florida

KATYA KNEW that if she lived to be a hundred, she'd never again feel as relieved as she did at that moment. She was back with Achilles, away from her captors and free of the belt. At least the explosive part. She still had a ring of burlap stuck to her skin. She couldn't keep her fingers off it.

"Give me two minutes," she said to Achilles, before kissing him quickly on the lips and running into the ocean.

The water was cool but far from freezing. It felt fantastic. Much better than the barn hose. She dove in to rinse her hair and swam underwater for as long as her breath held out.

Standing waist deep in the wavy water, she began working the burlap, gently at first, then with more gusto. She wanted it off. Needed it off. The cold helped to numb her skin and the salt water would cleanse the wound, right? She didn't really care. Not at that moment.

It didn't take too long, even though Omar had reapplied the glue only hours before. Where there's a will, there's a way. She emerged from the ocean feeling spiritually cleansed.

Achilles had no shirt to dry her with, but he wrapped her in another tight hug and ran his hands over her body.

"I'm okay," she said, looking at him and then her waist. "Fantastic even." There was a bit of blood, but mostly just angry pink skin. She was fine with that.

"This may sound like an odd question, but did you hear any talk of eggs and potatoes? Or see any?" Achilles asked.

"The only farm product I saw was chickens. Tens of

thousands of chickens. That's where they lived and kept me prisoner. A gigantic chicken barn with big fans at each end. But I did see lots of worktables and evidence of flat brown and enamel white paint."

"What's the relevance?" he asked.

"Eggs are enamel white. And potatoes are flat brown."

Achilles closed his eyes and threw back his head. "Of course! How did I miss that?"

"What do you mean?"

"Personal Propulsion Systems bought a bunch of paint. The receipt didn't say which colors, but I should have made the connection."

"Explosive eggs and potatoes fits everything I know," Katya said. "Does that help us catch them?"

"It will help us find the bombs once we know the target, but Miami is too big to be helpful. They have everything. A major airport. Sports stadiums. Luxury hotels. High-rise residences. Office towers. Concert halls. Colleges and universities. We tell Vic eggs and potatoes in Miami and he's got nothing."

"So what do we do? Should we drive around looking for the farm? See where they sent trucks?"

"How closely can you estimate the location? Can you find it in the next hour?"

"Probably not."

"Then we need another way. A second data point. Did you hear any talk of Cape Canaveral? Or Disney?"

"No, but they always spoke Arabic."

"Locations would sound the same."

Achilles was right, but that wasn't helpful. She hadn't—

"The only English words I heard were *serenity* and *tranquility*. They repeated those several times on different days."

Achilles perked up. "What was the context?"

"It was during some excited discussions, but I don't know more than that."

"Those are both spiritual words. Could it have been part of a prayer?"

"Why use English words then?" Katya asked. "Surely there are Arabic equivalents."

Achilles cocked his jaw. "Could those be proper names? Maybe religious retreats?"

"The Serenity Center and the Tranquility Center," Katya said, trying the idea on for size. "That could be it. Targeting a specific religious group certainly fits the terrorist mold. We should Google it."

"Agreed. But my phone died."

"Do you have a charger in the car?"

Achilles shook his head as his mind worked the puzzle. "They would have to be huge retreats, right? We're talking tons of eggs and potatoes."

"Twelve pallets worth," Katya confirmed. "And probably a lot more than that. I'm thinking the explosive pallets were mixed in with regular ones. Otherwise, the two trucks would have been far from full."

"That approach would also add camouflage. Good point. Who needs that big a shipment of eggs and potatoes? All at once?"

"The Army needs enough to feed an army?" Katya suggested. "Is there an army base in Miami?"

Achilles abruptly stopped walking and started looking around. Clearly excited, he quickly spotted what he wanted, said, "Follow me," and took off running.

Katya sprinted after him toward two people lounging on the sand. Big guys in their early twenties.

Achilles reached them first and said something she couldn't hear. She didn't catch their reply either, but their body language wasn't encouraging. "I just need it for a minute," Achilles said as she caught up.

"It's almost halftime," the closer guy said.

Achilles wanted their phone.

"It's really important and urgent," Achilles said. "Look, commercial," he added, pointing at the screen.

"One minute," the guy stood and handed Achilles his phone.

"Siri, where is the ship tranquility."

Siri thought. "Here's what I found. Does that look good?"

Katya couldn't see the screen.

Achilles said, "Siri, where is the *Tranquility of the Seas?*"

"I'm sorry, I don't know that location."

"Siri, where is the cruise ship the *Tranquility of the Seas?*"

"I'm sorry, I don't know that location."

"Okay, guy," the phone's owner said, holding out a beefy hand, palm up. "You can plan your cruise later, on your own phone."

"Siri, what cruise ships are in Miami, Florida, today."

"Okay, here's what I found."

Katya watched with great anticipation as Achilles clicked a link to cruisecal.com. *Could it be that simple?* An alphabetized spreadsheet of cruise ships popped up, listing their current port and arrival and departure times.

The other college football fan stood and waded in close. "Dude!"

Achilles began scrolling the list, zooming in when he reached S. "*The Serenity of the Seas* departs Miami at four p.m. today."

"And the Tranquility?" Katya asked.

"Departs Port Canaveral, also at four p.m."

101
The Split

Florida

AS ACHILLES CHECKED HIS WATCH, the phone's owner snatched his property back. The football fans were amped up now too, but in a very different way, twitching their shoulders and leaning in. Katya was pleased to see Achilles deflate them with a simple "Thanks a lot," before turning her way. The boys had no idea.

"We can still stop them," Achilles said with a determined look she knew well. He grabbed her hand and began jogging toward the parking lot.

"We?" Katya asked. "We should call the police."

Achilles looked her way but didn't slow. "I went through the whole Tip Line discussion with the FBI yesterday. It's like going to the DMV. They're inundated and understaffed."

Katya found that hard to believe. "But we've got details!"

"So do the paranoid, schizophrenic and deranged. We'll sound exactly like a thousand other calls they get each day when we start talking of exploding eggs."

"Thousand other calls?"

"The FBI Tip Line gets over two thousand a day. I'm guessing half are from nut jobs."

Katya felt foolish. She'd made the mistake of confusing life with a television show. The real world revolved around overworked, underpaid people on the ground who were directed by politically motivated superiors and bogged down by bureaucracy.

"There's another reason not to make a call, and that's Oz."

"I don't follow."

"Think about all his planning. It's been meticulous."

Katya thought back to her hostage situation. The headphones, the blindfolds, the padlock, the belt. The chicken farm, the sheriff's cars, the uniforms, the black box. "No doubt about that. But so what?"

"He might not risk the chance that his hopes, dreams and hard work all get flushed by a phone call."

"How could he prevent it?"

"Easily enough, given that most of the passengers will soon be aboard. He could send someone to both ports with instructions to blow the bombs if the ships begin an evacuation."

"Which is exactly what would happen if the port authorities believe a phoned-in bomb threat."

Achilles nodded grimly as the severity of their situation descended upon her. "No doubt his scouts will be tuned to the police band on the radio as well."

"Couldn't the police just jam the signal?"

"Even if they knew the proper wavelength, which they don't, that's much easier said than done, especially in a place as wired as a military installation. And there's always the chance of a passive trigger. One that goes off if the signal is broken."

"That's what they put on my belt," Katya said. "So what do we do?"

"We drive to the cruise ships and make the case in person. We ask to see the head of security and then we present him with the details—including our concern that evacuation will trigger the explosion. Since we know where the bombs are, they can work to disarm them without alerting Oz's observers."

"Makes sense, but which one do we pick? Which is closer, Miami or Port Canaveral?"

"They're both about two hours away. One north, one south. We have three hours before the ships depart. I think we should hit both."

Katya was more than a little shaken from her recent experience, but still quite capable of basic math. They couldn't— "You want us to split up?"

"I don't want us to split up. I don't want to ever let you out of my sight again. But we double our chances of reaching someone reasonable that way. Who knows what we'll run into in Miami or Port Canaveral. Best to try both."

He led her to a metallic blue car with an uneven paint job. "You painted the white car?"

Achilles opened the rear door and pulled the key from between the cushions. Then he grabbed his wallet from beneath a floor mat. "Here's a Visa card for gas, if you need it. The car has a full tank. The road we're on goes to the highway. Just turn south toward Miami and follow the signs to the cruise terminal. At the cruise terminal, look for signs to *The Serenity of the Seas*. Then ask for the head of security for the ship, not the terminal, but the ship."

Achilles was talking fast, but her mind was also in overdrive.

"You can abandon the car wherever it's most convenient. Here's my phone. The battery is dead, but charge it when you can so I can call you."

"Is there any special code I should use or something like that?" Katya asked. "I'm not certain they'll take me seriously. I don't even have identification."

"That's just as well, because there's a warrant out for your arrest. Use a friend's name, but don't let them bog you down with that bureaucratic stuff. Make it clear exactly what happened. What you witnessed as a hostage of Middle-Eastern terrorists. Whatever happens, insist they inspect all the ship's eggs and potatoes immediately. I'll do the same thing with the *Tranquility*."

"Even to me, that sounds crazy."

"What choice do we have?" He gave her a strong hug and a forceful kiss, then ran off.

Katya took a deep breath, then dropped into the driver's seat. It needed a lot of adjustment. Putting her feet to the pedals, she was reminded that she didn't even have shoes.

102
Crippling Conclusions

Florida

SEPARATING FROM KATYA after such a short reunion was the next-to-last thing I wanted to do. The last was watching two cruise ships loaded with happy families explode—knowing I hadn't done everything in my power to prevent it.

To get to Port Canaveral, I took advantage of an unwitting accomplice. The man who had peed on the parking lot donated his aged BMW to the cause.

Call it a hefty fine.

I'd hoped to find a cell phone in his car, but that search yielded no fruit. Being disconnected was frustrating in general, but exceptionally so at a time like this. I considered stopping to buy a burner phone or charger, but didn't want to get off the highway. I was cutting it critically close as it was.

At least I'd gotten the call and video in to Vic before going dark.

I started the drive thinking through my opponent's plan. Oz was doing what the original Osama had done. Turning a routine, mass transportation operation into a mind-bending, morale-crushing act of terrorism.

If he succeeded, the impact might surpass that of 9-11. Casualties on the two ships could rival those from the Twin Towers. The whole cruise industry would go down in flames. Worst of all, the world would learn that explosives could be hidden from the best detection system. Once that word got out, no crowded place would feel safe. No mall, no stadium, no office, no school.

I simply could not fail.

A construction zone made worse by an accident gave me a lot more thinking time than I'd planned. With dire conclusions coming faster than mile markers, I found myself rocking forward and back while fire flowed through my veins.

Questions popped up like clay pigeons on a range. Was Oz that good? Had he outsmarted the system as adeptly as his fellow Saudi? What was I missing?

One train of thought finally captured my full attention. *What did I really know?*

Oz had cleverly used a jetpack company to acquire the ingredients for military-grade explosives. Then he'd camouflaged his bombs. He'd molded them into egg and potato shapes. That was certainly innovative, but was it sufficient to beat the system?

Drug and explosive security at ports revolved around dogs. To beat the canines, Oz would have to remove or camouflage the explosive's scent. I pictured the operation as Katya had described it, adding in what I knew from Oz's purchase history.

He set up his finishing operation in a chicken barn. That meant constant fan flow coupled with lots of odors and odor-absorbing materials. First, he coated each explosive nugget in Flex Seal, an air- and watertight sealant. Then he probably coated them again. He'd bought a thousand dollars' worth of the stuff. Finally, he added layers of paint. First enamel white—probably several coats. And then flat brown for the potatoes. On top of that, everything was cartoned up and wrapped in plastic. All in a room full of molting chickens.

Would that be enough to defeat the dogs?

I didn't know. But I was virtually certain that Oz would have tested it to find out.

The traffic was maddening.

At one point, I considered opening my door to knock a passing motorcyclist off his bike so I could steal it, but the situation kept promising to improve. I contemplated asking a responding policeman for his phone, but that would be hit-or-miss on a good day, and these officers clearly weren't having one of those. They were dealing with congestion and casualties. In the end, traffic delays killed half my buffer. Thirty minutes.

Port Canaveral was enormous. In addition to hosting the world's second busiest cruise port, it boasted a booming day-cruise business plus large Coast Guard and military operations—each with its own section of the sprawling facility.

The all-aboard blast was sounding as I arrived at the *Tranquility's* berth.

I drove to the passenger drop-off and left the borrowed BMW running right there in the turnaround. I ran inside looking for a cruise line employee, rather than someone who worked for the terminal.

A woman with the appropriate uniform and name badge caught my eye. She was clipping a red velvet rope in place beside a sign that read, "Check-in Closes at 3:00." That was thirty minutes ago. Far behind her, I saw that the check-in stations were either empty or serving their last guests.

"I need to speak to the head of the *Tranquility's* security right now," I said, attempting to come across as authoritative despite being dressed like a traveler who was already making use of the Lido Deck bar.

"Are you a passenger?" she asked, her voice friendly but her eyes understandably skeptical, given my beachgoing attire.

"No. But I need to speak to the head of the *Tranquility's* security right away."

"Is there a problem?" She asked.

"Who runs security on the *Tranquility?*" I asked.

She crinkled her nose, but answered the question. "That would be Mr. Briggs."

What were the odds of that? Was the captain's last name Helms?
"Please use your radio to call Mr. Briggs. Tell him Mr. Achilles has—"

"You can't leave your car there!" a man said as a hand clamped onto my shoulder.

"Tell him Mr. Achilles has an urgent matter requiring his

immediate attention," I said to the lady.

"Sir, your car is what requires immediate attention."

"Tow it," I said, turning toward an officer nametagged as Jarvis. "Or just remove it to the parking lot. Key's inside."

"Sir, that's a serious security violation. Cruise terminals are restricted areas."

Jarvis's white uniform indicated that he was with the port police. Not the right force for my needs. Furthermore, although he was sizable in stature, my size and then some, Jarvis was young and junior in rank. Not a decision maker.

I looked back at my lady, but she'd moved on. Jarvis' hand had not.

This was not going as planned.

"I'm going to have to arrest you if you don't move your car. Right now," Jarvis pressed, clamping tighter while his free arm moved toward his handcuffs.

If he took me to port security, I was more likely to end up in a holding cell than in front of anyone in authority. At least in the short term. I couldn't risk that. Not with only minutes remaining before the ship sailed.

Without a word, I headed for my car, walking at a pretty quick clip.

Officer Jarvis followed.

103
New Job

Florida

I DIDN'T HAVE TIME FOR JARVIS.

The *Tranquility's* passengers didn't either.

Oz would likely have timed his bombs to detonate shortly after the ships sailed, probably while they were still in or near the port. That would cause maximum damage and ensure excellent video coverage.

A small white Seaport Security car with a green stripe and flashing yellow lights was parked right behind my borrowed BMW. To some, it would signify trouble. To me, it looked like a backstage pass.

I got into my car and pulled straight away, hoping he'd follow.

I was driving blind. Normally, I'd have studied the site of an upcoming op, even if just a little bit as I'd done with Stuart Beach. Enough to get the lay of the land. But I'd had no time for reconnaissance in this case. Even worse, the presence of military bases made guesswork particularly risky.

Instead of heading for customer parking or the port exit, I drove toward the employee lot.

Jarvis followed.

I wasn't blocked by a badge reader or ticket dispenser. I was simply advised by large red lettering that this was Employee Parking and unauthorized vehicles would be towed.

I found a spot near the rear of the lot, behind two large SUVs. As I got out of my car, Jarvis pulled up.

I ignored him and began walking toward the exit.

He got out of his car and yelled.

I turned and spread my arms. "What is it this time, officer?"

"You can't park here. This is for employees."

"I am an employee."

"What?"

"Do you see me wheeling a suitcase? I'm starting with the cruise line Monday. In security. Guess that means we'll be colleagues, of sorts."

Now Jarvis was confused. "But you're not an employee yet?"

I turned back toward him. "The papers are all signed, so I am an employee. I just haven't started." I wanted him preoccupied with legal minutiae rather than his present predicament.

"What was it you wanted from Becky back there?"

"This," I said, holding up my left hand while my right blasted him in the solar plexus.

Jarvis doubled over.

I slipped around his back and applied a rear naked choke, scissoring his carotid arteries and baroreceptors between my left forearm and biceps. I squeezed hard and I squeezed fast, prompted by the urgency of the situation. The change of pressure and lack of oxygen caused my opponent to pass out after just a few seconds.

The good thing about chokehold-induced syncope is that it's fast acting, when properly applied. The bad thing is that the victim remains unconscious for only about thirty seconds. Not that I needed additional prompting to rush.

I used the first third of my allotted time unbuttoning his shirt and another ten seconds pulling it and his T-shirt off. He was already coming around by the time I got his wrists cuffed behind his back.

I gave him another choke.

That one was sufficient to get him naked and into the BMW's trunk. But just barely. He was already shouting by the time I slammed the lid.

At least I knew he'd be fine.

The jig would be up and the alarm would go out as soon

as someone walked close enough to hear his cries or thumps. But in any case, this was all going to be over less than an hour from now.

I changed into his clothes, everything but the shoes. I just couldn't part with mine. They weren't shiny, but at least they were black. Enough to raise an eyebrow, but not sound an alarm, I figured.

I raced back to the *Tranquility's* terminal in the Security Service car, but this time drove into the restricted access area around back. The gap between the ship and the building I'd just been inside. It was crawling with forklifts and people in reflective jackets. Not surprising, given the amount of cargo that had to be loaded and unloaded during the few short hours the ship was at dock.

I took a second to contemplate the enormity of the operation taking place before me. The logistics of a cruise ship turnaround. First there was the unloading. The passengers, their bags, the solid trash, the liquid waste. Then came the loading. Countless tons of supplies and provisions. Many thousands of passenger bags. All delivered to a designated location—without losing a single piece of luggage or dropping one egg.

Overhead was the covered gangway the passengers used to go from the check-in operation onto the ship. It was empty. I considered climbing up and boarding that way, but saw that it was already closed at the ship's end. The gangway was drawing back.

Boarding had completed.

I'd have to sneak aboard with the cargo.

THE TRICK TO TRESPASSING is acting like you belong. Body language is half the battle, with clothing bridging much of the remaining gap. The rest is luck. Getting both noticed and reported depends on who's paying attention and how much they care. Given that X factor, you want busy people and a bustling atmosphere.

When I parked in a spot conveniently designated for security, I got both.

The long narrow scene sandwiched between the enormous ship and the servicing port facility resembled a military base on invasion day.

Or so I thought at first.

On second glance, it was clear that the invasion was ramping down. The lifts were forking the last of their pallets. The longshoremen were wiping their foreheads. The loading bays were starting to close.

It got worse. People weren't boarding with the cargo. There were ground crews and ship crews. The two didn't mix. Worse still, they weren't dressed the same. The dock workers wore mismatched casual clothes, whereas those on the ship were all uniformed in dark blue coveralls or two-piece gray outfits. I matched neither in my stolen white uniform.

My basic plan was to get aboard, find either the eggs or the potatoes, then send someone to fetch the head of security. Dressed as I was, and placed where I'd be, that should work much better than my first failed attempt. While waiting for Briggs to arrive, I'd dig in, looking for Oz's counterfeits.

But first I had to get aboard. Unchallenged at least. Unseen at best.

The loading bay doors were about eight feet above the dock. Easily within forklift range but more than a casual jump. The lifeboats were about thirty feet further up. Then the first promenade deck. I didn't spot any dangling ropes or chains. No suspended painting or porthole-washing platforms.

I can climb stuff that looks impossibly steep, but that requires friction. Friction on my feet, which climbing shoes provide, and friction on the surface. That was where the ship left me short. Seabreeze-slicked steel has a coefficient of friction next to zero.

As I scanned for an accessible entryway, I reflected on how much easier it would be to walk into the middle of the dock and shout, "There's a bomb on the ship!" But I couldn't risk the very real possibility that Oz or his colleague was watching or listening with a detonator in hand.

I spotted a gap and ran for it.

One forklift had just delivered its last load from the ground, and a receiving forklift had just picked it up. As the first drove away and the second turned around, I ran and jumped and pulled and rolled. I couldn't tell if I'd been spotted from behind, but at the moment nobody on the storage deck appeared aware of my presence.

I rose and started walking, wanting to distance myself from the door. A white Seaport Security uniform looked a bit like a naval officer's, but I doubted it would fool any but the greenest of crew. They were undoubtedly well aware of the positions and ranks associated with each color and style of uniform. It was human nature to compare, and probably part of their training.

The deck I'd rolled onto was horizontally expansive but vertically limited. I could easily touch the ceiling. It had clearly been designed to store pallet-loads of food without wasting space. Cardboard boxes were everywhere, all very neatly and systematically arranged.

Unfortunately, I didn't know the system.

The packing pattern was gridlike, for easy forklift access. Reminded me a bit of the food storage vault in the bunker. I began wandering, looking for potatoes and finding everything but. I wasn't surprised to discover that vacationers consume a lot of beer, but sheesh. You'd think this was a football stadium on Super Bowl day.

I'd just dodged a forklift while moving from taco chips to salsa when I bumped into a member of the ship's security detail. His black uniform contrasted with my white, as did his demeanor.

Without missing a beat, I said, "Glad I found you. Can you take me to the potatoes?" I knew that last bit sounded stupid, but I said it with conviction.

He whistled like few people can. Very shrill and loud. "Got him!"

I could have dropped the guard and run. A quick, crushing uppercut. But my goal wasn't to escape, it was to get the right people performing the right inspection. I read his name tag and said, "Jackson, I need to speak to your boss."

"I'm sure he'll want to speak with you, too. Turn around and give me your hands."

A long horn blast accented the demand. The ship was about to leave port with me aboard—in handcuffs. I'd really screwed this up.

Instead of presenting my hands, I raised my fists. "Not until I speak with your security chief."

Two more guards arrived as I spoke. One showed his cell phone to Jackson then said, "You gave your real name to my colleague at reception. Your unusual name."

He turned his phone around and I found myself looking at my picture. Not a surveillance photograph. My picture.

"Kyle Achilles, there's a warrant out for your arrest. I'm sure the U.S. Marshals Service won't have trouble finding an agent willing to pick you up in Nassau. Meanwhile, we have a private room for you."

I repositioned my feet into a more aggressive stance. There was little chance I could fight my way to freedom, but escape wasn't my goal. "Call your chief. Now!"

The second of the new guards pulled a Taser.

My heart shriveled at the sight. About the only chance of defending against a Taser strike is to prevent both barbs from connecting. That's not easy, but it's nothing like swatting a bullet either. Barbs fly slower than bullets, and more importantly, they have trailing wires. If you know that someone is about to shoot, the smart move is to wave your arms around before your center mass like a madman, attempting to deflect, dislodge or break a connection before the electricity starts flowing. Because once it does, fuggedaboutit. The blast is an overwhelming, all-consuming festival of pain. Unless, I've heard, you're cranked up on coke or meth. Which I wasn't.

"Call your chief, now!" I repeated.

105
Bombs Away

Florida

A VOICE BOOMED from behind a pallet of oranges, answering my demand. "The chief's here."

Ironically, Briggs wore a white uniform—but with black shoulder board and gold braid. He looked more like the classic British detective than a bouncer, which I took as a good sign. He was followed by a dozen men or more, which was considerably less encouraging.

"Listen up!" he said, addressing his crew. "I've just gotten off the phone with my counterpart on the *Serenity*. We have a credible bomb threat. Explosives are believed to be hidden among the eggs and potatoes."

"Three pallets of each," I said, as an eager but leashed German shepherd moved into view. "Packaged the same as the rest, and painted to resemble the real thing, I believe."

Eyes darted back and forth between me and the chief.

"There's no time to waste with identification," Briggs said, his voice both decisive and commanding. "We have ten minutes to get all the eggs and potatoes off the ship. But due to fear of remote detonation, we can't evacuate the ship. Not that there's time anyway. We also can't sound an alarm, and we can't make any shipwide announcements. We need to push all egg and potato pallets into the bay from the starboard side ports, so the dumping won't be witnessed by an observer on land. If anything gets in the way, push it overboard too. Now go!"

To the chief's credit, his crew responded like firemen to a five-alarm inferno.

Except Jackson and the Taser-toting guard. They stayed

on me.

Briggs locked his baby-blue eyes on mine. "Tell me what you know."

I gave him the two-minute version. The jetpack company and chicken farm. The dumpster full of potatoes and eggs. The detonators. The molds, Flex Seal and paint. The trailer swaps. The repeated use of the words *serenity* and *tranquility* during Arabic conversations. I ended by saying, "It's not just explosives. They also bought large quantities of white phosphorus."

"White phosphorus burns at 5,000 degrees," Briggs said, momentarily closing his eyes. "My hull melts at 2,750."

"I'm thinking some of the eggs and potatoes are RDX, but most are Willie Pete. The blast will consume their protective coating and scatter them around. Your ship will look like a floating fireworks store that caught fire, and it won't stop burning." I didn't like sounding overdramatic, but couldn't have him underestimating the threat.

Briggs nodded and said, "Heaven help us. The timers on the *Serenity* were set for 16:30."

I looked at my watch. 4:18 p.m. Twelve minutes to detonation.

"Come with me," Briggs said.

We ran starboard toward where sunlight was streaming through open side ports. The forklifts were going at it bigtime as the land sailed by. They weren't using the careful one-by-one lifting procedure I'd seen earlier. They were bulldozing whole rows of pallets. The sight reminded me of paratroopers leaving a plane.

"The captain has us over the deepest part of the channel. Just one truckload, right?" Briggs asked, skipping around as his mind jumped.

"Almost certainly."

"That's thirty pallets. We picked up eighteen pallets of eggs and a dozen potatoes. You say the supplier wasn't in on it?"

I was sure Katya and I would be answering the same questions many times in the days to come. If there were days to come. "That's right. They're innocent."

"That's all the potatoes!" a forklift driver shouted.

It was 4:26 p.m. Very impressive. But we'd all be vaporized in less than four minutes if the explosive eggs were still aboard.

I expected Briggs to run toward the second hive of activity, but he didn't. No point, I realized. He'd just be a distraction. Good commanders trained their people well, then got out of the way while they worked.

"What happened on *The Serenity?*" I asked.

"Your girlfriend led my counterpart to the explosives. She chose a considerably less dramatic means of alerting him, by the way. She just asked for him at reception. They found sophisticated active and passive receivers in addition to timers, which are set to detonate at 16:30."

"*Are* set? You didn't disarm them?"

"Cruise ships don't keep bomb disposal crews on hand. But they got a bigger buffer than we did. They found the first pallet at 15:30. That gave them enough time to covertly load the six pallets onto lifeboats and haul them out to sea. They're still towing the bombs toward deep water, on a very long line, but will let go any second."

Briggs looked at me, and I looked at him. I had no doubt that we were thinking the same thing. If his crew didn't get the eggs out in time, we'd never know it. We'd just vanish. Turn to vapor in the blink of an eye.

I didn't want to die.

In what might be the last seconds of my life, my thoughts moved on to Katya. She had made it! She'd also saved thousands of lives.

I didn't want to die.

I wished I'd been able to propose, to hear her say "I do," to make and raise beautiful kids, to see the world as tourists do and grow old by her side.

I didn't want to die.

I wished this hadn't happened to us. The bunker. The kidnapping. The cross-country chase. But in retrospect, we were lucky that it had. Because if it hadn't—

106
Caution

Florida

I DIDN'T DIE.

I did feel the underwater explosions. At the time I was bracing myself against crates of bananas while looking into a British detective's baby-blue eyes and thinking how far that setting was from my ideal parting scene.

The exterior video I saw later was much more impressive than the inside experience. Big shock waves raced across the top of the water like rings of turbocharged whitecaps, followed by white geyser-like plumes, then darker-lower-wider blasts of frothy water and finally eruptions of black silt which rained on ship and shore like the muds of Hell.

Then it was over.

Oz killed a lot of fish and caused one nonfatal heart attack, but his clever creations failed to take a single human life. Not the least of which were Katya's and mine.

In Florida, that was.

Nevada was a different story.

That was the sum of what I knew when a pleasant-faced man of some forty years with graying hair and a matching suit walked into the Port Canaveral security office where I was being detained. I'd never seen him before, but I knew who he was the instant our eyes met. "Special Agent Link."

As the door clicked shut behind him, Vic slid into the chair just vacated by the Navy captain who ran port security. He opened by answering a question the colonel had repeatedly ignored. "Ms. Kozara is on her way here now," he said by way of opening. "My Miami counterpart is escorting her up on his plane."

My heart leapt at the news, and I let it show. But that was only half the story. The least important half. "Thank you. What's her status?"

"Same as yours. She's a person of interest."

That was good news, if not definitive. While Katya had committed no crimes, a warrant had been put out for her arrest by the man across the table from me now.

Same for me.

While I hadn't committed the crime for which Vic had issued the warrant, I had racked up a serious slate of potential charges since. Not the least of which was assaulting and kidnapping officer Jarvis.

Not wanting to go that way, I asked the big question. "Did you catch Oz?"

Vic met my eye, then extended his hand across the table. "We did. All four of the people from your video and a fifth whom we've identified as the chicken farmer are now in FBI custody. As is the cryptocurrency flash drive. We don't have the password yet, but we'll get it."

The flash drive! I'd all but forgotten about the money. A temporary lapse, to be sure. I was less confident than Vic regarding their ability to coax the password from Oz. The Saudi struck me as exceptionally resilient.

I wondered if my flight prediction had proven correct. "Charter flight?"

"They rented a corporate jet."

"Where?"

"We caught them in Orlando. Their current location is *undisclosed.*"

My thoughts moved on to the number of prisoners. Given that all five had been flying out, either nobody had been watching the ports or Oz had additional accomplices.

"Your expression tells me you've landed on my immediate concern. Do you have any reason to believe there were more than the five of them involved?"

I'd given Oz's team a lot of thought while planning my big gambit. The beach exchange. "Given the controlling and analytical way the Saudi operated, and his focus on secrecy, I think he limited involvement to family. You should see if either he or Sabrina have other relatives around."

"One step ahead of you there."

"Good. There were probably contractors as well. People who supplied this or that without knowing about the larger plan."

"On it. Katya is helping with that," Vic added.

"And then there's the source Oz threatened me with. The one I told you about. His supposed friend high up in the FBI. You should ask him about that."

"Oh, don't worry. I will."

Something in Vic's expression compelled me to add, "I didn't believe him, but I couldn't be sure. I hope you're not offended that I proceeded with caution."

My words drew a smile. I wasn't sure why until Vic spoke. "Mr. Achilles, your definition of *caution* varies greatly from most."

The Cake and the Castle

One Month Later
Half Moon Bay, California

WE HAD A SMALL CEREMONY ON A BEACH. A Northern California beach, not a central Florida beach. It wasn't extravagant from a society pages perspective, but it was perfect. Mother Nature brought us her best, as did a string quartet and talented florist.

Standing there with the sun setting and the waves crashing, looking into Katya's loving eyes, I reflected on how close we'd come to missing that moment. If Jarvis had delayed me another few minutes or Briggs hadn't been top shelf, Katya would have become a widow without ever being a wife.

I couldn't control my tears.

Katya didn't seem to mind. But she did stop them—with a kiss.

Our reception was catered by none other than Cinquante Bouches, with the compliments of the owners and chef. While that had been offered and arranged in advance, we did have two surprise guests. Or maybe it was one—with an FBI escort.

Vic approached me while his charge was talking on his phone. "Congratulations!"

"Thank you."

"Before we get to the interesting stuff," Vic said, gesturing toward the other man with his head, "I wanted to bring you up to date on the investigation."

"Please," Katya said.

"Osama told us everything. In short, there were no

watchers on the docks, and he was bluffing about having a source within the FBI."

Vic spoke definitively, but I had to ask anyway. "How can you be certain?"

"Director Brix cut a special deal with him. He made a few minor if unorthodox accommodations in exchange for complete cooperation. If anything proves untrue, Oz and his crew go straight to death row."

As my internal alarm began blaring, Vic hastened to add, "In any case, the Saudis will spend the rest of their lives behind bars."

"We're relieved to hear it," Katya said.

I was about to inquire regarding the unorthodox accommodations when Vic's companion joined us.

"Governor Rickman," I said, shaking his hand.

"Congratulations! And please, it's Whip." He pulled a stack of fancy white envelopes from his suit coat pocket and presented them to us with both hands.

Katya flipped through the pile at his prompting. They were all addressed to Mr. and Mrs. Kyle Achilles.

"From our fellow captives," Whip said. "The genuine ones. All forty-three of them."

I looked over at Katya who was beaming with a pleased but perplexed smile.

"They're genuinely grateful, given what they now know," Whip added. "As am I." He handed me another envelope. One that differed from the rest. It was long and thick.

"What's this?" I asked.

"It's not a check. It's a thank you card, of sorts. I'd call it a token of Florida's appreciation, but it's more than a token. It is, however, both fitting and appropriate. Have a look."

I opened the envelope and pulled out a sheaf of stapled papers. An official document, complete with stamps and seals. "A property lease?"

"Look at the address," Vic said, unable to hide his excitement.

I recognized it immediately. "The castle?!"

"Forfeited to the state," Rickman said. "I couldn't give it to you outright, but it was within my power to offer you a lease. Ninety-nine dollars for ninety-nine years."

Before I could find a reply, Vic handed me another envelope. This one much smaller but just as thick. "A little something from the Orlando Field Office of the FBI."

"Where Mr. Link is now the SAC," Rickman added.

I didn't need to open the second envelope to know what was inside, but I did. A stack of one-dollar bills. "Let me guess," I said, ceremoniously passing it along to Governor Rickman. "Ninety-nine."

Both distinguished visitors turned to the bride. Rickman said, "The two of you will always be welcome in the Sunshine State. We hope you'll visit often."

"With kids," Vic added.

"Sounds like a plan," I said, turning to my wife. "Honey, why don't we get to work on that?"

Epilogue

Location: Undisclosed

OZ SUCKED in the fresh unfiltered air as he looked out the open window at his sapling tree. A lone elm. The view was simple, flat and otherwise bald, but undoubtedly one of the most expensive in history.

It was also the last he would ever see.

Oz was not complaining. Much to the contrary, he was pleased with his stroke of genius. The tree and the window were luxuries. Two of the four that blessed his life.

When the FBI surrounded his party just minutes before their departure from Orlando's Executive Airport, his plans and dreams had gone up in steam. Vaporized water, not smoke. That was the appropriate classification given that hours later, a new plan rained back down—bringing a very different dream. One much more modest, but infinitely better than any conventional alternative.

His brainstorm came in the form of a negotiation tactic. A quid pro quo scenario that ultimately became a contract signed by the big man himself, FBI Director Bobby Brix.

Oz gave the venerated politician everything he wanted in exchange for a single demand—with three parts. His was a simple ask. Easy to grant. Costing nothing and camouflaged accordingly—but giving Oz everything a man needed to be happy in life.

The Federal Bureau of Investigation got the list of all his accomplices—of which there were none—and the password for his cryptocurrency drive. A phrase worth ninety-two million dollars, less a few final operational expenses. Brix also got to avoid a trial that would expose the FBI's shortcomings and weaknesses, and he got to quash the public revelation of Oz's dog-defeating methods. What's more, Washington got complete control of the message, and it was a good one. *Justice has been swiftly rendered! The perpetrators have been locked up for the rest of their lives.*

Oz got life in a cell with a barred window he could open, looking directly onto a healthy tree not more than thirty feet away. A cell he was permitted to share with Shakira, Omar and Sabrina.

Oz could breathe fresh air. He could chat with his friends. He could watch his tree blossom and his wife grow old.

Or he could hang himself in the shower. That jury was still out.

AUTHOR'S NOTE

Dear Reader,

Are you curious about how I come up with my stories? To get the inside scoop and stay informed of my new releases, email me at TwistAndTurn@timtigner.com.

If you're skeptical about anything you read in this novel, please turn the page. I believe you'll find the supporting documentation linked there to be both interesting and enlightening.

Thank you for your kind comments and precious attention,

NOTES ON TWIST AND TURN

Please find below the web addresses for articles and videos supporting many of the key concepts and elements in Twist and Turn. All these and more are also available on my Pinterest page: **www.pinterest.com/ authortimtigner**/research-for-twist-and-turn-achilles-4/

- For more information on extravagant **bunkers built by Preppers**: thepreppingguide.com/underground-bunkers/

- For a story of incredible fraud and **deceit within the startup medical device industry**: en.wikipedia.org/wiki/ Theranos

- For the video of an **actual jetpack** in use: www.youtube.com/watch?v=gCYSWyHDpfU

- For a video of t**he real castle** on the beach: vimeo.com/ 230266711

- For a video of the **garage door opening trick** Achilles used at PPS: www.corporatetravelsafety.com/safety-tips/ how-thieves-break-into-homes-by-the-garage-door/

- For a video of a **modern chicken farm**: www.youtube.com/watch?v=4bvXR0NaJoY. The one physically described in the book is located near Cairns, Australia.

- For information on the real **Saudi Purge** that motivated the fictional Oz and Sabrina: en.wikipedia.org/wiki/ 2017_Saudi_Arabian_purge

- For information on the **coverup of Saudi Arabia's involvement in 9-11**: foreignpolicy.com/2016/07/18/what-we-know-about-saudi-arabias-role-in-911/

- For information on the **FBI tip line**: www.usnews.com/ news/best-states/florida/articles/2018-02-16/a-look-at-fbi-call-center-that-failed-to-flag-tip-on-shooter

- For a quick video showing the logistics of **provisioning a cruise ship**: www.youtube.com/watch?v=27258DIjIY4

WANT MORE ACHILLES?

Twist and Turn is book #4 in the series. Pushing Brilliance, The Lies of Spies, and Falling Stars came first, as did the prequel novella Chasing Ivan. Learn more at timtigner.com or amazon.com/author/tigner.

ABOUT THE AUTHOR

Tim began his career in Soviet Counterintelligence with the US Army Special Forces, the Green Berets. With the fall of the Berlin Wall, Tim switched from espionage to arbitrage and moved to Moscow in the midst of Perestroika. In Russia, he led prominent multinational medical companies, worked with cosmonauts on the MIR Space Station (from Earth, alas), and chaired the Association of International Pharmaceutical Manufacturers.

Moving to Brussels during the formation of the EU, Tim ran Europe, Middle East, and Africa for a Johnson & Johnson company and traveled like a character in a Robert Ludlum novel. He eventually landed in Silicon Valley, where he launched new medical technologies as a startup CEO.

Tim began writing thrillers in 1996 from an apartment overlooking Moscow's Gorky Park. Twenty years later, he's still writing. His home office now overlooks a vineyard in Northern California, where he lives with his wife Elena and their two daughters.

Tim grew up in the Midwest. He earned a BA in Philosophy and Mathematics from Hanover College, and then an MBA in Finance and a MA in International Studies from the University of Pennsylvania's Wharton School and Lauder Institute.

Printed in Great Britain
by Amazon